Let You Love Me

BOYS OF RIVERSIDE

GRACIE GRAHAM

To all single mommas or ladies who find themselves alone and pregnant. You're so strong and so amazing. I hope you, too, find your HEA.

Chapter 1

TEAGAN

ONE YEAR AGO, IF you would've told me I had my own personal Judas Iscariot living right under my nose, I would've told you to get the fuck out.

My band of friends were loyal. Solid.

Raised on the football field together, we grew up with a ball in our hands.

Broken bones, concussions, girls, and our first can of beer, we did it all together. We weren't just friends or teammates, we were brothers. And although we didn't share the same blood running through our veins, it sure as hell felt like it.

So when I found out Knox—my boy—was the one who assaulted my sister in high school, I lost it. I almost fucking killed him. Some days, I wish I would have.

This is one of those days.

I stare down at the news article on my phone, oblivious to the men around me, too lost in my own thoughts and the conflicting emotions at war inside of my head to focus on anything else.

Gripping the phone tighter in my hand, I skim the article as a combination of relief and anger swell inside of me.

After my family—a.k.a. my parents and Brynn—decided not to pursue criminal charges against Knox, I tried to find peace with it, but the fact that his actions would go unpunished didn't sit right with me. Every time I picked up a football or spoke with my sister or saw her face, I imagined that fucker putting his hands on her, and I lost it.

I know Brynn is happy now. She's healing, has closure, and is at peace; it's everything I could ever want for my twin sister, but it wasn't enough for *me*.

I needed more.

I needed him to pay.

The boys—Atlas, Graham, and Jace— and I were all in agreement. The asshole needs to be taught a lesson.

So, a couple of weeks ago, we solicited Calvin Scott, Graham's dad, for help in getting Knox relieved of his position at Virginia Tech. Since fucking up his relationship with Graham, Mr. Scott has been clamoring to make amends, and this was the perfect opportunity. As a former NFL-star with money and connections, he had all the pull we needed.

He made some calls and two weeks later, Knox was no longer playing for the Hokies.

Fuck me, it worked.

My gaze continues to scan the article and my mood darkens.

As it turns out, once Calvin Scott informed the administration of Knox's questionable past, several reported assaults from girls on Knox's campus started to make a lot more sense.

I read the last line of the article, and my jaw clenched.

"Though the investigation into several sexual assaults on the Virginia Tech campus are still ongoing, Knox Brian is being questioned as a prime suspect."

Yep, should've killed the fucker when I had the chance.

We let him get away with what he did, and, lo and behold, he did it again.

But this time, he'll pay.

Still, that shit doesn't sit right with me.

I quickly forward the link to the news article to the guys in our group chat, typing out a quick message—*Did you see this shit?*—then hit send.

"Nichols, eyes up here!" a voice snaps.

I grit my teeth and lift my gaze, stuffing my phone back into the pocket of my joggers, as I meet Chance Lockhart's cold stare with one of my own.

I know he's our quarterback, but something about the fucker rubs me the wrong way, and I'm not in the mood for his shit tonight.

We're gathered outside the Bowman Center on campus for what I hope will be the last hazing ritual of the season. Shot-gunning beers, streaking across campus, and waking at the ass crack of dawn to run bleachers are all good and fun, and we've done them all, but none of them will get us any closer to a NCAA Division I Football Bowl championship. We're one month into our season, and our record is good. We're strong as fuck, but I don't see how a gaggle of rookies loitering on campus on a Saturday night, post-win, is going to help us any.

When I signed on to play with the Wildcats last year, I'll admit, Chandler a.k.a. Chance the Chancelor Lockhart was half the reason. He's known on campus as the God of football. Who wouldn't want to play with him at the helm?

But I'm quickly growing tired of his egotistical shit. The douchebag plays games both on and off the field, and I don't like it.

"What are we doing here, Lockhart?" I ask, tone weary.

"Oh, I'm sorry, Nichols. You got somewhere else to be?"

Actually, yeah.

I keep my mouth shut, jaw locked.

Pissing Chance off is a bad idea.

Beside me, my roommate Tommy, stiffens. "So, you called us here after a game, on one of our only nights off, for another initiation stunt?"

Chance smirks. "We do this every year with the rookies. Do you want to be a part of the Wildcat family or not?"

Tommy scratches his head, the crease in his forehead deepening. It's clear to me he thinks this is as stupid as I do. Hazing and pranks like drinking and running naked through campus are one thing. Dicking around with the cars in the staff parking lot, like Chance wants us to do, is quite another.

"But if we get caught," Tommy continues, motioning to the cameras on the lampposts above us, "we could face suspension."

Chance rolls his eyes. "They're not going to suspend you. It's a simple prank, but if you're too much of a pussy–"

"Come on, man. We're not rushing," I say, my tone lazy as I add, "this isn't a fraternity. We've already made the team. What's the point here?"

A few of my teammates shoot me a nervous glance. I know they seek Chance's approval, but Coach Turner runs a tight ship, and I can't imagine a world where get caught dicking around with a professor's car would go unpunished.

"Are you questioning me, freshman?" Chance's dark gaze snaps to mine and I shrug.

I have a lot of things I'd like to say, but I don't out of prosperity. I might be dumb, but I'm not that dumb. Making an enemy of your quarterback is a bad idea, especially one as powerful as Lockhart.

"Listen," he sneers, "you can either participate or not. Just know we've earned our place as a Wildcat family. The rest of you have yet to prove yourselves. And don't forget Coach relies a lot on my insight as captain, especially when it comes to the rookies. So, do it or don't. Just know, we're taking note of who the *real* team players are."

I grit my teeth, the muscle flickering in my jaw.

This is stupid.

"Come on, man," Greene, one of our running backs, murmurs from behind me. With a nudge, he adds, "Just . . . play along."

"Yeah. You're pissing him off," Ben, one of our defensive linemen, mumbles under his breath.

"Tommy started it." I shrug.

"Listen up!" Chance snaps. "If you wanna be a pussy and leave, fine. Do it or don't, but you have exactly ten minutes to remove all four tires of the cars in this lot, place the vehicle on cinder blocks, then dispose of the rubber in the courtyard fountain. That's your mission. Anyone bailing, do so now." He eyes us through narrow slits.

I mash my mouth into a tight line and turn to face the other freshmen. "What'll it be, boys? I say we either face it together or walk, but we're a team."

Tommy lifts a shoulder. "It's just a harmless prank, right?" Then quieter, so Lockhart can't hear, he says to me, "If Chance wants to pretend we're back in high school trying to be part of the cool kid club, I say we just fucking do it and get it over with."

The other men, nearly two dozen of them, all nod their agreement.

"All right, then. We do this, and we do it as a team." I point toward the six guys closest to me and bark out their names. "Stand guard, let us know if anyone is coming. The rest of us will remove the tires, two on one car, so pair up. Let's get this shit done and get the hell out." I turn. "Tommy, you're with me."

I spin back around to find Chance smiling. "Me and the boys will be at Patsy's Pub across the road. You have only ten minutes to complete this mission and send us photographic evidence. Then another five to get your ass to the bar." Chance lifts his head to the sleek black Jaguar in front of us. "This one's yours, Nichols."

I arch a brow.

"Later, ladies," Miller, a senior tight end, says as he winks and turns.

"If they want to haze us so badly, why the hell aren't they staying to watch?" Tommy mumbles under his breath.

Because they're setting us up.

I brush the thought aside. If the boys want to do this, so be it. If I'm anything, it's a team player, and I'm not going to bail on them on or off the field.

I turn to find everyone paired up.

"Time starts now," Chance calls out, then backs away.

Everyone rushes into action at once.

Tommy and I hurry to the Jag.

I take one of the back tires while he rounds the front. Living in a small rural town, I've changed my fair share of flats, a skill I didn't expect to come in handy here.

Only two minutes pass before the first tire is off, and Tommy helps me stack the blocks beneath it before he removes one on the front.

Two down, two to go. With any luck, we'll finish this and put this fucking hazing shit behind us.

The second front tire comes off and we're down to mine. A rusted fucking lug nut is making it tough as shit to get it off, but I'm determined. Still, time is winding down, so I tell Tommy to take his to the fountain while I work.

"You sure, man?"

A glance around me tells me most of the guys are wrapping this shit up.

I grit my teeth and grunt as I put all my weight into the lug nut. "I'm sure," I grind out as Tommy takes off with one of his tires.

Finally, the nut starts to turn slowly as I hiss out a breath.

By the time Tommy returns, I'm wrenching it the rest of the way off. "Get the last tire and go," I say, breathing heavily from the exertion. "I'm getting it off now, but everyone else is done. Make sure the guys are all together and head to Patsy's," I say, removing the tire. "I'll be right behind you. All I have to do is dump this and take pics."

"I can stay—"

"No." I shake my head. "Get them and go before someone sees us and busts our asses. I'll be there in two minutes," I say, starting to stack the blocks underneath the last axel.

"Okay. See you in a few." He darts off, yelling for Ben and Greene to follow him, sneakers slapping on the pavement as he gathers the rest of the guys.

I stack the final block and pick up the tire when a shadow looms over me from above.

For a moment I think it's one of the guys, determined to help. But when they clear their throat, the hairs rise on the back of my neck and I instinctively know it's not.

Very slowly, I get to my feet, turning at the sound, and all the blood drains from my face.

I've been caught red-handed.

And not by a pissed off professor, receptionist, or staff member.

It's the Wildcats' head coach, *my* coach, and the look of condemnation he gives me may as well be a death sentence.

Fuck. Me.

CHAPTER 2

LANE

AFTER I TIE THE laces of Sophie's shoes, I hand her the large ball I bought at the convenience store this morning and straighten. She'd been bugging me for a new one ever since hers blew away in last week's thunderstorm after we left it outside.

"You're sure you can't stay for brunch?" my mother asks, hovering by the door. "Chance will be here any minute."

All the more reason to get the hell out of here.

"Can't. Sorry," I say, feigning disappointment. "I promised Gabby I'd help her with a psych paper while Sophie plays at the park."

Mom crosses her arm over her chest and watches me. "You're always so busy. It would be nice to see you relax a little."

Right. Because sitting across from Chance Lockhart at brunch is the epitome of relaxation.

I glance back to Sophie and my lips quirk as I watch her struggle to peer around the large pink ball in her arms. It's nearly half the size of her squat frame, and all I can see while she's holding it are two stubby legs and the halo of light brown curls that fall in wild tangles down her back and around her face.

While she may have gotten the shade of her ocher locks from her father—mine are a vibrant auburn—she certainly got her waves from me, along with all her other prominent features like her thick lashes, bright blue eyes, and full lips.

"Maybe next time, Mom," I say, already heading out the door while I take one of Sophie's little hands in mine.

I ignore the answering sigh behind me and guide Sophie toward the edge of the yard to the mailbox where the roof contractor was supposed to drop off my estimate earlier that morning.

I raise my head and lift a hand in a wave to Mrs. Miller, our neighbor and Sophie's babysitter, then once we reach the end of the yard, I flip open the mailbox and find the envelope tucked inside.

"Come on, Mom," Sophie wines, tugging on my arm.

My brow creases as I glance down at her, then back to the envelope in my hands. "Yeah, okay, we're going."

The emblem for Redd's Roofing is stamped in the corner, and I say a little prayer as I open it, keeping Sophie to my right and away from the road while we walk.

Please don't be high.

Please don't be high.

Please don't be high.

I remove the estimate for the new roof on the lake house and unfold it, my gaze homing in on the numbers and the amount totaled on the bottom of the page. As I read the amount, my stomach sinks.

It's high.

"Shit," I hiss before I remember myself and slap the paper over my mouth. "Sorry," I mumble, "Mommy said a bad word."

"*Mom*," Sophie singsongs.

She drops the ball on the sidewalk, watching it bounce, then runs to catch up with it while my heart leaps into my throat as I envision her stumbling onto the road. "Soph! Wait until we get to the park, okay? It's too hard to bounce it and walk. It'll roll out into traffic."

"I can do it."

I sigh, not in the mood for an argument as I clutch the letter, the estimated total heavy in my hands. "I said no. You can wait a few more minutes."

If I have to walk the two blocks to the park with her bobbing the ball the entire way, it'll take us years to get there, and I want to be as far away as possible when Chance shows up.

When I shoot her a sharp look, Sophie once again hugs the ball.

As we walk I wonder how I'm going to manage to come up with fifteen thousand dollars for a new roof when I was lucky enough to afford the house in the first place.

It was a foreclosure. I'd fallen in love with it years ago, and when it went for sale more than six months ago, I jumped. Luckily for me, I saved every dime I received after I graduated high school, including my parent's gift, as well as money working from home doing data entry, so I'd been able to afford the down payment.

To be fair, I knew the lake house was a fixer upper when I bought it, but because it was a foreclosure I couldn't inspect it or go inside, so I had no idea the roof was leaking in several places. All of the wood will need replacing, along with some of the plasterboard on the ceiling, which means I can't move in until it's fixed, not with Sophie.

But unless they're willing to accept Monopoly money, I don't have extra to spare. Any money I had in my savings is long gone, and between a full course load at college, working from home part-time, and being a full-time mom to Soph, I'm spread thin as it is. If I worked more hours, I'd never see her, and on top of that the burden of childcare would lie on my mother's shoulders because I sure as hell can't afford to pay anyone to look after my daughter.

I groan, feeling discouraged.

I should've waited to check the quote until later because now I'm just going to fret over it for the entire day.

It's times like these I wish I had waited to do adult things until I was an adult. I should've saved sex for when I was older, maybe even until marriage, done things right. Then I could've had the cute house, white picket fence with a dog in the yard, and the whole nine yards.

Instead, I'd been a doe-eyed fool. Naive. Lovestruck.

And though I love Sophie with all my heart, and I wouldn't give her up for anything in the world, I can't say it's been easy. Quite the opposite. Getting pregnant shortly before my seventeenth birthday had more than a few drawbacks, and I've been questioning every decision I've made ever since.

Rather than living with my parents, maybe I should've skipped college until Sophie was older. Maybe I should've worked until she was school age, and then I could've enrolled in night classes. It might've taken me twice as long to get a degree, but at least then I'd have money and insurance.

At least then, I might not feel like I'm being run ragged from the stress of trying to do it all, though I suppose I only have myself to blame. Since having Sophie, I've made it a point to ask for help as little as possible. Some might say I'm independent to a fault, but my parents didn't choose to have a pregnant teen, so the last thing I want is to constantly inconvenience them because of my mistakes. It's one of the reasons I fought so hard to get my own place. Now I just needed to make it habitable and I'll finally be out of their hair. They can have their lives back.

I chew my lip and mull over my options.

I can shift some money around but I still don't have enough for the roof, and with my paltry income, it'll take six months to save for it. As it stands, I've only set aside money for paint and a few extras, things I thought were necessities before moving Sophie in, and nothing more.

There's only one way I can think of to earn more money to pay for the roof, and it's the last thing I want to do.

I groan as I think of the student assistant position my father offered me last year. I'd turned it down, but it has remained open ever since, and I can't help but feel like he's holding it for me in the hopes I'll reconsider.

The position pays well, and since I'd technically be a part of CU staff, it means I'd have access to the campus day care center, which is a free perk for all employees. Currently, I pay Mrs. Miller to watch Sophie while I'm at school, and though she gives me a criminally low rate, free childcare would still save me a pretty penny each month.

The assistant spot is flexible, too. Late afternoon practices are the only time I'd have to be there. Otherwise, I can decide when I prep the equipment and uniforms for the following day as I long as I get the work done.

Childcare.

Better pay.

Flexible.

It would be the perfect job, if it weren't for one thing. One very *big* thing.

Taking the student manager spot for CU's football team means seeing Sophie's father every single day.

I groan as I glance down at Sophie. She tosses the ball in her arms and catches it.

I promised myself I'd have us in the house after the holidays, but if I can't fix the roof before then, it'll be impossible.

I'm in between a rock and a hard place and I know it.

"Look, Mommy, watch what I can do!" Sophie drops the ball in front of herself, and it bounces off the paved sidewalk, hitting a rock and careening into the yard beside us.

"That's great, but didn't I tell you to hold onto the ball?"

Sophie runs to grab the ball, then peers at me over top of it. "I can kick it, too!" Her little foot kicks out, the bright red lights on the heel of her shoe blinking as she makes contact with the ball and it surges forward. I wait as she chases it down someone's driveway, trying my best to remain patient when she clutches it to her chest, and again, bounces it out in front of her.

I bend down and snatch it up, ignoring her protests when she drops herself onto the sidewalk in a pout, her little hands balled into fists and a frown pulling the soft curves of her lips.

I sigh and close my eyes. Why can't she cooperate today? I'm stressed as it is, and if the telltale throbbing in the front of my head is any indication, I'm about two seconds away from a monstrous tension headache.

I inhale a calming breath before I open my eyes and cross the space between us. Kneeling in front of her, I peer into her bright blue eyes. "I'll give you the ball back, but no more bouncing."

Her gaze darts to the ball and she starts to smile, but I hold it back. "Promise? I'm serious this time. No. More."

When she nods, I hand it over.

Great mothering, Lane, give her everything she wants and she'll always throw a fit.

I give my inner critic the middle finger as we continue our walk, resentful at my sour mood. My nerves are worn thin already and we're not even at the park yet. I'm so preoccupied with my loathsome thoughts on how I'll pay for the roof that when Sophie drops the ball and it bounces off my foot onto the road, it takes me a second to react.

Sophie darts toward it and I reach out, grasping for her, but come up empty at the same time I see a flash of red—a car—headed straight for her.

Time slows and bile rises into my throat.

I lunge forward but I can't reach her, and one thing becomes clear.

I don't have enough time.

I'm not fast enough.

CHAPTER 3

TEAGAN

THE SUN BEATS DOWN on me as I push out from beneath the canopy of trees onto the last leg of the trail. Sweat rolls down my back and beads my brow. I swipe at it with my forearm, focusing on the burn in my muscles as I push myself harder, faster, pumping my legs and arms until my chest heaves.

The rhythmic sound of my sneakers slapping the pavement increases in pace, and the fire building in my lungs is nearly enough to silence my toxic thoughts and the worry that comes with them as I wonder just how fucked I really am after last night's antics. Six miles and I'm still every bit as stressed as I was when I started.

We're not the first freshman class to be initiated into the Wildcat family, so it stands to reason I'm also not the first to get caught doing something stupid.

Although I am willing to bet I'm the first one to steal Coach's tires.

Fuck.

How was I supposed to know that was his car? It certainly wasn't the little red sports car I've seen him driving to and from practice.

But Chance knew; he had to. He's played for Coach for three years now, not including their time together in high school. No way he didn't know whose car it was. He set us up, plain and simple, and no one can convince me otherwise.

Ultimately, it's my fault. My instincts told me something was off. I should've listened to my gut and walked away, but I didn't want to look like a poor sport or like I'm not a team player when I pride myself on both of those things. Add to that the Knox news, and I wasn't exactly thinking straight.

Had Coach arrived only a minute earlier, he would've caught all of us.

It's a lot harder to punish nearly a dozen recruits than it is a single person.

As it is, he only found me so I shouldered the blame.

Coach is no dummy, though. He knew there were more of us involved, but when he questioned me about it, I refused to rat my teammates out. I'm a lot of things, but a snitch isn't one of them.

Instead, I retrieved every single tire dumped in the fountain myself and replaced them before he let me go with the reminder that this was the first strike against me; I've only got two more.

I don't doubt him. Coach Turner is a notorious ball buster, the strictest coach in the league. He doesn't play around, and the kind of antics college football players get away with at other schools isn't tolerated.

I should probably take the warning and let it go, but I don't feel right about how I left things last night. He was pissed and I was stressed the fuck out. Hell, I don't even know if I properly apologized.

The end of the trail comes into view, where it bleeds into the sidewalk flanking the road that leads in and out of the park. A car passes and I offer them a curt nod when they wave, though I want to tell them to slow the fuck down. Everyone around here rips through these roads despite the playground to my left, just past the grove of trees.

The joyful shouts of children reach my ears as I near it, and the sound reminds me of my little sisters back home. A pang of longing hits me in the chest, but I smother it and focus on the other sounds around me. A dog barking. Music from an open car window. The rustling of leaves on the sidewalk beneath my feet.

I lift my gaze at the same time a flash of pink catches my eyes on the edge of the sidewalk. It's a bouncy ball, and it rolls past my feet onto the road in front of me as another car, again moving way too fast, heads straight for it.

I wince, anticipating the squashed rubber a moment before another blur of color joins it on the road, and it only takes me a split second to realize it's a little girl.

Panic seizes my chest, and I open my mouth to scream, to tell her to move as the SUV careens toward her, but my voice won't work.

Instead, I surge forward. My feet hammer the ground. My heart slams against my ribcage as the blare of a horn and the screeching of tires fill my ears, and I lunge for her. I'm airborne, arms outstretched as I fall to the hard pavement with a bone-rattling thud, enveloping the child in my arms and rolling us out of the way.

Using my body as a shield, I curve around her as the car flies past, horn blaring while the driver shouts something out their window, just barely missing us.

If it weren't for how badly I'm shaking, I'd flip them the bird, cuss them out.

Asshole.

The breath rasps in and out of my lungs. Rocks and debris from the pavement stick into my bare skin and my joggers are wrecked, but it's a small price to pay for the little girl still pressed against me, trembling like a leaf but safe.

I lie my head back on the sun-warmed concrete while relief swells inside me. I'm still trying to catch my breath when another figure appears above me, and the world stops.

A woman leans toward us, her expression horrified, and it's like being struck with an anvil. Like that fucking cartoon with Road Runner and Wile E. Coyote.

All I can do is stare, my body numb as the sunlight shimmers over her auburn hair. Eyes dark as denim meet mine, and the breath snags in my throat.

She's so beautiful my chest aches, and everything inside my head goes blank.

I forget where I am and what just happened.

I forget about Coach and Chance fucking Lockhart.

Nothing matters as I blink up at her, my gaze sliding down the rest of her face, over her pert nose and full mouth. The soft curve of her jaw and the sharp contours of her cheekbones are so glorious, I have the sudden urge to draw her. Though I don't have an artistic bone in my body, I'd do just about anything to commit her to memory.

Instead, I just stare.

At some point I decide I'm hallucinating; I must be, because she's a real life, auburn-haired Little fucking Mermaid.

And everyone knows the Little Mermaid is fucking hot.

Shit. Maybe she's an angel.

Maybe I died and this is heaven.

Fuck. Did I die saving the little girl?

A hysterical sob bursts from the tiny body I still hold in my arms, morphing into an all-out wail so loud it startles me from my trance.

I jerk to attention as I release the little girl at the same time the woman above me scoops her up into her arms, cradling her against her chest like she's a doll.

I swallow, mustering what's left of my dignity after staring at her like an idiot and rise to my feet with a groan.

No doubt every muscle in my body is going to fucking hurt later. Practice tomorrow should be fun.

Now that I'm upright, my gaze flickers down her body, past the tight athletic leggings I have no doubt hug her ass to perfection, paired with a loose T-shirt and sneakers.

My brain cells slowly come back to life and I guesstimate she's about my age, maybe a little older, a revelation that suits me just fine.

A flush of warmth shimmies down my spine that has nothing to do with the six miles I just ran and everything to do with the chick in front of me.

"Oh God. Thank you. Thank you. Thank you," the woman says on repeat, squeezing her eyes tight and depriving me of those gorgeous baby blues.

My breathing slows as I come back to earth and realize I've yet to say anything. I'm still staring at her like a lovestruck idiot. Or a fucking psycho. Take your pick.

I shift my weight on my feet and nod. "Hey, it's no problem," I say before I turn around and zero in on the girl's pink ball. My mouth flattens at the sight of the deflated rubber.

Striding over to it, I pick up the floppy material while the woman behind me scolds the little girl. "You know never to run out onto the road," I hear her say.

"I'm s-s-sorry," the little voice trembles on a sob.

"You scared the crap out of me, Soph."

I return to them and offer up the deflated ball with a grimace. "Looks like we didn't save the ball."

"Better the ball than Sophie," the woman says, a hitch in her voice as she takes what's left of it.

The little girl's chin wobbles as the woman sets her on her feet, clasping one of her hands tightly as if she might take off again when she meets my eyes. "I can't even imagine what would've happened had you not been there." The woman shakes her head, glancing down at the pink material in her hands. "I was distracted, thinking about something else, and she kept messing with the ball . . . I should've been paying closer attention. I should've been holding her hand. I *always* hold her hand," she says like she's afraid I'll think her irresponsible.

"Hey," I nudge her arm, "things happen. It's okay."

Hell, the number of times my little sisters, Trista and Sabel, have given me a heart attack . . .

"I know, but I—"

"Beating yourself up over it won't change it now."

She inhales, her whole body puffing up, and I can practically see her worry de-escalating as she exhales. "You're right." Her gaze flickers to my tanned chest, and the darks of her eyes dilate before she meets my eyes again, a flush in the apples of her cheeks.

She clears her throat, jerking a thumb behind her. "Anyway, I, uh . . . we should probably go, but thank you. Seriously. Thank you."

I nod. I should go, too, but I can't seem to move my feet because if I leave now, I may never see her again, and that would be criminal. I can't allow that to happen.

My heart lurches as I try to think of something to keep her here.

She begins to back away as my gaze darts around us, then back again as I settle on her T-shirt—a Wildcats football T-shirt—and I motion toward her. "Are you just a fan, or do you go to CU?"

Her lips part. Startled, she glances down at her shirt as if she's forgotten what she's wearing. "Oh. I, um . . . both?" She scrunches her nose and it's so damn cute, my heart fucking flutters inside my chest.

I grin. "Same, although it's my first year. What about you?" Not exactly the most nonchalant way of finding out how old she is, but I'm not really in the business of giving a damn about being casual.

She hesitates before she answers. "I'm a junior."

Which makes her roughly . . . twenty, twenty-one?

Perfect. I just turned nineteen so the age difference is nothing, though she could be thirty and a fucking professor at CU and I'm not sure I'd care.

My gaze flickers to the little girl tucked under her arm.

Damn, that's some age gap. At twelve years difference between me and my sisters, I know what it feels like to play the overprotective sibling role.

"So, you're a Wildcats football fan, then?" I ask, not yet ready to let her go.

She hesitates before her lips quirk. "I was practically raised on football."

She's gorgeous *and* loves football.

I'm completely fucked.

"So, you go to the games?"

"Most of the home games, yeah. You?"

I grin. "Again, it's my first year, but I tend to go to most of them." Nodding to the park behind her, I ask, "You're headed to the park?"

She arches a beautiful brow. "For a stranger, you ask a lot of questions."

I shrug, smirking a little but saying nothing.

Sighing, she says, "We *were* headed to the park. Looks like we're doing so now with a busted ball."

"Sucks you have a busted ball." She shifts, as if preparing to leave, and I panic. "I didn't catch your name," I blurt.

"That's because I never gave it." The upward slant of her lips tells me she's teasing.

I smile, dimples popping as I cock my head and wait.

She laughs and rolls her eyes. "Lane. My name is Lane." She glances down at the little girl. "And this is Sophie."

"Lane," I repeat, feeling it roll over my tongue like velvet. "And your last name?"

"Are you always this nosy with complete strangers, or just the ones you save in the park?"

I chuckle. "Is that a deflection?"

"Maybe."

"Okay, Lane-with-no-last-name, I'm Teagan Nichols."

"Well, Teagan Nichols," she says, taking a step back, "thanks again."

I shove my hands in my pockets and shrug. "Anytime."

I watch as the pair turn and leave, heading for the playground, while an unexpected jolt of longing settles in the pit of my stomach.

Turning, I head to my car and slide behind the wheel, then grab the T-shirt I left on the passenger seat and tug it on before I start the car and take the road toward the mini-mart a couple blocks down.

Ten minutes later, I park back in the lot with a brand new ball in hand.

Butterflies swarm in my stomach as I contemplate my next move.

Will she think I'm a fucking creep if I find her on the playground?

What's meant to be a sweet gesture could very well come off as trying too hard, or worse.

The last thing I want is for her to think I'm some kind of stalker, but the idea of leaving the park without her number doesn't sit well with me, so consequences be damned. I step out of my car and head toward the grove of trees.

Once I step onto the playground, my gaze scans the faces. Children dart around the swings and slides, climbing the jungle gym like ants on an ant hill. I spot a flash of auburn hair and my stomach turns in knots.

Making my way over to them, my guts tighten with nerves. A moment passes before I clear my throat, and bright blue eyes meet mine.

Her eyes widen in surprise before glancing down at the ball in my hands.

"I thought she could use this." I hold it out, offering it up as she shakes her head.

"Oh, no. We can't accept that."

"A ball!" Sophie yells and reaches for it but I hesitate, unsure of whether I should give it to her when Lane whispers, "Soph, we can't just accept things from strangers."

My mouth twists.

A stranger? Great. She totally thinks I'm a fucking creep.

Lane straightens and offers me an unreadable look. "It's okay. She can live without a ball."

"But I want the ball," the little girl cries.

"Please just give it to her," I say. "It's the least I can do."

"The least you can do?" Lane arches a brow. "You did just save her life, remember? I'm the one that should be thanking you."

"Then thank me by taking it. Seriously." I motion with the ball. "I have little sisters so I know how disappointed she probably is."

"There's really no need—"

"Do you always argue so much when someone does something nice?" I ask, my grin spreading as I squint down at her.

"Please?" Sophie tugs on her arm.

"But . . . why?" Lane blurts.

"Why what?" I narrow my eyes, not following.

"Why would you do that? Go get her a new ball. It's . . ."

"Weird?" I say, because it's a much better adjective than creepy.

"Well, yeah," she blurts.

I understand her skepticism. Hell, if my sisters popped a ball and some rando at the park went and bought them a new one without being asked, I'd be suspicious, too. I'd probably deck their ass. So, if anything is going to save me, it's the truth.

"Would you believe me if I said I had a really crappy night last night and I was out here trying to shake off the funk, so doing something nice for someone helped lighten my mood?"

She stares at me warily.

"What about the fact that I'm trying to figure out what to do to correct a mistake I made and running to the store to fetch you a new ball was a distraction?"

She purses her lips and I can practically see the wheels spinning, see her assessing me as if she's trying to decide on the chance I'm some kind of stalker.

"Or how about the fact that you're the most beautiful woman I've ever laid eyes on, and the second you turned for the park, I panicked because I couldn't stand the thought of not getting your number. And I thought maybe if I went above and beyond, you might do me a solid and give it to me?" I hold my breath, waiting.

She nods, her shoulders sagging with the movement, and I can breathe again. "Okay," she drawls, "you can have it." For a moment, I think she means her digits before Sophie skips toward her and squeals as she takes the ball.

"So, do you always hang out in parks where you can play Superman to little girls?"

"Just another Sunday." I shrug, and when she chuckles, it feels like a reward.

Maybe I can win her over yet.

"This is the part where you ask how you can make it up to me," I say.

She arches a brow, her posture stiff as she angles herself toward me and scoffs. "And how can I make it up to you?"

My lips quirk. "By giving me your number."

"My number," she says like she's never heard of such a thing.

"Yeah, you know. Those ten digits you put into a phone when you want to call someone."

"And why would I do that?"

I bark out a laugh. "Ouch. Point made."

She shakes her head, clearly flustered. "No. I didn't mean . . ."

"I guess I hoped you might think the gesture of buying a new ball was sweet."

"So it's bribery?" Her brows quirk.

"Maybe." My lips curl. "I also hoped you might find me charming. Or if not charming, then blown away by my sexual prowess and brooding good looks."

She bites her lip, and I can't tell if it's to fight a smile or because she's contemplating what I said. "I don't usually give out my number."

My stomach sinks. "Boyfriend?

"No." She shakes her head. "No boyfriend."

I frown. "A girlfriend, then?"

There's no fucking way this girl is single.

She snorts out a laugh, and it's the cutest fucking sound I've ever heard.

"No girlfriend, either. I'm . . . it's . . . my life is complicated."

I cross my arms over my chest and offer her a grin. "I can do complicated."

She stares at me like she's never seen a human before. Like she landed on Mars and doesn't know what to make of me.

She opens her mouth and closes it a couple times, then asks, "But . . . why?"

"You ask that question a lot." I grin and step forward, and though I know I should keep my hands to myself, I just can't seem to help myself as I reach out and tuck a lock of hair behind her ear. "Complications make life interesting. Simplicity is boring. And let's just say, I know myself well enough to know I'll be thinking about a certain redhead long after I leave this park."

"Oh," she breathes.

I cock my head, watching the emotions play over her face—surprise, flattery, confusion—while marveling at the obvious fact that this girl isn't used to such blatant admiration, which, quite honestly, is fucking mind-boggling. She should be. Every hot-blooded male in this park should be chasing after her.

"Yeah, *oh*," I say, and when her eyes soften, I know I've won.

A second later, she's rattling off her phone number while I punch it in my phone, then walk away feeling like at least one thing in the last twenty-four hours has gone my way.

After a shower to wash the run off me, I change and sink down onto my bed. I can hear Tommy in his bedroom talking to someone on the phone. The dude has proven to be a good roommate, all things considered, but I've quickly discovered he's loud as fuck. If I weren't convinced Chance had set us up to get caught Saturday night, I'd peg us getting busted on Tommy. No matter where he is, his voice carries. I could be standing right beside him or three hundred yards away and the dude would burst an eardrum.

I click open my texts and find the group chat, the one where I sent my buddies the link to the article about Knox and scroll through their reactions, which are essentially a mirror of my own.

To know someone feels the same way I do helps ease the sting of injustice a little bit. I guess there's comfort in numbers, and the kind of friendship I have with them can't be replaced. Though I get along just fine with my new teammates, I don't see myself getting close to any of them. Blame it on Knox's betrayal and my inability to trust new friendships. Either way, I can't seem to get past the fact the fucker lied to my face for years.

I trusted that asshole with my life, and he broke that trust.

Ever since, I've found myself putting space between me and my new teammates. I'm a little less forthcoming, a little less friendly.

If Knox could completely blindside me, I don't want to see what a mere acquaintance, someone who hasn't earned my trust, can do.

It fucking plagues me all the time.

I think about it when I wake and when I go to sleep at night, like a bad dream I can't shake.

Only two months have passed since the revelation, and I find myself constantly questioning the new people in my life. Trust is something I don't feel equipped to give. Doubt is my instant reaction to most anything.

Maybe with time, I'll adjust. Maybe now that Knox is paying for what he did, I can move on. But for now, my go-to for advice and an open ear is and always will be my boys from Riverside. Each and every one of them had been just as shocked and hurt as I was when we discovered the truth about Knox, especially Jace since he's in love with my sister.

Next to me, Knox was always the sensible one of our group, the most rational and even-keeled, so his betrayal came as an even bigger shock.

My mood shifts. I need to get my mind off him.

I can't go down that rabbit hole, not today. Not when I'm already stressed as fuck.

I shove the thought aside as my fingers fly over the keyboard, in need of an ear.

I frown at the number I don't recognize. For a moment I wonder if it's Knox, that somehow, he got a new number and infiltrated our new group chat.

The flash of fear strikes me like a lightning bolt, then quickly dissipates when I realize that can't be right. Jace was the one that started the chat this morning, and Knox would've had no way of adding himself.

As if reading my thoughts, the next text comes through, and I snort.

Atlas:

Who the hell are you?

Me:

Wondering the same before I spill my guts.

Jace:

Chris, what the hell?

Chris? The name sounds vaguely familiar, but I can't place it, so I type:

Me:

Who's Chris?!?!?!

Unknown:

What?

Graham:

Can someone tell me what the hell is going on? Who is Chris and how is he in our group chat?

Jace:

Chris is my jackass roommate. How did you . . . wait . . .

Unknown:

Okay, so I might've swiped your phone off the kitchen counter this morning and added myself to the chat.

Graham:

Um . . .

Jace:

WTF? Why the hell did you do that?

Unknown:

I figured you were down a friend now, and I wanted to see what it is you're texting your friends about all the damn time. In truth, I wanted to see if you're bitching about me.

Jace:

I have far better things to talk about than you. Trust me.

Unknown:

Well, I'm here now. Might as well stay. Carry on . . .

I drag a hand down my face.

Me:

Okay, I don't have time for this. For the sake of brevity and so I don't have to referee whatever kind of catfight you two are about to have, I'm adding Chris to my contacts.

Atlas:

Seriously? We're doing this?

Jace:

Chris is cool. Sometimes.

Unknown:

YES!!!

Jace:

But you're banished from my phone. I'm changing the security code right now and I don't even WANT to know how you knew what it was.

I quickly tap on the unknown number and add Chris's name in my contacts, then return to the texts.

Me:

Anyway, can we get back to my problems? I don't even remember where we were.

Chris:

The guys assumed you're just fucked in the head, but I, on the other hand, was giving you the benefit of the doubt and thought maybe you got your dick wet.

This guy . . .

I pinch the bridge of my nose, trying to focus my thoughts.

My lips quirk at the name of the British exchange student that I'd been obsessed with as a freshman in high school.

Atlas:

As much as I hate to admit it, I'm with Chris. Merry-whatever was before my time at Riverside, so I need some context. Give us a visual. How hot is hot?

Me:

Does it really matter? That's not why I'm texting.

Jace:

Abso-fucking-lutley.

Graham:

It matters. It always fucking matters.

I sigh. How did we get off on this tangent?

Chris. I blame Chris.

Me:

Slim, petite build with curves. Long auburn hair. And she has these eyes, these huge fucking blue eyes framed by ridiculously long and thick lashes.

I sound like a sap. I don't even know anything about this chick other than the fact that we go to the same college, she likes football, and has a little sister. Regardless, I am *not* about to fill them in on her peach-shaped ass or how well she filled out the tight little Wildcats t-shirt.

Jace:

You always did have a thing for gingers.

Graham:

True. Remember how he stole Brynn's Little Mermaid poster when they were six? He had that thing hanging on the wall in his fucking room for YEARS.

Atlas:

LOL! That's . . . Did you ask her out?

Me:

Not yet. She seemed a little spooked.

Chris:

Oof. Rejection happens to the best of us, buddy.

Jace:

True. Not all of us can have the Taggart Swagger.

I scoff.

Me:

Taggart Swagger? Did you just make that shit up?

Graham:

Dude, coining a phrase about yourself is a whole new level of loser.

Jace:

Whatever. Brynn agrees with me.

Ugh. My sister and Jace started seeing each other over the summer, and it's a development I'm still getting used to.

Me:

Please. Let's not talk about my sister.

Graham:

Back up. Out of all of us, you're a fucking cinnamon roll. How could she possibly get spooked?

Me:

I don't know. I got the feeling she's not used to guys hitting on her. Which I can't for the life of me understand because she's fucking gorgeous.

Chris:

Ah, I get it.

Jace:

???

Chris:

She's sweet but psycho. The super-hot chicks are always crazy. Guys probably steer clear of her.

Me:

What? No. That's not it.

Atlas:

Were you trying too hard? Sometimes that's a turn off.

Me:

No.

I answer instantly, then hesitate.

Shit. Was I?

Me:

I guess there's a slight possibility she thought I was a creep or something. But that's not even the real reason why I texted.

Jace:

Don't try and change the subject. This conversation is just getting interesting and I've been waiting forever to impart my words of wisdom on you.

I roll my eyes. The last thing I need are words of wisdom from Jace who was hands down the biggest player at Riverside. Just because my sister somehow rehabilitated him doesn't mean I want to listen to his advice on love . . .

At least not yet.

Maybe if I'm really fucking desperate.

Me:

I fucked up, and now I think my coach hates me.

Atlas:

Shit. Why?

Graham:

You're probably just being paranoid.

Me:

He caught me in the middle of stealing the fucking tires off his car.

Graham:

Okay, maybe you're not being paranoid.

Jace:

Yeah, you're fucked.

Chris:

Wait. Back up. Why would you do that? Even I wouldn't do that, and I do some dumb shit.

Me:

The upperclassmen have been hazing us on and off for a month now, and Lockhart got it into his head to make the rookies remove the tires off four cars and dump them in the school fountain. Just so happens one of the cars was our coach's and he caught me in the act.

Jace:

Shiiiiit.

Atlas:

Damn, bro.

Chris

Teagan needs our support, not our condemnation right now.

Atlas:

Who IS this guy?

Graham:

Of course we're going to give him shit. He stole his coach's fucking tires.

Chris:

You know what, I feel unappreciated by the group chat, so I'm leaving now.

Graham:

Okay . . .

Chris:

Seriously. I won't even come back to read these messages.

Atlas:

Anyway . . .

Chris:

I'm leaving.

Jace:

Carry on. What happened after he caught you?

Me:

I had to put all the tires back on the cars, and then he told me I have one strike against me. Sounds like I have two more before I'm riding the pine. You know what a ball-busting rep he has.

Jace:

Well, damn. I do love a good ride, but not on the pine.

Me:

Do you think I should go to his place and apologize? Or should I just leave it be? Last night was such a blur, I can't even fucking remember what I said.

Graham:

It's not a bad idea. It's always good to be a man and do the right thing.

Atlas:

It certainly won't hurt. He'll probably respect you more for it.

Jace:

Agreed. If there's one thing I've learned in the last month, it's that you need to own your mistakes.

I snort, knowing he's referring to how he hooked up with my sister and hid it from me.

Me:

Damn. Looks like it's time to swallow my pride.

Chris:

I totally didn't read these.

CHAPTER 4

LANE

I'M EVERY BIT AS distracted on the walk home from the park as I was on the way there. Only this time, Sophie's hand is tucked safely inside mine, and it's a certain boy occupying my thoughts.

Teagan Nichols.

I roll the name over in my mind, and I can't help but smile as I picture him in my head. The blond curls, his toned chest beaded with sweat, those piercing blue eyes, and the dimples. Oh, lord, those dimples. They're enough to bring a woman to her knees.

Which would explain why I gave him my number, because I don't give out my phone number. Ever.

I've been on the mom wagon for four years now, and any time a guy even gets a hint that I'm a single mom, they run in the other direction. Which is fine by me. I've never once been tempted to give any man access to me since becoming a parent.

My life is busy enough as it is between Sophie and school and work without adding another dynamic to it. I barely have time for friends, let alone anything resembling a relationship.

Yet I gave my number to Teagan. Why?

Because complications make life interesting.

I shake my head, a smile ghosting over my lips. Maybe he's right. Maybe complications *do* make life interesting. And maybe I'm about to find out because that's what any man entering my life would be—a complication—to me, to Sophie, and I'd certainly be a huge one for them. If I started something, I'd open not only myself up to heartbreak, but her, too. And even if I were willing to risk my heart, I'm not willing to risk hers.

She's lucky to have people who love her so unconditionally. She has no clue what it feels like to have someone in your life walk away from you because they don't feel like you're worth the hassle. But I do. And I'll protect her from that kind of rejection as long as I can shield her.

So, I wonder once again, what the hell provoked me to give him my number.

Because it felt good to feel desired?

Because for some reason, he came off as completely genuine in a way no one has in a really long time?

My gut tells me I can trust him, and tomorrow, I might very well wake up and regret giving him my number. But for now, I'm okay with it, even if I am dumbfounded by it. All I know is he saved Sophie's life today. I hate to think of what would've happen had he not been there.

I shake my head.

I won't go there. I won't think of the "what-ifs" when everything turned out all right in the end. Instead, I'll allow myself this rare moment of excitement and anticipation at the notion he might call.

Once we reach the house, I shove my thoughts of Teagan aside as I take Sophie through the garage, where we stow her new ball before entering the house into the laundry room.

I help Sophie take off her shoes, then watch as she runs toward the hallway for the kitchen as I follow close behind, finding my mother at the sink rinsing vegetables.

"Geema!" Sophia cries as she runs up to her and wraps her arms around her legs.

My mother curls an arm around her. "There's my girl. Have fun at the park?"

I hold my breath, waiting to see if she'll mention anything about Teagan or the ball. When she doesn't, I breathe a sigh of relief, then wonder why that is.

Before I can give it much thought, I help Sophie wash her hands at the sink, then head for the pantry as she runs into the living room. I find a bag of the cinnamon apple chips she likes and take them to her where she sits on the couch, waiting for me to put a cartoon on.

Between the adrenaline from Sophie's near run-in with a fender, my interaction with Teagan, and the stress of the roof estimate, I could really use some time to unwind. Maybe even close my eyes before I need to make Sophie her dinner. Which means I better get the conversation with my father over with before exhaustion sinks its teeth into me.

"Is Dad around?" I ask my mother as I enter the kitchen once more to find she's moved on to bagging the veggies.

"You know where to find him." She glances up at me with an arched brow, and I nod.

Of course. Though it's his day off, any spare time during the season is dedicated to work: watching game tape, going over plays, and assessing strategy for the week.

"Everything okay?" Mom asks, eyeing me closely.

I never have been able to hide anything from my mother. Even my pregnancy. She knew from the moment I discovered I was pregnant that something wasn't right. After weeks of trying my best to hide the truth, she wore me down until I caved.

The weight of the roof estimate is heavy in my pocket as I nod. "Yeah. Everything's fine. Just need to talk to him about something." I force a smile then turn, poking my head into the living room to tell Soph I'll be right back, but she barely acknowledges me, too preoccupied with the preening unicorns on the screen.

My father's office is at the end of the hall on the first floor, and as I draw closer, the familiar sounds of a football game reach my ears. The cheering fans, the sharp trill of the referee's whistle, the confident rasp of the sports announcer's voice. As weird as it is, those sounds offer me a weird kind of peace. I've been hearing them my whole life. I practically grew up on the football field.

The door is cracked but I knock anyway, knowing I need to give him a minute to take his mind off whatever thoughts are running through his head while the game plays on the screen.

I open the door further and step inside to see his gaze trained on the television, watching with rapt attention before he pauses it and turns back to me.

The rumpled state of his salt and pepper hair tells me he's been running his hands through it, a clear sign he's stressed.

"You ready for next Saturday?" I ask. It's the first game of the season and they'll be playing a team ranked higher than them.

He exhales and leans back in his desk chair, the leather squawking with the movement. "No. But we will be. It's gonna be a tough one. Alabama look really good this year, but so does Chance. He's strong, maybe stronger than ever."

Right.

I fight the urge to roll my eyes. Chance Lockhart, Daddy's claim to fame and his secret weapon. There's no doubt the talented quarterback is the reason for CU's winning season these last two years. He's also the reason Dad got the coaching position at CU in the first place. Although he doesn't know I know this, I overheard the conversation several years ago and clung to it, praying for his sake everything worked out, and it did. My father has dreamed of coaching at collegiate level for Cumberland ever since a college injury took him off the CU field, and I was thrilled for his sake that his dreams came to fruition, even if it was in part due to Chance's success.

I may be young, but I'm old enough to know not everyone is lucky enough to achieve their dream in this lifetime, and it couldn't have happened to a more deserving man. Both of my parents have been nothing short of incredible, supporting me through my pregnancy, withstanding the gossip and the scrutiny that comes with having a pregnant teen.

They lost friends over my indiscretion. Not to mention sleepless nights, stress, and money. Though I've tried my best to buffer any sacrifice on their part—because it was my actions that landed me here, not theirs—they inevitably paid a price for it. When you're seventeen and pregnant, and lucky enough to have the support of your family, you lean on them whether you want to or not; to some degree, it's impossible not to.

After Sophie was born, I took the full brunt of responsibility on my shoulders. I do everything in my power not to inconvenience them. I don't accept money. I have a sitter who stays with Soph when I'm at school. I buy groceries and pay my own car insurance.

I'm cognizant of the time they spend with her, ensuring it's the kind of quality time a grandparent would normally spend with their grandchild so as not to take advantage. I don't expect them to provide childcare. Both of them are in their midforties and still young. They have careers and a life outside of mine. The only thing I've regularly accepted from them since her birth is the roof over my head, because that I couldn't turn down. Not if I want to build a better life for us.

In short, I don't take handouts or favors. But I'm about to take one—a favor, that is. Or maybe it's not a favor so much as it's nepotism at play. Either way, it sits in my stomach like a lead brick.

"Lane?" he asks and I blink, noting the concern flickering in his eyes and realize he's been talking while I've been zoning out.

"Oh. Sorry. I just . . ." I shake my head. "It's been a long morning."

His brow furrows. "I was asking what I can do for you."

I clear my throat, fighting the urge to fiddle with my hands. "Remember the job you offered me last year?"

"The assistant spot working with Reid?" he asks, referring to the team's equipment manager.

I nod. "That's the one. Is it filled yet?"

"Not yet." He leans back in his desk chair, fighting a smile. "I may or may not have told him to drag his feet posting it, but I'm hoping that's about to change?"

It's a question. He must sense I'm about to cave.

The hope I see in his eyes should make me feel better about taking the job, but it doesn't. I hate feeling like I earned it only by name alone. I hate that people who have connections tend to get ahead in life, even if my father falls into the same category. It's such an unfair advantage to those who don't have any. I have no doubt the assistant spot will look good on my résumé, even if it has nothing to do with the degree I'm pursuing. My desire to major in sports therapy has everything to do with my upbringing and nothing to do with the fact that my father can get me a job as soon as I graduate. Hell, had I been a boy, I have no doubt I'd be playing college ball right now. But Mom and Dad didn't have a boy, and after my mother had me and needed an emergency hysterectomy a few months later, their shot at ever having another child went out the window.

"I'll take it," I say, thinking of the estimate in my pocket, thinking of Sophie. It'll make me far more money than my at-home gig doing data entry does. Plus, maybe if I'm smart with my time, I can still do both.

My father grins. Truthfully, he knows this will help me, but I also think he's just as excited to have me on the field with him, working side by side.

"It's about time. Glad to see you've come to your senses. This internship will make you a shoo-in for a job after you graduate. What made you change your mind?"

I shrug, racking my brain for a reason that doesn't involve the roof estimate, because he'll only offer to give me money. As a college coach to a team in the Big Ten, he makes a ridiculous amount of money, and when I refuse, it'll turn into an argument.

"I figured the extra income would be good for me if I want to fix up the lake house, and like you said, it *will* look good on a résumé."

Not a total lie.

"I don't know why you bought that place," my father grumbles. "You have a perfectly good roof over your head here. What are your mother and I gonna do with all this space by ourselves, huh?"

I grin. Dad didn't support my purchase of the lake house. Not because he thought it was a bad investment, but because he wants me to move out about as much as he wants a hole in the head.

"Oh, I don't know," I say, unable to help my smile, "walk through the living room without stepping on a Lego for once? Enjoy being able to watch something other than cartoons during the day?"

"I like cartoons during the day," he grumps. "Who's going to give me my shoulder rubs?"

"Dad, Sophie has the grip of a gnat."

"And how am I going to have an excuse to eat fruit snacks if she's not here? You know your mother won't buy any of that shit once she's gone."

I fight a smile as I step forward and press a quick kiss to the top of his head. "Dad, we'll only be ten minutes away. We'll still visit, have dinners on the weekend, and you can stop by anytime you want. And, hey, since I'm taking this internship, I'll see you all the time."

"During the season, anyway." He purses his lips. "I know your reasons for wanting to move out, and I may not like it, but I respect it. Can't say I'm not proud."

I swallow over the thickness in my throat. His words are what every child, especially one who's screwed up in the past, wants to hear from their parents. After I discovered I was pregnant,

I thought I'd failed them. At the very least, I wrote myself off as being a huge disappointment, so knowing I can still make them proud, even after I've made mistakes, fills my heart with joy. "Thanks, Dad."

"Only speaking the truth. I'll tell Reid you accepted the spot. Drop by and fill out the paperwork tomorrow, then start Wednesday. That gives you a couple days to get Sophie registered at the CU day care."

I nod as my phone pings, interrupting us, but when I check it, I see a text from a number I don't recognize and frown.

I swipe it open, prepared to delete it when my stomach leaps into my throat.

Unknown:

What's the minimum amount of time you have to wait before you can text a girl you're interested in without looking desperate or uncool? Asking for a friend.

Teagan.

I almost forgot about giving him my number, too distracted by the conversation with my father.

I bite my lip, fighting the smile threatening to split my face in two. Part of me is shocked Teagan's already reached out. This boy is a charmer, and I'm not sure what to make of it or his interest in me. It's not like I met him in class when I was alone. He knows I have a child, yet he's interested, anyway.

I don't know whether to be thrilled or skeptical, which is probably why I feel a little bit of both.

"What's got you looking so chipper?" Dad asks.

I glance up at him to find him staring and realize I'm smiling at my phone like a dope.

"Oh. Uh, nothing." I drop my smile. "Just someone from school." I hook a thumb toward the hall. "I better check on Soph."

I stare down at my phone, unsure if I should respond and what to say if I did. It's not like I have a ton of experience with men. I went from dating a little the first couple years in high school to falling in love—or what I thought was love—and getting pregnant. Whatever flirting skills I had are poorly developed at best and have long since dried up. Besides, now that I'm back home, the reality of my situation comes crashing in like a tsunami.

I can't *actually* date him even if I want to.

Earlier, I was on a high. A cute, flirtatious boy was interested. But now, I'm stone-cold sober. I have a daughter. I'm far too busy to date, and even if I weren't, I'm in a completely different phase of life than your average college student.

Most kids my age are only worried about their grades and which party they plan on attending over the weekend.

I'm worried about my mortgage, a leaking roof, and potty training.

Which is precisely why I shouldn't add him to my contacts, yet I find myself entering his name, anyway.

I'm still smiling when I enter the living room to find Sophie asleep on the couch. The sight of her so innocent and peaceful tugs on my heart, even if her napping so late in the day means she'll be up later tonight.

Deciding to take advantage of the rare time alone, I climb the stairs to retrieve the new romance novel I started the other night instead of catching up with laundry like I should.

I'm halfway up when the doorbell rings, and I almost turn back around to answer it before I hear my mother call out, "I'll get it."

I hold my breath, waiting to see if the sound woke Sophie, breathing a sigh of relief in the answering silence.

My feet hit the landing and I dart to my room to grab the worn library book, then head back for the stairs where I plan on sinking into the couch beside Sophie with a cup of cocoa, but I pause.

Below, my father's burly figure fills the doorway and I stiffen, half expecting it to be Chance Lockhart at the door. Those two are always going over plays and talking shop during the season. But when my father shifts his weight and crosses his arms over his chest, barking out a gruff response, I realize it mustn't be him.

Probably a solicitor or someone else from the team.

Thinking nothing of it, I continue down the stairs, turning to take the hall into the living room when I hear a voice I recognize and freeze.

A voice I heard only hours ago.

It can't be . . .

Risking a glance over my shoulder, my heart races at the sight of Teagan, partially obscured by my father's burly form.

For a moment I wonder if he's stalking me.

He must have followed me here.

It's the only possible explanation for how he ended up at my door.

The idea sends chills down my spine until I hear my father address him by name, and I frown.

He must know him. But how?

I take a couple steps back, hiding in the alcove beneath the stairwell so as not to be seen as I strain my ears to listen.

"Well, get on with it, then. What brings you here on my day off?" My father's tone is gruff, unimpressed while I strain to hear Teagan's response.

"I know I can't take it back now. What's done is done. It was stupid, and I never should have participated, but I just wanted to come again and apologize. Man-to-man, to your face."

Alarm bells go off in my head.

My mind races.

My father says nothing for a moment while my head spins. What on earth could Teagan possibly be apologizing for?

"So, you admit you weren't alone, huh?"

"No, sir. I wasn't. It was freshman hazing, but I'm asking you kindly to please not ask me the names of the others with me, because I won't tell you. I'm a team player, not a snitch."

A team player?

My body sags, the wall taking on the full brunt of my weight.

He must play football. He's one of my father's players.

You've got to be kidding me.

I wait until my father finishes, my brain buzzing with my thoughts as he closes the door, and I step out into the hallway. "Who was that?" I ask, trying to keep my tone as casual as possible.

Dad rolls his eyes. "Just one of my boys. Those guys were up to their usual pranks the other night, and this one got caught." He shakes his head while any hope that I might be wrong plummets.

I nod, schooling my expression into one of indifference as I wait until he brushes past me. I stare at the closed front door where Teagan just stood and fight the urge to peer out the little window to watch him leave, knowing I'm being ridiculous.

I never should've given him a second thought, but I did.

I turn and head for the living room while any notion I had of texting Teagan back goes up in smoke.

I don't date. But even if I did, no amount of charm would be enough for me to date a football player. Especially not one of my father's players.

The one and only time I broke that rule, I wound up pregnant with a broken heart.

CHAPTER 5

TEAGAN

THE LATE SUMMER SUN beats down on my back while I finish stretching, and my teammates wait beside me for Coach to show. Word is he's calling a team meeting, and I'd be lying if I said I wasn't slightly nervous at the prospect.

Showing up on his doorstep yesterday went about as good as expected; he gruffly accepted my apology, then told me we'd deal with it Monday on the field.

Well, it's Monday, and I'm no less nervous to see what he has in store for me than I had been the moment I got caught.

A whistle blows on the sidelines and my attention shifts.

Coach walks toward us with an air of authority that comes with being a weathered veteran of the game. Two of his assistant coaches flank him, along with Mark Reid, the equipment manager for the team.

Behind them, I spot several of my teammates, including Chance Lockhart, rolling four massive tires onto the field, and my stomach sinks.

There are two men to a tire, and even then, they're red-faced and sweating their asses off.

Another glance at Coach and the smug smile he wears like a badge of honor, and I know I'm fucked.

Something tells me this isn't a part of our normal workout today.

His eyes scan the men around me, pausing a second to lock eyes with me before moving on. "It was brought to my attention on Saturday night, as I'm sure many of you are aware, that the Wildcats like to do a little freshman initiation, or hazing, if you will. And since it seems Teagan Nichols, one of our tight ends"—he sweeps an arm in my direction—"likes to move tires, I thought we'd give him an opportunity to showcase his skills."

I groan as he turns a pointed stare at me, his closely trimmed beard twitching with his smile before he glances away again. "Now, I might be an old man, but I'm no fool. I know more than just one person is responsible for stealing and dumping the tires of those four cars, but only one was dumb enough to get caught."

Gee, thanks.

"So, if any of you are man enough to admit your involvement, you can join your friend Teagan here, and help him out with one of these tires. Otherwise, he will be responsible for flipping *all* four of them to the end zone *himself*."

My eyes widen, but I play it cool despite the string of curses I rattle off in my head. Those tires have to weigh four hundred pounds apiece easily, and from their position on the field, I'll need to flip each of them one hundred yards.

Beside me, Tommy starts to step forward, but I block him with my arm, giving him a subtle shake of the head. I already took the fall for these guys, and I'm not going to fuck it up now because Coach is a masochist.

Besides, something tells me this is more than punishment. It's a test. He wants to see how loyal I am, if I'm a team player or if I'll squeal under pressure.

If there's one thing you can count on from me, it's my fucking loyalty.

Some of these guys will share the field with me for four years. Many of them will become my brothers, comrades in battle, and you don't win by throwing each other into the gauntlet, even if it's to fight alongside you.

Or maybe he's testing everyone else.

Maybe he wants to see all of them step forward and take the heat as a team. But I know some of these guys and they're scared shitless of getting the boot and having their scholarships revoked. Not that I blame them. My love of the game aside, without my scholarship, I'd have to take out a shit ton of loans to get my degree.

Several other freshmen glance my way, a question in their eyes I try my best to answer as I step forward, chin held high.

I can feel Chance Lockhart burning a hole through the side of my face but ignore him. Something tells me he's loving every second of this, and I won't give him the satisfaction of getting a rise out of me.

"It was just me, sir," I say before anyone else can take the heat.

It needs to be one of us or all of us; there is no in-between.

Out of the corner of my eye, I catch Chance smirk, and let it boil my blood. I'll need the anger to motivate me if I'm to move these tires.

"Okay, then. Nichols," Coach snaps, "you better get started. We don't have all day and practice starts when you finish. The longer you take, the longer practice goes on."

Fucking fantastic.

I make a beeline for one of the tires, mentally preparing myself to push to my limit when Tommy calls out, "You got this, Nichols!"

"Use your legs," someone else shouts. "It's all in the legs and hips, baby. Come on."

I stretch my neck from side to side, then brace my hands on the first tire and begin.

The first couple of flips suck. The tire is heavy as shit, and I already feel the burn in my muscles, but the further I go, I begin to warm up and it gets a little easier.

I'm already breathing heavily by the time I get the first one across and head for the second.

By the third, it's no longer easy.

By the fourth, every muscle in my body is screaming like a fucking banshee.

About halfway down the field, my legs cramp. My forehead is slick with sweat as the sun beats down on me. My biceps burn, and I'm not sure I can make it.

I pause, leaning against the tire as I take a deep breath and reach deep within, calling on all my mental fortitude, reaching for anything and everything I've got to get me across the finish line. My anger at Lockhart. Knox's betrayal. A set of brilliant blue eyes and striking auburn hair.

Lane, the chick from the park, hasn't called or texted me back, despite sending her several texts of my own, and as fucking pathetic as it is, I imagine her waiting for me in the end zone. My own personal prize.

All I have to do is get there, and she's mine.

I grunt as I squat, using my legs to do the heavy lifting as I flip the tire over again and again and again while I growl, gasp, and curse. On final squat, I flip it once more across the goal line and collapse against it.

The acrid scent of rubber burns my nose as I catch my breath.

Applause erupts around me, followed by a hand clapping me on the back. "Damn, bro. Didn't know if you had it in you."

Tommy.

I lift my head, leaving behind a puddle of sweat on the black rubber.

He reaches out and clasps my hand in his, pulling me upright. "Come on, man."

I straighten and begin to walk.

My limbs feel like fucking Jell-O.

I place my hands on my hips while I try to slow the galloping in my chest, perfectly in tune with my teammates' applause.

Once I'm back on the sidelines, I bend, bracing my hands on my thighs for a moment while several of my teammates slap me on the back.

"Nichols is a *beast*!" Greene hoots.

In front of me Coach stares, offering me a curt nod before his eyes shift, flickering over each of us with the weight of authority while we wait for instruction.

"All right, listen up, boys." Coach's sharp tone cuts through the ambient noise, and the voices around me die. "Now that we've taken care of that nonsense, I've got an announcement to make and I need your full attention."

A ripple of curiosity spreads across the line. I exchange a glance with Tommy and wonder why the hell I'm so nervous.

"Starting this week, my daughter will be joining us as a student manager for the team," he announces.

The fist in my stomach disappears.

Thank fuck this isn't about me.

Around me, the boys exchange a look, and I can see the curiosity glittering in their eyes as Coach continues, "She'll be handling hydration, helping to bring equipment to and from practices and games, as well as cleaning uniforms and gear. But I want you to treat her with the same respect you'd show anyone on this team," Coach emphasizes. "She's here to learn and contribute. She's a hard worker and should be treated as a colleague, not as the coach's daughter. Is that clear?"

Chance Lockhart steps forward, his gaze narrowed on Coach Turner. Unlike the rest of us, he doesn't seem surprised at the news Coach has a daughter, which I suppose is to be expected. Chance and Coach have a history. But if the crease in his brow and the tight set of his mouth are any indication, the news Turner's daughter will be joining us agitates him.

He opens his mouth before he snaps it closed again, as if deciding against whatever it is he wanted to say.

Everyone around me nods in agreement. Beside me, Tommy nudges me in the ribs, grinning as he mouths, *Think she's hot?*

I snort, mumbling out of the corner of my mouth. "If she looks anything like Turner, not a chance in hell."

Tommy chuckles.

"There is one caveat," Coach continues, his gaze firm. "My daughter is off-limits, gentlemen. No dating, no flirting, no nonsense. I won't have you harassing her or giving her a hard time or placing bets on her back, or any of that other bullshit that goes on when a coach's daughter is dangled in front of a bunch of horn-ball athletes."

Tommy snorts, the sound so loud Coach glares at him. "*And* I also won't have you distracted. Your focus needs to remain solely on the field. We're a team, and that means staying focused on the game, not my daughter's personal life." He pauses, allowing the weight of his words to sink in.

"Oh, yeah," Tommy murmurs under his breath. "She's totally fucking hot."

I jab him in the ribs and he lets out an *oof* as Coach glances our way.

Does he not fucking listen?

"I've worked hard to build a program that demands discipline and dedication." Coach glares at us, his voice unwavering. "And I won't tolerate any drama that might derail us. If anyone here thinks they can test these boundaries, they're in for a rude awakening. And if I hear even so much as a rumble about you bothering her or breaking any of these rules, trust me when I say, you will regret it."

Shit. He means business.

Mission accomplished.

I'd rather cut my dick off than so much as look twice at the chick.

My gaze shifts behind him, and I wonder why the need for such a strong warning. Then again, I've been around athletes my whole life. We're a group of cocky motherfuckers, *horny* cocky motherfuckers, and I can see some of them viewing her as the ultimate conquest. Forbidden fruit just makes you want to take a bite all that much more.

"Are there any questions?" Coach asks. His gaze jumps to each and every one of us, and at our silence, he nods. "Good. I know some of you might be thinking this is a bit harsh," he admits, his expression softening just a fraction. "But I'm not just doing this for the team. I'm doing it for her, too. She's here for her own reasons and I won't let anything get in the way of that. Understood?"

"Yes Coach," everyone answers.

"Good." He cracks a smile for the first time since he stepped foot on the field, then shifts, revealing a slender figure waiting behind him.

My jaw unhinges.

I eat my words from moments ago as I blink at the woman hovering in the background with eyes I know firsthand are a brilliant cerulean blue because they've haunted my dreams in the two nights since we met.

I stare ahead at her, trying to convince myself she's a figment of my imagination. A mirage. Purely a product of my subconscious desires.

I've wanted to see her again ever since we parted in the park, and here she is. Stamped, sealed, and delivered right to me on a fucking die-if-you-touch-her silver platter.

My heart leaps into my throat while the sound of my pulse fills my ears so loud, I can barely register the words as Coach motions toward her with obvious pride and says, "Gentlemen, I'd like to introduce you to my daughter, Lane Turner."

Lane is Coach Turner's daughter.

Maybe if I say it to myself enough, it will sink in. Or somehow become untrue. The latter would be great.

She stands before the huddle of my teammates and gives a little wave while Coach stares each of us down, a warning in his eyes to punctuate the verbal one he just gave us.

I squint into the sun, sweat sliding down my forehead.

I feel like someone's playing a cruel joke on me. No way the girl I met over the weekend, the one I want so fucking badly, the one I can't stop thinking about, is the one girl I can't have.

My daughter is off-limits, gentlemen. No dating, no flirting, no nonsense. I won't have you harassing her or giving her a hard time. And I also won't have you distracted.

Fuck. He might as well have strung caution tape around her and nailed a stop sign to her forehead while he was at it.

Seriously, what the hell?

I stare at her, my gaze unwavering as I try to come to terms with this new piece of information.

If she was embarrassed by his impromptu speech, she gives no indication of it. If anything, she looks resigned as she stares into the sea of men around me with zero emotion.

I swallow as my gaze shifts, taking in her long legs and toned arms. She's wearing a pair of tight biker shorts and a tank top that showcases a small sliver of her midriff. She looks so fucking good, I want to eat her up while simultaneously shielding her from the probing eyes around me.

When my hungry gaze finishes its perusal and I return to her face, our eyes lock, and based on her cool stare, I'd guess she's not too happy to see me.

Did I imagine the chemistry between us?

When she glances away from me, I smother the disappointment churning in my guts.

Fuck me.

If Coach doesn't want any of the guys hitting on her, then maybe he should consider getting her one of those floral muumuus like my granny wears because what she has on is *not* sending the message that she's off-limits. If anything, it makes me contemplate throwing caution to the wind and completely ignoring everything Coach has just said.

Under any other circumstances, I might not heed his warning, I might pursue her anyway, but I'm on thin ice as it is after the hazing stunt over the weekend. The monstrous ache already blooming in my muscles is proof of that. I can't even imagine what he'd say if he found out I already had her number in my phone and several unanswered texts.

Hell, he'd probably have my balls in a vise grip and accuse me of harassment.

"Lane doesn't officially start until Wednesday," Coach continues, "In the meantime, Nichols will be staying after practice to help Mark with cleaning the gear."

I peel my eyes away from her and nod.

Fucking awesome.

"Now that we have that settled, let's get on with practice, shall we? We've wasted enough time for one day." Coach motions for the assistants to take the field and start us on drills while I try not to dwell on the girl talking to the equipment manager on the sidelines.

Practice lasts forever. Or at least that's what it feels like after the tire flips and two hours of busting my ass on drills.

By the time we finish, my muscles are wasted and I'm dog tired. Knowing I'm not finished only sours my mood.

"Nichols!" Mark, the equipment manager, calls out and when I glance his way, I find him still talking to Lane. "Take a minute to hydrate, then you're with me."

I nod. "Yes, sir," I grumble.

Frozen in place, I watch in a trance, unable to tear my eyes away from her as she hands him a packet of papers, then turns to leave.

I act on instinct, taking a step toward her. "Hey, Lane, wait up!" I call out.

Yep, that's right. After Coach's speech, I follow her off the field.

I'm either a glutton for punishment or just fucking stupid.

She didn't answer your texts, asshole. Clearly, she's uninterested.

Stupid it is.

"Lane, wait!" I call out one more time, praying Coach is otherwise occupied so I don't have to deal with his scrutiny and risk pissing him off any more than I already have.

He didn't say we couldn't talk to her, just that we can't pursue her.

Finally hearing me, Lane spins around, her face a mask of indifference. "What do you want, Teagan?"

Ouch. Not sure what I was expecting, but her greeting is even more frigid than I anticipated.

"You didn't answer my texts," I say as I come to a stop in front of her, matching her straightforward approach with one of my own.

"Is that a question or a statement?" She arches a brow while she waits, and I smile.

"Caught me. I guess what I meant to ask is, *why* didn't you text me back?"

She says nothing for a moment, shifting on her feet and glancing at the turf. "Listen, Teagan, you seem like a really nice guy—"

"Aw, shit." I groan. "You're giving me the brush-off?"

Her throat bobs as she meets my gaze, then glances away again, and it clicks where I've seen that exact shade of blue before—the blue hydrangeas my mother used to grow in the garden.

"Why didn't you text me back, Lane?" I ask again.

"My father is your coach."

A wave of relief crashes into me.

It's not personal. But it's also for reasons I can do nothing about.

"So, that's it? Don't shit where you eat?" I wince at my choice of words.

Seriously, Teagan. You're trying to win a hot chick over and you're talking about shit?

What the actual fuck?

"For lack of better words? Yeah." She shrugs and her lips twitch.

I rip my gaze from her mouth. "But you didn't know I played football until today, so why—"

"Your apology yesterday at my father's house was well-timed."

"Oh shit. You saw me?" I scrub a hand over my face when she nods.

"Listen, I'd better go." She starts to turn but I stop her with a hand on her arm.

Her gaze shifts from the point of contact to something behind us, and she stiffens.

Following her gaze, I find Coach talking to Chance on the sidelines, one hand on his shoulder, and I realize how this will look if he sees me.

Fuck. What the hell am I doing?

"He's just . . . overprotective," Lane explains, without being asked. "But if I were you, I'd lose my number."

This time, when she retreats I let her, watching her as she goes.

She's right. I should lose her number. Nothing good will come of pursuing her.

But I don't want to listen.

"What if I don't want to?" I call out, startling her.

She pauses, motionless as she glances over her shoulder. "Then you'll be wasting your time."

CHAPTER 6

LANE

I ALREADY WANT TO bury myself in a hole and never come back out, and it's not even my first official day of work yet. All I did was turn in my damn application.

My father's impromptu speech was bad enough, but dealing with Teagan *after* my father warned the team to stay away from me is a whole new level of mortification.

Still, I can't blame my dad for being overprotective. He spent the better part of the last year thinking I avoided this job because I was uncomfortable working with male athletes after falling pregnant to one of his players in football camp.

And he's not entirely wrong.

That *is* why I avoided this job.

But little does he know it's because the father's also on this field.

I swipe my bag off the bottom bleacher where I left it, ready to get the hell out of here and back to Sophie when a shadow looms over me.

Turning, I shield my eyes from the waning sun expecting my father or Mark, but instead, I find a stone-faced Chance staring down at me.

My heart jumps in my throat as I quickly take him in. His football gear only amplifies his muscular physique and broad shoulders. I've probably seen him in his football uniform and practice gear thousands of times, and still, the sight of him hits me like a hammer every single time.

He's like a vacuum, sucking all the air from the room, and I absolutely hate how he still affects me. The only difference between now and before is I rather enjoy breathing more than I enjoy his company.

He's beautiful on the outside, no doubt about it. Too bad he's rotten inside.

"Can I help you with something?" I ask, squinting up at him.

I can't help but wonder what he wants. It's not like we talk anymore.

"You can quit," he barks out.

My eyes widen in surprise before I school my expression into one of indifference. With a shake of my head, I sling my bag over my shoulder and step around him. "Sorry, but I can't do that."

A beat of silence passes before he calls at my back. "Lane, why the hell are you here?"

I pause in my tracks, fighting the manic laughter threatening to bubble from my throat. He, of all people, has zero right to question me about *anything*.

Spinning around to face him, I reign in the anger boiling my blood as I say, "I'm not sure it's any of your business, but isn't it obvious? I need a job and the money that comes with it."

"Not this one you don't."

I glance up at him, jaw tight as I fight the urge to cuss him out. How did I ever find him attractive? How could I have fallen for such an egotistical prick? And how dare he tell me where I can and cannot work.

"And what exactly is *wrong* with me working here?" I ask.

"How about the fact that it'll be uncomfortable."

"For whom? You, or me?" I arch a brow, arms crossed over my chest. "Because I find it hard to believe any part of you is worried about how I might feel."

"For *both* of us." He takes a step closer. Instinctively, I take one back. "Are you really telling me you want to see me nearly every fucking day?"

"No," I grind out. *Definitely not.*

"Okay, then there are plenty of other jobs."

I scoff, unsure of why I'm surprised. As usual, he's only worried about himself and how my presence will affect him, not how it might help me and my life. "I'd be hard pressed to find any other job like this one that will help me get the position I want after college, and certainly not one that pays this much for so little work, not to mention free childcare. Or did you forget I still have a child?"

"No, I didn't fucking forget," he snaps, and my brows rise.

He's so unflappable on the field and incapable of feeling, I almost forgot he's human.

"Is that why you're here?" he asks. "Is this some way of rubbing my mistakes in my face? You think I ruined your life, so now you want to ruin mine?"

Bile rises in the back of my throat, and I want to punch him so badly I fist my hands at my sides to stop myself from doing something I'll regret. "Sophie is *not* a pawn," I spit. "Don't worry, your dirty little secret is safe with me. No one knows you're her father," I hiss.

Relief flickers in his dark gaze and it's like a hot poker to my anger. He exhales and nods. "Okay. But I still don't like the idea of you parading around in front of all these guys."

I bite the inside of my cheek to keep from lashing out.

Since when has Chance ever been possessive of me? And what right does he have to tell me what I can and cannot do?

"I think my father's warning to the team was clear enough. Besides, you have no hold on me, Chance. We were never anything besides—"

"Don't say that." His expression morphs into something bordering on regret, causing me to blink as if I might be imagining it. "You know we had something real. I just can't have any complications or distractions in my life."

And there it is. The truth. Or at least part of it because not for one second do I think what we had was real.

Chance is a lot of things, but having a bleeding heart is not one of them.

A rueful smile curls my lips. "I'm all too aware of how you can't have 'distractions' in your life," I say, making air quotes with my fingers. "But as long as we're no longer together, you have no say in what I do with mine."

"You say that like I'm doing this just for me."

I snort and shake my head.

"I helped get your father this spot, didn't I?" He shrugs. "And who knows what the future holds. I might be able to get him something in the NFL one day but seeing you here every day won't serve me well if I'm to keep my head."

I narrow my eyes on his face. To hang my father's career over my head is cruel. I know damn well what got him here; it's why I've kept my mouth shut all this time, but we both know my father isn't moving to the next level with him.

I say nothing, waiting for him to finish his tantrum or whatever the hell this is.

"You know I still have feelings for you." He steps forward and I hold my breath.

When he reaches out and slides a lock of my hair through his fingers, I jerk away from his touch. "Don't act like we were more than we were, Chance. I was a fool once, but never again. I'm not the same starry-eyed teenager I was back then. I've grown up."

He licks his lips, gaze flickering over me. My stomach sours.

"That's too bad." His lips curl. "I liked that starry-eyed teenager."

Yeah, because you could so easily manipulate her.

God, I was a fool to think we were good together, that he loved me . . .

I swallow over the bile rising in the back of my throat and fake gag. "You're the same selfish narcissist you've always been, Chance. Some things never change."

"That's not fair. You know I want you, Lane, but I want football more. It would be a waste to squander my talent right now when what I need most is to focus. Maybe once I have a few years under my belt in the NFL . . ."

I fight the urge to dry heave again and instead laugh. "Let me just hold my breath."

Disapproval glints in his eyes. "Sarcasm isn't an attractive trait."

Neither is selfishness, but here we are.

I bite my tongue in an effort to save my energy.

There's no point in arguing; it's like going round and round on a Ferris wheel with no end in sight. So I save my energy. He's not worth it, anyway. All he'll do is say something in return to rile me up even more, and I've already had my temperature spiked enough for one day.

"Are we done here?" I ask at the same time my father takes the field. "Because I have a job to do."

Chance's gaze flickers to my father then back, and I know he'll retreat now that he's looking this way. God forbid my father discovers what a jackass he is.

As expected, he nods then steps away from me, snatching his helmet off the bench on the sidelines before jogging over to where my father stands, clipboard in hand.

I exhale, my stomach tight as a drum as I stare out into the football field. I hate that Chance still has the ability to mess with my head after all this time. I'm over him. Of that, I'm sure. Whatever we shared was a long time ago. My wounds have since been licked and healed over. The scabs might've formed scars, but I'm as good as new. At least, I'd like to think I am. I have no room in my life for what-ifs. I only have time for right here, right now.

I want people in my life who don't view Sophie's existence as some monumental hardship or sacrifice. I want someone who sees her like I do—a blessing. And if that means I have to live the rest of my days lonely and single, then so be it. I don't have time for half-assed feelings or relationships.

I turn and storm out of the stadium. Our conversation—his request that I simply find another job—really pisses me off. And the fact that he has any effect on my mood pisses me off even more.

Taking a cleansing breath and counting slowly to five like I do when I'm overwhelmed with Sophie, I reign in my anger. Once I've banished it to the back of my mind, I head for my car, more determined than ever.

I start Wednesday. I have a new job, and no one, especially not Chance Lockhart, is going to stop me from doing it.

CHAPTER 7

TEAGAN

B Y THE TIME I get back to the athlete dorms, I'm fucking spent. My legs and arms feel like rubber as I pick my way down the hall toward the suite I share with Tommy.

I try the doorknob to find it unlocked and enter the small living space between our bedrooms. CU doesn't have athlete apartments, only dorms, but still, the setup is a hell of a lot better than the regular dormitories, which feature only a single room and a bathroom on each floor. Instead, the athletes are set up with a suite that has a small common area big enough for the essentials—a small sofa, a bistro table, television, a mini fridge, and a single bathroom—which joins a bedroom on each side.

When I step inside, I find Tommy on the couch, one arm draped around Melissa, his girlfriend, a pretty cool chick who commutes from her parents' place nearby.

His attention shifts from the television to me, and his brows rise. "Bro, you all right? I told Melissa about the shit Coach put you through. You've got to be dead."

"That's one word for it." I kick my shoes off on the mat by the door, my duffle bag slung over my shoulder. "Is that pizza?" I ask, zeroing in on the takeout boxes gracing the counter.

Tommy nods. "We saved you some."

"Thank fu—" I start, then stop myself when I remember Melissa is here. "I mean, thanks," I say instead.

I drop my bag by the small table and tear into one of the boxes, lifting a slice to my mouth and taking a huge bite at the same time Tommy braces one arm over the back of the couch and turns to me. "So, that's some shit about Coach's daughter working with us, huh? Do you think something happened before and he felt the need to warn the guys off like that?" He shakes his head. "So fucking weird."

I shrug, grabbing a napkin from the table and wiping my mouth before I speak. "I don't know. It got me wondering, too, but you know how some of these guys are."

"Horny assholes."

"Exactly." I shrug. "Some will see her as a conquest."

"I guess I didn't think about it like that, but you have a point." Tommy frowns. "Back in high school, the basketball coach's daughter was super hot, and I remember hearing rumors about how the team had bets going on who could bag her first."

I stuff more pizza in my face, mostly because the thought of some douchebags making a bet like that about Lane chaps my ass. It almost makes me grateful for Turner's warning.

Or at least it would, if it didn't also apply to me.

My thoughts drift to Lane, and how indifferent she'd seemed. Damn if it doesn't make me want to try even harder to win her over.

I don't know what it is about her.

I can't explain it.

Obviously she's beautiful, but it's more than that. There's this intangible thing I can't put my finger on that draws me to her.

The sound of squabbling and slightly raised voices interrupts my train of thought, and I focus back on Tommy to see him arguing with Melissa. I arch a brow and grab another slice of pizza, plowing it into my face as I try my best to ignore their conversation.

"Come on, baby, you know I think you're the hottest chick on the planet," he murmurs in a soft voice.

Ah. I stifle a chuckle. *They're arguing over the fact he called another chick hot. Classic.*

Melissa picks up her phone in a huff and starts scrolling while Tommy glances back at me and rolls his eyes to which I raise my hands up in surrender.

Yeah, not getting in the middle of this one.

"How long have you two been together again?" I ask because they fight like a married couple.

"Officially?" Tommy glances over at Melissa with a soft look in his eyes. "It's been a year, but unofficially, it's been more like two."

"Unofficially?" I ask when Melissa laughs. "I'm sensing there's a story here."

Melissa lowers her phone, and any irritation she showed toward him a moment ago vanishes into thin air. "He's saying that because when he first asked me out two years ago, I said no."

"But I was persistent." Tommy grins like a dope. "I basically told her I'd wait until she was ready and settled into the friend zone."

I huff out a laugh. "Sounds like my buddy, Graham."

"It wasn't so bad. We were friends for a year, and then when she finally stopped dating the total douchebag she'd been seeing, I went for it. Struck while the iron was hot and mended her broken heart."

"So sweet," Melissa says drily.

"Nice play." I laugh and shake my head. "Settling for the rebound is risky." I finish my second slice of pizza and get up to retrieve a glass of water when it hits me.

That's it.

Coach said none of us could pursue Lane romantically. But he never said we had to stay away from her entirely. He never said we couldn't be friends.

Clearly Lane doesn't date football players, but that's not the only reason she has walls up. There's more to why she's so guarded. She said her life is complicated, which tells me it will take a hell of a lot more than a little charm and flirtation to scale those walls.

Someone as guarded as she is needs to build trust.

Just look at my sister, Brynn.

For years, she never let anyone in because of her assault in high school. She'd been so scared of getting hurt and being vulnerable and whatever the fuck else. It took someone she's known for years to break through those walls.

And while I don't have the advantage of time and history with Lane on my side, I can be a friend. I can earn her trust first and play the long game. Be the best fucking friend on the face of the planet, and with time, get her to open up to me.

Coach will see this, and not only will it work in my favor and put me back in his good graces, but I'll grow on him, too. He'll get to know me better as a man and not just one of his players. And slowly, so fucking slowly it'll probably kill me, I'll worm my way into her heart, and earn Coach's blessing while I'm at it.

It's the perfect plan.

I grin. What could go wrong?

CHAPTER 8

LANE

W EDNESDAY COMES FAR SOONER than I'd like, and after getting acquainted with the employee day care on campus I now have privileges too, I meet my friend Gabby at the student coffee shop, The Buzzy Bean. It's crowded, teeming with students heading to and from class, so while we wait to place our orders I fill her in on my weekend and everything she missed.

Once we finally have our coffees and croissants in hand, I take a large sip of mine as we step outside into the mid-morning sun, hoping the caffeine will help perk me up, or at least clear the fog hovering in my brain. Sophie woke this morning at five a.m. after I stayed up far too late reading, which was entirely my fault. Either way, both have me exhausted and regretting my life choices as I try to fight the brain fog dulling my thoughts.

"So, let me get this straight," Gabby says, waving her paper takeout bag around. "You met a hot guy at the park who was charming and didn't mind that you had your daughter with you, but you're going to completely ghost him now just because you discovered he plays football?"

Gabby eyes me like I'm crazy, one dark brow arched like a black cat on Halloween, but that's one of the things I love about her. I never have to guess what she's thinking; she wears all her emotions plainly on her face. It reminds me of when I was pregnant and she went around giving half the school the stink-eye for being judgmental about it.

When I got knocked up, most of my friends acted as though they'd stick by me while simultaneously turning around and stabbing me in the back. Rumors about the alleged father spread around the school, mostly fueled by these "so-called friends." Some of the things people said were so outlandish, I would have laughed if I hadn't spent the entire nine months punishing myself for making the mistake in the first place and scared out of my mind to become a mother at such a young age. They called me terrible names, flinging insults like frisbees, all while being nice to my face.

At least the boys openly stared and snickered. I preferred that to the two-faced girls who hid their condemnation behind empty platitudes and plastic smiles. Gabby was the only one who truly had my back. Our friendship grew closer as the weeks and months passed, and by the time I gave birth to Sophie, we both had someone in our corner I knew I could never replace no matter how crazy life got.

Now, she lives on campus with her new roommate, who would've been me if circumstances had been different.

The thought sends a stab of jealousy through my chest, but I push it down. It's not fair to begrudge her a normal college life, and I can no longer regret my choices either because they brought me Sophie.

And Sophie is *everything.*

Now I spend most of my energy on ensuring I'm the perfect mother and daughter. No more mistakes. No more decisions based on emotion that might put me in a bad place.

"You know I don't date football players," I say, eyeing her.

Never again.

"Besides, he *seemed* okay with me having Sophie. I don't really *know* anything. The idea of dating someone with a child and *actually* dating them and being cool with it are two entirely different things."

"Okay, you might have a point, and under normal circumstances, I wouldn't argue with the semantics behind football players being off-limits. I mean, your dad is the coach. That could potentially get messy, but you're never going to know if it would work if you don't try, right?"

I sigh. "I don't need to try to know it won't work. There are a million reasons why I won't give him a shot. Him being a football player is merely one of a dozen."

"But you *did* give him your number. There had to be a reason. I don't think you've done that, like, ever."

We take the curve in the sidewalk leading to her lecture hall.

She has a point.

"Temporary insanity?"

She snorts and I grimace.

Gabby's been pestering me to start dating for a while, and I know she means well, but I don't have time for anyone else in my life. Hell, I barely have time for her. We only ever hang out in-between classes and on the occasions she stops by the house to visit with me and Soph.

She pauses in front of Smithe Hall and scrunches her nose. "This is my stop."

I chuckle. "Don't look so excited."

"I know some people dig astronomy, but it's so freaking boring. Ugh. I fall asleep every single time." She shifts the book bag on her shoulder. "What do you have going on the rest of the day?"

"After this class, I have anthropology, and then I'll probably get an hour of homework in before practice starts and I show up for my first day as student manager for the team." I snap my mouth shut, eyes wide when I realize what I said. I'd yet to tell her about the student manager gig, mostly because I know she'll have *feelings* about me working in such close proximity to Chance. Even before I got pregnant, she disliked him, but after? I can't so much as say his name without her lip curling.

I press my fingers over my mouth. Maybe she didn't hear me?

"Say what now about being a student manager?"

I wince. "The estimate on the roof of the lake house is much higher than I'd hoped, and if I want to move in anytime soon, I need the money to fix it, and I refuse to accept financial help from my parents, so . . ."

"So you took your father up on the offer to get you that spot?" she asks, and I nod. Gabby squeals and reaches out, yanking me into a hug.

Her enthusiasm surprises me.

"That's amazing! And good for you for taking what you want." She squeezes my arms as she draws back. "You deserve it, and screw Chance Lockhart. You shouldn't be put out because he's an asshole. If you didn't take it, someone else with connections would. We both know how that goes, so it might as well be you. Don't go feeling all guilty. Everything you have, you've earned through hard work. You're the furthest thing from being a nepo baby."

My cheeks flush and I give a little shrug. Gabby knows me too well. "Well, we agree about Chance, but like it or not, taking the job in and of itself is nepotism, but it doesn't matter. I promised myself I'd have a place of my own and get out of their hair by graduation, and that'll be here before you know it."

"Wait." Gabby's brows knit. "If you're taking the student manager position, that also means . . ." She trails off as her eyes brighten. "You'll be forced to see Teagan nearly every single day."

"Don't remind me." I groan. "Though I'm sure it's a non-issue after ignoring his texts and telling him to lose my number."

He might've given the impression of being persistent but in my experience, guys our age lose interest, fast. No one wants to put in the amount of effort dating me would take.

Besides, it's not like we *really* know each other. We met *one* time prior to practice on Monday.

My gaze shifts, and it's as though our conversation conjured him when I see him rounding the corner of the student affairs building.

"*Shit*," I hiss and jerk my gaze away, dropping my head and praying he didn't see me.

"Lane, hey!" he calls out.

I wince, then proceed to cower behind Gabby's petite frame like I can hide from him, even though he's obviously already spotted me.

"Is it the insanely good-looking blond we're avoiding?" Gabby asks, her tone awed.

I nod, unwilling to glance up at him to confirm his proximity.

Gabby, however, has no problem staring. Her mouth curls as she checks him out.

"Stop that," I hiss-whisper. "Don't let him see me."

"For the love of all that is holy, that man is *fire*. Please tell me this is Teagan."

"Lane," the voice calls out again, only this time he's closer and slightly out of breath from his jaunt across campus to reach us.

I swallow. Hiding is useless, and when I lift my head, it's to the sight of his beautiful face.

He's even more handsome than I remembered, and it's as if my mind blocked out the memory as a means of self-preservation.

His blond hair is a mess of waves, trimmed neatly on the sides and back. I only saw him two days ago, yet it looks like he's gotten a haircut since then, and I hate that my first thought is how good it looks. How good *he* looks.

Ugh. What is it with men and freshly cut hair? Why is a well-groomed and put together man so sexy? I can't even remember the last time I had a haircut. Maybe a year ago?

When you have more responsibilities than time, you tend to let yourself slip. I'm not even sure I know the meaning of the term self-care.

Manicure? Pfft. My four-year-old does my nails now, which has the added benefit of painting the entire fingertip.

Pedicure? Ha! Haven't had one since my sixteenth birthday when Dad booked a spa day for me and Mom as a gift.

Don't even get me started on facials. I'm lucky to muster the time and energy to wash my face at night.

I run a hand self-consciously through my locks.

I bet he smells good, too.

I barely resist the urge to sniff him when I ask, "What are you doing here?"

"Uh, I go to school here, remember?" He stares down at me, a grin curving his mouth while he squints, his eyes crinkling in the corners.

"Right. I knew that." I shake my head, slightly flustered.

Of course I knew he went to school here. What a dumb question.

"What I meant to ask is why you're flagging me down after my father gave a clear warning to stay away from me and I told you to lose my number?"

Beside me, Gabby chokes on a sip of coffee.

Teagan turns toward her while I shoot her a glare and sticks a hand out. "I'm sorry, I don't think we've met. I'm Teagan Nichols."

Gabby beams at him as she shakes his hand a little too en- thusiastically. "Gabby Gonzolez. Lane's best friend." She grins. "You're hot."

"Gabby!" I croak.

Teagan chuckles and his dimples take that moment to make their appearance.

I want to smooth them out with my fingers, make them disappear. They're too fucking cute for their own good.

"Hey, Teagan!" Two long-legged brunettes call out as they pass.

He offers them a head nod while I fight a spike of irritation.

Of course. He probably has a million girls he strings along, just like the rest of them.

"Those your groupies?" I purr.

"Depends." He grins. "You jealous?"

I choke on a laugh when Gabby slaps a hand over my chest to stop whatever word vomit is about to spew from my mouth. "Do you like kids, Teagan?" she asks him.

I want to die.

Seriously.

Dig a hole and throw me in.

My entire face catches fire, but the worst part is that I find myself waiting for his answer.

But Teagan just chuckles like this is a question he's asked all the time and is not completely humiliating. "I love kids. Tiny humans are cool."

"See?" Gabby turns to me, eyes wide. "Tiny humans are cool."

"*Anyway* . . ." I drawl, trying to quickly change the subject. Not that I want to be discussing *anything* with him. "Didn't I tell you to lose my number?" I ask him again.

"Lane!" Gabby gasps, but Teagan remains unfettered.

He hooks his thumbs in the pockets of his jeans, the picture of easy confidence as his lips quirk. "I don't scare easily."

Beside me Gabby snickers, and I shoot her a glare that says, *Don't you have class?*

I toy with my coffee cup, flustered. "There has to be something that would turn you off."

"Just liars."

"Well, great. I'll make it a point to lie through my teeth from now on." Frustrated, I sigh and rake a hand through my hair. "Listen, I'm busy, and I'm not looking to date right now."

"So, if that's a lie, then you *are* looking to date?"

"What?" I shake my head. "No. I was just—"

Teagan laughs, and I roll my eyes.

"Relax, Lane. Who said anything about wanting to date you?"

You know a minute ago when I thought I might die of embarrassment? Yeah, I was wrong. Now is the time of my death.

My cheeks catch fire, and I want to crawl in a hole and die. How could I be so presumptuous? Of course he doesn't want to date me. I'm a college student and a single mom. I flat out told him my life is complicated. I'm basically a walking, talking disclaimer. Most guys don't want to touch me with a ten-foot pole when they find out I've got a child at twenty-one.

"Oh. I . . ." I snap my mouth closed. *What the hell do I say?*

If he's not interested in me, then what *does* he want from me?

"Right, sorry. My bad," I mumble.

He chuckles and bumps my arm with his. "Lane, I'm kidding." Then he rolls his eyes. "Of course I was interested. Have you looked in a mirror lately?" He reaches out and brushes a thumb over the heat in my cheeks, and I suck in a breath at the electric jolt of his touch. "You're so freaking cute when you're flustered."

"But . . ." I stumble over my words. "My father . . ."

Teagan grimaces at the reminder. "I know. Kind of put a hitch in my step, not to mention the fact that you're clearly uninterested. You and I probably aren't the best idea."

All the air leaves my lungs as if someone popped me like a balloon, and I feel a pang of disappointment deep inside my chest. Which is ridiculous. I don't want a relationship, but I can't deny that his interest feels nice.

"I couldn't agree more," I say, chewing on my lip.

Gabby's forehead crinkles, her eyes narrowing as she crosses her arms over her chest and asks, "So, what *do* you want from her, then?"

"Wait," I say as a thought occurs to me. "Do you want me to put in a good word for you with my father? Is that what this is about?"

After all, he had gotten in trouble with him, hadn't he?

"What? No!" Teagan flinches before shaking his head. "Listen, I know we barely know each other, so I won't take your question personally, but let me just tell you now, I am *not* that guy. I'm not a user. I wouldn't ask you to do that, and something tells me you wouldn't even if I did."

He's not wrong.

"But I don't give up easily. And you seem pretty cool." He bumps my shoulder like we're buddies. "I just thought we could be friends."

"*Friends,*" I say, like I don't understand the meaning of the word.

"Yeah." He grins, and when his dimples pop, I want to stick a finger in one. "You know, a person who someone talks to and maybe even admires in a non-sexual way? Someone you hang out with for fun?"

"I know what friends are," I snap, even though I might not have much time for them. "What I don't understand is why you'd want to be friends with *me*."

Wow. What a winning endorsement, Lane. Way to sell yourself.

Teagan's brows rise. "Well, after I realized you're clearly uninterested in me, I decided it was probably best to heed your father's warning. But it's hard to meet cool people outside of football, and I just figured, why not? I like you. You're funny and cute and I could do worse."

"Wow. Sign me up," I say, my tone dry while Gabby chokes on a laugh again.

Teagan rolls his eyes. "I don't mean it like that. I'm a freshman, remember? The new guy on campus." He shrugs. "You seem like a pretty cool chick, and I could use a friend."

I stare at him like he's a new breed of animal.

"And there's only so much testosterone I can take before I need a break from it, you know?" He screws up his face. "It would be nice to have a chick around whom I can talk to and hang out with when I have time. So, what do you say?"

All I can think is, *he used 'whom' properly*. If anything, that's reason alone to be friends.

"What do I say?" I stare at him for a moment, at a loss for words.

"Yeah. You can never have too many friends, right? So, is it a deal?"

Beside me, Gabby hip bumps me. "Yeah, bestie, what do you say?"

I frown over at her before I return to the intense cerulean blue of Teagan's eyes, unsure of what game he's playing. "I don't know. I barely have time for the friends I do have."

"You're talking to a division one football athlete, remember? And I'm currently in-season. Time is not an asset I have either, so you're not alone."

I hesitate, mostly because I can't think of one good reason to say no.

What does one more friend hurt? It's not like I'm making him any promises, and he seems completely genuine. My gut tells me Teagan Nichols is a good guy, despite whatever went down with my father and the team.

"Come on, Lane," he says when I don't answer right away. "I'm not asking for a proposal here. I'm just asking to chat here and there when we see each other on campus. Maybe we could study together. Talk before practice or grab a coffee occasionally . . ."

Gabby shoots me a pleading look. "Damnit, I have to go or I'm going to be late." She steps forward and wraps me up in a hug, whispering, "If you're crazy enough to *not* want to jump this boy, you better at least be friends with the poor guy." She pulls away, and I hate her a little when she winks and says, "If you don't, I will." She offers Teagan a little wave goodbye before she disappears into the building.

When I focus back on Teagan, I purse my lips. "And what if I say no?"

"I'll ask again tomorrow." He grins.

I huff. "Are you always this persistent?"

"When it comes to things I want." His eyes glitter, and my stomach clenches.

"Aside from school and work, I hardly ever leave the house," I warn.

"I get it." He shrugs. "If I'm free, I can come to you."

I open and close my mouth in one last-ditch effort to come up with an excuse to avoid him, but I'm all out of excuses. This boy has an answer for everything, and the truth is, I have no real reasons for why we can't be friends. So, I offer him a feeble, "But we hardly know each other."

He snorts and reaches out, giving my ponytail a playful tug. "Looks like we'll have to *get* to know each other. That's what friends do, right?"

I take a deep breath, eyeing him closely. "If you think this will lead to something more, I should tell you now, you're setting yourself up for disappointment. I don't have the capacity for more."

"Worried about me?" He cocks his head, his gaze warm as my heart leaps in my chest.

This is a bad idea.

I swallow. "No. Just stating facts."

He stares at me for a moment, some emotion I can't read flickering in his eyes. "Who hurt you?"

My eyes widen, and I take a step back. "What?"

"Someone did," he says so plainly, I want to ask him how he knows.

"No one hurt . . ." I trail off and scoff, evading his observation. "Guys can't *just* be friends with women. At least not when they're attracted to each other," I say, hating that I'm repeating back the words Chance said to me after practice. "You'll either come to want something or expect something in return. That's how it always goes."

"So you admit you're attracted to me?" he teases.

My lips part, aghast, before he steps closer and slings one of his muscular arms over my shoulder. "Oh, I can be friends, Lane Turner. I'm a giver, not a taker."

My heart seizes as my mind rolls completely into the gutter. *I'm a giver, not a taker.* My gaze drifts over his square jaw to the gentle curves of his mouth. His lips are full and pink and—*what the hell?*

I swallow when I realize he's waiting for me to respond, to say something. "As long as we're on the same page," I manage and barely refrain from patting myself on the back for forming words.

He gives my shoulders a little squeeze like we're already best buds. "Trust me when I say I won't expect anything from you. At least not anything you're unwilling to give."

"Teagan, if this is a game—"

"Damn," he gives his head a little shake. "You don't trust easily, do you?"

"No." There's no point in denying the truth.

"Well then, I'll just have to earn it, won't I?"

He drops his arm and takes a step back as he smiles down at me, an adorable crinkle forming at the corners of his eyes. "I'm a good friend, Lane. The fucking best. Just you wait and see."

CHAPTER 9

TEAGAN

I SIT DOWN AT one of the small tables at The Buzzy Bean with a sandwich and an iced coffee. A quick glance at my phone tells me it's almost seven o'clock. After practice wrapped up for the day, I showered and came straight here, hoping to get some homework and studying done until they close at nine because I'm one hundred percent certain the second I get to the apartment and sink down onto my bed, I'll be out like a light.

I suppose I have a right to my exhaustion. Between football, stressing over the situation with Knox, and now chasing after a girl, it makes sense I could use a little sleep.

When I told Lane I hardly had any free time to spare, I wasn't lying. A college athlete's schedule makes me wonder how the hell any of the guys can even find the time to date during August through January. Then again, most of my teammates are either already in a relationship or only care about no-strings hookups. Now I understand why.

Every morning, I wake around five-thirty, take a shower and examine my life choices while I eat breakfast, then get my shit together for the day. By six-thirty, I'm in the gym working on strength and conditioning with the boys. Afterward, I have just enough time to shower and hightail my ass to class.

A little after one o'clock, I get a break to take lunch, and then most days, we watch game film from two to two-thirty in the afternoon. By then, it's time to get taped up before practice where Coach beats our asses into the ground for the next two and a half hours, sometimes more if we need extra training or skill work.

Depending on the day, we wrap up around six or six-thirty, which gives my hangry ass time to eat something and do school-work before my head hits the pillow.

It's not an understatement to say a division one college foot-ball player eats, breathes, and sleeps football. It's my fucking job and I love it. I know my time with football is limited, and so I'm trying to soak up every minute, but I'm also tired as hell.

I open my Comparative Education textbook and stare at the pages for what feels like ages. I take a bite of my sandwich while I read, but I find myself having to reread the same passage more than once because my head's not in it. I'm too busy thinking about Lane to fucking concentrate. I've met the girl a mere three times, yet I can't seem to push her out of my thoughts. She's everywhere I look. I see her eyes in the bright blue of the sky, smell a hint of her floral citrus scent on the breeze, recall the flush in her cheeks with the blush of the setting sun. I've never wanted anyone as much as I want her, and I don't know what to fucking do with myself because it's so damn nonsensical. Still, no matter how much I try and make sense of it, I can't.

The only good news is, putting my focus on her takes it off Knox.

With a sigh, I give up on reading while I finish eating, content to just enjoy my food before I dive back in.

My phone vibrates from its perch on the table where I placed it facedown so it wouldn't distract me, but since I've given up on studying, I peek at the screen to see a message in the group chat from one of the boys.

Jace:

How's the lady situation? Fill us in and take my mind off my throbbing hamstrings.

Atlas:

Tell me about it, bro. In-season training is no joke. I just got back to my apartment.

Graham:

All is well over here. I only have one leg that's tired since moving to Chicago, and it's not the ones I'm standing on. ;)

Atlas:

Leg is an exaggeration, let's be fair.

Jace:

More like a pinky finger.

Me:

Naw, pinky toe is most accurate.

Graham:

Laugh it up, but I have TONS of energy at the end of the day for extracurriculars.

Chris:

Ooh. Are we making sex jokes?

I snort and begin to type, skipping past the part where Coach kicked my ass yesterday and start with an update on Lane since I can't get her out of my head, anyway.

Me:

Saw the chick again. And you'll never believe who she is.

Chris:

WHO?!

Me:

She's the fucking coach's daughter.

Jace:

Shit. That could get messy.

Graham:

Kind of like dating your best friend's sister?

Atlas:

Exactly like that.

Jace

Assholes.

Me

Especially when the coach spends twenty minutes introducing her and warning every single one of his players to stay the hell away from her, and that if any of us are caught asking her out or trying to hook up with her, we're done.

Atlas

Oof. Tough break.

Graham

That sucks, man.

Jace

You could always keep it a secret.

Atlas

How'd that work out for you?

Jace

I got the girl, didn't I?

Chris

He's got a point.

Me

Not sure it's that simple. This chick is guarded like Fort Knox, and she's not letting anyone break those walls. My guess is someone hurt her, but I have a plan that will solve the coach problem and get to let her guard down.

Chris

Damn, I love a man with a plan.

Graham

A shitty plan.

Jace

Hey, my plan was shitty, and I got the girl, didn't I?

Me

We're going to be friends.

Several minutes pass in silence and when no texts come through, I wonder if my last message didn't send.

Me

Hello? Did you all leave simultaneously to take a shit or something?

Chris

A group shit. Now, that's a new one.

Jace

I was waiting for the plan.

Atlas

Wait . . . is that . . . that's the plan? Be her fucking friend?

Teagan

Yeah, it's brilliant.

Graham

Aw, hell no. You friend zoned yourself? Trust me when I say that's a bad idea. I know from experience, bro, because I did NOT get the girl.

Atlas

Thanks for that, btw.

Graham

I would say fuck you, but I ended up with Sky, so . . . you're welcome?

Jace

Bro, noooooo.

Chris

Even I know that's a bad fucking idea and I'm a moron.

Jace

First time I've agreed with Chris.

Me

Wait and hear me out. I can't date her, right? Coach said she is off-limits, and I'm already on thin ice as it is. Plus, she's not looking to date, remember? She's got walls.

Me

So, I become her friend. Think of it as going undercover or infiltrating enemy lines. I'll be the best damn friend she's ever had. Coach will see that and get used to me hanging around her AS A FRIEND. She opens up, and then BOOM! Before she knows what hit her, I dial up the charm and swoop in and sweep her off her feet. It's perfect. By then, Coach will see my intentions are pure and he'll like me so much, he'll be more than happy to give us his blessing.

Graham

Yeah, somehow, I don't see it going that way.

Jace

Dude, has Graham not taught you anything? Once you enter the friend zone, you stay in the fucking friend zone. There's no coming back from that. You might as well cut off your dick and be done with it.

Chris

I agree. Before you know it, you're holding their purse while they pee in a seedy bar and giving them boy advice about "the other guy."

Atlas

Yup. I hate to say this, dude, but I agree with them.

Me

Okay, assholes. Do you have any better ideas? Because from where I'm standing, I can't see any other options.

Jace

Pretty much ANY other option would be better.

Chris

Show her your willy.

Atlas

Right. Because sexual harassment is a great way to win over a chick.

It'll work. It has to because this chick is different, and I can't get her out of my fucking head. She's not looking to date or hook up with other guys. In fact, I get the feeling she barely has a social life.

Chris

Ah, a social pariah, huh? I like it. Those chicks are wild in bed.

Teagan

What the fuck?

Jace

Ignore him. The only date he's had since I met him has been the standing one he has with his hand.

Chris

Rude.

Chris

But true.

Graham

I don't know, man. It could work. Just make sure to constantly hover the line and don't wait too long to cross it.

Jace

Shit. So we're going with this? It's a plan?

Me

We're not going with anything.

Jace

Fine. It's a fucking plan.

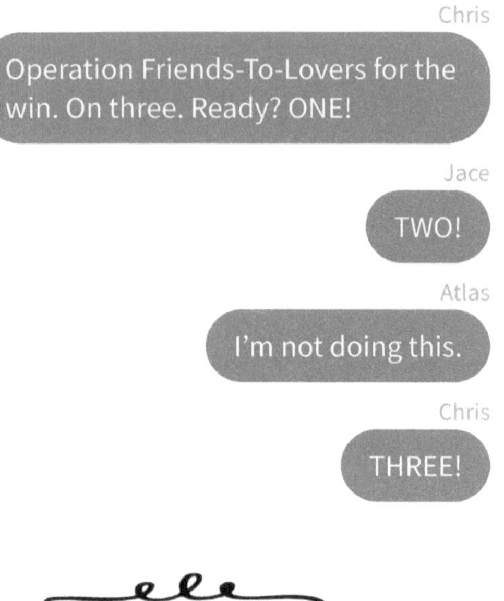

I jog onto the field with my helmet in hand. I busted my ass getting here early so I could talk to Lane before practice, but as I exit the tunnel, I catch sight of her and my stomach lurches.

Apparently, I wasn't the only one with a plan to get to her before practice, because she's not alone.

I slow my stride and curse under my breath as Chance Lockhart closes in on her.

Turning, I nod my head in greeting to Mark, but I'm distracted, and I can't seem to help myself from turning my attention back to Lane.

The stiff set of her spine, her tightly crossed arms, and the flattening of her lips indicate she's pissed off. I don't need to be an expert in body language to see it, and though it should bring me some sense of relief that she's not pleased to be the center of his attention, it doesn't. Instead, my head is flooded with a myriad of questions, things I want to know but can't ask.

I try not to watch them as I stretch, but my gaze gravitates toward her regardless.

What the hell is he doing talking to her?

Do they know each other?

Of course they do. Her father coached their high school team before getting the gig at Cumberland, which means they went to school together.

Grinding my teeth, I turn away from them when I can no longer take the rapid-fire thoughts.

I have zero right to be jealous. It's no secret Chance and Coach Turner are tight, so it would stand to reason Lane has some form of relationship with him. And it's none of my business what the parameters of it are. I promised Lane friendship, and there's no room for jealousy among friends.

For the sake of the cause, I swallow over the hot, sticky feelings swirling in my gut.

I'm more than frustrated when practice starts before I get the chance to talk to her, and by the time it ends, the effort to focus on anything but her nearly kills me.

She steps onto the field as the guys amble off, some shooting subtle glances in her direction as she helps Mark with the tackle dummies and strike shields.

The second Coach called practice to an end, he made a beeline for the tunnel to his office, so I know it's safe to approach as I jog toward her. Even if it weren't, I'm not sure I'd care.

Once I reach her, I draw in a breath and steady my racing heart. "Hey."

Lane glances over her shoulder and though she shakes her head, I take the subtle quirk of her lips as a good sign. "No tire flipping today?"

"Uh," I laugh and scratch my head, "no. I think I'll try and stay out of trouble, make that a onetime thing."

She helps Mark load the last strike shield onto his truck, then turns, her blue eyes sparkling as she says, "That's probably wise."

"What are you doing after this?" I blurt.

She brushes past me, heading for the hydration station where she begins collecting the water bottles and placing them in the baskets. "I have to finish up here, and then I'm headed home, but I still have some loose ends to tie up first. Busy, remember?"

"I remember." I smile. "I remember everything you say, but you still have to eat, right? Do you have dinner plans?"

She pauses. "Not specifically, no."

"Can I interest you in pizza across town?"

She grabs the last of the bottles and begins to load them in a metal cart with a pulley. "I have to go pick up Sophie, and before you ask, no, my father might work here, but he can't do it. If I know him, he'll be in his office for another hour."

I shrug. "So bring her."

Surprise flickers through her eyes before she schools her expression. "And this isn't a date?"

"Nope. I'll even let you pay for your pizza if you want." Though it will kill me to do so. Call me old-fashioned. Call me whatever the hell you want, but when I take a girl out, friend or not, I like to pay.

She stares at me for a moment, as if she's trying to dissect my thoughts, or maybe it's my motives she's after. Actually, I'm sure it's the latter. But I'm not sure I care because after a moment, she nods and says, "I need to finish cleaning up the equipment before I pick up Sophie. I'll meet you there in thirty minutes?"

CHAPTER 10

LANE

DID I REALLY SAY yes to pizza with a boy I barely know?

His slow spreading smile confirms I did.

Shit.

I blame it on Chance. He approached me *again* before practice and it's fucking with my head.

"Great." Teagan's blue eyes glitter like jewels in the fading sun. "You know where Slice is, the place right off campus?"

I snort. "Of course I know where it is. I'm a local, remember?"

"Right." He starts to walk backward toward the tunnel that leads to the locker rooms. "Six-thirty, it is. See you ladies, then."

I nod, watching him as he turns, brushing past several of his teammates when I notice Chance hovering just outside the opening. His gaze drifts from Teagan to me, his brow furrowed, eyes narrowed to slits.

I wonder if he thinks something is going on between us. Too bad I don't give a damn.

After our conversation Monday, and again today, I couldn't give two shits about what he thinks. Controlling bastard.

I arch a brow, mentally flipping him the bird as I climb onto the utility vehicle already loaded full of equipment, and head for the storage room, wondering if Chance Lockhart was going to be a problem.

As promised, I enter Slice with Sophie in tow at exactly six-thirty. Even though it's a weeknight, it's still pretty crowded thanks to its proximity to campus, so it takes me a few minutes to see Teagan in the corner booth at the back.

He waves me over, standing as we approach, and my belly tumbles over itself.

Even from here, I can see his hair is still damp, fresh from his shower. His blond locks curl on the top of his head, creating a halo over his otherwise angelic features. Sharp jaw. Clear, blue eyes. Pink, pouty lips with dimples I want to touch.

He's wearing a black button-down shirt rolled at the sleeves, with a pair of jeans that fit him to perfection. As I stop in front of him, the scent of his body wash, or cologne, or whatever it is, drifts toward me in citrus-cinnamon perfection.

My heart pounds, mind racing as I wonder what I'm doing here.

Date or not, I don't hang out with men in my free time, especially not with Sophie.

It's only pizza.

It's just food, nothing more, evidenced by the small human clutching your hand.

No biggie.

I clear my throat and glance down at Sophie. I'd told her on the way here we were meeting a new friend, but I hadn't bothered with specifics. I'm about to remind her of where we met Teagan when he surprises me by dropping to his haunches so he's at eye level with her, and says, "Hey, Soph, remember me?"

She nods, curls bouncing as her tiny grin eats up her face. "You bought me the ball."

"That's me. Good memory, kiddo." He winks and points to the little stuffed dinosaur in her hands, the one she's never without. "Who's this?"

"Oh," Sophie glances down at the stuffed toy. "That's Betty."

"Betty? That's a nice name for a cool dinosaur."

She nods, eyes wide. "She's a Brachiosaurus."

"Well, I hope Betty likes pizza."

Sophie screws up her face. "No. Betty's an omnivore. She doesn't eat pizza. She eats plants, silly."

"Oh. My bad." Teagan grins, then straightens as Sophie beams up at him like he's God's gift, and right now, I kind of don't blame her.

The knot of nerves in my chest tightens as he rises to his full height and his eyes lock with mine. "Hey," he murmurs.

"Hey," I say back, and he stares at me so intently with a slow spreading grin that I blush and glance away. "Um, are we allowed to sit?" I motion for the booth, and he jumps as if remembering where we are.

"Oh, yeah. Shoot. Sorry about that." He runs a hand through his hair and steps aside while I slide into the booth beside Sophie, chastising myself for the bubbling, giddy feeling building inside my chest.

I feel like a middle schooler with a crush, which is ridiculous.

"I'm thirsty," Sophie says.

"Okay, I know. We'll get you something, hon." I risk a quick peek at Teagan, wondering if he'll find her slightly whiny tone irritating, but I notice nothing amiss in his expression. If anything, he seems pleased by her presence as he folds his arms over the table and leans toward her.

"I'm thirsty, too. After practice, I could drink a gallon of water. Did you know I play football?"

Sophie shakes her head, eyes wide while I fidget in my seat. "You do?" she asks.

Teagan nods. "Which is also why I'm starving, and pizza is my favorite. I bet you don't like pizza."

Her blue eyes round even more, and she nods, offering him a toothy grin. "No, I do. I love it."

Teagan slaps a hand over his chest. "Whew. Man, I'm so relieved. For a second there, I thought maybe you were like Betty and hated it, and that would be terrible because I just can't be friends with a human who doesn't like pizza since I eat it *all* the time."

"You do?"

Teagan nods, his expression solemn. "I do."

"My mom says pizza is bad for you."

Teagan gasps in mock horror. "It is?"

"I don't know." Sophie turns to me as something tugs inside my chest.

"Well, in moderation it's fine, but you don't want to eat it too often."

"How much do you eat it?" she asks, turning back to him, concern wrinkling her brow.

"Hmmm . . . at least three times a week."

"Three times a week!" Sophie nearly screams, eyes flying wide.

Teagan grimaces. "Is that too much?"

"I don't know, but it sure sounds like it."

I chuckle, glancing between them. "Three times a week is crazy," I say, and even I can hear the humor in my voice.

"Ugh. You're probably right." He pats a hand over his flat stomach. "Does it show?"

Sophie tilts her head, eyes narrowing in consideration. "I don't know. I can't tell." Then even more seriously: "Let me see your belly."

I pinch my lips together to stifle a laugh. "Sophie, he doesn't—"

Teagan lifts the hem of his T-shirt and the words die in my throat.

It's only enough to expose his navel, nothing indecent, but the ripple of abdominals leaves me speechless.

I have no idea if he's clenching his stomach or not.

I have no idea if I even blink while I'm soaking him in.

I don't know much about abs because I have none.

All I know is I can't tear my gaze away from the hard expanse of skin.

It's not until Sophie speaks up that I manage to wrench my eyes away. "I don't know," Sophie says, her tone wary. "You have those weird lines and bumps all over. I've never seen those before." She scrunches her nose and glances up at me in question. "Is that normal, or is it from too much pizza?"

Teagan laughs at the same time I do, and our eyes meet across the table.

My cheeks flush as I cover my face with my hands for a moment, willing the blush away as I give my head a little shake. "Nope, Soph. That's not from pizza," I mumble through my hands. "Those are muscles."

As much as I don't want to admit it, I'm endeared by Teagan Nichols.

It's not just his chiseled abdominals—though, my God, the image of them is seared into my brain—nor is it his persistence.

I don't think I've ever met someone my age, let alone one of the opposite sex, who talks to Sophie like she's on their level. Most people either talk down to her, ignore her entirely, or use baby talk when speaking to her, but not him. Instead, he treats her like she's just another person, even stooping to eye level to greet her like he did today and the day we first met in the park. If I'm being honest, this one gesture alone makes me wish I were girlfriend material.

Because if circumstances were different . . . if we were both older . . . if Teagan were in a different place in his life . . . if he wasn't one of my father's tight ends . . . if I had more time and fewer responsibilities . . . then, maybe dating me would be easier. Maybe it could work.

He leans over the table, his long arms easily reaching Sophie's menu where she colors the pepperoni slices on the cartoon pizza while he shades in the other toppings, and for the first time in a long time, I feel myself relax.

I wasn't sure what I expected when he asked us to grab pizza with him. Awkward conversation? For him to ignore Sophie? Get annoyed with her when she spilled her milk?

Whatever I'd anticipated when I walked through the doors of Slice, so far, the evening has been none of those things. As it turns out, Teagan continues to surprise me at every turn. I might not have a ton of dating experience—okay, *any* experience—but he's different from any guy I've ever met.

It makes me wonder how the hell some unattached, single college girl with zero stretch marks or a need for a babysitter hasn't snatched him up.

"So, this must be a late night for her, huh?" Teagan asks, glancing up at me while I sip on my Coke, oddly content as we wait for our pizza.

I nod. "Yeah, later than I'd like, if I'm being honest." I glance over at Sophie with familiar fondness. "But it's not all bad. This job has its perks." *And giving Sophie a better life while letting my own folks finally live theirs is one of them.*

"Like seeing me nearly every day?" He winks, and my stomach dips like the freefall of a roller coaster.

"Of course." I huff, trying to shake the effect he has on me. "Can't forget that. But there's also the fact that I don't start each day until after one o'clock. Or that it's basically part-time hours with more pay than I can get anywhere else." I shrug. "I could do worse."

"Did you work before this?" Teagan asks.

"Yeah. Mostly just data entry stuff from home. It was super flexible, which was why I did it, but for those reasons, it also didn't pay much. And right now, I need the money."

Shit. Why am I telling him this?

"Oh, yeah? Saving for some big adventure?" he asks, eyeing me.

"Something like that."

"Something like that," he repeats, arching a brow. "That's it? That's all I get? Friends," he says, motioning between us. "Remember? Friends share things."

I try to restrain my smile as I shake my head and glance down at the table.

Am I really going to tell him?

Oh hell, why not? Something tells me he'll wring it out of me, anyway. Besides, I'm too excited not to share.

"Okay, fine." I bite my lip, unsure of what he'll think when I say, "I bought a house."

"Wow, that's..." He blinks, a hint of surprise and maybe even a little admiration shifting his masculine features. "Amazing," he finishes. "Not too many juniors in college can say the same. Tell me about it."

He smiles so wide, I can't help myself as I say, "It's actually off Drum Point Lake. This cute, yellow, three-bedroom house with a huge yard and lake view. It's a foreclosure, so it sat empty for almost two years. I found it one day on a whim while driving around the lakefront. Waiting for it to finally go for sale was excruciating, but it was also probably a godsend because it allowed me to save more money. By the time it got listed a few months back, I'd been watching and waiting for what felt like forever, but I was also ready, so I snatched it up."

"And so the extra money you make is for . . . ?"

"Repairs. It needs a little TLC, and in order to fix it up, I'm going to need money. But it'll be so worth it in the end if I can manage it. It's a diamond in the rough. Honestly, most first homes are just a starter homes, but I can't see myself living anywhere else."

I can already see Sophie chasing butterflies in the front yard and catching fireflies at night. I envision watching the sunset over the water from the back porch. On the weekend, I can take Sophie for a morning row in the kayak I've yet to buy. Sundays, having brunch with a view. Planting flowers in the spring. Summer BBQs. Birthday parties beneath the canopy of the large weeping willow. Decorating for Christmas. So many memories are waiting on us.

Teagan's eyes turn liquid as he stares at me with an expression I can't read.

I drop my gaze and self-consciously tuck a lock of hair behind my ear. For one infinitesimal moment, with the warmth of his eyes on me, I feel full in a way I haven't in a long time—maybe ever.

I shift in my seat, unsure what to do with this pressure inside my chest when our waitress arrives, saving me from the tension.

She delivers our pizzas, and Teagan thanks her with a dimpled smile before he turns his gaze back to mine, and my pulse flutters.

I wonder how many hearts he's broken with that smile.

The thought dissipates as quickly as it came to me, and I busy myself with fixing Sophie's plate, cutting her pizza in half so it's easier for her to pick up, while I try to ignore the heat of his watchful gaze.

"So, you're going to fix the house up yourself?" he asks, picking right back up where we left off. "That's a big undertaking."

His voice holds no judgment or disbelief, only awe.

"Some. I mean, there's a tutorial for everything on YouTube nowadays, right?" I laugh, and though I've given this a lot of thought, I don't want to bore him with the details, so I keep it short. "I can paint and spackle, hang doors, and change out locks and stuff like that. I'm even pretty certain I can manage any demo that'll need done, and some of the flooring. But the roof needs to be replaced first, and I'll hire out for the kitchen and bathrooms, too."

Teagan shakes his head, staring at me from underneath a thick fringe of lashes. "You really are something, Lane Turner."

I flush, giving him a small shrug. "A lot of people do it. I mean, I'm just like anyone else, trying to build a life for myself, and I *really* want to move out of my parents' house, finally get a place of my own, so it just makes sense. It's unfair to rely on them so much."

"Yeah, maybe, but you say that like you're a burden. I'm sure they love having you there. You're, what? Twenty-one?"

I nod in answer, and he continues, "So, you're not even out of school yet. You've got time. Most kids our age live with their parents. I'd probably do the same if I went to a university back home if it meant saving money."

I slide Sophie's plate in front of her and warn her it's hot before fixing one of my own while Teagan does the same. "Yeah, I guess. But my circumstances aren't . . . typical."

A crease forms between his brow and I can tell he's about to ask me about it. Seeing as how I'm not really in the mood to broach the subject of how I became a teen mom, I strike first. "Where *is* home for you? Tell me about it."

He lights up like a Christmas tree at my question, a warmth in his expression that was previously missing. "Riverside, Ohio. It's a small town outside the city and easily one of my favorite places. Maybe that has more to do with the fact that all my favorite people have come from there, but I love it regardless. My parents and little sisters are still back home. There's quite the age gap there, so it'll be a while until my folks are empty nesters, which takes a bit of the burden off my shoulders since I moved away. My twin, Brynn, was probably the hardest to leave, though."

"You're close with her?"

"You could say that. I guess we have the typical twin connection people talk about."

It warms my heart to hear he's close to his family, and the affection in his voice as he speaks about them isn't lost on me. It's something we both share. "And where is she at now?"

"Brynn? She goes to Ann Arbor University with my best friend Jace. They're"—he waves a hand out in front of him and his face twists—"kind of a thing now."

My brows rise, interest piqued. "Your sister and your best friend?"

"Yep," he says, taking a bite of his pizza. "Took a hot minute to get used to the idea." He grimaces, and I laugh.

"I can imagine, but he's your best friend for a reason, right? So obviously, you'd be happy he's with her."

He grunts and swallows. "Now you sound just like Brynn. But no matter how good of a guy he is, no one wants to think about his best friend"—his gaze flickers to Sophie, then back—"doing the horizontal mambo with his twin sister."

I snort. I can only imagine his colorful language if not for Sophie, and the effort to censor himself around her tugs at my heartstrings. Not everyone our age is as considerate. Even Gabby and my parents slip around her from time to time.

"As much as I hate to admit it, though, they're great together," he continues. "And he was already like a brother to me, so it could be a lot worse." He trails off, his eyes darkening before he shakes his head and shrugs. "Who the hell knows, maybe Jace will be my brother for real one day."

"That's sweet."

"You think I'm sweet?" He arches a brow, his tone teasing.

I lower my gaze, unable to help the smile splitting my face.

Are all guys this open and honest on a first . . . outing? I don't even know what to call this since it's not a date, but it has me wondering. Chance was the only guy I ever really fell for, and looking back, he wasn't exactly an open book where I was concerned. In hindsight, I'm not sure I should've been so shocked when he chose football over me—over *us*.

"So, why football?" I ask, taking a bite of my food.

Beside me, Sophie eats while she quietly flips through the dinosaur book I bought her a few days ago.

A crease appears between Teagan's brow as if considering his answer. "My father and I used to play together in the backyard and watch football on Sundays," he tells me. "In a house full of women, it was something just for us, which was kind of incredible. Then, as I grew older, I met some of my best friends on the field. Not a lot compares to the kind of camaraderie you gain from pushing yourself to the limit for your team and relying on each other on the field. Life can get crazy, but once you have a ball in your hand and your cleats in the dirt, it's as if all the threads of your life unravel. Nothing else matters. Everything besides the game just fades away until it's only you and your team with a single goal."

The depth and heart behind his answer surprises me. Then again, I'm starting to learn to expect the unexpected with him.

The apples of his cheeks flush as he grimaces. "Does that sound lame?"

"No," I shake my head. "Not at all. It sounds wonderful, actually, and I think my father would agree."

"Speaking of your father, I can imagine growing up with Coach Turner and living under the same roof as a ball buster was tough," he says, and his eyes immediately widen, then land on Sophie before he winces, "Sorry."

I chuckle. "Trust me, she's heard worse, but I appreciate it."

I know how the guys talk around each other, and Teagan is keeping it PG, something that's far more endearing than I'd like to admit.

"Can I have more?" Sophie interrupts.

I reach toward the pan of pepperoni and grab Sophie a fresh slice, then cut it and put it on her plate.

"To answer your question . . ." I sit back in the booth, considering. Coach Turner is a far cry from Ed Turner, the father. "He was strict growing up, that's for sure."

They had high standards for me, which I easily met.

I was the perfect daughter, until I wasn't.

"But as far as dads go, he's actually a big softie."

"Coach? *My* coach?" Teagan chokes out.

I nod. "I know it's hard to believe, but he has a bleeding heart. He's only tough as nails on the field."

"Give me an example." Teagan smiles, seeming to enjoy this insight into my father as he takes another bite of pizza.

I take a sip of my water, while my thoughts drift.

He's never been anything more than a giant teddy bear with me, even after I shattered his image of the perfect daughter. Overnight, his innocent little girl got pregnant, yet he never made me feel anything less than because of it. Though, I suppose, I did a good enough job of beating myself up. Instead, he accepted me *and* my mistakes while supporting me every step of the way. Even when I tested his limits and told him the father was a boy from California visiting for football camp, who wanted nothing to do with the baby and not to contact him, he took me at my word. He respected my wishes.

I still live with the guilt of that lie every day.

But I didn't feel as though I had any other choice. The truth would ruin everything and I'd already turned our world upside down; I wasn't going to ruin my father's future in college football, too. Getting pregnant at sixteen, then having a baby at seventeen was already a burden on them. No point in making an already hard situation harder, and the last thing I wanted was for my father to sacrifice his dream because of my mistakes.

Which brings me to Chance.

My father took him under his wing at the age of twelve when he coached him for the first time at a camp. Chance's parents had been out of the picture since he was young, leaving his elderly grandmother to raise him, so when Dad offered himself up as a mentor, Chance took it.

"Chance Lockhart, for one," I blurt, then wish I hadn't.

Bringing up the father of my child—my biggest secret—probably isn't the smartest move, all things considered.

"Chance?" Teagan blinks.

I nod, wishing I hadn't said anything. "By the time my father met him in junior high, he was being raised by his grandmother, who was older. She meant well and did her best, but it was hard keeping up with a young boy, so when Chance came into the program, my father sort of took him under his wing. He stepped up and became the father figure he needed."

Which is precisely why it would crush him if he knew Chance was Sophie's father. After everything my father did for him, for Chance to knock me up is one thing. For him to abandon us is unforgivable. And I don't want to be the one to break my father's heart. Just like I didn't want to crush his dreams of coaching for a division one college team.

"So, did he get Chance the full ride at CU?"

A slightly bitter laugh bubbles from my lips.

No, I want to say, *it's the other way around*, but I don't.

There are some things I'll take to the grave and my father getting the job on account of Chance is one of them; it's too closely tied to the reason I lied about him being Sophie's father. But the fact that I want to tell Teagan at all says something about his character.

I have no time and no energy, no room in my life for a male friend with questionable intentions, but Teagan's . . . different. It's the best way to describe him, other than to say I'm comfortable around him. Even with Sophie, which speaks volumes. I generally trust no one outside of my inner circle with her.

"So you must know him pretty well, then? Chance, I mean," Teagan says, and I get the feeling he's fishing.

"You could say that." I fidget with my napkin. "He was around a lot in high school, that's for sure." *A bit too much, actually.*

Teagan nods slowly, taking in this newfound information, and I wonder what he thinks of it. I wonder if he's questioning whether anything ever happened when he asks, "But you never . . . dated?"

I shake my head no at the same time his gaze flickers toward the entrance of the restaurant and hardens.

"Speak of the devil," he mutters.

I blink for a second, absorbing his words before my stomach sinks.

Turning, I crane my neck, knowing what I'll find when I zero in on Chance hovering around the hostess counter.

Shit.

I duck back into the booth and squeeze my eyes shut, praying he didn't see me. After the last two conversations we had, the last thing I want is for him to come over here and ruin our good time. Not to mention, I completely loathe him in Sophie's presence. The way he ignores her only serves to piss me off even more.

When I open my eyes, they lock with Teagan's.

He's watching me, and I have no doubt I look just as panicked as I feel when he says, "He's coming this way."

All the blood drains from my face.

I have no idea what Chance wants or what he might say. We don't make it a habit of interacting these days. In fact, our conversations at practice have been the first we've had in a very long time.

A shadow falls over me and I know it's him.

With any luck, he's here for Teagan.

Maybe it's something for the team, and he'll get whatever he wants, then go.

Teagan leans back in the booth, stretching his arms above his head, limbs loose and relaxed, even when Chance's eyes narrow to slits.

"Hey, man, what's up?" Teagan drawls.

"Didn't Coach warn us about fraternizing with his daughter?"

My head jerks to find Chance's sneer as he glances over at me, but when his gaze flickers to Sophie, his pupils dilate, like he's surprised she's here.

My hackles rise as I draw her into my side, further from view.

"No," Teagan drawls, then drops his arms back onto the table. "I believe Coach only warned us not to date her, hit on her, or harass her. This is none of those things because we're friends." He flashes me a dimpled smile. "Last I recall, he never said we couldn't be friends with her."

The muscle in Chance's jaw flickers, his eyes turning to gunmetal as he stares him down. A minute of silence passes, the tension pulling like a tightrope between us before he turns back to me, his posture rigid as he asks, "Can I have a word with you?"

I swallow. Across the table, I feel Teagan's gaze on me, and our eyes meet.

I wonder if he's questioning the parameters of my relationship with Chance? Maybe even drawing his own conclusions.

"I can't just leave Sophie . . ." I trail off, turning to where she's eating her pizza, still tucked into my side, mostly ignoring us as she flips through the pages of her book.

"I think she'd be fine for two minutes." He rolls his eyes, like anything otherwise would be ridiculous, and I want to deck him.

"No, Chance, she wouldn't," I grind out, "She's four, not—"

"Have your *friend* watch her, then." He arches a brow in challenge.

My nostrils flare. Loathing spreads through my limbs like long, broad strokes of a paintbrush, until I want to scream. How did I ever see this man as anything more than he is: a complete narcissist whose only concern is for himself?

Teagan slides from the booth, rises to his feet, and when he squares his shoulders, straightening to full height, his presence dwarfs everything else in the room, including Chance. "Maybe you should leave," he says, the playful edge in his voice gone.

Chance scoffs. "I don't think so, buddy. Not until I speak with her."

"Doesn't look like she wants to talk to you."

Chance's eyes narrow. "I don't take orders from freshmen," he says, and when he tries to sidestep Teagan, the latter stops him with a hand to the chest.

My heart jumps in my throat. Though I'm grateful for how readily he's come to my defense, I don't want to be the source of tension between them. Teagan's a good guy; I don't need to spend any more time with him to know that. But Chance will choose himself every time, and if there's any advantage to gain from tearing Teagan down, he'll take it. Teagan has already been given a warning from my father, and I wouldn't put it past Chance to cause him more problems because of his own wounded pride.

Chance's gaze darkens, his gaze homing in on Teagan's hand. "Awful protective of her for just a *friend*," he snarls.

His eyes lift at the same time I slide from the booth, coming between them. "We can talk," I say before I turn to Teagan. "Do you mind?" I nod toward Sophie.

Teagan's jaw clenches, but he offers me a curt nod and sits back down. "Not at all."

Steering Chance away from the booth, I storm toward the back of the pizza parlor to the alcove by the bathrooms. From here, I can still see their booth, but we're also far enough away that they can't overhear us.

Anger spikes my veins as I cross my arms over my chest. First, the conversations on the field, and now this. He's seriously stepping over some boundaries. I have no idea what's gotten into him, but he's about two seconds away from me releasing years of pent-up frustration.

"What are you even doing here?" I hiss.

Chance flinches. "What am *I* doing here? That's rich, considering I show up here to grab a takeout order, and I see you with my teammate *and* my daughter."

I jerk back as if I've been slapped.

Blinking up at him, I try and focus through the emotions ping-ponging inside my brain, but my pulse pounds so loudly in my ears, I can't think straight. "*Your* daughter?" A bitter sound escapes my lip, part laugh, part huff of disbelief. "Suddenly, after four fucking years, she's *your* daughter now?"

He shifts on his feet, spearing a hand through his hair. "You know what I mean."

"No. I don't. Being a sperm donor and her father are two very different things."

His mouth pinches, but he has the good sense to keep it shut, and I can tell by the way his eyes rake over me, he's contemplating his next words. "Okay, you're right," he says in a level tone.

I swallow over my surprise.

"But I still would like to know what you're doing here with Nichols. Are you just trying to fuck with me? Is that what this is about? Some sort of punishment after I pulled you aside and told you how I felt?"

Laughter bubbles in my chest. "Oh, you mean when you told me to get a new job? You're unreal."

I shake my head and try to brush past him, but he grabs my arm to stop me. "Does your father know you're here with him?"

I roll my eyes. "I'm not hiding anything, Chance. And if you must know, I met Teagan before I even agreed to work with the team." *Technically.* "He's my friend, like he said. Nothing more." I wrench my arm out of his grip, then glance toward the booth to check on Soph, only to see her showing Teagan something in her book. "And he wouldn't have even needed to give that little warning if I hadn't gotten knocked up by a jock at football camp," I grind out.

Chance swallows and his cheeks flush before he finally nods. "Fair enough. If you say you're friends, I believe you."

"I'm so relieved." I start to brush past him before I pause and look him square in the eyes. "And just so we're clear, I don't owe you an explanation, Chance. The only reason I gave you one was for Teagan's sake. But don't question me again, you hear me?"

Chapter 11

LANE

Despite Chance's exit, when I return to the table, it's awkward as hell. I have no doubt Teagan's wondering what Chance wanted, but I'm not about to tell him, so we spend the next fifteen minutes trying to pick up where we left off and failing.

I sit back in the booth, not yet wanting to leave but having no idea how to move past Chance's intrusion when Teagan clears his throat. "Did you know that Sophie can name every single one of these dinosaurs in this book from heart?"

"I did, actually." I tuck a lock of hair behind my ear, relieved at the diversion. "She's mildly obsessed with dinosaurs. We've watched every possible age-appropriate show on them millions of times and have tons of books. You want a direct line to her heart; dinosaurs are the quickest path."

"I'll have to remember that." He returns his gaze to Sophie, a twinkle in his eyes. "You know, when I was little I had an iguana named Bruce Willis? He always reminded me of a little dinosaur."

"Who's Bruce Willis?" Sophie wrinkles her nose, and he laughs.

"Just an actor. My father was mildly obsessed with the *Die Hard* films," he explains.

"Oh." Sophie turns to me, eyes wide. "Can I get an iguana?"

"Um . . ."

"Whoops. Didn't think that one through. Sorry." Teagan winces and I can't help but laugh.

"Do you have any pictures of him?" Sophie asks.

"I'm sure I do back home. I can probably have my mom send me a few."

"Cool." Sophie says over a yawn, then leans into my side, exhaustion evident in the dark half-moons beneath her eyes.

I check the time on my phone and see we've been here well over an hour. "It's getting late. I should probably get Sophie home," I say, reaching into my purse for my wallet. I'm pleased to see that while I was talking to Chance, Teagan stayed true to his word and had the waitress bring separate checks.

Once we pay, I slide out of the booth and scoop her and Betty into my arms while Teagan takes her book. The sky is clear and the air crisp with the promise of fall, but September in Cumberland is still warm.

Perfect porch-sitting weather, I think. And soon, I'll have one of my own where I can spend all my nights.

When we reach my car, I hit the key fob, and Teagan opens the door to the back seat where I gently sit Sophie inside.

"I had a lot of fun. Thank you for this," I say, unable to fight my smile.

Teagan turns back to me and slides his hands in his pockets. "Any time, *bud.*" He grins, offering me a playful punch to the arm, and I laugh.

When was the last time I felt this carefree?

"Thanks for tonight. You're . . ." I shake my head, at a loss for words.

"Sexy? Charming? Irresistible?"

I roll my eyes, and I'm rewarded with a peek of his dimples. For a minute I forgot what flirting feels like.

"I was gonna say easy to be around, but whatever makes you happy."

He scrunches his nose. "Not exactly sexy, but I'll take it."

"It's a compliment. Trust me. You're surprising, Teagan Nichols, in the best of ways." He bites his lip, drawing my gaze and making it hard to focus. "And, I'm, uh, sorry about Chance."

I tear my gaze from his mouth to see him staring at me. "Yeah," he says softly. "He's kind of a"—he steps forward to whisper in my ear so Sophie can't hear—"dick."

Heat washes over me, flushing my skin, before his words register and I take a step back, surprised. I'm so used to everyone worshipping Chance that the notion someone might not like him has never crossed my mind.

"Yeah, you could say that."

"I'm tired. Can we go?" Sophie's soft voice fills my ear, and her eyes droop sleepily.

"Sure." I lean down and buckle her in before I brush my thumb over the side of her face, whispering, "Just one more minute."

I straighten and close the door, leaving it cracked for some air.

When I turn back to Teagan, he scratches the back of his head and chuckles under his breath.

"What?" I ask, realizing I'm dragging this goodbye out. I should be gone already, headed home to put Sophie to bed. She's half asleep as it is.

"Nothing. It's just . . ." His lips quirk. "It's been a while since I've had a girl *friend*." He shrugs. "I don't know how to end a night out like this. I know exactly how I *want* it to end, but it's not a date, so I'm at a loss here. . ."

"You do?" I swallow. I imagine he'd kiss me if I let him, if Sophie weren't here.

The thought sends a flurry of butterflies floating through my stomach.

He nods, his gaze dropping to my mouth. "I do."

He takes a step closer before softly cursing and glancing in Sophie's direction. I follow his gaze only to find she's fallen asleep.

Teagan advances once more and I shuffle back, heart hammering in my chest.

Another step, and my back hits the side of the car as he leans into me, placing his arms on either side of my head, pinning me in place.

The soft rumble of his voice finds my ear. "If this were a date, I would *definitely* be kissing you right now."

I suck in a breath as he leans back far enough for me to meet his eyes, but my gaze homes in on his mouth instead.

Desire claws in my chest, a shocking sensation after four years of lying dormant.

I wonder what it would be like to kiss him. How soft his lips are. How his curls would feel between my fingers and whether he tastes as good as he smells.

What the hell am I doing?

I shift my eyes to his, only to find him searching for a green light I know I can't give. The small aqua flecks leave me stoned as I struggle to find my voice. "Friends definitely don't kiss," I say.

He exhales, tilting his head to the side, regret evident in those jewel-flecked orbs. "No, they don't, do they?"

I inhale, filling my lungs for the first time in what feels like minutes. Any moment, I expect him to retreat, but instead, he drops his arms around me, wrapping me in his warm embrace and smothering me in his citrus-cinnamon scent.

"I guess we'll have to settle with this, then," he murmurs into my hair.

I'm frozen in place. It takes five heartbeats just for me to sigh and sink into his arms before I'm engulfed in the heat of him.

His chest presses firmly against my own as strong arms hold me steady. Everything about him is larger than life, and this hug only proves it. He's everywhere. I'm surrounded by man, tiny in his arms, and I decide very quickly it's not a bad place to be.

If just a hug from him makes my head spin, I can't even imagine what a kiss would do. I'd be damn near catatonic.

Which is precisely why I need to take a step away.

I start to move and he releases me with a groan, his eyes hooded beneath a fringe of thick lashes.

Apparently, I'm not the only one affected by something as innocent as a hug.

He runs a hand down his face, his voice low and husky as he says, "Fuck. You give good hugs."

I chuckle though there's nothing funny about the way my blood simmers in my veins; it's simply the only sound I'm capable of making.

He clears his throat and shoves his hands back into the pockets of his jeans, looking sheepish as his eyes return to mine. "You know, I'm glad Sophie came along. She's a really sweet kid. Hanging with her made me miss my sisters. Be sure to tell her thanks for the paleontology lesson." He smiles.

Oh, my heart.

Any more and it'll be a puddle inside my chest.

"Well, she certainly seemed to enjoy herself, too. I think she's mostly impressed with your pizza eating skills." Then, because I can't help myself, I add, "You're great with kids, you know."

"Of course I am. I'm the ultimate big brother." He winks. "And you're a great sister."

His words slap.

It takes me a moment to register them as my stomach hollows out, and all the blood drains from my face. "Sister?" I say, slightly numb.

"Yeah . . .?" he says with less conviction than before.

I want to cover my ears with my hands, unhear his words, and if I can't do that, I'd settle for sinking into the asphalt.

He thinks she's my little sister. Not my child.

I quickly rewind through our previous conversations, trying to find the point in which I might have misled him or given him the wrong impression, but I find none.

Clearly, he misjudged the relationship merely based on age.

He assumes I'm a carefree, unattached college student just like him. And the only reason the fact that I'm a young, single mom didn't turn him off is because he didn't know.

He. Didn't. Know.

And once he does . . .

"I'd better go." Turning for the driver's side door, I swing it open.

"Wait!" He lunges forward, grabbing the door with his hands before I have a chance to slide inside. "What did I say? Are you not . . .?" He frowns, trying to meet my eyes while I do everything I can to evade them.

Any evidence of the smile I wore minutes ago has vanished, replaced with soul-crushing reality.

I hate that he misunderstood. And I absolutely hate how I thought for even a second that he might be interested in me—*me*, the single twenty-one-year-old mom who got knocked up at sixteen—when all along he had no idea.

This entire interaction and misconception reaffirm everything I already know to be true. That no one is going to want me with all my baggage. No one our age will ever want to be bogged down by a woman with a child. It's too much. We're too young. Guys my age want to party, sow their oats and have fun. They want to go to classes and plan their weekends without worrying about bedtimes and lunches, potty training, preschool, and cleaning up toys.

My mistake was forgetting.

But it won't happen again.

"Lane, talk to me. Did I do something? What did I—"

"She's not my sister," I blurt.

Meeting his gaze, I watch as he struggles to comprehend my words, and I take pity on him. "Teagan, Sophie is my daughter. I'm sorry if you misunderstood, but she's not my father's. She's *mine*."

Shock colors his expression and I hate it. I want to wash it away.

"But . . ." His eyes cloud, and I can practically see him counting back the years, trying to discern how it's possible.

"I was almost seventeen when I got pregnant." I force something resembling a smile, but it's brittle and weak and my chin wobbles.

I hate that, too.

"Bet you're glad we're just friends, huh?"

CHAPTER 12

TEAGAN

L ANE CLIMBS INSIDE HER car while I stand there, frozen.

Her words replay in my head as I try to make sense of them but for some reason, they won't compute.

"Lane, wait," I yell, scrambling for the car, but it's too late. She's already pulling away as I run after her and reach out.

I miss the back of her car, my hands finding nothing but air as she drives out of the parking lot and onto the road.

I'm too late. Took too long to process.

I'm a fucking idiot.

"Shit!" I shove my hands in my hair, the red glow of her taillights disappearing from view.

She's not my sister . . .

Teagan, Sophie is my daughter . . .

Bet you're glad we're just friends now, huh?

I close my eyes as the truth sinks in.

I'm a damn fool, a complete and utter fucking moron.

The evidence was all there. Lane never once led me to believe Sophie was anything but hers, and yet I just assumed, saw what I wanted to see.

The memory of the hurt flaring in her eyes stabs me in the chest.

Any chance I might have had of convincing her we should be more than friends has died with my blunder, I'm sure of it.

If you still want her . . .

Do you?

I do. Of course I fucking do.

My answer comes quickly, like a punch to the gut, along with the knowledge it's no longer as simple as wanting her.

She has a daughter. A four-year-old daughter. It changes things, whether I want it to or not, because it's not just Lane and me. There's another person to consider.

Suddenly, everything makes sense.

This is why she said her life was complicated. Why she insisted she has no time to date. The reason she's so guarded. The person who hurt her? I can almost guarantee it's Sophie's father, whoever he is—*wherever* he is.

The thought hits me like a Mack truck.

Somewhere out there Sophie has a father, and I know exactly zero about the situation.

Is Lane still in love with him? Is he involved in Sophie's life? What about Lane's? Does he share custody? Are there hard feelings, or did it end amicably? Hell, maybe it hasn't ended at all.

I scrub my hands over my face as my thoughts churn until they're one congealed mass of unknowns.

I reach into my pocket for my phone and pull it out. I want to text her, but I have no idea what the hell to say.

An apology feels awfully inadequate, considering the situation and my reaction to the news she's a mother.

On a scale from one to ten, I wonder how pissed she is.

Probably a ten, I decide. After all, she warned me I didn't want her, and my deer-in-headlights reaction to the news that she's a mother gave her zero reason to believe otherwise.

I slip my phone back into my pocket, deciding to wait until I have a clear head, then turn toward my car.

I need to think, to let the dust settle and figure out my next move. The situation is more delicate than I originally thought and reacting without forethought won't serve me well.

By the time I get back to the dorms, I'm no better off than I was standing in the parking lot of Slice. When I enter and find no sign of Tommy, I'm more than a little relieved. He knows I met someone in the park over the weekend, but I haven't updated him on the situation yet, so he has no idea that girl is Coach's daughter. I'm not about to tell him tonight when the situation just got a hell of a lot more complicated.

I make a beeline for my bedroom, needing the privacy in case he comes home.

Closing the door behind me, I walk over to my bed and settle down before I slide out my phone. I navigate to the Face-Time app where I start a group call to the boys, praying they're around.

Atlas answers first, followed by Graham and Jace, and I breathe a sigh of relief before I focus on Jace who, from the looks of it, is lying in bed with no shirt.

"What's up, man?" he drawls a second before I see a hand with bright pink fingernails slide over his chest, and I groan.

"Brynn is with you, isn't she?"

He offers me a sheepish grin as Brynn scoots further into the frame, her bare shoulders peeking out from beneath the sheets. "Hey, bro!"

I grunt and pinch the bridge of my nose as I fight for composure I don't have.

Knowing my little sister is with my best friend like that and seeing the evidence for myself are two very different things. "Seriously, man?"

"What?" Jace shrugs. "I *tried* to hide her."

Graham bursts out laughing, while Mackenzie pokes her head onto Atlas's phone, settling in beside him.

Do *all* my friends have to be so in love? Usually, I'm happy for them but right now, it's fucking infuriating.

"You could've gotten dressed or, I don't know, just not answered your phone. Now I have an image playing in my head that makes me want to blow chunks, and there's no erasing that."

Brynn rolls her eyes. "That's a bit dramatic."

Maybe. But I'm feeling a little raw right now.

With a sigh, I roll my head on my neck and take a deep breath. "Actually, it's good you're here. I could use your opinion."

"Oh my gosh! My big brother *needs* my advice?" Brynn jolts upright, taking the sheet with her and flashing all of us a healthy glimpse of Jace's pecker.

"Whoa!" Graham yells while I shield my eyes.

"I've gone blind," I choke out.

"I feel violated," Atlas mumbles beneath the throw pillow he's currently clutching to his face.

"That big, huh?" Jace wiggles his brows before he slides out of bed, giving us a glimpse of his bare ass this time as he tugs on a pair of boxer briefs.

"Seriously, man! What the hell?" I throw a hand up.

"Isn't he lovely?" Brynn murmurs dreamily.

"Not my choice of words," Graham chimes in.

"Eyes on the camera, Brynn!" I snap to which she tips her head back and laughs.

I groan and let my head fall back against the headboard with a *thunk.*

"Had I known we were gonna get a peep show, I would've grabbed some popcorn." Mackenzie snickers.

I scrub a hand over my face at the same time Atlas jerks in her direction. "Wait. You saw that? Don't look at that idiot."

Mackenzie laughs. "Jealous?"

Atlas frowns, which only makes her laugh harder as she says, "Call us even for the chick that flashed you at the game yesterday."

Atlas rolls his eyes with a grunt, then returns his attention to the camera.

"A chick flashed you her tits?" Jace asks, sounding impressed.

Mackenzie rolls her eyes. "Yesterday, at Georgia Tech. We were leaving the field, and some chick with a sign and Atlas's number, called his name, then just"—Mackenzie mimes lifting her shirt—"flashed him her entire mammary gland."

Jace winces. "Ew. That sounds . . ."

"Gross?" Atlas nods. "Yeah, that's why she's saying it that way. Makes it sound so fucking unappealing."

"I think it's the word *gland*," Graham muses.

"Definitely," Jace agrees. "Though the word mammary doesn't exactly tickle my dick."

I call them for advice and this is what I get. A long look at Jace's dick and a discussion about mammary glands. These guys are seriously unhinged.

"I keep getting flack for looking but what was I supposed to do?" Atlas shrugs. "Someone calls your name, it's instinct to glance their way. But as soon as I realized her ti—"

"Mammary glands," Mackenzie interrupts.

Atlas shudders. "Right. As soon as I realized *those* were out, I glanced away."

Graham laughs at the same time his girlfriend, Sky, pokes her head on the screen. "Did I miss something? What's so funny?"

Sky is technically deaf and only hears with cochlear implants so I have no doubt, if she wasn't focused on our conversation, she has no idea what's going on.

"Not much," Graham says. "Just Jace's flaccid dick and Atas ogling a random chick's mammary glands."

"Ew."

"Precisely." He grins.

"For the record"—Atlas holds a finger up—"there was no ogling."

"And flaccid or not, my dick is fucking fantastic," Jace says. "Admit it, boys. Between the high school locker rooms and college, we've seen a lot of wang, and mine tops them all."

A smug grin spreads his lips, and I shake my head.

"Why?" I slap a hand over my face. "Why did I call *you* guys in my time of need?"

"Good question," Graham says, his expression thoughtful.

There's a knocking somewhere over the line before a foreign voice calls out, "You decent?"

I frown, wondering who the hell that is when we're all here, when Jace turns his head toward the door and calls back, "I'm good."

I hear the creaking of a door and then: "Hey, man, did you see—" The voice dies suddenly before another face completely fills Jace's screen.

Chris, Jace's roommate.

His eyes widen, and he points an accusatory finger. "Are you guys FaceTiming without me?"

"Teagan needs advice," Brynn says beside him.

"Ooh. What about? I'm great with advice. Scootch in." He holds the phone out, glancing down at Brynn and Jace as he pushes his way onto the bed, flopping right down between them while Brynn clutches the sheet against her and Jace cusses him out.

Once he's settled, Jace glares at him. "Your eyes better stay fucking north," he warns.

"Chill, man," Chris says, his tone indignant. "I would *never*. Brynn is like a sister to me. Right, Brynn?" He turns and she nods.

The three of them are crammed into a queen bed like sardines. It's the weirdest thing I've ever fucking seen, but also, kind of funny.

At least, it would be, if I weren't in a pissy mood.

I need new friends that aren't jackasses.

"And since when are you good at advice?" Jace grumbles. "I don't remember any stellar advice when *I* needed it."

"Are you kidding me?" Chris spears him with a glare. "First, I told you to stay away from Brynn, that she was going to complicate shit and cause you problems. Sorry, babe." He glances over at her.

"Don't fucking call her babe," Jace snaps, but Chris just turns back to him and grins.

"*Then*, after it was clear you couldn't stay away from her, I told you to go for it because you were acting like a pussy. And when you expressed your concerns about messing up your friendship with Teagan, I told you to keep it a secret because he was in another state. What he didn't know wouldn't hurt him. You're welcome."

"Keeping it a secret was *bad* advice," Jace says.

"Looks like it worked out pretty well to me." Chris motions between them.

"Whatever," I grumble. "If you two assholes are done arguing, can I talk now? Or would anyone else like to chime in with any completely irrelevant information? Maybe what you had for lunch, the last time you took a shit . . .?"

Chris purses his lips. "My last—"

"I was kidding," I grind out. "No one wants to know." Chris shrugs.

"This about that chick, the coach's daughter you friend zoned?" Graham asks.

Jace rolls his eyes. "Of *course* it's about her. We told him that plan was a disaster waiting to happen."

"Yep, definitely about her," Atlas agrees.

I grit my teeth. "The *friend* plan isn't the problem, it's . . ." I trail off, suddenly unsure how to say it to these clowns in a way which will force them to be fucking serious for a minute. "I found out tonight that the little girl I've seen her with isn't her sister. It's her daughter."

There. I said it. Out loud.

And it turns out, I didn't need to say it any which way because I glance at the faces of my friends and there's not a single one of them who doesn't appear either completely sober at the news or shocked.

"Wait a minute. Hold up." Jace blinks. "She has a *daughter*? Like, a little human that came from her vagina and now relies on her for every-fucking-thing?"

Graham arches a brow. "Glad you didn't skip health class."

"Does she look like her?" Jace asks.

"What the fuck does that matter?" I snap.

"It matters," Jace insists.

I sigh, trying hard to keep my composure. "I tell you that my dream girl, the one I've created an entire, long game plan for, has a daughter, and *that's* your first question?"

Jace shrugs. "I'm just saying. It would be fucking weird if the kid looked like the father."

I reach back and massage my neck. "I don't even know who the father is, but other than Sophie's hair color, yeah, she looks like Lane."

"Lane," Chris drawls. "That's the chick's name?"

"Yeah," I answer with a nod.

"Sounds fucking hot."

For some reason, this makes me smile. "She is hot. We've established this, remember?"

"But she's also a mom," Graham chimes in like I need re-minding. "Are you sure you want to be involved in all of that?"

"That's a lot of responsibility," Jace adds, his tone serious now. "And it wouldn't ever just be you and her. It'll always be you, her, and her daughter; the three of you. With football and everything else, it's more than most could handle."

"Then if it doesn't work out, and the kid gets attached . . ." Graham shakes his head.

"That's tough." Chris frowns. "College football is insanely demanding. Making time for a relationship is hard enough, let alone trying to make a go of it with someone who has a kid."

Fuck. This conversation isn't going how I hoped.

My stomach sinks with every new reason they give me for why it's a bad idea.

But what did I expect? They're not saying anything I haven't thought of myself during the drive back to the dorms.

"I know it's bad timing. Hell, there have been days this first month where I've had no idea how I'm going to keep my grades up, excel on the field, *and* somehow find a sliver of time to spare for a social life so I don't go fucking crazy. Add a girl with a child into the situation, and, yeah, it complicates things significantly. Especially when she's every bit as busy as I am and armed to the hilt. Not to mention the fact that she's Coach's daughter.

"But she's also fucking amazing," I say. More so now that I know Sophie is hers. "I mean, she's managing to hold down a job, while going to school full time. She bought a house which she's currently in the process of flipping, and she's drop dead gorgeous. Though she's soft on the inside, she doesn't take any-one's shit either, and from what little I've seen, she's a fucking amazing mother. She's . . ." I shake my head and rub a palm over the subtle pressure unfurling in my chest. "She's unlike anyone I've ever met. Incredible doesn't even begin to describe her."

"*Ho-ly* shit," Jace stares wide-eyed at the screen.

"What?" I ask, shoving my free hand into my hair.

"He's got it *bad*," Graham says.

"You barely know her, and you're totally smitten." Brynn beams, and I roll my eyes.

"Struck by the love bug." Chris shakes his head, a dopey look on his face.

Jace smacks him in the arm.

"Ow!" Chris yelps and rubs it. "What the hell, man?"

"If you're going to join in our conversation, don't be a fucking cheeseball." He stares at him another beat and points to his own chest. "That's *my* job."

I snort at the same time my gaze focuses on Atlas, who's unusually quiet. Out of the four of us, he's always a little less vocal, a little more serious, but the tight set of his jaw and intense look in his eyes tells me he has something he's not saying.

"Atlas, you're quiet. What are you thinking, man?"

"I mean . . ." His jaw works as he stares off into space. Then as if choosing his words carefully, he says, "Out of the four of us, you're the only one with parents who aren't fucked up. I don't know, so it kind of makes sense to me that out of all of us, you'd be the one who could handle the complexities that come with dating a chick with a kid."

His answer draws me up short, and I can tell by the silence of the others, it surprises them, too.

"I mean, you come from a home where you're completely loved by two parents who were always there for you," he continues. "Which means you have a great example of what it is to be a role model and what healthy relationships look like." He glances next to him on the couch and reaches out to Mackenzie, who appears to be intently listening while staring at him, her expression soft. It makes me wonder if Atlas doesn't worry about having a family of his own one day, and how he'll do as a father since his own upbringing was so fucked up.

He glances back at the screen and shrugs. "If anyone can make this work, it's you. The question is, do you want to? Do you still want her, knowing all it entails?"

I feel the intensity of everyone's attention boring a hole through the screen.

Do I still want Lane knowing she has a daughter?

I feel like my answer should be no. I'm too busy, and I have no idea what the hell I'm doing. If you ask me if I'm ready to be a father yet, the answer is no. But Lane isn't asking me to be anything. Hell, I had to convince her to even allow me in her life enough to be her friend.

But I do know I can be a role model. Tonight with Sophie was fun, and Lane is fucking amazing. Her having a child changes none of that. Not one fucking thing. If anything, it adds another dynamic to her person, another layer for me to love.

She had a baby at seventeen.

That takes guts.

Grit.

Strength.

She didn't shirk her responsibilities. Instead, she dealt with them head-on and did it with fucking grace. I watched as she sat there tonight and cared for Sophie with love in her eyes instead of bitterness and resentment. She could have easily developed a chip on her shoulder after whatever happened with Sophie's father—assuming he's not in the picture—but she didn't. That much I can see from the little time I've spent with her.

I mean, sure, maybe she's a little distrustful of men, and maybe she's scared of relationships, but I get the feeling it's because she wears her heart on her sleeve, not because she's bitter about the things she's had to sacrifice to get to where she is. And *that* makes her even more attractive than I could ever imagine.

Hell, Graham is right. I *do* have it bad for this chick, and the crazy part is I've only known her for a week.

Do you still want her, knowing all it entails?

"Yes," I answer, and the fist inside my chest loosens, my mood lifts.

I don't care who the father is or whether she has a daughter. I still want Lane Turner all the same.

CHAPTER 13

TEAGAN

I T TAKES DAMN NEAR twenty minutes to track Lane down, which is a lot considering I'm in a time crunch. I know she starts work around two o'clock based on our conversation yesterday, and after searching the locker rooms, stadium, and surrounding grounds, I finally find her in the laundry facility on the ground floor of Wyndham Hall after asking Mark where she might be.

I think of the question in his eyes and his raised brow at my inquiry and grimace.

I can only hope he doesn't mention to Coach why I stopped by, but I find it hard to care as I step inside the murky basement and the clean scent of laundry detergent hits me in the nose.

I walk through the hall and down the stairs to ground level where I pass underneath an archway that leads to a large, well-lit space where I find Lane, standing at a wash basin wringing out uniforms by hand before slapping them into a large bin.

I clear my throat, and her head lifts.

Her eyes focus before her mouth parts, and several seconds pass before she asks, "What are you doing here?"

She lifts her chin as if preparing for my answer. Shoulders back, posture rigid, she's the picture of cool indifference. Any fissures I might have formed in her walls last night have long since closed thanks to my ignorance.

I take a step forward, slowly, as if she's a caged animal I'm afraid of spooking, and I wait until I'm only a couple feet away before I shove my hands in my pockets and swallow my nerves.

"I fucked up." With a shrug, I add, "I'm sorry. You never gave me a reason to believe Sophie was anything but yours, and I absolutely *hate* that my assumptions might have made you feel any kind of way."

"You saw what you wanted to see, Teagan. It's fine. Just forget it." She turns away from me, her tone dismissive, and I panic.

I'm not done, not even close.

"I didn't just see what I wanted, Lane. I mean, yeah, looking back, it was dumb as fuck to assume, but it was an innocent mistake. You're young, and I have sisters way younger than me, so I just thought..." I rake a hand through my hair with a growl, knowing I'm screwing this up. "The fact that Sophie's yours has exactly zero to do with how I feel about you."

She glances over at me, her brows arched. "But...?"

"No buts, Lane." I step closer, wanting to reach out and touch her, to pull her arms away from where they're crossed tightly against her chest. "I want you all the same."

"Friends," she chokes out. "You mean you want to be *friends*."

Fuck.

"Right," I say, nodding like an idiot now. "Friends."

Lane sighs, staring at me long and hard for several beats before she nods. "Okay."

"Okay?"

"Yeah, fine." She tries for a smile but it falls flat. "I shouldn't have gotten so upset with you, anyway. It was just . . ." She chews on her lip as if contemplating finishing her thought, and I want her to finish her sentence more than I want my next breath.

"Just . . . ?"

"*Nice*. It was just nice, thinking that you knew and didn't care. That you accepted me and Sophie and—" She bows her head, and the vulnerability in her voice grips my heart and squeezes.

Fuck, I'm in trouble with this girl.

"Lane." I close the gap between us and tip her chin, so her eyes meet mine. "I *don't* care. And I would've acted the same exact way had I known. Nothing changes now, I swear."

She exhales, her smile wan. "If you say so."

I do. I do fucking say so.

"Well, since we've established we're still friends, I only have about forty minutes left, but I thought maybe we could hang out."

"Hang out," she repeats like she doesn't know the meaning.

I nod. "Yeah. You know, two people who spend time together?"

"Teagan," she shakes her head, "I'm working."

"Right, I know. Maybe I can help?" I push my shoulders back and close the gap between us, nudging her out of the way where I take up wringing the uniforms in her place.

"You're going to help me wash uniforms?"

"Sure. Why not?" I place one of the wrung jerseys in the rolling bin, then move onto the next.

"But . . ." Her eyes track my movements. "Why would you do that?"

I sigh and pause, so I can stare her in the eyes. "Because I want to see you. So I can spend time with you however I can get it, and since my schedule is fucking nuts, this is the only way I can." I cock my head, staring at her stricken expression and wondering why the hell she's so shocked I might want to get to know her. I vow to make her understand just how amazing she is, how special. "I told you this already. Friends, remember?" I choke out even though friendship isn't the only thing I want.

"I guess I just thought . . ."

Since I discovered she has a daughter I'd want nothing more to do with her?

Well, she thought wrong.

I plunge my hands back into the mass of dripping uniforms and wring out another one, then glance down at her again with a grin. "Are you going to help, or . . ."

"Oh. Yeah, of course." She shakes her head as if clearing it, then shifts toward the sink. "You really don't have to do this," she says, handling a pair of pants.

"I know. But I want to." My arm brushes against hers and I feel a zip of energy beneath my skin I try to ignore.

We work like this, side by side, for several minutes before she clears her throat. "I think if we're doing this, the whole friend thing," she says, sounding a little nervous, "there's something I need you to know and understand." Her teeth sink into her lower lip, and it takes everything in me to focus on anything other than how soft they'd feel against my own.

"Well, maybe a couple things," she adds.

I tear my gaze away and lean back against the wash bin, facing her. "I'm listening."

"First, I need you to know I'm not a slut."

The hell?

My eyes widen and I open my mouth to protest a world in which I'd ever think such a thing when she silences me with a finger to my lips. "I didn't sleep around in high school. Not that I'm saying anyone who did is wrong or . . ." She sighs and her free hand clenches into a fist. "It's just that I realize how young I was at the time, too young. And I shouldn't have . . . but I believed in the fairy tale because I was young and awestruck and foolishly in love with someone I thought I knew. He never gave me a reason to doubt him." Her throat bobs. "And I know it doesn't matter, but I was only with him twice before . . ." she trails off and waves a hand, her cheeks red as tomato.

But it's not her words that turn my stomach to knots; it's that look. I know it well. I've seen it on my own sister. In the dark days and months after Brynn was assaulted, she wore her shame on her sleeve, baring it for the world to see, and it fucking killed me. Which is also how I know nothing I say will convince Lane otherwise. Her narrative to herself is the only one that counts because when you are your own worst critic, changing your mind is next to impossible.

That shit—*healing*—takes time.

The muscle in my jaw ticks, but I somehow find it in me to nod and ask, "And the second thing I need to know?"

She meets my eyes, the blue deepening to sapphire. "Don't ask me about the father, because I won't tell you. All you need to know is that he was a boy I met at one of my father's summer camps and he moved away. And, yes, he knows about Sophie. I'm not the kind of person who would hide that from someone. It was his choice to walk away."

She lifts her chin, continuing, "And I don't regret her. Not ever. The only thing I regret is believing in him, trusting him to be there for us. So, I won't apologize for having her when she's one of the best parts of me."

An ache blooms behind my ribs throbbing with an intensity I fear she can read in my face. "Okay." My voice is a gravelly rasp as I say, "But now you're going to listen to me."

I step forward and she sucks in a breath as I place my hands on either side of the wash bin behind her, caging her in. But she doesn't back down. Instead, she straightens, steeling her spine as her eyes lock with mine, and I fucking love that about her.

She's the strongest, most vulnerable woman I've ever fucking met, with the exception of my sister. Which is why I'm beyond pissed that she could think, for even one second, she's anything less than incredible.

Her breathing grows shallow, even more so when I lean just a little bit closer, my voice low, an ominous rasp in the otherwise quiet room.

"Not for one fucking second would I ever think anything poorly of you because you're not a virgin. That's fucking bullshit, Lane." My brows rise. "You think I'm that much of a hypocrite? Because I'm not, and just because you wound up having to face the consequences of your actions, it sure as hell doesn't make you any less than me. You don't owe me or anyone a fucking explanation."

My chest hovers above hers so close, I can feel the heat radiating from her skin. The space between us is palpable, almost painful.

"And second, how you can think that what you've done with Sophie at such a young age is nothing short of fucking courageous is beyond me. You're incredible, Lane. I don't need to know you any better to see that, and anyone that can't is blind as a fucking bat." My gaze drops to her mouth.

Fuck, I want so badly to taste her.

"But you're wrong about one thing."

Conflict flickers in the depths of her eyes before she pushes her shoulders back and scoffs. "One thing? I feel like you just gave me a list."

My lips quirk. "Sophie isn't the best part of you." I shake my head. "She might be amazing, but *you* get to claim that title all on your own. Don't dim your light just because you're under some misguided notion you're somehow tarnished now. Fuck that. And fuck regret. I'm sorry he, whoever he is, left you to handle this all on your own, but he's an idiot. I don't need his name to know that much. Just like I don't need to know who he is to tell you I'm nothing like him."

Her chest heaves with the force of her breath, her eyes dilating to midnight while she white-knuckles the wash bin behind her. It would take zero effort to dip my head and claim her mouth, to run my hands up her sides and bury them in her hair.

I burn for her, yearn to touch her.

But I won't.

I refuse to follow my statements with anything that might prove to her I'm just another guy out to get something from her.

So, even though it takes monumental effort, I step back and drop my arms. "Sorry about the language," I say, gripping the back of my neck. "I was just . . ."

"Trying to get the point across?" she asks, breathless.

I nod. "Yeah."

"Point taken."

CHAPTER 14

TEAGAN

COACH BARKS OUT AN order and I jerk to attention. My mind has been anywhere but football for the last hour—namely a gorgeous ginger—but I better fucking focus before I get called out.

No sooner than the thought leaves my brain does my gaze flicker to the sidelines where Lane helps Mark break down equipment. She lifts her head and when our eyes meet, I swear I can see the flush in her cheeks from here.

Making Lane blush will never get old.

Grinning, I turn my focus back to Coach.

"All right, boys, no more dancing around. This isn't fucking ballet. Let's make this one count," Coach calls out. "Tank," he says to Tommy, "you're the heart of this defense. Show 'em how it's done!"

He moves down the line, each step slow and deliberate as his gaze skims across us. "Teagan—"

My ears perk, attention focused. "Yes, sir?"

"You're distracted and sloppy."

Fuck.

"Show me why the recruiters said you had hands like vise grips and the agility of a heat seeking missle. Show me you're not just a fuck-up rookie that likes to steal tires."

Harsh. I mash my mouth into a thin line. But I guess it's a cheap shot I deserved. "Yes, sir."

He addresses several others, and then I line up, positioning myself in the offensive backfield. Crouching down, I brush the grass with my fingers as I focus on the play at hand.

When Coach Turner blows his whistle, Chance barks out signals and we break. I split out, taking the left of the V-shape formation, my feet carrying me down the field where Chance lets it fly.

I turn right where the ball should be to find it spiraling right toward me. I reach out and catch it, then tuck it under my arm as I spin and dodge a defender with a mix of finesse and strength.

With my head down, I move my feet, flying over the turf as I barrel toward the end zone.

When another defender appears to my right, feet before the goal line, I know he'll get to me before I can cross, so I launch myself into the air, soaring like a bird and crashing straight into him.

The pain from the collision is immediate, thundering through me, but it's mitigated by my desire to score.

I plummet to the ground like a stone, *over* the goal line.

The impact knocks the air from my lungs, but it only takes me a moment to recover before I'm getting to my feet, the ball still clutched in my arms.

A grin spreads over Coach Turner's face before he quickly smothers it with his usual stern expression. "Now that's what I'm talking about."

With a jolt of pride, I jog back toward the line of scrimmage, trying to catch my breath as beads of sweat roll a path down my forehead, underneath my helmet, and over the back of my neck. My gaze flickers to the sidelines, and I'm pleased to catch Lane staring. A flush of pleasure surges through me before I tamp it down, a secret smile curling the corners of my mouth as I focus on the next drill.

When practice is over, my teammates and I file off the field. Tommy runs to catch up with me, his breathing still ragged from the squat jumps Coach had us do to close practice. I barely glance over at him, too busy watching Lane pack equipment into the Gator to pay much attention. "Shit, man. I need a shower, a hot meal, and about a week's worth of sleep."

"You're not kidding." I remove my helmet and run a hand through my sweat-damp hair. "Cafeteria tonight?"

Tommy grunts. "I guess so."

"I'll meet you there," I say, but my focus is already on Lane. "I just have to—"

"Nichols!" a voice calls out from behind.

I stiffen, recognizing the deep timbre and pivot on my heel.

Chance Lockhart advances toward me with a frown, and I sigh. "Lockhart."

His lips thin, forehead furrowed as he stops in front of me. "You have a minute?"

Not for you, I want to say, but he's our quarterback and our captain. I can hardly refuse him, so I mutter, "I can spare one or two."

"Good." Chance shifts on his feet and crosses his arms over his chest as Tommy leaves us to talk. "I just wanted to touch base with you."

"What about?" I ask, even though I know exactly what this is about.

"Lane." His eyes narrow. "Listen, I don't know what your intentions are with her—"

"I thought we cleared this up last night," I interrupt. "Lane and I are friends."

He scoffs. "Lane doesn't have guy friends."

How the fuck would you know?

I don't know what it is about Chance Lockhart that rubs me the wrong way, but my ass has been chapped since before the tire stealing incident. And after last night and the way he spoke to Lane, I'm fucking rubbed raw.

I stare at him, wondering what his game is when I decide it doesn't matter and offer him a shit-eating grin. "I guess she does now."

The muscle in his jaw twitches. "Well, I don't know if you know this, but you could say I've been a part of her family for a long time. Coach Turner mentored me for years and—"

"She told me," I say through gritted teeth.

Chance's brows rise as if surprised she shared this particular piece of information with me.

"Then you can understand where I'm coming from when I say I just want what's best for Coach's daughter."

My lips flatten into a thin line. If he has a point, he'd better damn well get to it.

"Lane has been through a lot." His gaze flickers up and down my body, sizing me up. "As you're aware, she has a daughter. She's in a completely different place in her life. I don't want to see her get hurt, especially by some freshman who's still sowing his oats."

"Pretty presumptuous, aren't you?"

He shrugs, his tone unapologetic as he adds, "Just calling it like I see it."

I step a little closer, searching his expression for any clue as to what the hell his angle is because I'm about done with the games. "Well, while we're calling things as we see them, maybe I should point out that you're awfully invested in her personal life for a family *friend*."

Anger flickers in his green orbs. "You heard Coach. He doesn't want any of you dickheads messing with her. Maybe he'd buy your bullshit excuse about being her friend, but I don't. I see right through you, Nichols." He sneers. "I see the way you look at her, and it doesn't look particularly friendly to me."

I lift a shoulder. "Why don't we let Lane be the judge of that? She's a big girl, and from what I've seen, she can handle herself."

His lips curl, his tone ominous as he says, "Tread lightly, Nichols. I'm watching you. It'd be a shame to get on Coach's bad side as a rookie."

I scoff, amazed I can loathe this douchebag more than I already do. "Is that a threat?"

He shrugs. "Consider it a promise." He brushes past me, bumping into my shoulder hard.

Fucking asshole.

I turn, and like a glutton for punishment, I watch him make a beeline for Coach, who's hovering outside the tunnels talking to Lane. Both of them turn to Chance, but while Coach naturally leans toward him like a flower drawn to light, Lane takes a step back.

This observation, however, does little to ease the knot tightening in the pit of my stomach because two seconds later, Chance says something to make Coach laugh, and he's waving her over.

I turn my attention away from them, and not for the first time since our encounter at Slice, I wonder what kind of relationship he and Lane had these last seven years. I'd also like to know why he seems to think she's his business. He certainly has an opinion on Lane's personal life, and something tells me she would be none too pleased about him interfering without her knowledge.

But it's not like I can ask her.

Her fiery independence combined with the walls I've yet to scale mean I'm not privy to answers. Which leaves me questioning: How much of a problem is Chance Lockhart?

CHAPTER 15

LANE

I REMOVE THE FRESHLY laundered uniforms from the massive drum of the dryer, placing them in the basket before hanging them in preparation for tomorrow's game as Teagan props a hip against the counter, watching me.

When he came to apologize yesterday for mistaking Sophie as my sister, I thought his helping me was a one-time thing, so imagine my surprise when he showed up today, too. "Will you be at the game tomorrow?" he asks.

I try to go to home games if I can make them, but I hadn't planned on going tomorrow. Since taking on the student manager job, I have so much stuff at home to catch up on, but something about the pleading look in his eye when he asks, makes me want to try.

"I might be able to catch at least the first half of the game," I say, tucking a lock of hair behind my ear.

His face splits into a wide smile, which turns my stomach into a whirlpool of quickly moving water and conflicting currents.

I keep my head down and focus on hanging the football jerseys until the feeling passes. Every time I'm around Teagan, he has the ability to make me feel torn up inside. My mind says one thing while my body tells me another.

"What are your plans for tonight?" He steps closer so he can help, and our fingers brush.

The jolt of energy shoots straight to my chest but I ignore it.

I inhale sharply, somehow forcing my words. "Not much. Just hanging out at the house. I'll be solo tonight. My parents have plans."

An extremely rare occurrence during football season. Not that it makes much of a difference. I'll still be doing what I always do: Make Sophie dinner, play for a bit before bath and bedtime, and then sit alone on the couch catching up on laundry and schoolwork. If I'm lucky, I'll have time to read. And though a Friday night at twenty-one spent doing such mundane things sounds boring to most, after how busy my week's been, I'm looking forward to it more than I'd like to admit.

God, I sound so boring.

Teagan's brows rise to his hairline, and he blinks. "Wait. Your father is going *out* the night before a game?"

I chuckle. "I know. It's unheard of. He misses holidays, weekends, barbecues, and basically anything not football related come fall, but my mother's high school reunion is tonight, and he promised her he'd go with her, even if for a little bit. Of course, that was a year ago when Cumberland was ranked at the bottom of the NCAAs and he first started. Now that you're climbing rank, he's panicking about taking the night off."

"Yeah . . ." Teagan laughs and shakes his head. "I can't imagine Coach going out the night before a big game. Think he'll actually follow through?"

I know all about tomorrow's game because I've heard about it all week at home. He and my mother went back and forth for hours over it. We play Alabama, who is currently ranked tenth. Securing a win will be really tough, but would also bolster our rankings, and my father thinks we can do it. Normally, he'd spend hours into the evening studying game tape and going over the playbook.

I smirk. "Oh, I'm not sure he has much of a choice if he wants to stay married."

Teagan snorts. "Say no more. I know how that is. My parents have been married twenty-five years."

I smile over at him and grab another jersey from the pile. "Yeah, mine were high school sweethearts and married right after college. There was a time I thought I might follow in their footsteps, but then . . ."

I discovered Chance Lockhart never really loved me.

I swallow, realizing how close I came to slipping up.

What the hell is wrong with me? I never do that.

His baby blues narrow as if he can see right through me.

I clear my throat. "Anyway, my mom has sacrificed *a lot* to support my dad's dreams and his love for the game, so this was her one stipulation. She's giving Thanksgiving to football and the rest of the holiday season, but not this. I wouldn't say my mother outright gave him an ultimatum, but let's just say it was highly implied." I chuckle, imagining my father's long face. "I have no doubt he'll be chomping at the bit to get home."

Teagan crosses his arms over his chest. If he noticed my diversion from what I almost shared, he doesn't show it. "What time does it start?" he asks.

I peer up at him, brow knotted. "Seven. Why?"

He shrugs and goes back to hanging, but not before I catch a hint of a smile. "Just curious."

After I finish washing the last of the dishes from dinner, I'm about to grab the novel I've been reading and settle in, when the doorbell rings.

With a frown, I hurry across the kitchen and through the open concept living room for the door, afraid the sound will wake Sophie, but one peek through the peephole has me raring back.

Teagan.

I inhale a sharp breath, unsure of what to make of his presence here on a Friday night just before a big game. *Is this why he asked when my parents would be gone?*

Before he can ring the doorbell again, I steady my hand on the knob and wrench it open. The sight of him sends a flurry of butterflies dancing in my chest.

He stands on the stoop in front of me, hair damp from the shower. He's in a pair of athletic shorts and a navy-blue shirt that clings to his muscular chest, and my first thought is how good he smells. Like soap and citrus with a hint of spice.

"Teagan, what are you doing here?"

He glances behind me, craning his neck to peer inside as he whispers, "Is your father gone?"

"Yeah," I drawl. "I told you, they're at the reunion. What are you doing here?" I ask again, sure there must be some ulterior motive for visiting me when he knows they'll be gone.

He shrugs and the corners of his lips curl. "I just wanted to see you, so I thought . . ."

I arch a brow. "You thought you'd come to my parents' house while they're gone, after my father explicitly warned the team I was off-limits?"

"Something like that." He smirks and his dimples pop.

My skin rises to gooseflesh at the notion that this man, this beautiful, charming man, wants to see me, and is willing to risk himself to do it.

"You either have balls of steel or you're really stupid," I blurt.

His head cocks. "I'm partial to the balls of steel theory, but in truth, I might be a little bit of both." He motions behind me. "*So*, are you going to invite me in or not?"

Not.

I should definitely *not.*

"I don't know . . ." I stall because the idea of being with Teagan, alone, in my own home makes my stomach do weird things.

"Lane," he scolds. "How are we supposed to be friends if you keep pushing me away? Friends hang out, don't they?"

I know what he's doing, and I want to call him out on it. He can call us friends all he wants, but we're not. Aside from the fact we hardly know each other, we're something in-between friends and more, some indefinable entity that doesn't exist. Which is ridiculous when I think about it. But ridiculous or not, it's the truth.

Or maybe I'm just so damn starved for male affection, I'm reading into things that don't exist.

I frown at the thought, then clear my throat and step aside. "It's your funeral," I say, because my father coming home early is a very real possibility.

He tentatively steps inside, turning back to ask, "How long do we have?"

"He compromised at leaving around ten, but if I'm right, they'll leave before that."

"That gives us two hours, maybe less if I'm being cautious." He grimaces. "Which I probably should be."

I shake my head, shocked he's really here, and I really let him in. We're doing this. Hanging out at home on a Friday night. Alone.

God, I feel like a preschooler.

"Shouldn't you be prepping for your game?" I ask, trying to get a reign on my nerves.

Teagan shrugs. "There's more to life than football."

His statement hits me like a load of bricks.

Now there's a newsflash. I almost forgot someone who loved the game could even feel that way. Most of my life, I've had it drilled into me that football was the be-all and end-all, the only thing that mattered. Sometimes I wonder how my mother puts up with it when it seems she's married to a game and not a man that's flesh and blood. But then she gets her husband back in the off-season, and my father dotes on her. They take trips together and fill their weekends with date nights, making up for the time they lose the other half of the year. And if that works for them, who am I to judge?

But even if Chance hadn't broken my heart and proved to me that someone like him will always put their love of the game first, I wouldn't want that kind of life for myself. Day in and day out, I have to be present for my daughter, and I don't want anyone who's only half-in. I want someone all-in or nothing.

"Besides," Teagan continues, breaking through my thoughts, "I'm ready. I did all my prepping this week, and the night before I like to take my mind off it. Otherwise, the pressure would eat me alive."

I ingest what he's saying as he kicks off his shoes, ignoring the way my nerves flutter with renewed life at the intimacy of him walking through our foyer in socked feet.

The hallway opens into the kitchen and living room and Teagan makes a beeline for the large island, which is when I notice the plastic grocery bag in his hand for the first time.

He stops in front of it and pulls two containers from the bag, placing them on the counter. "Where's Sweet Sophie?" he asks, and my heart does a little flip at the nickname.

His blue eyes flicker over his surroundings but are left wanting when he glances back to me. "I brought dessert, a treat for her since we didn't get to have any at Slice the other night." He points to one of the boxes. "First, I got her this chocolate mousse cake, but then I realized I didn't know if she had any allergies, so I picked up this one, too." He shoves a pale, crumbling cake toward me as he reads the label, "It's allergen friendly. No nuts, soy, wheat, eggs, or dairy." His face twists, and I laugh. "I'm sure it's delicious," he deadpans.

I slowly shake my head, eyes wide as I stare at him like he's one of the seven wonders of the world. "You bought *two* cakes?"

He shrugs, his gaze flickering back at me seriously. "I know peanuts are a pretty common allergy, but a lot of kids nowadays can't have wheat, or dairy, and . . ." he trails off. "What? Why are you looking at me like that?" he asks, dragging a hand over his face. "Is there something on me?"

"No. I just . . ." I swallow, and my heart twists. "You bought a special dessert for Sophie just in case she has an allergy?"

"Well . . . *yeah*," he says like it's no big deal when it's actually a very, very big deal. At least, to me.

No one except my parents ever even thinks twice about Sophie. But here's this man who's spent time with her only twice, and he's going out of his way to accommodate her. For me.

My eyes fill with tears, and I blink them back, sniffing as I glance away from him, mortified at the rare display of emotion.

Get it together, Lane.

When I turn back to him, he's staring at me like I have a third head. "Um, is everything okay? Did I do something wrong?"

I shake my head while I fight to speak over the lump in my throat. "No. No, everything is great. And Sophie can eat either cake. She doesn't have any allergies. It's just . . ." My throat constricts, and I purse my lips.

Damn you, Lane. He's going to think you're nuts, crying over something as simple as cake.

"It's, uh, just not every day—" *Or ever,* "—that someone shows they care about Sophie." *Or me.*

"Oh." He exhales and the tension in his posture loosens. "Well, I guess you'll have to get used to it. Best damn friend you've ever had, remember?" He grins, twin dimples beckoning me forward. I want to reach out and hug him, squeeze him, to make sure he's real. "Anyway, you might wanna just toss this one," he says, shoving the allergy friendly cake away from us with a grimace. "It looks like cardboard."

I laugh but inside I'm screaming because, as ludicrous as it is, I want to save the cake. Remember it. Place it on my nightstand where I'll see it every morning and night as a reminder that men like him exist. Ones that go the extra mile. Ones that care and actually give a damn.

I'm completely hopeless, a total freak, but he's making it hard to care.

"There's only one problem," I say with regret. "Sophie's already asleep."

"Damn it, seriously?" Teagan's shoulders slump forward as he glances down at the cake so forlornly, I can't help my responding chuckle.

"Are you more upset that you missed her or that you feel like you can't eat cake now?"

His mouth drops and he scoffs. "Of course I'm upset that I don't get to see her." Then he tilts his head and adds, "And, okay, maybe I'm a little sad I can't have cake."

I shake my head, fighting a smile, but it's impossible. "Pizza several times a week *and* cake. It's a miracle you have the body you do," I say without thinking.

Teagan's brows rise at my statement, and my cheeks burn.

"You checking out my body, Turner?" His eyes glitter with mischief as he comes around the island and steps closer. "You like what you see?"

I swallow, glancing down at the marble countertop as I open my mouth, trying to find something clever to say in response, some way I can shrug this off, but with his close proximity, I draw a blank. Instead, all I can focus on is the memory of his toned chest that day in the park and the glimpse of his six-pack when he lifted his shirt inside Slice.

God, even now the outline of his muscles and contour of his biceps are visible through the soft material of his shirt.

He steps closer, and the heady scent of citrus and spice hits me in the nose.

My mouth goes dry, like it's filled with cotton. "I . . . uh . . ." I press my lips together and reach toward the cake. "You can have a piece. Sophie won't care. She'll still be thrilled in the morning."

She can have cake for breakfast, and I'll win mom of the year.

Teagan's low chuckle rumbles through my chest as I step away from him, needing the space to breathe. I busy myself with grabbing a plate and utensils, then cut him a slice, hoping he doesn't notice the way my hand shakes.

What the heck is wrong with me?

Teagan wants to be friends. Period. Do I not remember how friendship works?

You don't ogle your friends and tell them they have a hot bod. Ugh.

I cringe.

He watches me with predatory eyes as I slide the slice of cake toward him. "You're not having any?" he asks.

"Maybe later?" When he frowns, I add, "I'll have some with Sophie tomorrow."

I couldn't choke anything down right now if I tried.

Thankfully, my explanation seems to appease him because he grabs the plate and takes a bite at the same time he notices the video monitor on the counter. "Is this Soph?"

"Yeah. I know she's four, but sometimes she still wakes during the night, so . . ." I shrug off the rest of my sentence because "and I'm paranoid" doesn't seem particularly attractive.

Not that I care about being attractive.

He swallows a bite of cake and grins at the black-and-white screen, then chuckles. "The only thing you can see is a lump and all that wild hair."

My heart thrums at the affection in his voice, a warning to change the conversation to something a little more innocuous and less . . . heartwarming.

I clear my throat and pick the monitor up, motioning for Teagan to follow as I make my way into the living room. He follows me while I remind myself how to breathe and pretend I know how normal humans in this situation behave.

I sit down on the sofa and turn on the television, unsure of what to do with myself as Teagan joins me on the couch, his tone chipper. "What we watchin'?"

I glance over, gaze trailing the length of him from his broad muscular shoulders to his socked feet propped up on the coffee table. He's completely made himself at home, and I can't help but wonder if his easy confidence comes naturally or if he's every bit as nervous as I am.

"Uh, just *Grey's Anatomy* reruns," I say, but when I glance over at him again, he's not even looking at the screen. Instead, his gaze is focused solely on the smooth, wooden surface of the coffee table. Before I can even process what he finds so interesting about it, he bends forward and scoops up the stack of scrapbooks perched in its center.

"Oh, no. No!" I practically shout. "You don't wanna look at those."

"What? Why?" He yanks back, away from my grabby hands.

"Because they're . . . they're . . ."

A wolfish grin spreads his perfect mouth. "Are they embarrassing photos or something? Now I *have* to look." He turns, already cracking the top one open.

I make a play to grab it from him, but he easily shifts his giant body further so they're out of reach.

"They're not embarrassing." *Per se.* "They're just—" He hesitates in his perusal, glancing at me over his shoulder. "—I don't know, boring, and okay, maybe there are a *few* pictures I don't want you to see."

"Not making me wanna look any less." He chuckles, turning his attention to the photobooks in his hands, then: "Oh shit. Are these from when you had Sophie?"

I sigh and drop my arm, knowing I've likely lost this battle. His broad shoulders and muscular back might as well be a brick wall. Even if I got the scrapbooks off him, he'd easily overpower me and grab them back. I'm starting to realize in Teagan's presence, I'm not in control of anything—my body, my emotions, my reactions, or my train of thought.

As if in agreement, a ball of fire unfurls inside my chest as I watch him turn the page, the muscles in his forearm twitching with the movement.

I blush, willing the fire to recede at the exact moment he shifts and peers over his shoulder. His left dimple appears. "You're so damn cute when you blush." He says it like he's reciting the weather, like it's nothing, just a fact he's pointing out.

He reaches for me and brushes a thumb over the warmth in my cheeks I imagine are now candy-apple red.

Swallowing, I remind myself to breathe when he pulls his hand away just as quickly, focusing back on the book again. "Wow. She was so tiny," he says, staring down at the very first picture which is an enlarged photo of Sophie seconds after she was born. "And look at all that hair!"

I blink, slightly whiplashed from his touch as I scoot a little closer so I can see and focus on the present. "She did have a lot of hair. After she was born, everyone was amazed I didn't have heartburn while I was pregnant."

He glances at me, a furrow in his brow, and I laugh, explaining, "They say that's a sign your baby has a lot of hair."

He nods and returns to the photo. "Did you have morning sickness?"

I shake my head. "Not really. Maybe a little bit of queasiness at first, but nothing major."

"I remember my mom's pregnancy with my sisters well because I was older, and she was sick as a dog for a while. Fucking sucked for her. I felt so bad."

I bite my lip and stare at his profile like he's a riddle I'm trying to solve. He's so fucking perfect; I wonder if he could possibly be real. Then again, my experience with men is limited. All I've ever known are the immature guys from high school: Chance and the boys my father coached. It's not like I've had much time in the last four years to date or form any friendships with members of the opposite sex.

Maybe this is what the majority of men my age are like, though I doubt it. Something tells me guys like Teagan don't come along too often.

Which is why you should grab him and hold on tight.

I shove the errant thought aside. I'm not in a position to even entertain a relationship, but that doesn't stop me from slyly taking in his masculine features. The thick, long lashes and the bump in the middle of his nose that makes me wonder if he broke it at one time. His angular jaw below chiseled cheekbones. The tiny freckle right above the corner of his full lips. The mess of loose, blond curls, ones I want to run my hands through but know I shouldn't.

My gaze shifts again and our eyes lock, only for mortification to set in.

He caught me staring.

Oh shit.

I should be embarrassed and look away, but somehow, I can't. I'm transfixed. Under his spell.

His blue orbs deepen to midnight, and my pulse wallops in my ears like the steady beat of a drum.

As if he can hear it, his gaze shifts to my neck, then north where he homes in on my mouth, and my lungs freeze.

All the air is sucked out of the room. I'm in a vacuum and I can't breathe.

As if to emphasize this point, my heart rages behind my ribs, racing like a jack rabbit on speed.

Am I having a heart attack?

He shifts forward, leaning toward me, and he licks his lips.

Bump-ba-bump-ba-bump.

Yep. I'm definitely having a heart attack.

His focus narrows further, and everything inside me tightens. My throat. My chest. My thighs.

My hand flies to my chest, clutching at my shirt, afraid it might beat straight through my skin as I try and orient myself.

In an act of self-preservation, my gaze falls to the page he's on and I cringe.

He notices.

But then, he seems to notice everything about me, doesn't he? I'm starting to wonder if he's intuitive.

He brushes a finger against the photo. "You were beautiful." He says it like a prayer, and I stare down at the photo to see what he sees. It's me in a hospital gown, pulled down low enough for Sophie to rest on my chest, but not so much it's indecent. It was taken shortly after I gave birth, before they whisked her away for a bath and testing and the millions of things they do to tiny humans once they enter the world.

I can still remember how protective I felt, how much I wanted to tell them no and keep her in my arms.

It might've been an incredible moment—one of the most incredible ones of my life—but an incredible photo of me, it is not.

I choke out a laugh, and it's like breaking the seal on a soda bottle. The pressure from moments ago dissipates. "You're kidding, right? This was three a.m. in the morning, and I was exhausted after fourteen hours of labor. I was swollen and red-faced and sweaty and miserable."

"And the most beautiful thing I've ever seen."

I open my mouth to protest.

He's just being kind, saying what I want to hear. But a seething glance from him tells me otherwise. It's a warning not to argue because he'll win, so I snap my mouth shut.

"What was it like? After you had her? Were you scared?" he asks.

I stare down at the album, transporting myself back to the day I went into labor with Sophie. I had yet to turn eighteen, and I was only a couple months away from graduating high school. I'd been in class when the first contractions started.

"Scared out of my mind is a good way to describe it," I say, watching as he turns the page, listening. "And I guess, embarrassed, too. I had to tell my teacher I didn't feel well to get excused from class, and then I went to the school nurse where I had the joy of informing her I thought I was going into labor. I suppose I should be grateful my water didn't break. That would have been much worse. By then, it's not like my pregnancy was a secret, but it didn't matter much. The disapproving glances, the whispers in the hall, the shame, they were still there, along with all their judgments.

"My dad was already at the school since he was the high school coach. He rushed me to the hospital where my mother stayed by my side in the delivery room. Honestly, she was amazing." So amazing, I barely missed Chance's presence, hardly gave him a second thought.

If either of my parents ever felt embarrassed by me, they never showed it, and for that, I'll be eternally grateful. Still, when I look back on that period in my life, I can't help but wonder.

It makes me wish I could repay them; show my gratitude for all they've done.

Which is why moving out is so important to me.

It's time to give them their lives back.

"What specifically scared you?" he asks, his voice soft.

"Honestly? Everything." I shake my head and lift my gaze to the ceiling, remembering. "Getting an epidural. Something going wrong and needing a C-section. Something *being* wrong with the baby. The pain. All of it." I swallow. "I was so young. How could I care for a baby when I still felt like a child myself? I wasn't ready. I wanted more time. More money. More wisdom. It took me a while to come to terms with what having a baby at my age would mean. All the things I would have to give up. Things I might miss out on, and even though I chose this, I was terrified that I might resent her. That when she was born, I'd feel nothing at all. Or worse, that I'd be angry with her. But I didn't. I wasn't."

A vise grips my throat, and I clear it to speak. "When I heard her cry, everything changed." I meet his eyes. "In one single second, everything changed. It was like someone turning the chapter in a book or flipping a switch. They laid her in my arms and sleepy, unfocused blue eyes blinked up at me and the world stopped. I knew, even if any of my fears were valid and I would have to sacrifice everything, she was worth it. It was *all* worth it. Like someone cleaved my chest open and filled all the empty spaces with love for this tiny human I had only known for seconds."

I inhale, feeling a little shy and wondering if I said too much. "There's no other way to describe it," I say with a shrug. "I don't know if that's what it's like for everyone, but it's what it was like for me."

Teagan swallows and brushes a lock of hair off my face, tucking it behind my ear in a move so tender, it makes my chest ache. "Did you have any help other than your parents?"

I shake my head. I know what he's asking. Did I have help from the father? Was he ever involved?

"No. Just them, and I'll admit, they were my rock. I leaned on them, especially emotionally, but I also made it my goal in life not to rely on them too much. They both have full-time jobs and their own responsibilities. Sophie was my choice. She's mine, and I didn't want to put them out."

"Does he know anything about her? Like how amazing she is?"

We're skirting around the topic of who the father is, and Teagan knows it. He turns his attention back to the scrapbooks and flips a page, focusing on the photos—taking in Sophie's first outfit and my first time strapping her in the car seat before I brought her home. I can practically feel the unspoken question he wants to ask the most radiating off him: *Who is he? Why isn't he here?* The only questions I told him to never ask, and the only ones I won't answer.

"I'm not sure how to answer that," I say because Chance has seen Sophie throughout the years, he just chooses to ignore her. "But probably not. He knows of her, and he's seen her—"

"Through photos?"

"Mmm-hmm," I murmur a noncommittal response and push away the guilt accompanying it. "He's just too focused on himself to care much, I guess."

A muscle in his jaw twitches, and we sit in silence for a few minutes while he finishes flipping through the album. He flips past photos of her first bath and first bottle after I had to stop breastfeeding when I started college because pumping and nursing and going to class was too damn much. He turns over another page to reveal her first taste of carrots, crawling, and those miraculous first steps just before she turned one. All of my memories, each one special.

Gabby and my parents are the only people who have ever seen these photos. Not necessarily by design, but they're the only ones who have ever cared enough. And as Teagan finishes, I realize just how intimate this feels, sharing these moments in time with him. To anyone on the outside looking in, they're just photographs, but to me, they're more than that. They're the struggle. They're all the sacrifices it took to get here. They're pure love and joy and maybe even a little bit of pain, too.

Motherhood summed up in a nutshell is a Tootsie Pop. You have to get through the hard outer shell to get to the good part.

Once he's finished, he closes the scrapbook and sinks back into the cushions, lifting the arm closest to me to rest across the back of the couch and behind my shoulders. I turn toward him expectantly, but the intensity in his expression makes me squirm.

He stares at me like I'm a new discovery under a microscope he wants to study. Like he wants to pick my brain until he's memorized every nook and cranny, every thought. "Do you know how incredible you are?"

"Oh, I don't know." I keep my tone light, shifting attention to my peeling nail polish. "I just did what anyone else would do."

"No." He shakes his head, his tone firm. "Not everyone would make the choice you did, and even if they did, it doesn't mean they'd be the person you are, the mother you are. Do you ever give yourself any credit?"

I glance up at him, mouth gaping.

"I'll take that as a no." Reaching between us he takes my hand in his and threads our fingers together.

My stomach plunges like a diving swan. I contemplate his long fingers, the strong masculine hand wrapped in mine, and the rough feel of calluses sends my heart racing all over again.

"Lane, look at me," he says, and there's no arguing his tone. It's a deep baritone, a command.

I glance up at him and hold my breath, afraid for reasons I can't comprehend.

"You're an amazing woman." He draws tiny circles on the back of my hand in a dizzying rhythm. "And an amazing fucking mother. What you've done with your life, with Sophie, is nothing short of incredible. What you did was brave and hard, and you should be fucking proud. Don't dim your light just so you can be at everyone else's level."

I swallow. *Breathe.* "Okay."

His eyes narrow. "No. Not just *okay*. I want to hear you say it like you fucking mean it. Repeat after me: I, Lane Turner, am fucking proud."

"Teagan—"

He cuts me off with a glare so sharp, I inhale and mutter, "I, Lane, Turner am fucking proud."

"Good. Now say, 'I am a fucking amazing mother.'"

"I am an amazing mother."

"No." He shakes his head and his whole body vibrates. "*Fucking* amazing."

My lips quirk. "I am a *fucking* amazing mother!" I yell, and a laugh bursts out of my chest.

Teagan grins. "Good."

His gaze dips to my mouth. "I'm sexy."

"Are you making a statement or—"

When he glares, I snap my mouth closed, but I can't hide the smile lifting my lips as I drawl, "I'm sexy."

"Fuck, yes, you are." Our eyes lock and my smile fades. "And smart."

"And smart," I repeat, heart pounding as his thumb continues its dizzying rhythm over my skin.

"A hard-ass worker, *worthy* in every single way, and I deserve every fucking amazing thing this world has to offer."

I swallow. "A hard-ass worker, *worthy* in every single way, and I deserve every fucking amazing thing this world has to offer."

Like you.

He holds my gaze for several tense moments before he finally smiles. "Good. After I leave, write that down, and then repeat it to yourself every night before you go to bed, and every morning when you wake up. And if for one fucking second, you start to doubt yourself or question how completely and utterly fucking perfect you are, you say it some more. It's your new mantra, Turner. You hear me?"

"I hear you," I say because it's the only words my mouth is capable of forming.

"And don't let anyone ever tell you otherwise." He glances down at the watch strapped to his wrist while I stare, lost in him and his words and the way they make me feel.

"Shit. I should go."

The statement deflates the hot air ballooning in my chest, and I nod.

To think I hesitated to even invite him in, and now, I don't want to let him go.

I rise to my feet, and he follows. His departure is a good reminder that though Teagan Nichols might make me feel desirable, at the end of the day, it changes nothing between us. I'm still a twenty-one-year-old mother to a four-year-old with a world of responsibility, while he's barely nineteen and completely unattached with years of oat-sowing ahead of him. Not to mention, he's a college athlete and one of my father's players. His dedication to his football career comes first.

Bottom line: it would never work out.

Yet he was here on a Friday night before an important game.

I shake the thought away as I walk him to the door.

The whole reason he's hurrying off is so he doesn't get caught by my father.

Football is his priority.

We're at opposite junctures in our lives, and a little—okay, *a lot*—of attraction can't change that.

I'm off-limits, and even if I weren't, I'm more hassle than I'm worth.

It's best if I remember that.

He might be my friend, but that's all we'll ever be. His allegiance lies with football and mine is with Sophie.

CHAPTER 16

LANE

GABBY SCURRIES TOWARD ME in the darkened basement of Wyndham Hall, two coffees clutched in her fists. The heady scent reaches me before she does, and I hurry to take one off her hands like the caffeine fiend I am.

"Why am I meeting you down here again?" she asks, glancing around the basement like it's a dungeon.

"Because I switched my work hours slightly, so I don't have to talk to Teagan. Which also means I had no time to make coffee because I left the house earlier than normal, and I needed a caffeine fix." I wave my hand in the air. "It's a whole ripple effect. Thank you, by the way." I lift the cup, then bring it to my lips and take a tentative sip.

"And why are we avoiding Teagan?"

I swallow and grimace, but it has nothing to do with the taste of the coffee and everything to do with the fact that I'm either foolish, a coward, or really smart. Maybe a little of all three. But after watching the first half of his game on Saturday from the safety of the box with my mother and Sophie, I hurried off before Teagan could realize I was there.

Watching him play was a lot like watching a sea turtle discover water for the first time. Like he was born to play football. The second his cleats hit the turf, instinct took over, and everything else was just . . . inconsequential.

I thought about him for the rest of the day, and when I woke on Sunday, I knew. The best way for me to keep my sanity and not make a mistake is to keep my distance. Hence bumping work up to when he's unavailable.

I'll still see him at practice, of course, but if I get there just as they're taking the field and ensure I'm nowhere to be found when it ends, there will be little opportunity for him to speak to me, if any. It's not like he can just jog over in the middle of practice and ask for a chat. My father would hand his ass to him.

"It's . . . complicated."

Gabby hums under her breath. "Maybe so, but this place gives me the creeps." She shivers, casting a wary glance toward the industrial ceiling at the same time my phone pings with an incoming text.

I slide it from my pocket and my stomach twists. It's another text from Teagan.

Ever since Friday, he's been texting me my new mantra. Saturday morning, I thought it was a one-off, but when he texted me again that evening and the next day, I knew I was in over my head.

I turn the phone to Gabby so she can see. "*This*!" I wave the phone in front of her. "This is why."

Teagan: I, Lane Turner, am fucking proud. I am an amazing fucking mother. I'm sexy. Smart. A hard-ass worker, worthy in every single way. And I deserve every amazing fucking thing this world has to offer.

"*Uh*," Gabby's lashes flutter before she glances up at me like I've lost my mind, "and we don't like this because we don't like being told we're fucking amazing, worthy, and nothing but the best?"

"Well," I nod like a bobblehead, feeling as crazy as I probably look, "*yeah*."

Gabby pushes my phone toward me while I briefly explain everything that happened last week after I last spoke with her. Including the night at Slice and Friday night at my house and why he's sending me these texts and at which frequency. When I finish, she stares at me before closing her eyes and pinching the bridge of her nose.

"So let me get this straight. He proved, once again, that he's amazing with Sophie and actually enjoys being around her. *Then*, he shows up at your place of work"—she blinks her eyes open and motions to one of the filthy football jerseys—"and helps you wash these stinky-ass uniforms, a job *you're* getting paid for, just so he can spend time with you and talk? And then he shows up at your house and risks getting busted by your father, who's also his coach, *and* brings Sophie a treat? Not just one, but two in case she has a fucking allergy?"

She punctuates each new point with a step toward me, while I shrink back. "And he tells you in not so many words that you are fucking amazing and better start believing it, to which he's now texting you reminders twice daily, and you're *avoiding* him?" Her eyes bulge. Soon, she'll be scooping them off the ground. "Sure, makes total sense!"

I exhale like a deflating life raft prepared to sink. "But don't you see?"

"That he is an absolute catch, who also happens to be infatuated with you? Yeah, I'm seeing it clear as day. Are you?"

"No." I shake my head, because I refuse to believe it. Or maybe I'm afraid to, I'm not sure. "He left Friday night in case my father came home early. We're *friends.* Football is his priority. And even if it weren't, I barely have time as it is. I can't get involved with anyone, let alone a guy who is married to a sport. Hell, I see what my father's career has been like for my mother, and maybe she's a better person than I am, but I just can't do that. I'm spread thin as it is, I don't have the time or inclination to play second fiddle."

Gabby stabs an angry finger toward my phone. "Bullshit."

"What?"

"You don't believe a damn word he's saying in those texts, do you? That's the real problem here, and the most amazing thing is, *he* sees it and he's only known you a week!"

"That's not true." I stiffen, feeling my defenses rise. "I know I'm a good mother."

"It's not just about being a good mother, Lane. Yes, you're a fucking amazing mother, like he said. But the point is, you're not just a mom. You're an amazing *woman.* A beautiful person, inside and out, who is worth every fucking good thing this world has to offer."

I say nothing, gritting my teeth.

Because I know that.

Of course, I know that.

Yet I want to argue; a rebuttal sits precariously on the tip of my tongue.

"You want to know how I know you don't believe it?" she asks, her tone softer now.

I sigh. This is not how I thought the conversation would go. I thought Gabby would agree with me, make me feel better. Instead, I feel infinitely. . . worse.

"How?" I ask.

"Because if you believed it, you'd give him a chance to prove to you that it's more than just words. That he believes it, too, because any man that does isn't going to have you play second fiddle. They'll put you front and center in their life like the shining fucking star you are, Lane."

I glance away from her, emotion welling in my throat.

Is she right?

"We're friends," I say feebly.

"Yeah. Friends who want to jump each other's bones. Or at least, you should."

I shoot her a glare. "I barely know him. Be serious. I don't know what to do here."

"Yes"—she steps forward and grabs my hand—"you do. You wanna know how I know?"

I nod.

"Because you don't let a damn person near Sophie unless you're sure of them. You may not know everything about this man, and you may have just met him, but you trust him, Lane. If you didn't, you never would've met him last week at Slice, and you sure as hell wouldn't have let him through your front door with your baby girl upstairs." She squeezes my hand. "You and I both know this friend thing is only a cover, a convenient cover for the way he really feels in case your father noses around. And it serves as a nice and cozy security blanket for you in the process because I have a feeling Teagan knows you better than you think. Which is how he also knows becoming your friend first was the only way he'd get near you with a ten-foot pole."

I stare down at her hand in mine while the knot in my chest tightens.

She's right; Gabby knows me better than anyone. Other than my parents, she's the one person to stick by my side. She's been with me through everything. And I trust her.

"So what are you suggesting?"

"I'm suggesting that you open that stubborn little head of yours"—she taps the side of my head—"to the possibilities, that's all. And at the end of the day, if you just want to be friends, if that's what's comfortable for you, then fine. Be friends. But since when do friends hide in a creepy-ass basement and avoid each other?"

I suck in a breath, knowing she's right.

"Just . . . give it some thought."

Chapter 17

TEAGAN

I KICK THE DOOR to my dorm room open then slam it shut behind me, glad Tommy decided to catch dinner with his girlfriend after practice. The stale scent of pizza fills the air and makes my stomach rumble, so I drop my bag on the floor beside the door and make my way toward the kitchenette.

The soles of my sneakers squeak over the linoleum, announcing my arrival, and when I swing the fridge door open, the light from inside glows in the din of the room, reminding me I hadn't bothered to turn on the light.

That's okay. The darkness matches my sour mood.

Grabbing a protein drink, I give it a quick shake, then crack the lid open at the same time my phone rings.

With a groan, I dig it out of the pocket of my athletic shorts, not really in the mood for conversation, unless it's from the one person I want to hear from.

Brynn's name flashes over the screen, and after a moment's hesitation, I answer. "What's up?" I say, my tone gruff.

I should be at the top of the world, vibrating with excitement.

We beat Alabama over the weekend by a field goal, pulling our rank. We're now thirteenth in the fucking country. Yet I can't seem to give a fuck because Lane's ghosting me.

"Whoa. Everything okay? You sound like shit."

"Feel like it, too," I grumble.

It's only been five days since I've talked to Lane, I remind myself. Five fucking days. I need to chill the fuck out, but I can't seem to figure out how.

"What's going on?" Brynn asks, her tone soft.

I exhale and tip my gaze to the ceiling. "I think I pushed too hard and scared Lane off," I blurt.

"*Ah.*"

"What do you mean, *ahhh*?" I ask, annoyed.

"Nothing. It's just I should've figured this was about her. So, I think it's safe to say the ol' friends plan isn't working?"

I grimace. "I mean, it was. Kind of. Until I pushed my way into her house and proceeded to gush over her, and then send her texts twice a day, every day since Friday night reminding her how fucking amazing she is."

Brynn whistles.

"*Yeah.*" I take a drink of my shake, wishing it were something stronger.

"You are hook, line, and sinker for her, aren't you? This is worse than I thought."

I swallow, then screw the cap back on my drink and set it on the counter when my stomach rumbles in protest.

I thought I left Lane's place on a positive note. I thought things went well, but now I have no idea what to fucking think. I haven't seen her since that night, and when I showed up at Wyndham Hall on both Monday and Tuesday to help her with the uniforms, she wasn't there. All I found was the rack of cleaned gear, which meant she'd deliberately moved her shift to avoid me. And when I inquired about it via text because I was too chicken shit to try and call her, she just gave me some vague response about having some appointments this week.

I drag a hand down my face. "I don't know what to do. Obviously, I came on too strong and spooked her. What do you suggest?"

To say I feel like an asshole is an understatement. It's only been a couple weeks since I met her in the park that day, and I knew she had walls up. I should've eased into friendship, but something about Lane makes taking things slow seem like a Herculean effort.

"Maybe there's nothing to do, T."

"What the hell does that mean?" I snap.

"Maybe you just need to give this time. It was your idea to do the friend thing, so take a step back and give her some space. Don't take her silence personally. When she's ready to be friendly again, she'll find you."

"So, just do nothing?" I stare at the door to the dorms, mulling this over.

"Yeah. She has a child, remember? There's a lot going on in her life. She might need more time to process, or maybe she's just busy. Maybe she's not getting enough sleep or it's her time of the month or she's exhausted from potty training. There are a million reasons she might have to keep her distance, and you pushing her won't help."

Fuck, Brynn's right.

I need to take a step back.

"Put the ball in her court," I say.

"Exactly. From the sounds of it, she knows where you stand, so let her work through whatever is going on and I guarantee she'll come back around. Sometimes persistence means patience."

"Damn. You're good at this."

"*Duh.*" I can practically hear her eye roll over the phone, and it makes me smile.

From here on out, patience is my middle fucking name.

"Teagan!"

I pause, frozen at the sound of her voice. I'm almost afraid to turn around and look in case it's not her and instead it's some sort of mirage or my brain playing tricks on me.

Several heartbeats later, I hear my name again and I pivot. A vise grips my chest at the sight of Lane hurrying to catch up with me. Two cups of coffee are clutched in her hands, her auburn locks trailing over her shoulders as she spans the distance.

Relief unfurls inside of me, spreading through the length of my body like a growing vine as I wait, hands tucked into the pockets of my jeans.

She inhales, slightly winded from her jaunt across campus as she steps in front of me. "Shit," she breathes. "Maybe I need to start working out."

My lips quirk, and when I take a quick inventory of her in black leggings and a loose-fitting Wildcats T-shirt that falls off one shoulder, I beg to differ. She's nothing short of perfect.

I meet her eyes once again, and her cheeks flush. "Hey," I say as if the last five days she's been avoiding me haven't been pure torture.

"Hey." She offers me a soft smile.

"Tired?" I motion toward the cups in her hands.

"Oh." She jolts, as if remembering them and holds one out. "This one's for you."

I arch a brow. "You bought me a coffee?"

"Yeah." She shrugs, and I take the offered cup. Our fingers brush, and I marvel at the resulting sparks from the simple contact. "Consider it a peace offering since I had to switch my schedule and haven't seen you all week. I felt bad you went looking when I wasn't there, and, well . . . I feel bad about hardly texting you back. I've just been so busy and—"

"Lane?" I dip my head, catching her eye again.

"Yeah?" she whispers, dark lashes fluttering.

"*Breathe.*" My lips quirk as she audibly exhales.

"Right. Sorry." She reaches into the front pocket of her messenger bag and pulls out a little baggy filled with creamer and sugar packets. "I wasn't sure how you took your coffee, so . . ."

"This is perfect," I say, raising my cup. "So, does this mean you're done avoiding me?"

"I wasn't—" She bites her lip, cutting off her words. "Okay, maybe I *was* avoiding you a little."

At least she's honest.

I chuckle. "Is that a yes or a no?"

"Yes. I'll be at Wyndham Hall at one, if you're interested in coming to hang out while I work."

I grin. "I think I can find the time."

"Okay, great." She takes a step back, eyeing me as she bites her lip. "Oh, and uh, good game on Saturday. My dad won't shut up about it."

His eyes brighten. "You watched?"

She nods. "Of course I watched." Then she bites her lips as if debating on whether to say more. "I went to the game and stayed until half time, and then I took Sophie home and watched the rest on TV. You were . . ." She shakes her head. "*Amazing.*"

Joy spikes my bloodstream like a fucking drug. One positive affirmation from this girl and I'm on a high.

Shit, I'm screwed, but I'm finding it hard to care because Lane Turner was there, watching me play, and she wants me to know it, too.

"I know." I wink and when she laughs, I want to do it again.

"If only everyone had your confidence."

You will, once I'm through with you.

She flashes me one last smile, then turns and starts walking away while I unabashedly check out her ass as she goes.

"Oh, I almost forgot!" She whips back around and almost catches me as I jerk my gaze back to her face. "Sophie said thanks for the cake."

The next week and half go something like this:

Training.

Classes.

Football.

Working with Lane.

More football.

And when I'm lucky enough, Lane again.

Between schoolwork and busting my ass on the field, I see Lane whenever I can, mostly in the laundry room before practice, but occasionally in the evenings, too. We've gone to Slice twice more with Sophie after practice—once last week, and again this week—and I'm starting to wonder if this won't become some new tradition, one I'm quite fond of.

I wring a pair of practice pants out, then hand them to Lane, who takes a soft bristled brush to the grass stains, grinding in the oxygen booster and stain remover before they go in the wash with industrial strength detergents to get the stains out.

We've formed a routine in the last week and a half, working in tandem. She no longer has to direct me, and I no longer have to ask.

"I suppose you won't be going to the game tomorrow?" I ask. It's an away game, and I can only imagine how hard it would be to take Sophie on the road for what would be a long and boring weekend for her.

"Nope. We'll be sitting this one out. I'll still be watching, though. In fact, Sophie asked me if we were going to see you on TV." She glances over at me and shakes her head, a grin spreading across her glorious lips. "Between you and my father, she's going to be one heck of a football fan when she's older." She chuckles. "Though right now, she loses interest after about five minutes."

Damn. I fight the surge of disappointment she'll be absent from the stands.

Catching sight of her cheering us on last weekend was like a hit of valium, and two plays later, I scored a touchdown.

"A girl after my own heart. So, what are you doing tonight, then?" I ask, trying to keep my tone casual, despite how much I crave spending time with her.

"Tonight, I'm meeting the contractor at my house." She beams as she glances over at me and takes the damp jersey from my hands. "I got my first paycheck, so I finally feel comfortable putting the deposit down on the roof and getting started. He'll come over, I'll sign the contract, and if I'm lucky, I'll have a new roof in a couple of weeks. Which also means I can finally start work inside now that I know it won't get ruined by leaky ceilings."

I frown. "How bad is the roof?"

"It's already leaking in a couple of spots, nothing too bad, but enough that if we get a huge storm, I'm worried about the integrity of it. The roofer said the leaks are new, and so as long as we nip them in the bud, they don't pose a mold risk. He'll remove the entire thing and replace some of the damaged plywood on the water damaged parts. Then once he's finished, I found a drywaller to patch the ceilings where they've leaked. Like I said, it just needs a little TLC."

I nod, but my mind is working overtime, focused on the idea of her going to this house alone and meeting a contractor. I know he's a professional and so he's most likely trustworthy, but after what happened to my sister, I trust no one.

I shift on my feet, angling my body toward hers and taking a defensive posture as I cross my arms over my chest. "So, you and Soph are going to the house *alone* to meet this contractor? Is it just him or a team of guys?"

Not that I'm sure it makes a difference. Either way, I can't stomach the thought of her going by herself, though I'm not sure how she'll react to my concern. Will she take offense? Think I'm controlling or overprotective?

She lifts a shoulder. "Since he's not doing any work, I'm sure it'll just be him. But he's a friend of the family. It's probably the only reason he agreed to meet me outside of normal work hours. Why?"

Friend or not, meeting her outside of work hours is just another reason to be suspicious.

Knox was a friend once, too.

"I don't like it," I say, bracing for an argument.

Her brows rise, and it's a moment before she says, "Wait. Are you worried about me being alone with him? The guy is harmless. My parents have known him for years. Besides, I met him myself the first time around, too. Single, working, college mom, remember?"

And your father was okay with that? I want to ask but don't. I have no doubt my line of questioning won't go over well. She's not a child; she's very much a grown, capable woman. Of that, I'm well aware.

But still . . .

I don't like the idea of her meeting him alone at night.

I tug on the back of my neck, contemplating my next move and how I can assert myself into the situation without coming off as overbearing.

Fuck it. There's no tiptoeing around what I want.

"I'd feel a lot more comfortable if you let me go with you."

She stares at me for a moment, forehead furrowing as my words sink in. "You want to spend the Friday night before your away game hanging out with my daughter and protecting me from harmless contractors?"

Sounds perfect.

"I mean, that's what I want, yeah." I shrug, and she shakes her head slowly.

"But *why*?"

I can't tell if she thinks I'm crazy or if she's in disbelief or . . .

Before she can refuse me, I step forward and grab her hands, threading her delicate fingers through mine—*God, we fit so perfectly*—as I look her in the eyes. "I was hoping we could hang out, anyway. But knowing you're meeting this guy—some stranger—alone, worries me. My twin sister was assaulted in high school, and it haunts me every fucking day that I didn't stop it, that I wasn't there for her. So, *please*, even if my worries are in vain, let me tag along?"

She sucks in a breath, and emotion flickers in the blue depths of her eyes. "Oh, I—I'm sorry." She squeezes my hands. "But you know whatever happened wasn't your fault any more than it was hers, right?"

I clench my jaw, saying nothing because the truth is, I don't know what the fuck to think. Part of me does still harbor a little bit of guilt over that night. How could I not when years later, it turns out I not only knew her attacker, but he was one of my closest friends? I should've kept an eye on her that night. I should've noticed when she slipped away from the dance to meet him.

The thought curdles my stomach.

I might not be able to change the past, but I can change the future. So, I focus on Lane and convincing her to let me help because it's not lost on me that she still hasn't agreed.

"I can entertain Sophie while you're talking to him," I say, ignoring her question entirely. "That way, you won't be interrupted."

Her eyes search mine, and I let her read me because I have nothing to hide. "All right," she says after a moment.

I blink. "All right? I can go?"

I don't know why I thought she'd put up more of a fight. Maybe because I've been seeing her so much lately as it is, or because she's so fiercely independent and hellbent on doing everything herself?

"Yeah. If you want to come, it'll be fun." She glances down to the jersey she's scrubbing with a private smile and adds, "I'm actually planning on spending the night there, so that tomorrow, I can get up and start prepping walls for paint. I planned on doing it while watching the game. You can even stay after I put her to bed, if you want?"

Joy unfurls in my chest at the invitation. Though it won't be my first time hanging out with Lane alone, it's the first time she's invited me.

The prospect of it has my heart pounding like a fucking teenager.

I place a heart over my chest, willing it to calm the fuck down as I say, "Lane Turner, are you asking me if I want to spend time with you alone?"

Her blush is instantaneous and so fucking adorable, I want to lean down and kiss the cherry-red tinge skating across her cheekbones.

"You're right." She waves a hand in dismissal. "Forget I said—"

"Lane," I place my fingers under her chin and tip her face to mine, "you're insane if for one second you think I don't want to get you alone."

She tugs her lower lip into her mouth with her teeth, and the resounding spike of yearning I feel is like a mule-kick to the chest.

I step even closer, until I can feel the warmth of her breath feathering over my neck. "And for the record, you don't even have to ask. Just say the word and I'm there." The red in her cheeks deepens. "In fact, it'll be the highlight of my week."

A moment of tense silence follows before she exhales and rolls her eyes, pushing me away. "Oh, yeah. I'm sure it'll be thrilling, hanging out with the single mom and her daughter."

"*Everything* about you is thrilling," I admonish.

She swallows before she groans, and I decide I like seeing her flustered. "Stop. I'm sure you say that to all your female friends."

"Nope." I wink before I lean forward and whisper into the shell of her ear. "I'm not in the habit of having friends that are girls. Only you."

CHAPTER 18

LANE

I HOLD MY BREATH as we pull into the gravel driveway of the lake house. *My* lake house.

Sometimes I can hardly believe it's mine, but as I take it in with fresh eyes, I can't help but wonder what Teagan will think of it when he arrives.

The pale-yellow siding is in need of a good power wash. The roof is covered in moss and water stains, seemingly patched together in spots with tar. Overgrown and weeded landscaping surround the little bungalow, growing wildly by the front door where the small porch has long since been torn off, too weathered and worn to be safe.

Inside, I know firsthand how much more work has to be done. Old kitchen cupboards, stained carpets, and water-stained ceilings. But behind the house, the lake unfurls like a ribbon of spilled ink. A craggy old dock in need of repair connects the large backyard to the strip of blue, which sparkles in the fading sun like a bed of diamonds.

The mere sight of it calms me, fills me with an indescribable amount of peace. This one, unmarred, beautiful thing allows me to see past the house's flaws and imperfections to the beauty within.

It's been months since I closed on what is to be my new home, yet every time I come here, it still feels like a dream. It's surreal that it's mine.

I step out of my old Honda and retrieve Sophie from the back seat, unbuckling her harness so she can climb out. The second her feet touch the gravel driveway, she runs to the corner of the yard beneath the shelter of the weeping willow.

I've only brought her here a handful of times and already, I can see it's becoming her favorite place to play. I don't blame her; it's an amazing spot. I, myself, have imagined summer days out here, dappled in the shade of its branches, curled up with a good book and a glass of lemonade.

I pass the time, waiting for Teagan and the contractor while I walk the property, pulling up a few weeds and dreaming, envisioning the house with a new front porch. Maybe one that wraps around the house for a panoramic view. Or an outdoor fireplace. A gazebo by the water. The possibilities are endless.

The crunch of gravel draws my attention, and I turn in time to see Teagan's car coming up the drive. I holler at Sophie to stay put and meet him halfway, straining to see his reaction through the reflection of the fading sun glinting off his windshield.

A flash of a smile has the fist of nerves releasing in my stomach before he cuts the engine. His door flings open and he steps out. "This is amazing." He waves toward the house. "Just look at that view. Damn, Lane, you did good."

I bite my lip, turning to sweep my eyes over what he sees, then back. "It's pretty great, isn't it?"

His blue eyes glitter like the sea, allowing no room for doubt. "I don't know what you got this place for," he says, "but even with all you'll have to put into it, it's worth it. Just for this yard and the lake and that view." He shakes his head, awestruck in a way that sends a rush of warmth unspooling inside me like a skein of yarn.

"I know. If only I had more time and money," I say, my tone wistful. "Then we could get it to where we need it, so we can move in."

If it were just me, I'd stay here now. But with the leaky ceiling and musty carpets, I'd rather wait for Sophie's sake.

All in good time.

"Once football season is over, I'll have a lot more time to help," he says.

My eyes return to his. He says it like it's a given. But I won't hold my breath. After the season ends, he'll be exhausted and ready to just be a normal college student.

By then, he'll want to cut loose. Party and start dating. Do all the things other guys like him do in their spare time that he can't do right now because of his commitment to football, and none of those things include helping a single mother remodel her house.

I hum a noncommittal sound under my breath. We might be "friends," but friendship also has boundaries. What will it be like once he's dating someone and he brings her around? How will I feel when I see him with a girl on his arm?

My stomach sours at the thought.

"Did you guys have dinner yet?" he asks.

I run a hand through my hair, ignoring the wave of nausea my train of thought has brought on. Food is the last thing on my mind but I know Sophie is probably hungry, and she's already turned her nose up at the snacks I brought.

"Um, no. We came straight here from the field. I was too worried the contractor might get here early and not wait. What about you? If you're hungry, maybe we could pick something up or order . . ." I trail off when he holds up a finger and turns, bending into his car to retrieve something before he straightens, a large, insulated bag in hand.

He holds it out like a trophy and gives it a little shake. "Figured as much, so I hurried like hell back to the dorms. Hope you like what is probably now lukewarm mac and cheese."

My heart flutters. "You made mac and cheese?" I say, dumbly staring at the bag.

He nods, digging inside to reveal a couple plastic forks. "Brought some plasticware and paper plates, too. Figured you didn't have anything here yet."

I stare at him completely immobile. Dumbfounded. If I don't say something soon, he'll start to wonder what's wrong with me. Maybe there is something wrong, because it's beyond ridiculous that I'm getting heart palpitations over a little box of carbohydrates covered in powdered cheese sauce. But I am. My heart totally does a backflip behind my ribs while butterflies erupt in my chest.

How many times has anyone ever taken the time to think about us—me *and* Sophie?

Never.

But it's not the first time Teagan's done it, either.

My gaze lifts to meet his again while I tread in a pool of emotions so over my head, I fear I might drown in them. If I've learned one thing about the man in front of me in the weeks I've known him, it's that Teagan Nichols is a man of action, not just a man of words. He doesn't just talk a good game. He says one thing and then follows through, and I have no doubt he's like this. Every. Single. Time.

A few weeks ago, when I turned down his advances and my father warned the team off me, he told me he was going to be the best damn friend I've ever had. And ever since, it seems he's dedicated to the cause, completely determined to make good on that promise.

He takes care of the people in his life.

He thinks about them.

And that's more than I can say about most people.

I glance away from him for a moment, trying to get a rein on my emotions. I'm on the verge of tears over something as silly as macaroni.

After what feels like minutes, but is probably only moments, I'm confident I can speak without my voice wobbling. "I'm sure we'll love it. Come on." I nod toward the house, then call out for Sophie. "The contractor should be here soon."

I scrawl my signature on the job bid before me as Jason from Redd's Roofing explains they'll start on the roof at the end of next week with a full crew, which means it will take them about three days to finish the work. I nod, more than a little thrilled they'll be starting so soon and thank him as he takes the contract in hand. After he removes the top sheet and hands me the yellow copy, I walk him to the door.

A burst of warm autumn air hits me when I open the door. It's the perfect night for porch sitting, an idea I file away for later as I return to the kitchen where I find Teagan and Sophie still perched in the same spot since our meager meal of mac and cheese.

I watch Teagan help Sophie slide a brightly colored plastic bead on the string of elastic from the bracelet kit I brought to keep her occupied while we're here. They've been at it for almost an hour, and his patience astounds me. I think they've made about a dozen bracelets already, and if I know Soph, she could make a dozen more.

Though Sophie has always been an easy-going child, I have to admit, it was nice knowing she was taken care of while I spoke with the roofer instead of having to split my focus. The freedom allowed me to get his opinion on a couple of other things the house needs.

Sophie instructs Teagan to put *only* heart beads on this one in a bossy tone only a four-year-old can master, and I smile as I slide out my phone to check the time. Almost eight o'clock, just past Sophie's bedtime.

"Hey, baby, the contractor just left, and it's past your bedtime. We should probably go get your bed ready."

"But I'm not tired," Sophie insists in a tone I recognize is perilously close to morphing into meltdown territory.

I grimace inwardly. The last thing I want is to deal with a tantrum in front of Teagan.

"Just a little longer?" she pleads, taking my hesitation for weakness.

With a sigh, I glance at Teagan who yawns and stretches his arms dramatically above his head. "Man, I'm beat. It's been a long day and I'm so tired. Maybe I should get going."

"No, you can't go yet." Sophie pleads. "You'll miss bedtime stories."

"Oh, well . . . I mean, I do love a good bedtime story, but if I stay much longer it'll be way past my bedtime too, and I don't think your grandpa wants me to be tired tomorrow." He winks at me before returning his gaze to her, and I stifle a laugh.

"Do you have five minutes?" Sophie asks, jumping down from her chair.

"I can probably spare it," Teagan says, his tone solemn.

"I'll just get ready real quick, so you can hear stories, too." She glances at me as if it just dawned on her that she might need my permission. "Mom, can he stay for stories if I get ready now?"

My lips quirk. "I'm okay with it if he is."

She turns to him, and the hope shining in her blue eyes is so obvious, it makes my stomach sink as I question whether this is a mistake—allowing Teagan around her so much when I know he won't always be here. "Then you're staying?" she asks.

"Anything for you, Sweet Sophie." He nods and reaches out a fist that she bumps with her own, a new trick he taught her earlier.

"Mom does the best voices," she says through a yawn.

"Does she now?" Teagan grins, and my cheeks flush. "I can't *wait* to hear them."

I groan. "Why don't you clean up, or no one is getting stories," I say motioning to the beads scattered about the table.

"You heard the boss." Teagan begins scraping piles of beads in his hands. "Let's clean up." He dumps a huge handful into the plastic tub while Sophie pinches one at a time between her little fingers.

After they're finished, Teagan scoops Sophie up with a growl while she squeals in delight. "Got you now," he grumbles before tossing her over his shoulder like a sack of potatoes.

I laugh as I follow behind them, directing Teagan to the first bedroom which is meant to be hers. "I just have to grab our stuff from the car."

"On it." Teagan sets Sophie on her feet, then starts to brush past me but I place a hand on his arm to stop him.

The swell of muscle meets my palm, and it takes everything for me to focus and not stutter as I say, "You don't have to do that. I can go."

"Nonsense." Teagan rolls his eyes, then holds his hands out and wiggles his fingers. "Keys?"

I hesitate only a moment before reaching into my pocket and placing them in his outstretched hand.

"Be right back." He winks, then disappears from sight while I focus on the mundane task of breathing.

I usher Sophie to the bathroom where I have her go potty and give her a quick sponge bath in the old, claw-foot tub I scrubbed last time I was here. By the time I finish, Teagan knocks on the door and tells me the duffle bag I brought is outside the door.

I step out, grabbing the overnight bag with our stuff and quickly help Sophie change into PJs and brush her teeth.

Once she's ready for bed, we return to the bedroom and I freeze.

The inflatable bed I brought with us for Soph sits in the corner of the room, all set up with her lavender sheets, unicorn bedspread, and pillow. In the outlet nearby, Sophie's rainbow night light is plugged in and glowing, casting color onto the bare walls.

Something tugs on my chest and when I find Teagan messing with the baby monitor in his hands, my stomach turns in on itself, kicking my heart into my throat.

At our approach he turns, his forehead puckered. "I think I did this right, but—" He taps a button and his forehead smooths when the screen comes on. "Oh, there. I think I got it. You might want to check it just to be sure . . ." he trails off when he notices me staring.

For the second time today, this man—this beautiful, wonderful man—has me next to tears. First, it was boxed food, and now this.

I'm losing it.

That must be the reason.

I've gone completely insane.

Or maybe I've just been Teagan'd.

The thought makes me snort.

The truth is, I'm so used to doing everything myself; having to struggle solo through nights like tonight where I'm already exhausted by the time I put Soph to bed, leaving me drained. And though it's partly my own doing—my refusal to ask for help—I can't help but be moved by Teagan taking the initiative. He doesn't act like Sophie's a chore or a burden. Instead, he seems to enjoy helping.

"What?" Teagan grins as he does a double take to the bed and back. "Did I do it wrong?"

I shake my head, my throat tight. "No. I uh—" My voice cracks, and I have to clear it before I can speak. "Sorry. No, it's just . . . it's perfect. Thank you."

His shoulders curve in relief, and I almost laugh at the fact he was worried I might be upset he took charge and set up her room without me. The thought is quite comical.

"Ready, Soph?" I glance down at her, afraid that any moment, I might throw myself at Teagan's feet.

Sophie nods and runs to the bed, giving it a little bounce when she jumps on. "It's comfy!"

I smile as I drop the duffle bag from my shoulder and remove the two small books I packed, then ease myself onto the edge of the inflatable bed beside her while Teagan takes a seat nearby on the floor, leaning his back against the wall.

Without preamble, I crack open the first book and start to read, trying my best to ignore Teagan's probing gaze. More than once, I glance over at him, self-conscious of the inflection in my tone as I read in different voices. But each time, he just grins, his dimples winking at me from his perch on the floor.

Once I finish, I lead Sophie in a couple of prayers, then give her a kiss and a hug, noting the way her eyelids are already drooping heavily with sleep.

"Night, baby," I say, pressing Betty the Brachiosaurus into her arms before I head for the door. "I'll be just outside here, and I'll have the monitor if you need me."

"Teagan, too?" she mumbles.

My chest tightens, but I nod all the same. "Yeah, Teagan, too."

"Night, Sweet Sophie," Teagan says.

My heart kicks the way it did the first time I heard his nickname for her as I head out into the hallway.

Sophie's quickly becoming attached, growing used to having Teagan around.

Panic accompanies the thought, bubbling behind my breastbone. But as long as I can keep it contained, I'll be all right.

Besides, he's only been around a few weeks, and he's just a friend. I'm not hurting anyone.

I close the door behind us, neither of us speaking until we're back in the kitchen, away from the door.

The soft static of the monitor fills the silence between us as I turn to face him. Nerves jump in my chest, and I clear my throat, grateful I had the forethought to grab a bottle of wine before I came.

A little relaxation and liquid courage are precisely what I need.

I head to the ancient refrigerator wedged in the corner of the kitchen and open it, pulling out the bottle of Chardonnay, then grab two paper cups off the counter and hold them up. "Want to have a glass and sit out back?"

Teagan smiles and draws closer, each step slow and languid like an animal stalking its prey. I swallow, and the pulse leaps in my throat. His eyes flicker to my neck as if drawn to the movement before he stops an infuriatingly acceptable distance away and leans against the counter. "I don't drink before games."

"Oh. How could I forget?" I blink, feeling slightly foolish.

Of course he doesn't drink before games.

I start to turn and set one of the cups back. "Sorry, I—"

"*But,*" he says, reaching out and taking the cup from my hand, "I can make an exception this once and have half a glass."

I exhale and a flush of pleasure creeps up my neck. I need to get a grip. I'm so nervous, I feel like I'm sixteen again, pining over my first crush.

The thought sobers me; that first crush was Chance, and we all know how that ended.

With that in mind, I crack the twist top off the wine and pour both our glasses before holding mine out with a smile. "Fancy, I know."

Teagan chuckles. "Trust me. It's not my first rodeo. I've drank booze from my fair share of paper cups before."

Right. I'm sure he's gone to hundreds of parties between high school and college. Not everyone is stuck at home with a baby at seventeen.

I clutch my cup to my chest, like it can serve as a barrier between him and my heart as I guide us to the small sunroom off the kitchen that leads to a set of sliding doors.

I step outside, and the balmy evening air greets me. At seventy-five degrees and humid, it's above average temperature for early October. The sky above us is clear and dark with only the moon and stars to light our path to the lake.

"I don't have any furniture out here yet," I say, glancing around me at the barren stone patio. "But do you want to sit by the dock?"

It's a simple question, yet it somehow feels monstrous, like I'm putting myself out there.

"Absolutely." He reaches out, and his long, warm fingers curl around my hand, shooting tingles up my spine as he pulls me down the grassy slope of the backyard to the lake below.

The soft grass beneath our feet turns to the craggy wood of the old dock. Our footsteps thud heavily over the weather hewn surface, joining the throaty bellows of bullfrogs and the chirring of crickets.

When he releases me so we can sit, I settle onto the edge of it and dangle my legs over the edge, staring out at the silvery reflection of the moon rippling over the glass-like surface of the lake.

"They're so much brighter from down here," he says.

I glance over at Teagan to see his head tipped up to the sky, so I do the same and hum in agreement, my mind drifting. I close my eyes for a brief moment, allowing the soft breeze to ruffle my hair like fingers softly combing through my locks.

The last few years might have been challenging, but they led me right here, to this moment, sitting beside a new friend at a house I intend to turn into my dream home. It may have been a long road, and it may not be over yet, but moments like this make the struggle worth it.

I take a sip of my wine and open my eyes once more, allowing the velvety feel of it to coat my tongue and loosen my words. "Thank you for everything tonight. For dinner. For playing with Sophie. Setting up her bed . . . just, everything."

I see him shrug in my peripheral vision. "No big deal."

But it is a big deal. He has no idea how those simple acts have left their mark, how they've burrowed a place in my heart.

"She's amazing. You know that, right? I mean, other than my sisters, Sophie is seriously the coolest kid I've ever met, and so damn easy to be around."

I glance over at him, to the strong set of his jaw, the soft slope of his nose, his serious expression, and I realize he *means* it. He's not just blowing smoke or saying what I want to hear or being polite. He means every single word he says. Teagan is not the type to hear himself speak.

"Yeah, she's pretty special," I say. "I got lucky."

He turns to me now, his dimples on full display. "There's no luck about it, Lane. You made her that way. You're the reason she's so awesome. You know that, don't you?"

Do I?

I swallow through the ache in my chest. "How do you do that?"

"Do what?"

"Say all the right things at all the right moments." Things that pierce straight through my heart. It's like somebody gave him a roadmap to my fucking heart.

God, I'm in so much trouble.

I know it. My heart knows it. My entire body knows it, which is probably why the palms of my hands are growing clammy by the second and my throat is as dry as the dessert despite another swallow of wine.

I hardly ever drink, and it's been a while since I've had even one glass, which is probably why the pleasant buzzing inside my brain is already starting.

I reach out and grab the bottle, refilling my cup. With Sophie safe inside and the monitor clipped to my hip, I can afford to imbibe since I'm not going anywhere until later tomorrow. But Teagan's another story.

He has a game tomorrow and if I'm smart, I'd ask him to leave, and then go to bed, or choose paint colors. Anything other than what I'm currently doing because he and I can go nowhere. I'm flying down a road I know is a dead-end. But I can't seem to stop myself.

"Do you think if you'd never had Sophie, you and her father would still be together?" he asks, cutting the silence.

I stiffen for a moment, worried he can see straight through me before I force myself to relax. I might not have history with Teagan but as crazy as it sounds, I trust him, even if I can't tell him the specifics about the father.

"I don't know," I answer honestly.

Would Chance have wanted me if I hadn't gotten pregnant? Would we still be together?

It's a question I never allowed myself to ponder because the answer is irrelevant.

Teagan's throat bobs, his gaze searching the water as he absorbs the honesty behind my answer.

"But I don't think so," I add.

Chance's first love was football. Looking back, I'm not sure he had room in his heart for anything else. Including me.

"It doesn't matter, anyway," I say.

"How so?" He glances at me, his expression earnest as he waits for my answer.

I shrug. "Because when I found out I was pregnant, he showed me who he really was. And I don't want to be with someone who doesn't want Sophie, too. We're a package deal."

"The best of packages," he says, and I smile down at my cup as he continues. "Whoever he is, he's an idiot. He has no idea what he's missing out on."

But he does.

He just doesn't care.

"Oh, I don't know," I say. "I mean, there are times when I resent him for leaving me when I needed him most, but I also can't fully blame him, either. We were so young. He was scared, not ready to be a father, and I made the decision to keep Soph. He never really had a choice. I can't blame him for not wanting to change his whole future to suit me."

Teagan quirks a brow. "I hope you're kidding. He's a fucking tool for leaving you, Lane. I don't give a shit if he was scared or not. You step up. It takes two people to make a baby, and the second he laid his hands on you, he knew what he was getting into. He should at least be here for you in some capacity. Hell, even if it's only monetarily."

I don't know if this is his way of asking if he's paying me some sort of child support, but I balk at the idea. Even if Chance gets drafted to the NFL, which I know he will, I don't want his money. It's all or nothing with me.

"Maybe I want to do this on my own."

"You're stubborn." Teagan frowns.

"And maybe a little selfish, too. If he doesn't want me, then I don't want him. And with him uninvolved, even financially, I don't have to share Sophie. She's all mine, and that's the way I want to keep it."

Teagan rolls his eyes. "Nice try, but there's not a selfish bone in your body, Lane Turner."

I take a large swallow of my wine, wondering how Teagan can so easily take what I say and turn it into a compliment.

"You know so much about me, and I feel like I know very little about you. Tell me more about your family. I know you're close . . ." I say, steering the conversation away from me.

He nods, and if he recognizes the deflection for what it is, he doesn't say so. "I had a typical childhood, I guess. Probably pretty similar to yours, from the sounds of it. My parents are pretty great. They've been married for a long time, and both run their own businesses, yet somehow managed to be there for all of us and make it all work. My mom runs a catering business that she started when we were in diapers. She's pretty determined in that way, starting something she loved from the ground up, with sheer will and determination. You remind me of her in that way; strong and unyielding. You'll stop at nothing to reach your goals and build the life you want. And you won't apologize for it, either. Kind of like this," he says, glancing around him. "Not many people our age would see through the dreary exterior of this place to the gem beneath, but you do. And even if they did, they sure as hell wouldn't put in the work to get what they want."

I clear my throat, once again redirecting. "You said you have three sisters?"

He laughs. "Yeah. My father and I have been outnumbered for quite a few years now."

That makes me smile, and I nudge him with my arm. "It probably explains why you're so good with women."

His teeth flash in the moonlight. "You think I'm good with women?"

I roll my eyes. "You know you are."

His gaze drops to my mouth, the blue turning liquid.

"Tell me about your friends," I say through the vise grip on my chest. "You said you're really close to some of your old teammates from your hometown, right?"

"Yeah. Jace, Atlas, and Graham. Atlas is the newest of our group, but we're more like brothers than anything. Over the summer, I lost a friend, though. Knox Brian." He shakes his head. "Turned out he betrayed us all, really pulled the wool over our eyes and he wasn't the man I thought he was. I've had kind of a hard time opening up to some of the guys at CU because of it, and don't get me started on secrets and lies and . . ." He trails off, and his throat bobs. I can tell whatever he's referring to cuts deep. "Well, I guess you could say lying is a hard no for me."

I remember the day he chased me down on campus. He mentioned then he couldn't handle liars. Looks like he was serious.

"I think I mentioned that Jace is dating my sister?" he says, tearing me from my thoughts.

"What's that like?"

"Fucking weird."

I bark out a laugh.

"Seriously. I mean, it took some getting used to the idea, especially because in high school my best friend was known to be a player. But somehow, he's just what she needs, and she's everything to him."

"I couldn't imagine being away from my family. Do you miss them?"

"Yeah, but we talk a lot, and we'll get together when we can. I guess distance is all a part of growing up and getting older."

"All your friends play college football?"

"Well, we all used to. Graham sort of . . . burned out. His father was kind of brutal and really put him through the ringer. It just wasn't in his heart anymore. Only Atlas and Jace still play. Both for Big Ten schools, too. We already played Jace at AU this year and somehow lost. We're slated to play Atlas at OSU—"

"At the end of the season," I finish for him. "Yeah, I know."

Grinning, he lifts his chin. "Look at you memorizing the schedule." When I laugh, he adds, "Atlas is already talking shit about bringing us down a peg, since we're vying for their spot."

"I can't imagine what that would be like, playing *against* them when you're used to playing *with* them."

"It's weird, for sure. As athletes, we're all a little cocky, so you think you're the best and want to kick their ass, but you're also proud as hell when they excel on the field. I have no doubt Atlas will get drafted, and Jace has a pretty damn good chance, too."

"And you?" My heart clenches. I have no claim to him. We've only known each other a short time, yet the thought of him leaving after his four years are up saddens me in a way it shouldn't. It's a good reminder to keep my walls up. No matter how good of a friend he becomes, Teagan's future in football will likely dictate his life.

He shrugs. "I don't know. I mean, I'm not gonna lie, I've thought about it. I think anybody who loves a sport enough to essentially dedicate eight years of their life to it between high school and college has thought about it. You'd be crazy not to imagine what it would be like, to dream of being drafted. But at the end of the day, it just comes down to two things."

"Which are?"

"Talent and drive. Are you good enough, and how bad do you want it?"

I already know he's talented or my father wouldn't have him on the starting lineup. I want to ask him how bad he wants it, but the words don't come. They stick in my throat, heavy and leaden on the tip of my tongue.

Instead, I glance back out to the water. Maybe I don't want to know the answer. All I've done the last four years is look ahead to the future. It's what I had to do to ensure I could provide for Sophie and give her the life she deserves.

But I'm tired.

For once, I want to just be Lane Turner, a twenty-one-year-old college student with no inhibitions. I want to be free and maybe a little bit reckless. I want to experience the kind of things I missed out on during the last four years because I had to grow up so quickly.

A breeze ripples the dark surface of the lake, and I wonder how cold it is. How the water would feel against my bare skin.

"Have you ever gone skinny dipping?" I blurt.

I can feel his eyes on the side of my face, heating my skin, and I have to bite my lower lip to keep the blush from rising to my cheeks.

"Yes," he answers.

Of course he has.

"I haven't. I haven't done a lot of things." Except sex. I've done that. I had sex twice, and here I am—the product of that choice is sleeping peacefully in her bed inside the sliding glass doors.

Before Sophie, I was shy. I was also a rule follower. I never would've gone skinny dipping or parked somewhere to fool around with a boy. I never even drank under the age of twenty-one, too nervous and scared of getting caught.

Hell, the only reason I even lost my virginity so young was because I completely trusted Chance. He was always around, like he was already part of the family. Most days, my father treated him like a son, and that summer, Chance saw me in a new light. He made me feel like a woman. Desired. And I thought he loved me. I believed him when he said every part of me was safe with him.

I was naive.

Then after Sophie, I had no time for anything else. Even if I had the time and opportunity, I've spent the last four years desperately proving I'm not irresponsible. I've done everything in my power to escape further judgment.

Whether it's the boy beside me emboldening me or the wine loosening my limbs, I rise to my feet, an idea unfolding.

I kick off my sandals, and Teagan's lips quirk, clearly amused. I'd love nothing more than to wipe the smile from his face so before I can overthink it and change my mind, I reach for the hem of my shirt and lift. In one swift movement, I pull it up and over my head. It dangles from my fingertips a moment, then falls.

The little flecks of green in his blue eyes burn in the darkness, almost catlike as he tracks my every move. The smile slips from his lips and a surge of satisfaction chases my ability to make it vanish.

I've never been more grateful in my life for the fancy underwear Gabby gifted me for my twenty-first birthday because, if the expression on Teagan's face is any indication, he more than likes the purple lace bra I'm wearing.

My fingers move to the buttons of my shorts next, and Teagan's eyes home in on the movement. "Lane, what are you . . .?" The gravelly rasp of his voice verges on desperation, and I laugh, drunk on the attention.

"It's warm out, and I'm going skinny dipping. What does it look like I'm doing?" Somehow, in the last few minutes, I've become the bold one, and it's so disorienting it makes my head spin.

Or maybe that's the wine.

I shimmy the shorts down my full hips, standing in front of him in nothing but my matching bra and panties while a thousand insecurities rise to the surface. I have stretch marks. Birthing hips. I could stand to lose a few pounds and haven't worked out since Sophie was born.

But I shove them all away as his eyes rake over me.

His Adam's apple bobs, and the dimples I love so much are nowhere to be found as his jaw tightens, the muscles flexing in his cheeks.

"Are you going to join me or sit there staring?"

His nostrils flare, eyes brightening at the challenge, and he stands so fast, he's a watercolor of movement. Gripping his shirt behind his neck, he yanks it up and over his head in one fluid motion. His abdominals ripple before me, his chiseled chest flanked in shadow.

I want to reach out and touch him, to trace every groove and line with my fingers, to feel them clench and undulate beneath my touch, but I don't. Instead, I settle on unclasping my bra and let the material slide slowly from my shoulders, my breasts, focusing on the decadent way the night air whispers against my skin. And when it falls to the wooden planks in front of me, Teagan's gaze turns feral.

He takes a step toward me, and my heart leaps before I turn and step to the edge of the dock where I quickly shed my panties, then dive into the cold, dark depths of the lake.

CHAPTER 19

TEAGAN

I SPIN AROUND AND shove my hands into my hair as I try to repress the image of Lane's full breasts and the milky smooth skin of her perfect ass from my mind.

Shit.

It's impossible. I'm a good man, but not *that* good.

Water splashes a few feet away, a reminder that Lane is within reach and completely nude. "It's cold!" she shouts with a laugh. "Well . . .?" A splash of water hits the deck behind me, spraying my calves. "Are you coming in, or are you going to make me swim alone?"

I exhale a shaky breath.

Does she have any clue what she's fucking doing to me?

I may be strong-willed, but I have serious doubts about whether I can plunge into the lake naked with Lane and not make a move on her.

So why am I turning around and dropping my shorts?

I watch as Lane's gaze shifts to my boxer briefs. I know she can very clearly see the effect she's having on me, and I smirk. Her face is flanked in shadows, but I don't need to see her expression to know her cheeks are a beautiful shade of pink.

I slide my thumbs under the elastic of my boxer briefs and tug them down, a little surprised when Lane doesn't turn away to give me privacy as I drop them. Then again, she's done nothing but surprise me since I've met her. Every single time I'm with her, she reveals some new layer of herself I get to unwrap like a fucking gift. And playful, uninhibited Lane is dangerous. I'm already all-in on this girl, but this side of her has the ability to make me fall to my knees.

Her eyes rake down my body, taking me in like I'm a prize horse she's considering buying. But I don't mind, not one bit. Lane Turner's eyes on me are something I could get used to, so I let her look, take her fill. Maybe she'll think of me when she's alone in bed at night.

I groan at the thought.

I'll sure as fuck be thinking about her.

She licks her lips, her gaze flickering over me one last time before suddenly turning and swimming a few feet away, which I take as my cue.

I dive into the water. The sharp cold bites at my skin, and I'm enveloped in darkness before the kicking of my arms and legs draws me to the surface.

I burst from the water and whip my hair from my eyes, only to find her a few feet away. Even from here, the mesmerizing blue of her eyes transfixes me.

Inhaling, I catch my bearings and close the distance between us, treading a foot in front of her. "Seems a little unfair, don't you think?" I murmur.

"What?"

"You've seen every inch of me, but you turned and dove into the water before I could get my fill." My gaze dips to her chest covered by the lapping of water, as if I can see below its surface to what's beneath.

She bites her lip, grinning as she shrugs, and damn if I don't want to reach out and pull her into my arms, remove the lip from beneath her teeth and tug on it with my own.

We stare at each other for a moment, both of us treading circles around the other when I ask, "So, how's it feel, skinny dipping? Is it everything you imagined?"

She hums, tipping her head to the sky for a moment as if contemplating my question. "I think it is, actually. I feel . . . *alive.*" She laughs, a shaky sound as she lowers her head again. "Or maybe it's just you that makes me feel this way."

Heat blooms inside my chest, filling the hollow ache as my gaze lowers to her lips where droplets of lake water cling to her cupid's bow.

I want to kiss her so damn bad it hurts. Make her forget her own name, erase the scars left behind by Sophie's father, ease whatever turmoil lurks behind her walls. And so I swim closer, until there's only inches between us instead of feet. Close enough to hear her subtle intake of breath.

"What are we doing here, Lane?"

Her throat bobs. "I don't know." She breathes.

Not exactly the answer I was hoping for, but I'll take it. For now.

I reach out and tug her to me, wrapping my arms around her and drawing her into my chest, so I can bear her weight, treading water for the both of us.

Her body pressed to mine in all the right places makes it hard to breathe. A vise grips my chest, and when she wraps her legs around my waist, it fucking squeezes without restraint.

I grunt, mustering every ounce of willpower I possess not to touch her in all the places hidden by the frigid water. "You're making it hard to be a gentleman here, Lane."

"I wasn't aware being a gentleman was a requirement when swimming nude among friends."

I close my eyes, mashing my molars to dust. "Well, I don't really make a habit of swimming nude with my *friends*," I grind out.

Fuck. I hate that word. Never hated a word more in my entire life.

Friends.

The word rattles in my brain like loose change.

Fuck being friends. I want to crush my mouth to hers, to taste her lips and slide my hand between us to the sensitive place between her legs, if only to see her reaction before I make her moan.

But I made Lane a promise and I'm not going to break it, especially not in the heat of the moment when she can't even define what she feels for me. And I sure as shit won't after she's had a couple glasses of wine.

When I finally kiss her, I need to be sure she wants me. I need to know beyond the shadow of a doubt, she wants more than friendship because when I take Lane Turner, there will be no going back. She'll be mine, every single piece of her. Body, heart, and soul.

She shifts against me, adjusting her arms around my neck and grinding against my hard length in the process.

I hiss, gut clenching from the contact, and her eyes widen. It's as if her power over me somehow shocks her even though I've made it completely obvious I want her.

"You're still. . ." She trails off, then clears her throat.

Obviously, she thought the cold water would take care of my friend from the land down under, but the chill of the lake has nothing on the sex appeal of Lane Turner.

"You have quite the effect on me." My mouth curves.

Her finger traces the lines of my collarbone, her tone soft as she asks, "Do *all* your girl friends have this effect on you?"

"I told you before." I shake my head. "I don't have friends that are girls. Only you."

"Why me?" Her eyes lift.

"I think you know."

She may have a buzz and we may be skirting a line we shouldn't here, but there's no point in pretending.

I want Lane.

I've wanted her since the moment I laid eyes on her, and I won't let her forget, for even a second, how desirable she is simply because I vowed to settle for friendship.

She hums under her breath, and the sound reverberates through my chest, sending more blood south.

Great. Just what I fucking need.

I grip her ass and shift her position so she's higher around my waist. I'm not sure how much of this I can endure. My self-restraint is a thin thread between us, growing weaker by the second as her bright blue eyes stare up at me, daring me to act on something I fear she'll regret later. Unfortunately for her, I know what she's doing. She's afraid, scared shitless, and she's trying to give me all the control and push me to make a move, so later on, when she freaks out—and she *will* inevitably freak out—she'll have someone to blame. But as much as I want her, Lane regretting me is the one thing I can't handle. And if I take advantage, the moment I leave tonight, all of her fears and worries and inhibitions will come rolling in like a roaring thundercloud.

"Damn, I want to kiss you," I whisper, brushing a thumb over the corner of her mouth. In case it isn't completely obvious, I need her to know. I don't want my lack of action to make her feel like I don't want her in every conceivable way because I do.

Her gaze homes in on my mouth, her hair drying around her face in thick, wavy ropes as she licks her lips. "Then do it."

"Friends, remember?" I say through clenched teeth.

"Friends are overrated."

Fuck yes, they are. At this moment, in particular.

"Lane . . ." I lick my lips, a warning lilt to my voice as I instinctively lean closer. Her breath cascades over my mouth, and I fist my hands behind her back.

"Teagan . . ." she mocks.

I swallow and press my forehead to hers, my breath heavy in my ears and mingling with the erratic beat of my heart.

My hands slide up her back, slick from the lake.

I close my eyes, inhaling the scent coming from her skin—brown sugar and something floral—and I want to drown in her, plunge into her depths and never surface.

A shaky breath parts my lips as her hands start their own perusal, gliding over the muscles of my back, my shoulder blades, up to my neck and raking into my hair.

I imagine what it would be like to crush my mouth to hers, to kiss her until those hands and fingers yank at my roots. I imagine her breathy moans, the contented sighs I'm certain I can coax from her.

And then her hands slide between us, tracing the muscles of my pecs, moving over the ripple of my abdomen clenching even tighter at her southward movement.

A breath hisses between my teeth as she stops just above my groin, pausing as if she knows what she's doing to me. How much she's torturing me.

I blink my eyes open to see her hooded gaze, clouded with lust in the moonlight, and I wonder if she's been with anyone since Sophie's father. If my instincts are right, she hasn't. Because if there's one thing I know about Lane, it's that she puts her daughter first above all else, even above her own pleasure.

And damn if I don't find that fucking attractive.

I want to be the one to give her *everything*, including a safe place to fall, but also the release she needs, the one she deserves. I want to see her come undone at my hand, be the one to make her unravel.

My breathing turns shallow as I fight my resolve.

Fuck, I'm going to cave.

I can feel it.

If I'm going to stop this, now is the time. Otherwise, I won't stop until my hands and mouth are everywhere and she's screaming my name.

I inhale, filling my lungs with a cleansing breath as I remind myself I'm playing the long game. This isn't about one time or one night. This is about wanting all of Lane, all of the time. This is about making her mine.

And she's not ready.

I know she's not.

I grip her thighs, ready to lift her off me and bracing myself for the inevitable rejection I know I'll see on her face when the monitor on the dock beside us crackles to life.

"Mommy!" Sophie's voice, small and afraid, cries out in the darkness.

The glazed-over look in Lane's eyes clears.

She blinks once, twice, then curses under her breath. "Saved by the bell," she says, then releases her hold on me and swims back to the dock.

CHAPTER 20

LANE

I STARE DOWN AT the bracelet in my hand and my heart clenches. It's strung together by a pink piece of thick, yellow yarn. Two beads forming the number thirty-seven are flanked by two heart beads on either side.

"Please, Mommy, we have to take it to him," Sophie whines.

"Soph . . ." I trail off, the words thick in my throat as the unbidden memory of me wrapped in Teagan's arms and pressed against him in the cool lake hits me out of nowhere.

I climbed that boy like a damn tree, and in those moments, I never wanted anything more than I wanted him.

It would be so easy to blame it on the wine, because, yes, for a lightweight, I had too much, too fast. My head was buzzing, my limbs weightless, but I wasn't drunk, and wanting him was all my own doing. The wine had nothing to do with the desire coursing through my veins; that was all me. It only made acting on it easier.

My cheeks heat when I replay the evening in my mind.

I'd been so bold with him, so different from the reserved girl I was with Chance back in high school. Then again, I was different then. I had to grow up fast.

What would have happened had Sophie not woken up?

It's the question I keep asking myself.

And still, I have no answer.

Would Teagan have pushed me away? I could see him teetering close to the edge of his restraint.

Or would we have done something I'd come to regret?

As it is, I'll have a hard time looking him in the eye when I see him next. I can't imagine how I would feel if we'd hooked up.

"He needs it. It's his good luck charm." Sophie blinks up at me, her expression earnest.

"I know, honey, but he's getting on a bus soon. Today's game is away. Even if we wanted him to have it, I'm not sure we'd make it in time."

"But we have to at least *try*." Her lower lip quivers and her eyes fill. "Pappy has his handkerchief," she says, referring to my father's good luck hanky. "He always has it, and Teagan has nothing."

"How do you know? Maybe he has—"

"No," she insists. "I asked him." She crosses her arms over her chest, fighting so hard against the wobble in her voice. "Please, Mom, he's my bestest friend. And he'll lose without it."

My ribs crack open, heart exposed.

If I didn't want Sophie to get attached, I failed.

A sob rips through her throat, and tears slide down her cheeks.

With a groan, I place my head in my hands, debating on what to do. If we take the bracelet to him where the buses pick them up, someone might see us, and the last thing I want to do is get him in trouble with my father. Even though I'd be willing to clear the air, I'm not sure I'd have the time before they leave for the game.

But Sophie is clearly devastated, and I'd be lying if I said a small part of me didn't want to see him. Part of me wants to look him in the eyes after last night, to make sure nothing has changed between us. As crazy as it sounds, over these the past few weeks, Teagan's friendship has come to mean something to me—*he* means something to me—and I don't want that to change because in the moment we'd gotten carried away.

Sophie hangs her head, swiping at her tear-streaked cheeks as I glance at the time on my phone. "If we hurry, we might catch him." I sigh.

"Really?" She blinks up at me, and the silvery tracks from her tears shine on the apples of her cheeks.

I nod. "But I can't guarantee it. We could be too late."

The sky overhead is cloudy and gray as we make our way to the stadium.

Sophie sits in the back seat, chattering incessantly the entire way. When I pull into the parking lot and peer up at the massive bus, I can see the silhouettes from within, which means they've already boarded.

Shit. How the hell am I going to get this to him without making a scene?

"It might be too late, honey," I say, my voice trembling from nerves.

"Nuh uh, Mommy, I see him. Right there!" She points to the tinted windows of the bus, and sure enough, I catch Teagan's profile toward the back.

Double shit.

A cursory glance around the lot tells me my father has yet to arrive because his red sports car is nowhere in sight. Maybe if I hurry . . .

"Okay," I say, biting my lip. "But let me text him and tell him we're here."

I grab my phone from the cup holder of the car and open my contacts, find his name, and start to type out a quick text.

Me

> Hey, I'm here at the school. Sophie wanted me to bring you something. Any way you can meet me outside the bus?

I hit send and watch as he glances down at something in his hands before his head whips up and he searches the lot , easily finding us.

I offer him a little wave, then wait as he drops his head once more.

Teagan

Be right there.

He rises from his seat, seemingly pausing to talk to someone halfway down the aisle, and then he disappears from sight as he dismounts the steps on the other side.

Opening my car door, I step out and start walking for the bus at the same time Teagan comes into view, and my brain bursts into flames. Teagan in a football uniform is hot, but Teagan in a suit is a sight to behold.

The black suit coat stretches perfectly across his broad shoulders, somehow amplifying his athletic build. A crisp white shirt and blue tie draw my eyes for a classic look. Everything about him is polished, masculine, and completely sexy. The only thing remotely out of place are the rebellious curls mussed atop his head.

Feeling paranoid, I glance back up at the bus, and any hopes I had that his teammates might not notice our little exchange vanish as more than a dozen faces turn in our direction, watching Teagan's approach.

"Hey," Teagan murmurs, drawing my attention.

His sapphire gaze melts into mine, stealing all my reservations. Suddenly, we're the only two in this parking lot, the only people on the planet.

I clear my throat, remembering why I'm here, and reach out, offering him the bracelet. "Sophie insisted you have this for your game. She said it's your good luck charm, and she was quite adamant."

He smiles and turns it over in his hands with a chuckle. "She asked me if I had a good luck charm, then made me put my numbers on this one but she said it was for her."

I grin. "Clearly, I've raised a fibber."

Teagan mock gasps. "You take that back. Not my Sweet Sophie."

My heart squeezes, the breath stalling in my lungs as he asks, "Can I thank her myself?"

"Of course."

I walk with him back to my car, focusing on putting one foot in front of the other while my mind wonders to last night, until the memory feels like a living, breathing thing between us.

When we reach my car, he swings open the back door to where Sophie sits and lowers into a crouch, the bracelet clutched in his hand. "Sweet Sophie, you sneaky little thing you. You told me this was your bracelet."

Sophie giggles, her eyes red-rimmed from her earlier crying jag. "I tricked you because I wanted it to be a surprise. Now you'll really win."

Teagan nods, his expression solemn. "Thank you. I always wanted a good luck charm, but never thought I'd have one so pretty."

He slips it over his large hand onto his wrist where it just barely fits, and Sophie nods her approval. "You can't take it off. Ever. Not until football is over. Isn't that what Pappy does with his hanky?" Sophie scrunches her nose, blinking up at me for confirmation.

I nod, my throat tight. "He carries it just about everywhere until the season is over."

"See?" Sophie says, like he might argue. "You have to leave it on."

Teagan covers the bracelet on his left wrist with his hand. "I won't take it off. I promise. I may have to cover it with wrist tape, though, since wearing jewelry is frowned upon. Would that be okay, Sweet Sophie?"

Sophie sobers, her expression turning serious as if considering this, before nodding. "I think that's okay."

"Good." Teagan's lips quirk, and then he leans in and gives her a hug, made slightly awkward by her car seat. When he straightens, he turns to me, a hungry gleam in his eye as tucks his hands in the pockets of his suit pants. "Thank you," he murmurs.

I swallow, trying for a smile, but my heart is racing so fast I can hardly manage it. All I can think about is nude Teagan from last night. All that smooth skin and hard muscle. How my legs felt wrapped around his waist, heart to heart in the moonlight. All the things I wanted to do . . .

Friends, Lane. You're just friends.

I clear my throat and fake punch him in the arm. "Sure thing, *buddy*," I say, and immediately want to die.

"Buddy, huh?" He grins and opens his mouth to say something else but is interrupted by the rumbling of an engine directly behind us.

I turn to see a flash of red, and my eyes widen. "It's my father," I blurt, turning back to him. "You better hurry if you want to avoid being grilled the whole way about why you were talking to me."

He takes a step back, but not before holding my gaze a moment longer, regret swimming in his ocean-hewn depths. "Damn. I wish we had more time."

A lone butterfly takes flight in my stomach, tamped down by the fist of dread in the form of my father. "Go," I shoo him away. "You're already bound to have some explaining to do," I say, glancing pointedly at the prying eyes on the bus, and he grimaces.

"Nosy bastards."

Then he turns and jogs for the bus.

CHAPTER 21

TEAGAN

I KNOW I'M IN trouble the moment I step on the bus and all eyes swing to me. Then again, I've been in trouble since the moment I met Lane Turner.

Fuck.

I ignore the blatant stares from my teammates, grateful not everyone is here yet, particularly Chance. He already has a problem with me talking to her, so I can't imagine what he'd think of her flagging me down before a game.

I stroll toward my seat ignoring the obvious fact my teammates just witnessed me talking to the one girl Coach warned us all to stay away from. Tommy's brows rise across from me, a look that says *I hope you know what the hell you're doing* but I ignore it. Better to play dumb; it's less culpable that way.

"You got some balls of steel, Nichols," Greene says from behind as he claps me on the back.

I ignore him, instead focusing to my right as I watch Coach exit his vehicle with none other than Chance fucking Lockhart in the passenger seat.

I clench my jaw, hating how close he is to Lane's father.

My gaze shifts to where Lane stands by her car, turned toward them as they approach, and a ball of nerves fist in my gut. I know she's probably playing it off like she came to see her father—it's less suspicious that way—but the jealous asshole in me doesn't want Chance talking to her.

I can't read her lips from this angle, but whatever she tells Coach must do the trick. Only a moment passes before he draws her into a hug, then peers inside at Sophie before he turns for the bus.

Behind him, Chance follows, his gaze flickering over Lane in a way that makes my skin crawl. But he says nothing to her. Instead, he makes a beeline for the bus, and I exhale.

Mandretti, one of our defensive linemen, swivels in the seat in front of me and grins. "Cute bracelet." Not a second passes before Coach boards and his grin deepens. "You know you're gonna be fucked, right?"

I ignore him, my face a mask of cool indifference as I stare straight ahead while Coach addresses the driver and Chance continues down the aisle.

Across from us Bryce chortles. "The pink hearts are a nice touch," he says. "I suspected you might like 'em young, but damn, bro, this takes it to a whole new level."

"Shut the fuck up," I snap. I know they're just razzing me. Being a dick to your teammates and roasting their ass is par for the course, but I don't like him saying anything about Sophie.

"Ooh, touchy."

"You sure you want Coach to see you wearing that?" Greene from behind me.

"His daughter has a kid?" Tommy whispers.

Chance freezes, his gaze jerking to Tommy as he passes, then to mine where it homes in on the colorful bracelet on my wrist. Anger sparks in his eyes, a subtle change most might not notice, but it's a look I recognize from that evening in Slice.

Completely oblivious to the exchange, Mandretti asks, "Hey, Lockhart, you see this shit? Nichols's new girlfriend, here, made it a point to bring him a good luck charm."

"Probably so Coach doesn't beat his ass," Bryce says under his breath.

"Shut it down. *Now*," I grind out, and Mandretti raises his hands, palms out in surrender.

Chance brushes past me, glaring at me with malice in his eyes as he bumps into my shoulder, *hard*.

It's a warning; I have no doubt he knows exactly who the bracelet is from, especially after passing Lane in the parking lot.

Too bad I don't give a fuck.

The stadium buzzes with excitement, kicking the adrenaline in my veins into overdrive. The crowd roars as the line scrambles into formation. Only one and a half minutes is left on the timer until the end of the game, and we're three points away from winning.

The pressure is on.

Underneath the glare of stadium lights, I take my position, heart pounding with anticipation. The play we're about to run means the ball will go to me, and I'm ready. More than ready. Hell, I've been waiting for the opportunity all night.

My muscles coil as I bend down. My fingers sink into the sod as I ready for the snap of the ball.

"Set, hut!" Chance's command echoes across the field, and the play unfolds like well-rehearsed choreography. Receivers dash downfield skirting defenseman, while the offensive line forms a protective wall. I break free from my defender, exactly how I'm supposed to, my eyes fixating on the end zone.

I turn, arms outstretched and ready for the pass, when the ball sails over my head and to the left.

Shit.

This is no mistake. Clearly, it's not meant for me. Chance Lockhart is too good of a quarterback to miscalculate so poorly, and when the ball finds its mark in the waiting arms of our wide receiver, the crowd erupts in cheers.

He's taken down only ten yards from the end zone, which means we still have a chance.

My heart sinks, though I shouldn't be surprised by the turn of events. This isn't the first time today I've been overlooked. Chance is cockblocking me; that's all there is to it.

A million excuses have been given all night for why I haven't seen any action: Chance read the field and the wide receiver was the safer bet. I wasn't in position, even though I fucking *was*. He didn't see me open. The play didn't feel right. He went with his gut.

Amazing how many times his fucking gut told him *not* to give me the ball.

Disappointment gnaws at me as I hustle toward the huddle, trying to shake off the feeling of insignificance as Chance calls another play.

I nod, determined to make my presence known, to do something fucking noteworthy since I haven't had the opportunity all game.

Once more, the ball snaps, and I surge forward, running my route with precision and more speed than I can ever remember. I find an opening in the defense, a fleeting moment of opportunity.

But just as I turn to make the catch, someone shoves me from behind, throwing me off-balance.

Fuck.

I struggle to regain my footing, barely witnessing the moment Chance gets sacked, and the ball whizzes past, falling short of me. Greene fumbles for it, and when it lands, several defenders and offensive men dive for it.

Somehow, Greene comes out on top with the ball, managing to spring to his feet, and he takes a flying leap toward the end zone, falling to safety behind the goal line.

The cheers of the fans around me erupt to deafening levels.

We scored. Which means we won.

I *should* be ecstatic.

I pick myself up and force my feet to move, closing the distance between myself and Greene where several of my teammates are rushing the field. I reach a hand out and help him to his feet, clapping him on the back and congratulating him before we're engulfed by the rest of the team.

Several hours later and with food in hand, we're back on the bus, headed home.

It's late, everything cast in shadows as we take the highway back toward Cumberland. The excitement from our win has finally fizzled out with most guys leaning back in their seats, their eyes closed, earbuds in, and catching a nap on the six-hour drive home.

Not me.

I stare out the window, losing focus on the scenery as we pass. My thoughts are lost on the game when a voice brings me up short.

"Tough break today."

I turn to find Chance in the seat behind me, his expression smug as he meets my eyes between the seats.

"Amazing how that happened. Didn't get near a pigskin all game."

"Like I said," Chance chews on a piece of gum, his lips curling, "tough break out there."

My eyes narrow. On the field, I'd suspected all the diversions, change in plays, and unhappy coincidences were calculated, but now I *know* they were.

"Can I ask what exactly your problem is with me?"

Chance's eyes widen. If he's surprised I've challenged him, then he's dumber than I thought. Then again, he's so used to everyone kissing his ass.

"Sounds like you're the one with the problem."

"Really?" I tip my chin. "So today's game, all those times I was supposed to get the ball and didn't, those were just . . . coincidences?"

Chance chokes on a laugh, though his eyes are filled with anything but humor. Instead, they glitter with indignation. "Some people call me a god on the field, but damn, you're giving me more credit than them all." He narrows his eyes. "You think I can control a whole fucking game?" he seethes.

He's not entirely wrong to imply anyone who thinks a single person can control the game is an idiot. There is a whole hell of a lot out of his control on the field once the ball leaves his hands. But while he still has it, while it's in his possession? That's a whole other story.

He controls the narrative. Quarterbacks dictate the pace of the game, and oftentimes, the scoreboard. And they're sure as hell in control of calling plays and who they give the ball to. It's why pro quarterbacks are the highest paid position in the NFL;

the weight of responsibility lies on their shoulders the most out of any other position. Lockhart is playing dumb and it pisses me off, because he knows I'll see his answer for what it is—complete and utter bullshit—but there's not a damn thing I can do about it. Just like there wasn't a damn thing I could do about it today on the field.

"Cut the shit, Lockhart," I say, keeping my tone even, careful not to rouse any of the guys around us. "You can claim it was out of your hands for a few of the plays. The sack at the end was one. But the last-minute play changes, blatantly ignoring me when I was wide open and grounding the ball instead, passing it to Bryce and Greene every single fucking time regardless of whether I was in the perfect position to score? That's all you. Even when Coach told you he wanted me to have the ball, you found a way to deflect. You're just lucky we won today."

Chance grins. "Oh, come on now, Nichols. You and I both know luck has nothing to do with it." He winks. "I'm just *that* good. But don't be sour. There will be other games. It's not like this is your last. As a rookie, you should be grateful you're even getting so much play time."

I grit my teeth. Though he's not entirely wrong, we both know I'm a damn good football player. Otherwise, Coach wouldn't have me on the starting lineup.

"Speaking of luck, though . . ." His gaze travels down my arm to where Sophie's bracelet encircles my wrist, staring pointedly for a beat longer than I'd like.

My chest tightens, and I twitch to cover it up. I want to hide the brightly beaded bracelet from his probing gaze so I can somehow protect Lane and Sophie. But it's too late, and any such movement will only draw further attention. Besides, if the way he's staring at it is any indication, he already knows who gave it to me.

His eyes lift, his gaze icing over as a chill shimmies up my spine. "Looks like luck wasn't on your side today, after all," he says.

CHAPTER 22

LANE

I TAKE A SEAT on one of the cushioned benches of the mall's indoor playground and remove Sophie's shoes, then tell her to be careful as she runs off to climb a giant, rubbery whale.

"Now, let's talk about why we just spent an hour wondering around the mall eating a thousand calories in pretzels"—Gabby waves her cinnamon sugar pretzel in the air—"when I know darn well your mother made a massive brunch this morning."

She eyes me, one dark brow arching toward her hairline as I deflate.

Sometimes I forget how well Gabby knows me. My mother's brunches are a well-known tradition and honestly amazing. She could easily open a brunch-only restaurant and make a killing. But the moment football season starts, Chance seems to be at every single one of them, and since I make it a habit of avoiding him at all costs, that means I usually make myself scarce.

Like today.

If my parents have caught on, they've never said anything. Or maybe the conversation in-season is so hyper-focused on football, they barely notice my absence.

"You know why." I dish out a good dose of side-eye before glancing back to where Sophie climbs up the whale's spongy tongue which doubles as a slide.

"You'd think he'd quit going after . . ." She discreetly nods her head toward Sophie.

"Not in-season." I shake my head on a sigh. "He no longer comes around in the spring and summer, but in the fall, he just avoids us as much as possible while he's there."

Gabby grunts. "He's like a fucking sea urchin. All innocent looking at first sight, until you realize what a prick he is, and if you don't stay away, he'll fuck you up." I snort while Gabby stares off into the distance. "Gosh, I bet it'll be a relief once he's gone, won't it?"

"You have no idea." I sigh.

"Do you think the rumors are true? That he might get drafted early?"

"I don't know." *God, I hope.*

A little boy gives Sophie a light shove, and my stomach lurches. I start to rise to my feet, but pause when she tells him to stop, then moves to the other side of the playground. Crisis averted.

"Little rat. Gosh, I freaking hate kids," Gabby mutters. I chuckle at her candor because as much as Gabby loves Sophie, she's not a fan of children. "Except Soph, of course," she rushes to add. "She's an effing angel. You're so lucky to have her."

My lips curve, her words bringing me back to my conversation with Teagan.

There's no luck about it, Lane. You made her that way. You're the reason she's so awesome. You know that, don't you?

"So, how's it going with Teagan," she asks, as if she can read my thoughts.

When I don't immediately respond, she bumps my shoulder with hers. "Any new developments there? Did you heed my advice and stop avoiding him like a pus—"

"Gabby!" I hiss, then bark out a laugh. "Children, remember?" I motion around us.

I bite my lip, grinning wide while my thoughts drift to Teagan and everything that happened the other night at the lake house.

Gabby gasps. "Oh my gosh, something happened, didn't it?"

"*Shhhhh.*" I glance around us as if someone I know might hear. "Nothing . . . *happened,*" I say, even though I'm not entirely sure that's true. I mean, sure, we didn't actually do anything, but I wouldn't call skinny dipping and practically eye fucking each other nothing.

My face burns with the memory, and Gabby must notice because she bounces in her seat and says, "Spill, right now."

I shake my head, wondering how I can accurately sum up my feelings for Teagan and everything that happened the other night into words. "I don't know, Gabs. It's like he's . . . *perfect.*" I glance at her, my throat aching from the truth in my words.

"He's seriously everything. I had basically come to terms with the fact that I'd be single until Sophie was in high school because who would want to be hemmed down so young with a child? But he's messing with my head, making me rethink everything."

"Like what? That someone might actually *want* you?" Gabby stares at my profile while I gnaw on my lip.

"For one thing, *yeah*."

She scoffs. "Lane, I've told you that about a thousand times. You're fucking *amazing*."

I fight the urge to roll my eyes. "Okay, but it's an entirely different thing having your friends and family tell you that versus an insanely sexy man." *Damn, is he sexy.* "For another, he's making me think that maybe not all athletes are created equal. That maybe you can dedicate most of yourself to your passion but still have time for other things."

"Of course you can." Gabby reaches out and tucks a wavy lock of hair behind my ear. "Just like you can devote yourself to Sophie, but it doesn't mean you can't make room for something or someone else. Chance was just a dick, Lane."

I let her swear go with a grimace and swallow through the ache in my throat.

She's right; I know she's right, but . . .

"Did he kiss you?" Gabby asks when it's clear I've clammed up.

I exhale. "No." I shake my head, reliving those tense moments at the lake in my mind. "But I wanted him to. I *really* wanted him to. He came up to the lake house, and Gabs . . ." I turn to her. "He brought me and Soph dinner. It was just boxed mac and cheese he rushed to make before he came, but it was so freaking sweet, I swear. And then he played with Sophie for next to an hour, stringing bracelets together with her while I spoke with the contractor. He unloaded all our stuff from the car and set up her bed while I helped her change and brushed her teeth. All without asking. *And* he calls Soph 'Sweet Sophie,' and I swear it hooks my heart every single time."

Gabby's smile spreads, a mischievous glint to her eye.

"What?"

"Nothing." She shakes her head. "It's just that boy has it *bad*, Lane. He is *so* gone over you. I'm not sure I've ever seen anything like it, to be honest. I wish I could've been there the day he met you in the park because I'm betting he let some serious sparks fly. He's making a damn good case for love at first sight."

I scoff. *Love at first sight.* Sounds like a fairy tale. "You can't be serious."

"Even you have to admit, the boy sounds smitten."

A flutter of nerves awakens inside my chest like a flock of trapped birds.

"And then?" she asks, interrupting my thoughts. "That can't be it."

My cheeks flush, knowing what Gabby will think of the rest. "Then I had some wine." Gabby's eyes round. "I know," I say quickly in my defense. "I don't often drink, but I was at the lake and excited about the house and the prospect of moving in soon, and I wanted to celebrate."

"With Teagan." She wiggles her brows.

"I didn't even know he was coming until last minute." I scowl as Gabby takes a monstrous bite of her pretzel; eyes locked on me like she's watching her favorite scene in a movie unfold.

I stifle the rise of nerves and check Sophie's position before I continue. "Once Sophie was in bed, I opened the wine, and we took it out to the dock where we looked at the stars." I ignore the look she shoots me. "We talked for a bit, and then," I swallow and blurt out: "wewentskinnydipping."

Gabby chokes on a bite of pretzel, wheezing as she pounds her chest.

My eyes widen. For a moment, I imagine having to perform the Heimlich right here in front of all these children and the giant rubber whale when she finally coughs it up.

Wheezing, she presses a palm to her chest. "I'm sorry, did you just say that you, Lane Turner, went skinny dipping with that hunk of a man?"

I purse my lips, glancing away from her to watch Sophie climb a rubber crab with massive claws. "Yes."

"Holy shit." She blinks. "Was his body as incredible as I imagine it to be?"

I flush, struck with an image of a nude Teagan standing on the dock, and my body heats so entirely, I'm forced to close my eyes, to try to breathe through the fire in my veins.

Beside me, Gabby barks out a laugh. "That good, huh?"

I groan and turn to her. "He was so perfect, it's unfair."

"And what did he think of *you*, my dear?"

If the tent in his pants was any indication, he liked what he saw.

She watches me intently, searching for one of my tells, and whatever she sees must confirm what I'm thinking because her high-pitch cackle startles every person on the playground.

Several heads turn. Eyes probing.

"Could you be quiet?" I hiss. "We're in the presence of children," I admonish, mostly because the thoughts running through my head are bordering on indecent.

"Sorry. Sorry." She waves a hand out in front of her as if trying to gain her composure, though she doesn't *sound* sorry. "But this is the most excitement you've seen since sixteen, and you expect me not to be completely thrilled for you?" she whispers. "Not happening."

My mouth flattens.

"So," she continues, "you talk, have a little wine, strip down and get in the water, and then what?"

"And then"—I eye her in my periphery, knowing she'll have a field day with this next part—"he pulled me to him, and I sort of—" I clear my throat.

"You sort of . . ."

"Wrapped my legs around his waist while he held me snug against him, and we came damn close to kissing and who knows what else." I drop my face in my hands.

Gabby groans. "What the hell stopped you? Why didn't you go for the *who knows what else*?"

"I could tell he was hesitant." I raise my head and shrug.

Gabby frowns.

"Not because he didn't want me. That much was apparent."

"Then why?"

I laugh, but it's nothing short of bitter. "Let's see, probably because of my father and the warning he gave everyone. Teagan has a lot at stake by getting involved with me, so I think he's skirting the line intentionally. Also, maybe he was remembering the fact that I'd previously turned him down. Maybe he's not sure what to think." I run my hands through the length of my hair and exhale. "I don't know, but I think he would've caved if it weren't for Sophie waking up and crying for me because afterward, that was that. I had to get out of the water to get her, and he left. Perks of being *Mom*."

I offer her a droll smile. "At least he got a taste of what a relationship with a single mom would be like. Complete privacy is hard to come by. Interruptions and inconvenience are par for the course."

Gabby's gaze shifts to the playground where Sophie giggles with another girl. "Sophie," she tsks. "You little cock-block you."

"Gabs!" I laugh and elbow her in the ribs.

"What?" Gabby asks, eyes wide. "She should've taken one for the team, am I right? Suck it up, buttercup. Momma needs to get some."

I cover my face to hide the raging blush ripping through my cheeks. "Oh my gosh. *Stop.*"

After a good laugh and most of the blood returns to my chest, Gabby asks, "So, all joking aside, how do you really feel about him?"

The million-dollar question, one I've both avoided and asked myself a thousand times since that day in the park with no clear answer.

My emotions where Teagan is concerned are like a ball of tangled yarn. The more I tug and pull at the strings to try and unravel my feelings, the more they tangle. Pretty soon, the only solution will be to cut them loose. At least that way, I'll know where I begin, and he ends.

"I don't know. It feels . . . complicated."

Gabby huffs. "What isn't?"

Maybe she's right. Maybe everything in life is complicated, and maybe I'm just making things more difficult than they need to be by focusing on the hardness of it all. The problem is, it's not just me I have to consider. If it were, maybe my answer would be clearer. Maybe it wouldn't be so hard to define this ballooning in my chest when I think of Teagan.

We both fall silent, staring at Sophie as she laughs and plays.

"When will you see him again?" she eventually asks.

"I don't know." A twinge of worry gnaws on my gut. "I'm worried about Sophie. She's getting really attached, and if I could convince myself this thing with Teagan and I was purely platonic, and we could remain friends with no complications, maybe I wouldn't worry so much, but . . ."

A vise wraps around my chest, compressing the worry until it needles beneath my ribs. "I don't want her to get hurt, Gabs." I swallow. "I don't ever want her to know what it feels like to think someone chose you, only for them to walk away."

"Hey, Dad." I climb the porch steps with Sophie racing ahead of me.

She flings herself into my father's arms, going in for the kill before releasing him and running into the house in search of my mother.

"Have a seat." Dad pats the empty space on the porch swing beside him, and I oblige, sinking down onto the thick cushion.

"How was brunch?" I ask, my guilt getting the better of me.

"Good. We missed you, you know." I hum under my breath. "Chance was asking where you were."

My head jerks to him and I frown. "Really?"

Why the hell did Chance care where I was? It's not like my avoiding him is anything new.

My father nods. "I told him you'd be there next weekend."

The way he says it leaves no room for argument. Unless I want to put up a fight, I'll attend next Sunday's brunch. I may be a grown-ass adult now with my own child, but I am still living under their roof, which means, to an extent, playing by their rules. Or at least, that's how I feel. It's one reason, among many, why I can't wait to move into the lake house next month.

"You should've seen him yesterday, Lane. Damn, you'd have been proud. He was *fire*. There's no other way to put it. He made some last-minute decisions on the field because his gut was telling him something different from what I suggested. I was skeptical, but it paid off. We won."

A massive knot lodges in my throat.

"That's great, Dad," I say, but it falls flat.

As long as his success is tied to Chance's, I'll always be less than enthusiastic. I look forward to the days when Chance is gone and playing for the NFL, so I can finally talk to my father without my stomach tying in knots.

I listen while he explains in great detail all the things Chance did well. Twenty minutes pass with him singing Lockhart's praises like he's invincible. Twenty minutes of *Chance this, Chance that*, until I'm about to burst from frustration.

Anger crawls under my skin as the urge to scream rises inside of me.

If I hear his name one more time, I might puke. Barf the cinnamon sugar pretzel I consumed with Gabby right onto the floor.

My hands fist at my side in an effort to restrain myself while I grit my teeth.

"I'll tell ya what," my father continues, "I wouldn't be surprised if he's top ten in the draft. That boy's gonna go far. He's turning into quite the young man."

"Yep," I somehow manage, but all I want to do is scream. I want to turn and tell him the boy he loves so much is the same one who got me pregnant. The same man who left.

I want to explain how the man he thinks is so fucking amazing is also the one person in this world my father despises the most; he just doesn't know they're one and the same.

But I do. I know, and it eats me up inside.

I'm so close to being free of Chance Lockhart.

One more season after this one and he'll be gone.

If I'm lucky, they'll draft him early.

There's no doubt Chance will go to the NFL; it's only a matter of when.

I listen for another minute, until I can't possibly take anymore and then I blurt out, "How about Teagan Nichols?"

My father's gaze flickers to mine, a question in his eyes I refuse to answer before he asks it. "How do you know Nichols?"

I shrug. "We have a class together," I lie. "We talk sometimes. I guess you could say we're friends." I don't hesitate with the label, knowing any kind of pause or inflection in my voice would be a red flag.

My father doesn't question me; I've never given him a reason to, or at least not one he knows about. "He did okay yesterday. Didn't see the ball much," he tells me.

I stare down at my hands, playing with a piece of loose thread on the hem of my T-shirt, unable to stop myself as I ask, "Do you think he has a chance of going pro?"

I know what Teagan said Friday night, but I can't help but wonder if he was being modest. Or maybe he was saying what I wanted to hear.

"Nichols is good, damn good." My father's mouth turns down. Most would think it's a frown, but I recognize it as his thinking face, and so I wait. "I've only just started coaching him, but Teagan is a dark horse. Not a lot of buzz around him. That's not necessarily a bad thing. If you ask me, the kid has everything it takes to rise to the top. He's quick. Smart. Thinks on his feet. Has the hands of some of the best tight ends in college football. I think if he wants it, he can earn his shot. I guess time will tell how badly he does."

My father's .

It reminds me of what Teagan said about drive.

It also reminds me of why I need to be careful.

A dull ache blooms inside my chest at the warning.

Teagan is only a freshman. He has four seasons to prove himself on the field and determine what kind of player he's going to be. Four years to dictate his future and potentially earn himself a spot in the draft.

His life is in a state of flux; he has his whole life ahead of him, and like most people our age, he has no idea where the path might take him. A lot can happen between now and then. I, on the other hand, already know where I'll be. My life will look the same today as it will five years from now.

The thought is the reminder I need.

No matter how good he is with Sophie or how much he makes my heart leap inside my chest, he's a wild card. He has zero responsibility to anyone other than himself, which means he can afford to be selfish.

He's an athlete first and foremost, which means he and I would never work.

I need to remember that.

I find Sophie in the kitchen with my mother, dropping big balls of cookie dough onto a lined cookie sheet. "Having fun?" I ask, smiling, despite the heavy weight taking up residence in my chest following the conversation with my father.

"Yeah! We added extra chocolate chips!" Sophie says, dropping another ball of dough to the sheet.

My mother glances up at me, her eagle eyes taking in my expression. "Uh oh. Your father talked your ear off about the game, didn't he?"

"I may or may not have sat through a thirty-minute play-by-play of Chance's performance in the game."

Mom winces. "Well, at least you missed the mini strategy session at brunch." She rolls her eyes, and I laugh.

I don't tell her I'll have the joy of hearing it next weekend. If I have any say in it, I'll find a way out of brunch with Chance.

Stepping forward, I take a little piece of raw dough and pop it in my mouth. "You'll get sick!" Mom swats at me, but I dodge her easily.

"I've never heard of one person getting sick from raw cookie dough."

"You say that now . . ." The corners of her mouth curl in amusement. "Gosh, you've done that since you were a kid."

"And we've had this argument ever since." I laugh.

"Old habits die hard." Mom smirks and pats Sophie's head. "My sweet girl here is as patient as the day is long. It's remarkable, really."

Sweet Sophie.

A private smile tugs at the corners of my mouth at the thought of Teagan's nickname for her, then I groan and run my hands through my hair.

Is everything always going to remind me of him? Am I destined forever to think of him every single time he's not around?

"Everything okay?" Mom asks, arching a brow as she turns to put the pan of cookies into the preheated oven.

"Yeah, yeah. Fine. Sorry. Just thinking about something."

"Anything I can help with?"

I wish.

I remember the days when my problems were so small my parents could solve them all. It's been a long time since then.

"Nope. It's fine." I sigh.

Nothing I can't handle, anyway.

My phone dings and I glance down at it, noting a new text from Teagan. "Um, I'll be right back," I mumble, grateful both Mom and Sophie are preoccupied with loading another cookie sheet.

I wander from the kitchen and up the stairs toward my bedroom as I click open the text and read.

Teagan

> Do you have plans for the day? I was hoping to see you.

I bite my lip, debating.

Should I answer or ignore him?

I crack my neck, a habit I've had for years, then begin to type.

Me

> I was just out with Gabby and Soph. We'll probably stay in the rest of the day. Sorry.

Not even a minute passes after I hit send that my phone starts to ring.

I suck in a breath.

He's calling me.

Shit.

Do I answer?

Of course I have to answer.

He obviously knows I'm around because I just texted him back.

Shit, shit, shit.

"Hello?"

"Why stay in when you can go out with me instead?" Teagan asks the second I answer.

My stomach tightens at the same time the rush I feel whenever I'm with him floods through my veins, begging me to give in and say yes.

My head spins from the whiplash of emotions as I try to remember the reasons I can't. "I don't know," I hedge. "Soph and I should probably stay here."

"What? No. You most definitely should *not* stay there."

"Teagan . . ." I close my eyes, my head warring with my heart. I want to see him, but I know I can't. Friends or not, it'll only lead to disappointment.

"Lane . . ." He mocks.

"It's just that you've spent a lot of time with Sophie lately. I think you should probably keep a little distance, you know?"

"No, I don't know. Explain."

I sigh and shove a hand through my hair. *Why can't he just make this easy? Take my answer as a no and move on?*

"I don't want her to get hurt, Teagan. She's already growing attached, evidenced by the bracelet she begged me to bring you yesterday, and I think a little of that is okay. Our weekly pizza night at Slice is fine, but I've been thinking, and it's probably best if we limit our interaction to just that, once a week."

As it is, that'll be too much. I know, because I already find myself waiting to see him each day on my shift and counting down the hours until the next one.

Sophie's no different.

The more time she spends with him, the more she talks about him. Just yesterday, after we delivered the bracelet, she asked when we'd see him next, and the idea of her becoming attached and losing him scares me more than anything.

"That's bullshit, Lane. I would never do anything to hurt her, and I want to see her."

"I know that, but when things go south with us, I'll have to explain—"

"*If.*"

"What?" I blink and shake my head to clear it.

"*If* things go south. You said *when*. And for the record, that's one of the reasons we're only friends, right? How could things possibly end poorly among friends?"

I swallow over the lump in my throat. The word "friends" suddenly seems wholly inadequate to describe the flowy feeling I get when I think of him, like someone turned on a spotlight inside my chest, lighting me up and chasing the darkness.

When I say nothing, he adds, "You should know I don't just abandon my friends, Lane. Best damn friend ever, remember?"

I huff out a laugh. Of course I remember, and so far, he's living up to the title. But that's part of the problem, isn't it? The more amazing he proves himself to be, the worse it'll hurt once he's gone.

"Do you want references?" he asks.

I bark out a laugh. "What?"

"References. I can give you the numbers of all my friends and you can ask them about what kind of friend I am, how loyal, trustworthy, whatever."

I scoff. "Don't be ridiculous. I don't need references, Teagan. I need . . ." I growl in frustration, "I don't know what I need."

But I do know; I just don't want to say it.

I *need* space but I *want* him, and I feel my resolve slipping by the second under his persuasion.

"So it's settled, then."

"What's settled?" I lift my free hand and pinch the bridge of my nose.

"We're friends, which also means we're hanging out today."

"Teagan, I don't think—"

"Be at your house in thirty. Be ready and dress casual."

"No. Wait—" I start, but the line goes dead before I can finish.

I hold my phone out and stare at the blank screen, stunned as I rewind our conversation in my head, wondering how we got here. From the moment I found out I was having a baby, I had to grow a backbone. I'm no longer easily persuaded or influenced. I don't give into things on a whim. Instead, I'm headstrong and steadfast in my decisions.

But Teagan Nichols is an entirely different beast.

I've only known him for weeks and yet I can see he's a man who goes after what he wants and doesn't quit until he gets it.

And for reasons I can't explain, he seems to want me.

And for reasons I can't explain, he seems to want me.

CHAPTER 23

TEAGAN

I WAS FULLY PREPARED for Lane to freak out after Friday night and take a step back from me, so when she showed up on Saturday morning in the parking lot outside the stadium with a bracelet from Sophie, I was floored. Like a fool, I thought maybe we'd skate right past the awkward tension of almost hooking up and move on but based on the conversation I just had with her, I was wrong.

I don't mind waiting for her to come around. After all, I'm a patient man.

But I also won't take a back seat.

I have no idea what the fuck I'm doing when it comes to Lane, but I've never been passive a day in my life, and I'm not about to change now. Lane can take all the time she needs adjusting to the idea she and I are meant to be together. If she wants to be friends for the next year, so be it. Even if it means twelve months of cold showers and blue balls, I'll friend the shit out of this thing if I have to.

My guess is something must have happened in the last twenty-four hours to change her mind and plant a seed of doubt. Hell, maybe I'm paranoid, but part of me wonders if Chance somehow got to her. With the way he acted at our game, I wouldn't be surprised, and it has me once again questioning just what in the hell their relationship is, and why he's yet to squeal to Coach.

Whatever the reason, her shields are up and stronger than ever, but I won't let that get me down. Rather than allow her to strengthen them further, I need to attack. Complacency will get me nowhere. Instead, I need to work on finding a way through the armor around her heart, and I can't do that sitting in my dorm room twiddling my fucking thumbs. Especially not when I'm on the cusp of a breakthrough, and if Friday is any indication, that's exactly where I am.

Operation Friends-To-Lovers is working. It's still the best shot I have at breaking down her walls and getting her to trust me, all without pissing off Coach.

I pull into the driveway of the Turner residence and take a steadying breath as I stare up at the large brick house with the perfectly manicured landscaping. Showing up here is a bold move. Even if Lane has told her father we're friends, I have no idea what his reaction was, and I haven't had a chance to ask. Yet here I am.

All I can do is pray he doesn't kick my ass when he sees me standing here, waiting for his daughter.

I swing open my car door before I can second-guess myself and hop out at the same time Lane appears on her doorstep, a sweater wrapped around her slender figure as she stares at me with reproach. "Teagan, you shouldn't have come."

I grin. "Didn't we settle this on the phone?"

"Yeah, I said I didn't think it was a good idea," she hisses.

"Right. And I said I'd be here in thirty minutes and to be ready." My gaze flickers down the tight black leggings that showcase her curves then back to her face again, and I stifle a groan. "You ready?"

Her lips twitch, which I take as a good sign. "You're incorrigible, you know that?" She blinks at me until I step onto the porch. "My father might see you."

I shrug, feigning indifference even though my stomach tightens with my nerves. "We've been hanging out for weeks. We're friends. He's bound to find out at some point. Might as well be now."

It's true. Maybe I'm a glutton for punishment, but if Friday night proved anything to me, it's that Lane and I have everything it takes to leave the friend zone, and we're closer than she's willing to acknowledge, which is why she's scared. Hell, we're light-years ahead of where I thought we'd be.

More proof I'm right for her.

Lane exhales and tucks a lock of hair behind her ear, avoiding my eyes. "I told him, but still . . . I don't just hang out with guys, like, *ever*."

I reach out, placing my hand on her stiff shoulders. "It'll be fine. Trust me."

"Teagan . . ." She exhales.

"Oh, honey, who's at the door?" a female voice I can only assume is Lane's mother calls out.

"Um, no one. Just a salesman," she yells over her shoulder.

I arch a brow at her and my lips quirk. "A salesman? What exactly am I selling again?"

"Tell him we don't—*oh*!" A woman with chestnut colored hair peeks around Lane, eyes wide as she takes me in.

"I've got it, Mom." Lane tries to close the door, but her mother isn't having it and blocks it with her forearm.

"What's he selling?" she asks.

"Nothing."

"But I thought—"

Lane turns and gently pushes her mother away from the door. "Don't worry about it. I've got it under control."

"Well, whatever he's selling, sign me up," her mother mutters loud enough so I can hear.

I burst out laughing, and Lane stops, mouth gaping beneath cheeks red as a sunburn. "Mom!"

"What?" her mother asks innocently.

I take that as my cue and step forward into the foyer of the Turner home, stretching out a hand toward her mother and clearing my throat. "Hi, ma'am, I'm Teagan Nichols, a friend of Lane's from school."

Lane crosses her arms over her chest. "He's also one of Dad's tight ends."

"*Ahh*," her mother says like she gets it now, and I wonder if she knows about her husband's warning to the team, or Lane's apparent aversion to socializing with football players, maybe both.

Whatever it is, she doesn't seem to care as she takes my hand with a spreading grin. "Nice to meet you, Teagan. I'm Dolly. Come on in." She waves me inside and Lane groans. "So, I'm confused. Are you also selling something?"

I chuckle. "Nah. Lane was just messing with me. You know, Lane, always a little jokey jokester," I say, reaching down and ruffling her long hair with my hand until it tangles like a bird's nest atop her head.

Lane swats my hand away while her mother watches on with amusement. "Interesting. So, you two are *friends*?" she asks, pointing between us.

"If you could call us that," Lane says dryly at the same time, I reply:

"The *best* of friends."

I rock back on my heels, a smile plastered to my face while Dolly laughs. "Well, that is just wonderful to hear." She claps her hands together. "Lane could certainly use more good friends in her life."

"*Mom.*" Lane scowls.

"Ed!" Dolly calls out, and I stiffen for a moment while Lane shoots me a vengeful look. "Ed, come here and say hi to one of Lane's friends."

Footsteps echo down the hall, and the next thing I know, Coach Turner rounds the corner, his eyes blinking with surprise when he sees me standing here in his foyer on a Sunday afternoon. Beside him, Sophie clutches his hand, but when her head lifts and her eyes lock with mine, she drops his giant mitt like a hotcake and dashes straight for me.

"Teagan!" She flings her arms around my legs and squeezes.

My hand finds the top of her hair, which is braided into a halo around her head. "Hey, Sweet Sophie."

Beside me, Lane visibly softens while Dolly looks as though she might pass out from sheer joy, and Coach stares at me through narrowed eyes. The three couldn't have more opposite reactions if they tried.

"Well, I see Sophie already knows you well." Dolly glances between us, failing to hide her approval. "Just how much have you two been hanging out?"

Coach crosses his arms over his chest and lifts his chin. "Yeah. How much *have* you been seeing my daughter and granddaughter behind my back?"

"Ed," his wife admonishes.

He turns on Lane, ignoring her. "You made it sound like you only saw each other in class."

I clear my throat, and nerves dance in my stomach when I open my mouth to speak at the same time Sophie releases me and spins around.

"We get pizza at Slice!" she blurts, beaming. "Mom says we can only have it one day a week, even though Teagan has it *three* times." Dolly chuckles while Coach's brows rise. "*And* he came to the lake house the other night to play with me."

Oh shit. I wince.

Stiffening, I glance at Coach to gauge his reaction.

His cheeks redden, and if the muscle flickering in the side of the jaw is any indication, he's pissed. *Really* pissed.

Fuck, I'm screwed.

I rack my brain for something to say, something to make this sound better than it does, like I'm not trying to date his daughter, which in the grand scheme of things is exactly what I'm doing.

I step forward, but Lane places a hand out to stop me when she glances at Sophie. "Pizza once a week is plenty," she says to Sophie. Then to her father: "We were talking on campus and I mentioned how Jason was doing me a favor by meeting me at the lake house after practice to go over the contract." She shrugs. "Teagan didn't like the idea of me and Sophie meeting him alone at night."

Dolly clutches her hands in front of her chest, looking a little like she's praying. Even Coach seems to relax a little.

He shifts on his feet and turns toward me, his arms dropping at his side as I clear my throat. "I have sisters, sir. I guess I'm kind of used to thinking about those things."

"Well . . ." Coach nods in my direction while Dolly beams. "I appreciate it. That's . . . smart," he says, almost begrudgingly as he glances back at Lane. "Even though Jason has done work for us before, Teagan probably has a point. You shouldn't have been meeting him alone. But all you had to do was tell me, and I—"

"Would've stopped watching game tape to come with me?" Lane smirks, her brows rising.

Coach gapes, shame sliding over his features.

"That's what I thought." Lane snorts but reaches out to pat him on the back. "Anyway, it worked out fine. Teagan was able to stop by and entertain Sophie while I got the contract signed. It's all good, and I'll have a roof in the next few weeks."

"That's lovely." Dolly reaches out and squeezes my arm. "It's so nice to know Lane has someone else looking after her best interests, isn't it, Ed?" She glances pointedly at her husband, a warning in her tone.

I bow my head, swallowing over the guilt rising in the back of my throat. An image of Lane with the moonlight glittering over her bare skin just moments before she plunged into the water slides through my head.

If by looking after Lane's best interests she means ogling her naked and imagining all the things I'd like to do to her, then, sure, I'm a fucking saint.

"It is," Coach says, hesitating before he adds, "he's on the team, you know?"

I inhale, more than a little relieved.

"Yes, he told me," Dolly says.

Coach brightens and I have to blink to make sure my eyes aren't playing tricks on me. "Damn good player, too. A lot of talent. Lane and I were just talking about him a little while ago, weren't we, Lane?"

Lane's eyes widen and her cheeks flush.

"Were you now?" I drawl.

So maybe that's where the sudden bout of doubt came from?

"You just came up in passing," Lane waves it off as if it's nothing.

"Well, to be fair, you asked me what I thought of him." Coach rocks back on his heels, so serious I want to burst out laughing because if Lane's squinty eyes are any indication, she wants to kill him.

"You were asking about me, huh, Turner?" I ask her, my tone smug.

Lane's throat bobs before she shoots her father another scathing look.

"Teagan, why don't you come in and have a seat?" Dolly asks. "Have some coffee?"

"I'd love to—"

"Oh, no, no, no, no." Lane grabs my arm and steers me toward the door. "We'd better get going or we're going to be late."

She pauses, then reaches out to Sophie. "Come on, Soph. Let's get your coat and shoes on."

"Oh, so soon?" Dolly asks in a sorrowful tone. "Where are you off to?"

"Uh . . ." Lane glances at me in question. "Teagan's taking us to, uh—"

"It's a surprise," I say, having mercy on her.

"Do you need us to watch Sophie, dear?" Dolly asks, directing the question toward Lane, her knowing gaze so loaded with meaning, I snort as I glance away.

"No. We were planning on taking her."

"*Lane*"—Dolly shoots her a look only a mother can give—"you can leave her with us once and a while, you know?"

"But I want to go," Sophie nearly cries.

"It might be nice to just have some grown up time," Dolly adds.

"Actually, Mrs. Turner," I start.

"Dolly," she interrupts.

"Right. Dolly," I say, kindly. "Actually, the place we're going to is definitely somewhere we'll want to take Sophie."

"Oh." A flicker of something passes over Dolly's face before she nods. "Well, if you're sure."

I glance at Lane. "We're sure," she says.

"In that case, the three of you have fun."

CHAPTER 24

LANE

"YOUR MOTHER IS LOVELY. Seriously a peach," Teagan says, his tone chipper as he walks us to his car.

I elbow him in the ribs, hoping my mother isn't watching from the window.

Knowing her, she is.

"I hate you," I say, though there's no conviction in it.

"No, you don't," he crows. "You love me." He winks, and a flush instantly creeps up my neck.

Dammit, he's right.

"I can't believe you show up here unannounced and, literally, win both of my parents over in a matter of minutes." I shake my head, still in disbelief my father didn't give him a harder time. Then again, I had warned him that Teagan and I were friends just a couple of hours ago.

"You sound surprised by that."

I arch a brow in response.

"Face it, Turner, I'm a charmer." He grins, but when I stop beside my car, he frowns. "We're taking my ride."

"Car seat, remember?"

"Oh, shoot. Right. Of course." He shakes his head and waits while I fling open the door to the back seat and unlatch Sophie's car seat.

Once I have it in hand, I lug it over to his car, fully prepared to hook it into the seat myself when he takes it from me and starts to work. Without fumbling or asking me how, he begins securing the bottom strap of the seat.

"How do you—"

"Little sisters, remember?" he glances back at me, and I nod, once again taken aback by his take-charge attitude.

When he's finished, I help get Sophie strapped in then take the passenger seat, suddenly aware this is the first time I've been in his car.

I'm unsurprised to find it neat and tidy, just like him. Not a speck of dust covers his dashboard or a hint of dirt on the floor mats, a far cry from the toy-riddled, sticky mats in my own.

His citrus-spice scent mingles with the scent of leather up-holstery in an intoxicating combination. I want to close my eyes and breathe it in, drag it deep into my lungs like I'm taking a hit of it, and I would if I didn't think he'd notice.

"In all seriousness," he says, interrupting my thoughts on how I could bottle his scent and take it with me, "your parents are great."

"Yeah, they are pretty great," I say. I've spent the last four years, in fact, thinking how lucky I am to have them in my corner. "But you should probably be worried."

"Worried? Why?" With one hand braced on the steering wheel, he leans back in his seat, concern creasing his brow as he glances over at me.

"Did you see the way my mom was eyeing you? She's probably browsing wedding invitations right now. No doubt when I get home tonight, she'll grill me with a thousand questions about you, right down to your blood type."

"O positive," Teagan deadpans.

I laugh and poke him in the arm. "I'm serious."

Teagan chuckles. "And that's a bad thing?"

"Uh, *yeah*. That's a very bad thing, Teagan, because we're *friends*." I flick my gaze back toward Sophie.

"Right." Teagan drums his fingers on the steering wheel, and I sense there's more he wants to say on the matter. In fact, I wonder if he'll contradict me when he changes the subject. "About that, thanks for the quick thinking with your father. You saved me."

He's not wrong. Dad looked pissed.

I shrug. "I just told him the truth."

"Maybe, but your quick thinking is what saved me from getting my butt benched come Monday."

"You don't need to thank me." I smile, but it's like trying on clothes that don't fit and are a little too tight. "Besides, that's what friends are for," I say, ignoring how at odds the words feel with the growing ball of warmth in my chest. "Now, tell me where we're going."

I stand in front of the expo center, Sophie's hand clutched in mine, staring at a massive banner proclaiming *Dinosaur World* stretching across its entrance.

My eyes find the giant T. rex the same time as Sophie, and she gasps. "Dinosaurs?" She glances up at me, mouth agape, eyes wide like the moon.

I look to Teagan for confirmation, and he grins down at her, taking her hand. "This is Dinosaur World, and I've been told they have *very* realistic, life-sized dinosaurs inside, including some that you can ride."

"Teagan . . ." I say, wanting to protest because I know how much these things cost, and it's entirely too much for this single mom on a budget.

When he shrugs, his expression turns sheepish, and I don't have the heart to tell him. "What? It's only here for three weeks before they move locations, and the second I heard the ad for it on the radio, I knew we had to come."

The sentiment is so sweet, I swear my heart melts into a puddle inside my chest.

"Come on!" Sophie tugs us forward, each on either side.

I take one step in front of the other, trying to figure out how the hell I'm going to pay what will probably be one hundred dollars just to get in, not to mention any food or refreshments Sophie may want.

We head underneath the high archway and through a large set of glass double doors to the lobby with a ticket booth on the right, and a station to the left where they check your tickets before letting you inside the expo center to view the exhibits.

I squint up at the sign, trying to see how much this will cost me when a cold sheen of sweet pricks my back.

Adults: $60.

Kids: $40.

Teagan tugs me to the left, stealing my attention. "Come on . . ."

"Wait. We have to buy tickets," I protest.

He shakes his head. "Nope. Already bought them."

"Teagan." I stop and narrow my eyes.

"What? I figured it was faster than waiting in line."

"Well . . . fine." I hope Sophie doesn't mind peanut butter and jelly for the next two weeks. "Just let me know what I owe you."

Looks like no lattes from The Buzzy Bean this week.

"Not happening." He shakes his head. "This was my idea."

"Just because it was your idea, doesn't mean you should pay." I cross my arms over my chest. "What happened to going Dutch, remember?"

"*Mom,*" Sophie whines and tugs my arm, "Come on. I wanna go in."

I sigh and glance down at her. She's practically vibrating with excitement as she bounces on her toes.

"Consider it an early birthday gift to Sophie." Teagan steps toward the counter and holds his phone out to the attendant where they scan our electronic tickets, then unclasps the large velvet rope that leads to the doors inside the dinosaur display.

"I already had a birthday," Sophie proclaims loudly.

"See?" Teagan grins, his ridiculously adorable dimples popping. "I missed it. Consider it a belated birthday gift." He glances down at her. "Which also means birthday dinner at the Omnivore I." He points out a sign that proclaims: *You can eat like a dinosaur, too!*

I groan because there's nothing worse than paying fifteen dollars for subpar chicken fingers, and because I know there's no use talking him out of this. "Fine. I'll just have to pay you back another way."

Teagan's brows rise, and I instantly flush. "I didn't . . . that's not what I . . . I meant . . ." I groan and palm my forehead. "You know what?" I shake my head, trying to cool my heated cheeks. "I'm just going to shut up now. Forget I said anything."

"No can do. It'll take a lot to strike that one from my memory. I'm already thinking of all the forms of *repayment*," he says with a wiggle of his brow.

I try not to smile. "Stop."

"I'm serious."

"I'm sure you are." I grin and roll my eyes, then we push through the massive oak doors into the darkened exterior of the exhibit.

By the time Teagan pulls into the driveway of my parents' house, the sun is setting low in the sky, just barely kissing the horizon. Another thirty minutes and it will set completely, flooding everything in darkness.

When the car comes to a stop, he puts it in park, and glances behind him to where Sophie quietly sleeps. She's passed out in her car seat, a T. rex balloon clutched in her hand.

His gaze softens as he takes her in, wrenching something free inside my chest until it rattles around behind my ribs like spare change. "She's exhausted," I say, trying to ignore it.

"That's the understatement of the century."

I smile. "I wouldn't be surprised if she sleeps for days."

Teagan meets my eyes, a grin splitting his full lips, and before I can stop myself, I reach out and grab his hand. His eyes round, gaze dropping to the point of contact, and I swallow. "Thank you for today." His eyes lift. "She loved *every* second, and I'm sure she'll talk about it for months." I peer out the windshield with a sigh. "I guess I better get her inside," I say, aware I'm still holding his hand and am in no rush to move it.

I need to go inside. The night is over. But I find myself wanting to draw it out, to stay in his car with him a little longer.

"Do you want me to carry her?"

I shake my head and take that as my cue. Seeing Sophie passed out in Teagan's arms would be too much to handle. Already more than a dozen times today, I glanced over at him and her together, and my ovaries nearly exploded.

"I got her," I say.

He nods, somehow knowing not to push the issue. "I'll get her car seat out while you're inside and put it back in yours, then."

"That would be great. Thanks." I offer him one last lingering look before I pull my hand from his, already resentful for the loss of contact when I slip outside.

A breeze ruffles my hair as I open Sophie's door and scoop her up. She rouses slightly, mumbling something unintelligible as I guide her head against my shoulder and start for the porch.

The front door swings open before I even make it there, and my mother steps aside. It's no surprise she watched for us, and I offer her a smile of thanks as I pass and take Sophie upstairs to her room.

The house is quiet as I lay her onto her bed, trying not to jostle her too much as I remove her shoes, socks, and jeans, leaving her in nothing but her T-shirt. I mentally cringe at the fact we haven't brushed her teeth. But I'm in a hurry to get back to Teagan, afraid he'll leave before I have a chance to say good night. Certainly, one time won't hurt, and I'll brush them extra well tomorrow morning.

I lean down and press a kiss to her chubby cheek, heart clenching when she whispers, "I love you" before she curls onto her side with her favorite stuffy, Betty.

The second my feet hit the landing, my mother rounds the corner, waiting for me. "Did you guys have fun?"

"Yeah." I can't help my smile as I add, "He took us to Dinosaur World at the expo center. Sophie had an absolute blast."

"And what about you? Did you have a *blast*?" She hip checks me, and I know where this is headed.

"Yes, Mom." I roll my eyes. "I had fun."

"He's so cute, isn't he? Like a blonder, curly haired Hemsworth brother." She hums while I gape at her.

"*Mother*," I gasp

"What? I do have eyes, dear."

I chuckle and cross my arms over my chest, my gaze shifting to the front door, itching to get back to him but not wanting to seem too eager. "It's not like that."

She tilts her head. "You sure?"

"Yeah, of course." I shrug. "We're just friends."

"A male friend whom you haven't known your whole life takes you and your daughter to an exhibit nearly all day that's solely for *her*, and he just wants to be friends?" Her brows rise. "Bullshit."

"*Mom*!" I gasp.

Dolly Turner never swears.

"Just saying, dear," she pats me on the side of the arm. "It might be something to think about."

"There's nothing to think about." Though the lingering ache in my chest says otherwise, and judging by her sly grin, she knows it. "Besides, Dad would kill him, and it would totally ruin his chances on the team."

"If you say so."

I know she doesn't believe me, but there's no point in standing here trying to convince her, so instead, I simply say, "I should probably go out and say good night. He switched Sophie's car seat, and I don't want to keep him waiting."

"Yes, you do that." Mom flashes me a thumbs up, then casually glances at her watch. "Hey, it's early, only seven o'clock. Why not go out and have some fun?"

I pause at the door, searching for a reason to say no. "I probably shouldn't in case Sophie wakes up."

"I raised one child perfectly fine. I think I can handle my grandchild."

"Yeah, but I have class tomorrow and he has practice—"

"Oh my gosh, Lane." Mom steps forward and gives me a little shake. "Would you, for once, stop acting like an old lady and let loose a little?"

I stiffen. "I am *not* acting like an old lady."

Mom crosses her arms and glares at me with a look that says *Prove it.*

"I have responsibilities. I have to wake up early, and Sophie—"

"Will be just fine asleep in her bed with me to watch over her." Mom places her hands on my arms and spins me around toward the door. "This is the perks of having grandma nearby."

"But, Mom—"

"No buts. Go. For once, let someone help you out. For once, do something for yourself and spend some time with that beautiful man out there."

"I don't want to be selfish," I say, peering at her over my shoulder.

Big mistake. She glares at me so hard, I physically wince.

"It is *not* selfish to do something just for you sometimes, and it's also not irresponsible to accept help. I *want* to be with Sophie. Now, act like a young college student and go out with that fine young man."

"Are you sure?" I ask, doubt creeping into my voice.

"Absolutely. Even if it's for only an hour. Even if you're just *friends,*" she says, emphasizing the word as if she doesn't for one second think that's what we are.

"I don't even know if he'll want to. Maybe he needs to get back to the dorms." Suddenly all my insecurities come rushing in. "Maybe he has other plans," I add as I pull the front door open, and Mom practically pushes me out.

"Oh, he wants to. Trust me." Mom nods behind me, then closes the door and locks it, leaving me more than a little disoriented. I turn to find Teagan leaning against the front of his car, legs crossed at the ankles, his hands in his pockets.

My heart takes the opportunity to run a marathon inside my chest, and after a moment of dumbly staring at him, I realize I should probably move.

I close the gap between us, searching for something to say and feeling like this is my first time talking to a boy.

Luckily, he saves me from myself.

"Did you get her down okay?"

I nod, my mouth dry. "She's out like a light."

"Good," he says but makes no move to leave, which is both a relief and unnerving.

"Did you, uh . . ." I swallow and the words stick in my throat. *Why the hell is this so hard?*

"Did you wanna maybe go somewhere for a bit?" I ask. "Sophie's covered, so if you want . . . I mean, I'll understand if you don't but—"

"Fuck, yes, I want to." He reaches out and takes my hand. No discussion. No question. One moment, he's leaning against his car while I mumble like a stuttering baboon, and the next, he's yanking the passenger door of his car open for me and waving me inside.

Why is that so hot?

I pinch my shirt with my free hand, fluttering the material to cool the heat coursing through my veins while I slide into the passenger seat, watching as he rounds the hood, giving it a little tap before he slides in next to me.

Blue eyes meet mine, and he says, "I know just the place we can go."

CHAPTER 25

LANE

THE PARKING LOT IS completely empty when we pull into Arrowhead Park.

I glance over at Teagan, wondering what his plan is. He gets out without a word, opens my door, and pulls me out.

The muscles in his back flex beneath the soft cotton of his shirt as he heads for the entrance of the park where a large metal gate blocks the pebbled walkway. A sign that reads: *Closed at dusk. Violators and Trespassers will be prosecuted,* hangs askew.

"They're closed," I say, motioning toward the sign. "We're not supposed to be here."

Teagan glances back at me, one brow quirked. "And?"

And he's forgetting he's with the rule follower, a Careful Carol. *Okay, I just made that up, but does he not remember the night we went skinny dipping and I confessed I'd never done most things before?*

Well, that includes trespassing and breaking into state parks after dark.

"It's just . . ." I shift on my feet, glancing around me as I bite my lip. I feel like, at any moment, one of the park guards is going to jump out of the bushes and put me in cuffs.

Teagan smiles. "Do you *always* follow the rules?"

"Generally," I admit with a grimace, but is that really a bad thing? "Rules exist for a reason."

"What if I promise you it'll be okay. We're just going to sit and watch the sun finish setting. That is, if we make it." He presses his lips together and glances at the horizon, then back again, and if the deepening of his dimples is any indication, he's trying not to show his amusement at my fear of getting caught.

"Look, we're not harming anything, so we won't get in trouble. Even if someone sees us, at most, they'll just tell us to leave."

I narrow my eyes as he steps over the knee-high gate, holding a hand out to me. "Do you trust me?"

I inhale, allowing a cleansing breath to ease the knot in my chest, and I nod, because I do. I really, really do trust Teagan, and the knowledge of that strikes me with enough force I move my feet.

Once they're planted firmly on the other side of the gate, Teagan steps back and shakes his head. "Lane Turner," he says, his tone teasing, "skinny dipping *and* breaking into the park. What a rebel you are."

"Are you making fun of me?" I ask archly.

"Only because you're so damn cute."

I shake my head, biting my lip as he draws me to his side, wrapping an arm around my shoulders in a friendly gesture that makes me question if he really does only see me as a friend.

"Whatever shall we do with you." He guides us past the grassy knoll toward the playground, over a walking trail, and through a grove of trees until we reach a bench that overlooks a vast, green field that the park uses for recreational sports.

"It's not the lake," he says, sitting and tugging me down with him. "I'm sure your place has a much better view, but it's quiet and pretty all the same."

He's right on both counts.

I take a seat beside him. The sun is already a dipping fireball in the sky, but from our spot on the bench with the field stretched out before us, it seems to go on for miles.

I'm quiet as we watch, both of us settling into a companionable silence and decompressing from the excitement and chaos, as fun as it was, from our time spent at the exhibit. I bite my lip, wishing I could lean into him and lay my head on his shoulder. But that's something a girlfriend would do. And I shouldn't wish for things like that because it'll only end in disappointment.

As if he can sense the direction of my thoughts, he reaches out, only hesitating a moment before he laces his fingers through mine.

And this isn't something a boyfriend would do?

I give my inner voice the middle finger and close my eyes, focusing on his touch, the warmth of his hand, the rough bite of his calluses against my palm.

"Tell me what you're thinking?" he murmurs, and when I blink my eyes open, I find him staring down at me, a hunger in his eyes that takes my breath away.

My thoughts scatter, my mind a minefield. One wrong move and I might detonate. So I shake my head, clearing my throat as I rip my gaze from his. "Nothing."

He doesn't push.

Instead, I see him shift in my periphery to stare back out at the last of the sunset. "You asked your father about me?"

My mouth hitches. "I was wondering when you'd bring that up."

"What did you want to know? You know I'd tell you anything." He gives my hand a squeeze to emphasize his words, and I nod.

"It wasn't like that. I wasn't . . . prying for information," I say for lack of better words. "I just asked him about how he thought you were doing. How far he thought football might take you. If he thought you had a shot to go pro, that's all. I was just, I don't know, wondering after our conversation the other night."

Teagan hums. "And what did he say?"

I jab him in the ribs. "Fishing for inside information, Nichols?"

He chuckles, a soft rumble that vibrates through me even from a distance. "Just curious," he says.

It shouldn't bother me if he wants to know. Of course he craves his coach's approval, but there's a tiny part of me that fears the second he finds out my father sees his potential and believes he could make it all the way, he'll be gone. Just another Chance Lockhart who once held a piece of my heart.

And therein lies the problem.

Teagan Nichols was never supposed to have a piece of my heart in the first place. And fuck it all to hell if he isn't bulldozing his way in and staking claim.

It's with this in mind that I say, "In not so specific terms, he basically said he thinks you have the potential to go wherever you want football to take you. He called you a dark horse."

I can see the sheer pleasure this brings him, the way his eyes brighten a little more, and his smile widens, deepening his dimples.

My heart lurches. "That pleases you," I say, then cringe because it sounds more like an accusation than a statement.

He glances down at me with a frown. "Should it not?"

"Of course. I just . . ." I snap my mouth closed, but he's not letting me get off that easy. Instead, he pulls my hands closer to his chest, running the pad of his thumb over my knuckles in a dizzying rhythm.

Friends, Lane.

You're friends.

It doesn't matter.

"Did this conversation have anything to do with you refusing to go out with me this afternoon when I called?"

I shrug, saying nothing. He's too damn perceptive for his own good.

"*Lane.*"

I exhale, my lungs shaking with the effort. "Maybe a little. It's a reminder, one I needed. It's important I remember that no matter how good of a friend you become, you'll be leaving. Your future is elsewhere," I say, even though I'm fooling myself. I already know that what I feel for Teagan is more than friendship.

All the more reason to keep him at arm's length. Because I can't go there. Not with him. It'll only end poorly.

He says nothing for a moment, staring down at me while I do everything I can to avoid the heat of his pointed gaze. "I'm not going anywhere," he whispers.

"You can't say that." I rise from my spot on the bench, forcing him to drop my hands. I need to breathe, need to think without his touch muddling my brain.

Friends don't hold hands.

Friends don't look at you like that—like they're drowning and you're the only one capable of carrying them to shore.

"Why not?" He stands alongside me, his expression a mask of frustration. "I should know."

I whirl on him, an atomic bomb building inside of me ready to explode. I'm a living, breathing, exhibition in frustration and anger and *want.*

Because as much as I don't want to admit it, as hard as I've been trying to avoid it, I *want* Teagan.

Which is fucking ridiculous.

I have zero right, not when I've only known him a few weeks, and certainly not when we're at two different junctures in our lives.

"Are you really telling me that if you got an offer from the NFL, you wouldn't take it? Are you really telling me that you plan on staying here after college when all your family and all your friends are elsewhere?"

"Lane, I'm not going to sit here and say I've never thought about what it would be like to get drafted. Hell, I'd be lying. Every single guy I know in my shoes has thought about it. You can't commit yourself so fully to one thing for so many years and not think of the possibilities, but dreaming about what it would be like and the reality of it happening are two very different things. Have you even thought about asking me if I'd go? Have you ever thought that I might not want to?"

I snort. "Of course not. Why wouldn't you want that? You'd be crazy to pass up an opportunity like that."

Teagan stiffens, his jaw flexing. I catch a flash of disappointment before he glances away from me, out into the fading watercolors on the horizon. "I see. So, if I told you that I'd rather stay here, that all I've ever really wanted is a simple life, one where I earn an honest living teaching and coaching high school football, that would be *crazy*? A waste of an opportunity? Is that how you see it?"

Guilt grips my stomach while the rest of me free-falls, unable to stop the impact as he continues.

"Is it so wrong to just want a normal life with a family and friends? One where I'm not destroying my body day in and day out. One where I'm not always on the road for half of the year, away from the people I love? A life where I live for the people in it instead of my work?"

"I . . . no. It's not . . ." I shake my head. How could I think what he's saying is anything short of amazing. Hell, it's the path my father took until he reached his ultimate dream of coaching at the collegiate level. "*Is* that what you want?" I ask, my voice small.

"Yeah, Lane. It is. It's what I want."

I turn my head, gazing out at the darkening horizon, the sun so low in the sky now it's merely a fireball dipping below the trees. "But that still doesn't change the fact that at the end of four years, you'll leave. You have nothing keeping you here."

"I could have *you*, Lane."

"Teagan." I scoff, glancing down at my hands.

He doesn't know what he's saying.

He doesn't. He can't possibly mean that.

Even if he does, he might change his mind. About me. About Sophie. Just like Chance did, and then what?

His fingers slide beneath my chin, tipping my face up toward his until our eyes lock. "What if I told you I wanted to stay here after graduation?"

I shake my head, tears blurring my vision.

Oh God. Do not *cry.*

"Do you even know what you're saying, Teagan? That would be c-cr-crazy."

The corners of his mouth curve, affection in his tone when he says, "There's that word again."

I inhale sharply. "You can't stay for me."

"Why not?"

"We barely know each other. It's barely been a month since we even met."

He cocks his head as if assessing my argument. "Maybe. But you can also know someone for years only to discover you don't really know them at all," he says, his mouth tightening in a way that tells me he's talking about Knox. "Trust me, I know."

I do, too.

Chance was coming by our house for years prior to hooking up. My father took him under his wing fresh out of grade school, and if someone would've told me he would get me pregnant only to leave and abandon me in my time of need, I would've said they were crazy, too.

"You can't just say things like this, Teagan. It's not just about me."

"You don't think I know that?" he says, waving a hand around him. "Haven't I proved I have room in my life for Sophie, too?"

My chest inflates, too full for comfort. "Is that what today was about? What all of this is about? Proving yourself?"

"That's not fair." He shakes his head, the muscle in his jaw flexing. "You're trying to start a fight, Lane, to find some flaw, and it won't work. I won't fight with you. Not over this."

He's right.

That's exactly what I'm doing.

But I don't know what else to do about the way I feel, and that's the problem.

The one and only time I followed my heart instead of my head, I'd been wrong. Terribly, horribly wrong.

I can't let that happen again. Not with Sophie involved.

I scrub my hands over my face, only for them to tremble and shake when I pull away. I'm so fucking scared, I can't see straight.

"I'm sorry," I say, because I have no idea what else *to* say, and I'm about two seconds away from breaking.

"My parents met when my father moved to Riverside their senior year in high school. They knew each other only weeks before they started seeing each other, and they were engaged not long after graduation, married a year after that. They've been together ever since, so I know it can happen just like this, Lane. Crazy or not, it *can* happen. And, yeah, maybe you have a daughter, and maybe that complicates things, but as soon as I found out about Soph, I asked myself if that was something I wanted to take on. If I cared your life was one step ahead of mine, and I don't. I decided then and there that I'd catch up. Lane, I want you just as you are, daughter and all, and I don't give a damn who knows it, including your father."

My heart riots as those sapphire eyes stare straight through me. *How is he so freaking calm? How is he so . . . steady?*

Teagan is a rock—unyielding, immovable, and solid as the day is long—and if I'm brave enough to let him, he'll be *my* rock.

I clench and unclench my hands by my side in an effort to contain the emotions raging inside of me. How many times have I heard the expression, *when you know, you know*?

Teagan has done nothing but prove himself to me this last month.

But the part of me petrified to risk Sophie won't let go. My self-preservation clings to her. "What happened to just being friends?" I ask, but my voice is brittle, as weak as my thinning resolve.

"Does this feel like just friendship to you, Lane? The other night, in the lake?" His eyes heat, and he takes a step closer, "Did *that* feel like friendship? I proposed the friend thing because I knew it was the only way you would let me into your life. But make no mistake, I've never wanted to *just* be your friend. I've always wanted more."

My breathing grows shallow. The thread of my restraint is thinning, ready to snap.

"None of that changes the fact that there's a good chance you and I"—I motion between us—"this won't work. And I don't want Sophie to know what it feels like to have someone she thought loved her walk away."

He blinks, understanding flickering through the green-blue flecks of his eyes. "I get why you're afraid, Lane, and if you tell me right here, right now, you don't want me—*us*—then I'll walk away." He reaches out, cupping my face in his hands. "But if you do . . ."

"I just don't understand why you want *me*. Of *all* people, why me?" I whisper. It's the same thing I wondered about Chance. I remembered thinking how lucky I was, and in the end, he *didn't* want me, not as long as I had Sophie.

What if Teagan changes his mind and decides I'm not good enough?

Teagan shakes his head, his tone fierce. "I swear to God, Lane, one of these days, I'm going to make you see what I see. I'm going to make you see just how special you are and how fucking lucky I am, or anyone else is for that matter, to have whatever piece of yourself you're willing to give."

"Teagan, I—" My voice cracks.

I snap my mouth shut, unable to finish the sentence, unable to cut him loose and set him free, yet unable to claim him.

It's wholly unfair; I know this, yet I can't seem to force myself to either take a step back or forward, too scared of making the wrong move.

He lets out a tremulous breath, the muscles in his neck straining as if the effort of holding himself back is too much. "If friendship is *still* what you need, I'll take it. I said it before, and I'll say it again." He straightens, his gaze steady on mine. "I'll take whatever piece of you you're willing to give. For *now*.

But make no mistake, Lane." He steps forward and tucks a stray lock of hair behind my ear. "I'll prove myself to you. And when I do, you *will* be mine."

CHAPTER 26

TEAGAN

"**I** FORGOT TO ASK you something. Are you dressing up tomorrow?" I lean back against the wash basin. Tomorrow is Halloween and I have plans to trick or treat with Lane and Sophie, something I've been looking forward to ever since I bulldozed my way into their plans last week.

Lane turns to face me. She's done with the uniforms, her shift officially over until she needs to be at the field later today, which leaves us approximately five minutes before I have to get my ass to class.

A week has passed since our argument at the park, and neither of us have mentioned it again. I haven't pushed, haven't so much as laid a fucking hand on her even though I want to *every* second of *every* fucking day. Each time I'm with her, not kissing her, not holding her hand, fucking kills me.

Her mouth curves into a grin. "I usually dress up, yes, but nothing extravagant. This year, I'm just wearing white, using the fuzzy bunny ears from Sophie's easter basket last year, and painting a bunny nose and whiskers on my face. Why? You're not worried about it, are you? Most parents I see don't dress up."

"Oh, no. I already got something." I flash her a smile. "I was just wondering if you wanted me to pick you up a costume, too."

Her eyes brighten. "You really got a costume?"

"Sure did. Sophie's going as a T. rex, right?"

Lane nods. "What did you get?"

"It's a secret," I wink. "You'll just have to wait and see."

She chuckles, then grunts. "No fair." She fake pouts before asking, "What are Tommy and the others doing?"

I shrug. "A party."

"You don't want to go?"

"No." I reach out and tug on a silken lock of her hair. "I'd rather be with you and Soph."

She shakes her head like she's afraid to believe me, like she's stunned I'd rather spend time with her and Sophie than go to a party. Little does she know I'm over the whole party scene. I don't need it. I had my fill in high school, and I'm not saying I don't ever like to unwind and have a good time, but in truth, it's lost its appeal. There's nothing fun in getting wasted and feeling like shit the next day. Besides, there's not much time for it in-season, anyway. Not unless you want to be sluggish as shit on the football field.

Lane bites her lip, and it takes everything I have not to reach out and pull her to me, claim her mouth with mine when my phone buzzes in my pocket, saving me.

I stifle a groan. "That's my alarm, which means I have to go."

"Come on. I'll walk you out." She motions toward the hall and guides us outside into the cooling autumn air.

"I'll see you at the field later?" I ask.

She nods, though we both know just because we'll see each other, it doesn't mean we'll get to spend time together.

We pause outside the door behind the cover of a small maple as a breeze rustles its branches. Most of the leaves have fallen, covering the sidewalk in a living watercolor beneath our feet. Above, the sky is gray and threatening rain, and a cursory glance around us reveals no one is watching. Students pass with their heads down, rushing to class to avoid the inclement weather, and I wonder what we look like to them. If we look like a couple.

My gaze falls to her mouth, but I quickly tear it away again because staring at her lips won't do me any favors when I promised I'd behave.

As if sensing my inner turmoil, Lane reaches out and cups the side of my face with her hand, her thumb brushing over my jaw.

I lean into her touch, pathetic and lovesick, like a stray dog begging for pets.

She worries her lower lip with her teeth, then steps closer, and maybe I'm crazy, but when her blue eyes shift to my mouth, I think maybe she wants to kiss me, too. Instead, she leans into me with a sigh.

Pressing her forehead against mine, she whispers, "Thank you."

"For what?" I choke out.

"*Everything.*"

CHAPTER 27

LANE

I PUSH BACK FROM Teagan, blushing as I nudge him in a muscled bicep when what I really want to do is kiss him.

"Later?" he asks and I nod, regret turning my stomach as he walks away.

I stare after him, biting my lip as he goes, knowing I probably look as smitten as I feel. Part of me wishes I could just give in—for once, be reckless—but the other part of me, the one with an iron will, is too scared of what will happen when I do.

God, do you hear yourself, Lane?

When, not if.

It's like I'm already preparing for the inevitability of us.

Teagan's made a lot of promises, but I know how easily promises can be broken. His intentions are pure, of that, I'm sure. But intentions don't matter when the end result is still the same.

With a sigh, I shift and start down the walkway when I jolt to a sudden stop.

Chance steps directly into my path. I have no idea where he came from or how long he's been standing there when his impenetrable gaze locks on mine.

A rock sinks into my stomach, and I say a quick prayer he didn't see me talking to Teagan. I can't imagine how we looked—me cupping his face, my forehead pressed to his.

Swallowing, I clear the bile rising to the back of my throat.

I expect him to say something. To call me out. Anything.

But a moment passes before he breaks eye contact and pivots, walking in the opposite direction like his feet are on fire.

With my heart pounding in my throat, I stare after him as the cold blade of fear slices through me.

Shit. Shit. Shit.

He wouldn't say anything to my father, would he?

Even if he did, I can handle it. My father already knows Teagan and I are friends, which is the truth.

Either way, I hate to think of how this might affect Teagan if Chance tries to read into things and make a big deal of nothing.

I blow out a slow breath, trying to calm my racing heart as I start down the walkway again. I have thirty minutes before my next class, so I decide to grab a coffee from The Buzzy Bean to ease my nerves.

I can't help but feel like Teagan and I have been inching our way up the steep incline of a roller coaster since the day we met, and now we're cresting the hill, teetering on the edge before the fall.

Lord knows I'm trying to stay there, to put on the breaks and keep him at arm's length, but each time I'm with him, it feels a little harder to just be friends. A little more impossible with every longing look, every brush of the hand, and the way he seems wholly devoted to me despite me giving him very little in return.

My walls are up, but I feel them crumbling. And I'm not sure there's a damn thing I can do about it.

I zip the back of Sophie's dinosaur costume up, then spin her around and soak in the sight of her with a grin.

"Do I look scary?" she asks, holding her arms up like a T. rex.

"Ferocious," I say, even though she looks anything but in the soft green, plush costume. "Are you sure I can't get you to eat more spaghetti before we go?"

"No." She shakes her head. "I can't eat spaghetti, Mom. T. rexes are carnivores, remember?"

I arch a brow. "There's meat in the sauce."

She grimaces as if the thought repulses her, and I roll my eyes. Whatever. I guess the three bites she ate at dinner will have to sustain her until the inevitable binge of candy.

"Can we go now?" Sophie asks, tugging on my sleeve.

I slide my phone out of my pocket and glance at the time. Practice just ended. "Teagan will be here soon, and then we'll leave. Until he gets here, why don't you help grandma pass out candy to all the early birds."

"Good idea!" Sophie beams and turns for the living room while I follow behind.

Even though trick or treating started thirty minutes ago, I told Teagan we'd wait for him to leave. At Sophie's age, starting forty-five minutes late won't hurt when she'll barely last an hour, let alone the two allotted for trick or treaters.

I wander into the living room behind Sophie to find her making a beeline for my mother who's sporting a giant black witch hat and clutching a huge basket filled with chocolate candy.

Sophie growls ferociously and claws at my mother's back, clearly in character, while I stifle a laugh.

With a dramatic gasp, Mom jumps back with wide eyes, the picture of fear itself as she whispers, "Oh, please, T. rex, don't hurt me."

Dropping her arms, Sophie cocks her little T. rex head and says, "*Grandma,* it's just me, *Sophie!*"

Mom covers her heart with a hand and closes her eyes. "Oh, thank goodness. Sophie, you scared me."

Sophie chuckles. "Do you think I'll scare Teagan when he comes?"

My mother quirks a brow, her gaze sliding to mine.

Pressing my lips together, I say nothing as she stares.

"Teagan's coming?"

I shrug, shoving my hands in the pockets of my white jeans. "He's meeting us here in a few minutes, yeah."

"That's lovely. He seems pretty solid, yeah?"

I know what she's getting at. Teagan is reliable, present, a far cry from the love 'em and leave 'em type like the guy who knocked me up. So, I clear my throat with a smile I don't have to force as I say, "Yeah. He's different."

And I have to hand it to her, she doesn't push.

Instead, she just turns back to Sophie and asks her about all the candy she's going to get while I watch on, feeling pretty damn lucky.

CHAPTER 28

TEAGAN

P RACTICE KICKED MY ASS.

Every single one of us is still catching our breath when we head through the tunnel into the locker room.

Tommy sidles up next to me, jogging to keep up.

"Shit, Nichols, where's the fire?"

"Sorry, man. I'm in kind of a hurry."

"You going to the party at Beta Tau tonight?"

I shake my head.

"Seriously, bro? You've barely hung out with any of us in the last month," Tommy whines.

I glance over at him. "Isn't Melissa going to be with you?"

"Well, yeah." He shrugs. "So?"

"So, you won't miss me." I clap him on the back with a laugh.

Tommy rolls his eyes. "You got a chick you're after or something?" he asks, and I can't blame him for the inquisition. We may not be as tight as my friends back home, but we get along well and are certainly closer than we've been lately. I have no doubt he's starting to wonder what the hell's going on.

"Something like that," I mutter.

"Oh shit." He sucks in a breath. "It's Turner's daughter, isn't it?" he whispers. "I mean, I should've known, what with the whole bracelet thing last week, but I guess I thought you valued your life a little more than that."

I snort at the same time Chance appears from behind, his blue eyes glacial on the side of my face before he slams into my shoulders and walks past.

Fucking asshole.

My eyes narrow like knives on his back as Tommy whistles. "You steal his Wheaties or something?"

Or something . . .

"Lockhart's a dick," I say, not giving a shit if anyone hears me.

Tommy's eyes widen, and I break away from him before he can ask any more questions, making a beeline for my locker. I have no more than ten minutes to get my ass out of here and to the Turner residence or I'll be late.

I enter the combination into the lock at the same time Coach's voice calls out behind us. "Oh, boys, really quick." I glance behind me, hoping this doesn't take long. "Chance made a suggestion I agree with. Tomorrow we're watching game tape for twice as long, so we start at one. If you have class, you're excused. Otherwise, I expect you to be there. We're this close"—he holds his forefinger and thumb an inch apart—"to taking the number ten spot. So, we're going to give it our all on Saturday. That, and if you get wasted tonight at that Beta Tau party, it's on you. I happen to have extra bleacher runs scheduled tomorrow."

Everyone groans, including me, not because of the warning about bleachers or partying too hard, but because the extra session watching game tape means I won't get to see Lane.

Shit. This keeping our distance fucking sucks when all I wanna do is spend every waking moment with her.

Too much too soon? Probably. But I can't seem to help myself.

I turn away from Coach but not before I catch a glimpse of Chance, a smirk aimed in my direction. "Coach, can I have a word?" he asks, then turns away from me and to Turner while I try and push my paranoia aside.

Whatever he wants to talk to Coach about, it can't possibly involve me.

I turn to face my locker, cradling the combination lock in my hands and quickly scroll through the numbers, then pop it open at the same time something falls off the top shelf. In a blur, the object careens toward me, hitting my mouth and crashing to the ground.

"Fuck!" I jump back at the sound and the sharp stab of pain in my lower lip.

The acrid sting of alcohol fills my nose. The room falls silent, and when I glance down, I'm shocked at the sight of a shattered whiskey bottle.

The hell?

"Nichols!" Coach yells. "You better have a damn good explanation for what that's doing in your locker."

My head snaps up and my eyes widen as I take in Coach's pointed gaze, his face red with anger. I open my mouth to protest, to tell him I have no idea how it got there, but the words won't come. I'm too stunned.

My ears ring in the quiet that follows as I try and grapple with what the hell just happened.

I take a step forward, and my cleats crunch over what I assume is the shattered glass, but when I glance down at the floor, I discover it's my phone. It must've fallen out of my locker, along with the bottle.

"Oh shit." Someone nearby chuckles.

You've got to be fucking kidding me.

My nostrils flare, but I tamp down my quickly rising emotions as I glance back up at Coach. "Sir, I swear I didn't—"

"I don't give a flying fuck about your excuses. Get that shit cleaned up, you hear me?" He moves toward me, his stride clipped as he points in my face. "This is strike two."

"Coach—"

"We'll handle this on the field tomorrow," he snaps with a stab of a finger in my face. "You wanna drink on my watch? You want to use your locker as your personal wet bar? Then you can run *everyone's* extra bleachers."

I shake my head. "Coach, I swear—"

"I *said*, we'll handle this tomorrow." Then he turns and walks out the door, slamming it closed with an ominous thud.

"Fuck," I hiss, raking my hands through my hair as I stare down at the mess.

Everyone eyes me with varying degrees of surprise, humor, and irritation as Tommy moves in front of me, blocking me from view. "That's not yours," he says.

Tommy knows me well enough by now to know I don't drink in-season, let alone during practice, and I'm sure as shit not dumb enough to keep the evidence in my locker even if I did.

"No shit." I exhale, placing my hands on my hips while my mind whirrs.

It's a trick, a prank; it has to be.

Unless someone stashed it here with the intention to come back for it, but the possibility doesn't compute.

"Who would have your combination?" he asks, reading my thoughts.

I glance up at him, my teeth clenched so hard they feel as if they might crack. "Hell if I know."

"Damn, bro. This shit is fucked up. Coach's car and now this?" Tommy whistles, and I pinch the bridge of my nose.

"Thanks for the reminder," I say between gritted teeth.

I know exactly how screwed I am. Particularly because this will make it all that much worse when he finds out I want more from Lane than friendship.

Tommy turns toward his locker, and my gaze focuses on Chance who hasn't budged an inch since Coach left. My eyes narrow.

He was the one to suggest the extra strategy session tomorrow, coincidentally during my time with Lane. Just like *he* was the one to stop Coach before leaving the locker room. If it weren't for him, Turner never would've been in here when the bottle fell. But Chance gave him ample time.

As if sensing the scrutiny, Chance lifts his head and when our eyes lock, his answering smirk curdles my blood.

His fingerprints are all over this; I'm fucking sure of it.

I don't know how he knows Lane and I spend time together on my lunch break, or how he got into my locker. But I have places to be, so rather than dwelling on it, I turn away from him and bend down to start cleaning the mess beneath my feet.

I pocket my phone first, then hurry to gather the shattered glass. Piece by piece, I pick it up and collect it in the palm of my left when a large chunk slices clean through my flesh to the bone. "Shit!" I hiss and drop it as the coppery tang of blood scents the air, the red substance bubbling to the surface of my skin, quickly coating my palm and dripping down my arm.

I shoot to my feet and kick my locker with a bang, startling everyone around. "Fucking hell!"

I yank a clean T-shirt from my locker and wrap it around my palm to stanch the bleeding while Tommy's eyes flare. "Dude, that's a *lot* of blood."

Bryce peeks over my shoulder. "Fuck, man. You need stitches."

Thank you, Captain Obvious.

I lean my forehead against the cold metal of my locker as I try to come to terms with the situation. The simple fact is I'm supposed to be at Lane's in less than ten minutes and if I stop for stitches, I'll never make it. I don't have time to clean up this mess, let alone get myself to the ER and back.

I inhale, hoping clearer thoughts will prevail as I debate my options. I can't even text Lane to let her know what happened because my phone is shit, and I don't have her number memorized.

Fucking technology.

I curse as I envision Lane waiting for me at her house with Sophie dressed in her costume, and then I imagine her disappointment when I don't show.

She'll think I don't give a shit.

She'll think I forgot or chose to do something else instead.

I know Lane well enough to realize all her defenses will rise, and it won't matter how much I reassure her after the fact that it couldn't have been prevented, my not showing up for her when I told her I'd be there will plant a seed of doubt.

I glance over my shoulder to the back of Chance fucking Lockhart's head as he chats with Manzetti.

I have no idea how the hell he would know I have plans with Lane tonight. Maybe it was just a coincidence, or maybe it was carefully calculated. Either way, I'll be damned if I let him win.

I grind my molars and crouch back over the glass, this time, taking it a little slower as I pick up the glass with my good hand, keeping the now blood-covered shirt clenched in my other.

Once I finish cleaning up the glass, I quickly set off to find Mark and try to convince him to help me use some butterfly bandages to help close the wound.

"It needs stitches," he insists.

I nod, my mouth tight. It hurts like a bitch and if the fucking gallon of blood I've lost is any indication, it's obvious I need stitches but I don't much care. "I know. But I have somewhere to be, so if you could just help me and take care of it, that would be great."

"Man, you really need to go to the ER."

"*Please.*" I clench my jaw, breathing through my nose as I try to calm myself. "Just . . . do this now and I promise I'll get stitches in an hour or two, as soon as I'm able."

He stares at me for a moment before he sighs, and I know I have him. "Fine," he says, "but if Coach finds out about this and asks, I did no such thing. I'm not taking responsibility if you don't make good on your word and your hand is fucked up in the morning."

I nod as he unwinds the T-shirt wrapped around my palm. "Absolutely. It's all on me, but I'll take care of it, I promise."

CHAPTER 29

LANE

HE'S LATE.

He's late, and I'm standing here waiting on him, when for all I know he may not even be coming.

I pace back and forth beside the door as I bite my thumbnail, trying to keep the intrusive thoughts at bay. But it's hard. I live on doubt and thrive on speculation the longer I wait.

Anything could've happened. A car crash, late practice, or a dead car battery. There are plenty of reasons he could have for not being here, yet my mind goes straight to the worst of them because the past has told me to expect it.

When you're a parent, you show up. You don't have a choice, and I can't help but think he chose something other than us.

Not that I blame him. It's not like I've been forthcoming, or he owes me anything.

"I thought you said Teagan was coming?" Sophie says, glancing up at me, her mouth turned in a pout.

"He is. Or, he was." I grimace, then huff out a breath and glance at the time on my phone. "We'll give it a few more minutes, then we'll go."

My mother returns from refilling the candy bowl in the kitchen, and her eyes soften as she asks, "He still hasn't shown?"

I shake my head, my throat tight.

"I'm sure he has a good reason."

"Yeah, sure."

But then why didn't he call?

Teagan's a grown man, perfectly capable of sending a text, and if he wants to be involved in my life—in Sophie's life—he needs to learn to be accountable.

I pass the mirror in the foyer and catch a glimpse of my reflection, suddenly self-conscious in my face paint and bunny ears.

I want to rip them off, to yell and scream because I did the one thing I promised myself I'd never do. I relied on him to show up, and now I'm allowing my faith in him to ruin a special moment with my daughter when I should be enjoying it. The last thing I want is for her to be disappointed because a man I brought into our lives—*a friend*—didn't do what he promised, not when I can be enough for us both.

I shove aside the sinking anvil of disappointment and reason with myself. Maybe he is genuinely running late. Maybe he has a good reason. Or maybe he doesn't. Either way, it's time to stop waiting around for him.

The doorbell rings and Sophie joins my mother, grabbing a couple pieces of candy for the trick or treaters. "We'll go after this one, Soph" I say, but when my mother swings the door open, I freeze.

While my mother's face splits into a smile, mine fades. "Oh, Chance, honey, Ed isn't here yet. Do you want to come in and wait?"

I cross my arms over my chest, annoyed he chose this moment to show up.

My mother moves aside as he steps in beside her. "Do you want candy?" Sophie asks, and I stiffen, waiting for Chance to acknowledge her.

He hesitates for a beat, as if he has no clue how to interact with a little human, before he nods. "Uh, sure. Thanks," he says, and when she hands him a candy bar, he smiles.

I hate it.

"Come on, Soph. Time to go." I motion toward her pumpkin bucket, suddenly in a hurry to get the hell out of here. Chance knows my father always stays at his office for more than an hour after practice. He's never back this early, which makes me wonder why he's really here.

I'm not sure I want to stick around to find out.

Sophie hurries toward her basket and scoops it up while I ignore the way Chance is staring at me. I remember a time when his attention was all I wanted. When it made me feel special.

My stomach twists at the memory.

"I figured you'd already be out," he says.

I hum a noncommittal response, then say, "We got delayed."

With her pumpkin bucket in hand, Sophie skips to my side and beams up at me. "We finally get to go now?" she asks, bubbling with so much excitement it ties my stomach in knots. I never should have made her wait.

"Yep. Let's go, honey." I reach down and clasp her hand, brushing right by Chance without a second glance as my mother stops us at the door.

"Wait, Lane—" She grips my arm, while I try to stanch my frustration. All I want to do is get the hell out of here and away from Chance, but her bright-eyed expression tells me I'm not going to like what she's about to say. "Why don't you take Chance with you? That way you have company while you walk house to house."

Yup, absolutely loathe it.

My stomach twists like a towel being wrung dry. "No, Mom, it's fine. I don't think—"

"I'd love to," he interrupts.

My head jerks toward him and the blood drains from my face. "That's really not necessary."

"Nonsense. Your father won't be back for at least another thirty minutes. Chance might as well go and kill the time," my mother insists. "Come on, it'll be fun."

Fun.

I want to laugh because nothing about Chance accompanying me while trick or treating with *our* daughter—the one he made very clear he never wanted—sounds fun.

"I don't think that's a good idea." I shake my head, afraid of showing my hand but also not in the headspace to give a damn.

Mom's smile falters, a hint of uncertainty as she says, "Don't be like that. I know this evening isn't turning out how you wanted, but it's still salvageable." She shrugs. "If Teagan shows up, I'll tell him it was getting late and you couldn't wait."

I clench my jaw and glance away from her.

If she knew the truth, she wouldn't be so quick to pair me up with Chance. But I say nothing of the sort. Instead, I leave the house in a hurry, all while squeezing Sophie's hand a little tighter than necessary.

Maybe if I walk fast enough, he'll take the hint and get lost.

Our feet hit the paved sidewalk, and Chance jogs to catch up. *No such luck.*

I say nothing as we walk to the neighboring house for candy while I mash my lips together, refusing to be the first to speak.

"So, Nichols, huh?" he says, after a moment.

My gaze darts to his and my eyes narrow as Sophie takes the stairs of our neighbor's porch, then rings the doorbell. I had hoped in vain he missed what my mother said. The last thing I want is for him to know I was stood up by one of his teammates, even if it wasn't a date.

"Don't look at me like that." He scoffs. "I knew the second I saw you guys at Slice he wanted to be more than just friends."

"Why would you think that?" I hate that I even want to know, but I can't deny how much I do. Maybe there's some truth I can glean from his words which will explain why Teagan's not here.

"Besides the way he looked at you?" He shrugs. "Guys are never just friends with girls."

I stare at him for a long moment, absolutely hating that I'm reading into what he said.

Were Chance and I never friends? Had he always wanted more from me before we got together?

I shake off the thought. It doesn't matter. That ship has sailed and I don't want a repeat ride.

I cross my arms over my chest, keeping one eye on Sophie as she thanks the Smiths for the candy, then skips her way toward me.

"Listen, Lane." Chance angles himself closer, but I refuse to look at him. "I know you think you know him, but he's not right for you."

I laugh. Full-on tip-my-head-back and belly-roll laugh.

"Are you really telling me *he's* not good for me?" I say, ignoring the fact that we're not even together, not like that. "Seriously, Chance?"

"I'm telling you he's bad news."

I grind my teeth so hard my molars ache, cursing him even more when I have to force a smile at Sophie as she returns and places her hand in mine.

I guide her to the next house and down the long walkway, then wait as she knocks before I whirl on him. "What the hell are you doing here?" I hiss.

"I told you—"

"You *lied*." I roll my eyes. "So what's the real reason?"

The muscle in his jaw twitches, giving him away. Not that I didn't already know he was a liar.

"Okay, so maybe I didn't come to see your father. Maybe I wanted to see you. Is that so hard to believe?"

Anger rolls through me like a giant boulder rolling downhill, gaining momentum as it goes. "Yeah, actually, it *is* a little hard to believe, Chance."

I've been here the whole fucking time. I had his child, and there was a time in the beginning when I would've forgiven him. When I dreamed of those words—that he'd want me enough to make a sacrifice. But that time has long since passed and I don't genuinely believe him for a minute. If I've learned one thing about Chandler "the Chancelor" Lockhart over the years, it's that he never does anything unless it's for personal gain.

Sophie turns toward me, a triumphant smile lighting up her face, and I flash her a thumbs up and wait as she hurries back. She's so stinking cute in her fuzzy T. rex costume, her light brown curls tumbling out from underneath the hood, and Chance is like a fucking thundercloud looming over me, ruining it.

I spare him a look. "You need to leave."

He opens his mouth to argue, but I stare him dead in the eyes, my tone glacial as I say, "*Now*. I'm not even kidding. And stay away from us here on out."

He scoffs, placing his hands on his hips like this is a big joke—like I'm a joke.

"I mean it, Chance. If you don't, I'll tell them *everything*."

"Who?"

"You know who."

He flinches. "You can't be serious. Lane, we've known each other for years."

"Not one part of me cares." Most of those years were miserable; the others soured long ago. "I understand that as one of my father's players you'll be around sometimes. But no extra trips to the house. Nothing more than necessary. And don't *ever* try to seek me out again. Whatever this is—" I say, waving a hand between us and stepping forward to grab Sophie's hand. "—won't happen, so let's stop pretending it will. Are we clear?"

With Chance gone, my spirits lift as I walk Sophie to the next house. I can finally breathe again, hold my head high without him dampening my mood.

We climb the front porch of the large Cape Cod where Sophie receives a giant 3 Musketeers, her favorite. I help her down the steps and over a giant crack in the walkway, followed by a large tree root. Her little feet shuffle through the fallen leaves, kicking them like confetti, when I hear someone yell our names.

I pause, recognizing the deep timbre, but am afraid to look for fear that I'm wrong when he calls out again.

"Lane! Sophie!"

I suck in a breath, then turn, and my gaze instantly finds him. Teagan is leaning out the window of his black Honda with one hand on the wheel while he slows to a crawl on the opposite side of the road.

Our eyes lock, and an elephant sits heavy on my chest. He gives me a flash of a smile before it's gone again and he's slowly pulling over.

He cuts the engine and hops out, racing across the street toward us at the same time Sophie tugs her hand from mine and runs for him.

"Sophie!" I yelp, afraid she'll cross the road, but Teagan's there before she even has the chance.

He sweeps her up and into his arms like it's nothing, grinning from ear to ear while she squeals. "Why, is this a T. rex I'm holding in my arms?" he asks, peering at Sophie's little face and pretending he doesn't recognize her.

"*Teagan*." She giggles the same way she did with my mother. "It's me, Sophie!"

"Sophie," he gasps. "Is that really you?"

"Yes." She laughs some more while he feigns shock, and the elephant in my chest becomes a fucking stampede.

With a shake of his head, he sets her back on her feet and runs a hand over his chin in appraisal. "Yep. You're the most terrifying dinosaur I've ever seen. I still can't believe you're actually my Sweet Sophie."

"I am, I swear," Sophie insists, then turns and skips over to me. With a tug on my arm, she says, "Mom, did you see that? I tricked him. Teagan didn't know it was me," she says like I didn't witness their entire interaction firsthand.

"That's awesome." I cup her face, trying to contain the swooping, swirling feeling gathering inside of me that I can't name.

In my periphery, I see Teagan draw closer, and I inhale a steadying breath, preparing myself for what I know those warm, cobalt eyes will do to me when they lock with mine this close.

I lift my gaze and blood buzzes in my veins. "You came."

"Of course, I came." His gaze softens. "Did you really think I wouldn't?"

Before I can answer that question, he glances down at Soph and pats her fuzzy hood. "Did you really think T. rex could trick or treat without her caveman?"

It's then I notice his costume. I'd been too preoccupied with the range of feelings seeing him evoked to notice, but he is, in fact, wearing some kind of faux leather dress-like ensemble with a ragged hem, fake wooden club in one hand, and a thick white bandage on the other, which appears to be speckled with blood.

I press my lips together to keep from laughing. All my fears from earlier, and all my anger from my encounter with Chance, vanish in an instant. "That's"—I shake my head—"some costume."

Thank God for his muscles because it's the only thing keeping him from looking completely ridiculous.

I bite back a laugh when he grabs Sophie's furry hand and approaches, his dimples deepening with every step while I take him in.

My gaze drops to his mouth, and I'm suddenly hungry.

"You're not laughing at me, are you, Lane Turner?" He reaches out and flicks one of my furry bunny ears.

"No, of course not. I would never," I say, my tone solemn. With him this close, I can smell him—all citrus and cinnamon and a hint of sweat that is utterly enticing. My gaze travels to his biceps, forearms roped with muscle, and his firm chest. "Actually, you really should put on some clothes." I reach out and pluck at his caveman toga. "This is borderline indecent out here with all these children."

He dips his head to whisper in my ear, and his breath tickles the side of my face. "Wanna hear a secret?"

I nod, biting my lip in anticipation.

"I'm actually fucking freezing."

I bark out a laugh at the same time goose bumps cover my arms.

"Come on, Mom," Sophie whines.

"Okay, okay," I say, pulling away. "Let's get a move on. We have candy to get!"

"Yes!" Sophie's furry paw shoots in the air.

We walk to the next house with Sophie in-between us while she shows him the candy she's collected so far, babbling a mile a minute. Every so often, Teagan reaches behind her to touch me as a reminder he's here, as if I could forget.

A soft brush over the small of my back, fingertips whispering over my arms, a tug of my hair, brush of my neck, all while listening intently to Sophie.

A block later, Sophie starts for the door of another house, while Teagan and I hover behind her on the sidewalk, allowing the other children to pass.

"Sorry I'm late." He reaches his hand to mine, lightly brushing my fingers with his before intertwining them. Then he releases them just as quickly, leaving my stomach tangled in knots.

"I thought you weren't coming." I swallow, remembering how utterly disappointed I'd felt when I left the house with Sophie. How pissed I was at Chance for being there and stepping in. "What happened?"

I glance up at him as Sophie returns to our side and we start toward the next house.

"This happened." He lifts his bandaged hand out in front of himself with a grimace.

My gaze focuses on the blood-stained gauze, and I gasp as realization hits. It's real, not a part of the costume like I'd originally assumed.

I stop in my tracks, and a trick or treater behind me nearly plows into my back.

I mutter an apology as I grab Sophie's hand and keep moving, eyeing the white gauze. "Teagan, what the heck happened? That has to be a lot of blood for it to seep through the bandage like that."

We turn into the driveway, and I guide Sophie to a woman dressed like a princess, sitting with a bowl of candy propped on her lap.

"I cut it on a chunk of glass right after practice." Teagan shrugs it off. "I had Mark put some butterfly bandages on it for now."

"You need stitches." I frown.

"Probably." Teagan purses his lips as he avoids my gaze, but he has the sense to at least look sheepish. "But I wasn't about to leave you high and dry or—"

"Teagan, all you had to do was call. I would've understood."

I glance down to see Sophie receiving a bag of potato chips before we turn and continue walking.

Teagan reaches his good hand into the pocket of the athletic shorts he's wearing under his costume and pulls out his phone. The screen is cracked; a massive spiderweb over a black screen with a giant chunk missing, revealing the electronics beneath. To say it's destroyed is an understatement.

My mouth drops open, and I pause at another door while Sophie takes a step forward to get her candy. "What did you—"

"That's what a cleat does to a phone screen when you step on it. It fell out of my locker and I hadn't noticed. Saved it and brought it with me just in case you didn't believe me."

I exhale at the stab of guilt. "You didn't need to do that," I mumble, though deep down I'm not sure it's true.

Would I have believed him if he came here with an injured hand and nothing else? I'd like to think so, but my trust issues say otherwise.

Would I have believed him if it was something as simple as traffic or a road closure? I'm honestly not sure.

"Well, I'm glad you're okay," I say, meaning it. "But the second we're done here, you're getting that hand checked out."

Teagan reaches out and grabs my hand with his good one, lifting it to his lips and placing a quick kiss on my palm before Sophie turns around. Heat swells in my chest, and though he drops my hand a split second later, my heart swells.

Forty-five minutes of trick or treating and Sophie is ready to head home. We're a block from my house when I glance up at Teagan. "Thanks for coming, injured hand and all."

"Of course. I wouldn't have missed it for anything." He looks down at me and my heart flutters.

I swallow and glance at Sophie, a warning in my tone when I say, "Once we're home, you have thirty minutes to unwind, and then grandma's going to put you to bed, so I can go help Teagan with his hand. Okay?"

"Thirty minutes is a long time," Sophie says, and I laugh. Knowing her, thirty minutes will turn into an hour or more if my mother has anything to do with it.

When we reach our house, I pause on the sidewalk. "Do you want to come in while I get Soph settled? I won't be long."

"You know you don't have to come with me," he says. "Not that I don't want company, but I won't be offended if you don't want to spend your evening in the ER."

"I'm going," I say, leaving no room for argument. I almost never ask my mother for help, but I don't want him to go alone, and selfishly, I don't want our night to end just yet, so I'm making an exception.

Maybe my mother's right. Maybe I need to live a little.

His brow creases, and I realize there's something else. Something he's not saying. "Okay, but I should probably wait outside." He grimaces. "Somehow I don't think your father would be too pleased to see me with you tonight."

"What?" I ask, surprised. "Why?"

Teagan exhales and kicks at a rock on the ground.

"Teagan, what happened?"

Sophie tugs on my arm. "Mom, we're running out of time."

I sigh, torn between wanting an answer now and taking Sophie inside so I can get him alone. "Okay, we're going," I say to her, then turn back to Teagan. "Tell you what, she's exhausted and we're pressed for time. It's kind of a ritual for me to check her candy and see what all she got, but once I'm done, I'll get her settled with my mother, then meet you there and you can tell me everything."

"I hate to ruin your night, Lane. You don't have to—"

"I *want* to."

He nods, eyes locked with mine. "All right." He glances down at Soph, then ruffles the curls beneath her hood and smiles. "Thanks for letting me crash trick or treating. I had fun."

"Me too." Sophie beams, and though the affection I see in her eyes and hear in her voice should scare me, it doesn't.

"Catch ya later? Maybe at the lake house or our weekly Slice date?"

Sophie nods emphatically.

"Cool." He offers her a fist bump with his good hand before she lunges at him and wraps him up in one of her signature hugs. "G'night, Sweet Sophie," he says, and my heart clenches.

A little more than thirty minutes later, as promised, I walk into the ER only to find Teagan sitting in one of the waiting room chairs in the corner, his hand still wrapped in the same bandages he came in with.

My heart stalls at the sight of him, and I feel something shift inside my chest like tectonic plates.

He hurt himself, yet he came straight to me and Soph instead of taking care of himself first.

This knowledge sinks inside me as I start toward him, and the smile he offers lights me up from within. "I was hoping you'd be back there already," I say with a grimace as I glance at the blood-stained gauze.

"If this waiting room is any indication," Teagan says, nodding toward the people scattered about, "it's going to be a while. It's like a revolving door around here."

"Halloween." I groan. "People do careless things on holidays, get hurt, and wind up in the ER."

"Apparently. If I thought I'd be fine at practice tomorrow I'd leave and worry about it later. As it is, though, the impact of catching the ball in my hands and lifting weights will most definitely reopen the wound, and the last thing I want is to bleed all over the place and give your dad one more reason to bench my ass."

I frown, and I'm about to ask him again what happened when his stomach growls so loudly, the woman across from us stares.

"Hungry?" I laugh.

Teagan grunts. "Freaking starved. I haven't had anything since the protein bar I downed before practice this afternoon."

My eyes widen. "You didn't grab something before you came trick or treating?"

He shakes his head. "I was already late. I didn't want to be even later."

"Teagan ..." I admonish, though I can't really blame him. He was probably worried I'd think he stood me up and he wouldn't have been wrong. "Why don't I go out and get you something?"

He shakes his head, quickly grasping my hand and holding me in place. "Don't leave."

"Fine." I sigh. "But at least let me go see what I can find. There's gotta be some kind of food around here." I hate the thought of him being hungry when we could be here for hours yet.

Teagan hesitates only a fraction of a second before his stomach growls again, and he laughs. "Okay, go. If you don't, we might get a noise complaint."

I press my hand to the side of his face, cupping his jaw. I hate how I doubted him earlier today for even a moment when he's been nothing short of amazing.

"I'll be back in a flash," I say, then ever so gently, I lean forward and press a kiss to his cheek.

With a sheepish grin, I stand and hurry from the room in search of food.

Ten minutes later, I'm cursing myself for crossing the line with Teagan.

Why did I kiss him on the cheek?

I just had to go there.

It was innocent, but still . . .

I return to the emergency waiting room with a questionable turkey sandwich, chips, a granola bar, and some chocolate.

"This is all they had," I say with a grimace as I drop everything down on the small side table next to his chair. "The cafeteria was closed."

Teagan lifts the sandwich up for inspection and arches a dubious brow at the grayish color of the turkey.

"I know." I motion toward it. "Eat that one at your own risk."

He laughs and goes for the granola bar. "This will do. Thanks."

"Of course."

He takes a couple of bites, then grins. "You know, this wasn't really what I had in mind when I hoped I'd get you alone tonight."

My cheeks pinken. "Really? Sitting in the waiting room of the ER wasn't what you had in mind?"

His lips twitch. "Not quite."

I lean into him with a smile. "Well, I'm happy just being anywhere you are, so . . ."

"Yeah?" his voice softens, his hand in my hair.

I nod and bite my lip, lost in the simplicity of the moment together as I turn shyly away.

He eats the rest of his granola bar, then crumples the wrapper and shoves it in his pocket with his good hand before he turns to face me, his expression serious as he asks, "What were you like in high school?"

I think I know what he's asking. What was I like *before* Sophie?

I stare off into the distance, thinking about it. That time in my life feels so distant, it's like I can barely remember it. "I was carefree, but kind of quiet. Definitely a rule follower. I didn't go to parties or drink or stay out late. I never did anything rebellious." I glance down at my hands, trying to fight the stab of self-consciousness; I'm not exactly making myself sound cool. "I had a group of friends I hung out with on the weekends. I studied and got good grades. Kind of the opposite of what you'd expect from a girl who got herself knocked up at seventeen."

He narrows his eyes in disapproval of the latter, but it's the truth, so I don't apologize for it. Instead, I meet his gaze head-on, losing myself in his sky-colored irises. "What about you?" My gaze drops to his lips for a moment, and I find myself wishing we were somewhere more private. Somewhere I could possibly kiss him again, this time on the mouth.

I grunt and roll my eyes at myself.

Not gonna happen, Lane.

"What were *you* like?" I ask, steering my thoughts away from his lips.

I can only imagine Teagan in high school. He was probably the kind of guy who charmed all the girls in his grade, never had trouble finding a date, and ran with the "cool kids." Football on Friday nights. Parties on the weekend. Teagan Nichols strikes me as the boy everyone wants to be around, including me.

"I was a little different than you, not gonna lie."

I smile at this; it's what I expected.

"I certainly wasn't shy, though I *can* be quiet when I want to be. Hell, I'm definitely more reserved than some of my friends. But I wasn't an angel, either. In the summer, and often during the year, my friends and I were known for the parties we had at my best friend's cabin in the woods. If I had to put a label on it, I would call myself a *cautious* rule breaker."

"A cautious rule breaker?" I arch a brow.

"Sure. As in, I only broke the rules when I knew I wouldn't get caught."

I tip my head back and laugh, and Teagan's eyes flare at the sound.

Reaching out, he lifts my legs and places them on his lap, so I'm sitting half on the chair, half on him, and my breath catches.

"You probably had a lot of girlfriends," I murmur while his thumb strokes circles on my leg.

One muscular shoulder lifts, then drops. "Some."

I roll my eyes. "A lot."

"Maybe, but none of them were you." He reaches out and brushes the pad of his thumb over my lower lip and my stomach free-falls.

God, why does he have to be so damn perfect?

"You never would have gone for me in high school," I say, completely serious. "I was too quiet, too reserved. You probably went for the outgoing cheerleader types."

"*Wrong*," he says, his tone firm. "I would've fallen all over my feet to take you out."

I narrow my eyes and call his bluff. "I don't believe you."

"Why not?"

"Because . . . I'm different now, not the same woman I used to be. So, if you like me, the woman, you likely wouldn't have liked me, the girl."

Am I looking for reasons he's not perfect for me?

Teagan shakes his head, undeterred. "You're so much more than the person you give yourself credit for, and I have no doubt the Lane Turner you were then was every bit as amazing as the Lane Turner you are now. I like that you didn't date every guy that looked your way. I like that you're reserved, and I think it's fucking adorable you follow the rules. I also love that you're so close with your family, because I'm close with mine. They mean the world to me. And, yeah, parts of you changed with Sophie. That's to be expected." He reaches out and threads the fingers of his unbandaged hand through mine. "But that seventeen-year-old girl that faced adversity with fire in her eyes, that's the same woman sitting here with me right now. Your tenacity and strength are your most desirable traits."

One corner of his mouth hitches. "And I kind of love that you gave me a hard time at first. That you didn't just fall over your feet for me."

I swallow. "So, it's the chase you like?" I ask, deflecting from this growing, aching, need in my chest that's been with me all night.

"Of course not," he says, his tone soft as his thumb continues tracing over my skin. "I just found it fucking adorable that you've been trying to resist me. As if you ever had a chance. As if we wouldn't end up right here, regardless."

"We're not together, Teagan."

"*Yet.*" His jaw flexes. "Not together *yet.*"

I swallow. "How are you so perfect?"

"I'm not. But maybe I'm just perfect *for you.*"

I inhale a shuddering breath, because what if he's right? What if he *is* perfect for me? Maybe he and I were meant to be together all along, and my path, everything I've been through up until this point, was merely a journey to lead me to him.

What if fate exists? And what if I could actually have my happily ever after?

Look at me, believing in fairy tales.

I squeeze his hand in mine. "Come to Sunday brunch with me this weekend," I say, surprising even myself.

I promised my parents I'd be there this weekend, and it's the perfect opportunity to both see him again and have them get to know him better. My father can see he's so much more than one of his players. He can see for himself I'm safe with him. After threatening Chance tonight, he shouldn't be there, but if he does have the balls to show up, at least I'll have Teagan as a buffer.

"He knows we're friends," I say, so it shouldn't be too much of a surprise. Though I'm pretty sure my parents will see right through me and sense there's something more. Hell, my mother already does.

Teagan swallows, sorrow honing his features like rough-hewn granite. "This week might not be the best time. Somehow, I don't think your father would be too thrilled to have me there, friend or not."

I frown because I'd completely forgotten something happened tonight which he's yet to tell me about—the reason he didn't want to come inside and wait for me.

"Tell me. What happened?"

CHAPTER 30

TEAGAN

S ILENCE SURROUNDS US AS I collect my thoughts, and though I appreciate her giving me the time and space to explain without rushing me, I'm not sure where to start because I don't have any real answers.

"After practice, we entered the locker room like usual, except Coach came to tell us there's a change in schedule for tomorrow, courtesy of the Chancelor." I grit my teeth and move on. "At the same time as Chance pulled him aside, I opened my locker, and something fell from the top shelf. It caught me off guard, cracking me in the mouth, then falling to the ground by my feet. Turns out, it was a booze bottle. And of course, your father was there to witness the whole thing. Needless to say, he was pissed."

I huff out a breath, still frustrated as hell with the situation. "You know he runs a tight ship. A lot of other coaches in the league turn a blind eye to half the shit their players do, but not him. Anyway, add this to the hazing prank incident last month, and I have two strikes against me, as he so kindly reminded me. I think it's safe to say I'm on his shit list right now and I won't be getting off it any time soon."

Lane's brow furrows and she shakes her head as if trying to make sense of it.

Join the fucking club.

"I don't understand. If it wasn't yours, who would've put it there?"

"Hell if I know." I growl, pulling my hand from hers and shoving it through my hair. "Someone must've stashed it there, but the question is how?"

"Who all has access to your combination?"

"I assume Coach does and maybe the janitor in case there's a problem? Fuck, I don't know." I knead the back of my neck, and the muscles tense even thinking about it. "It's possible someone watched me put the combo in and kept it, but if that's the case—"

"You think someone set you up?" She frowns.

I exhale and drop my hand. "I don't know."

I'm not sure of anything.

"Maybe? Or maybe they literally stashed it there for themselves and never thought I'd see it. Maybe they planned to come back for it, then couldn't?" It's not plausible, but it's possible. I shrug. "All I know is your father is only going to give me so many chances, and who knows what he's thinking now. For all

I know, he thinks I have a drinking problem. At the very least, he thinks I broke the law and violated team policy. I can't imagine the reminder that we're friends and I've been hanging around Sophie will go over well with him."

"I can explain. I can—"

"No." I shake my head, adamant. "You can't fight my battles. It's not fair, and I'm not sure how much it'll help, anyway. Defending me might piss him off even more."

"So what are you gonna do?"

I sigh. "Lay low. Keep my head down and work hard, all while keeping my eyes open for trouble until I can somehow earn back his good graces."

"I hate that this happened to you."

I snort. *You're telling me.*

I scratch the edge of my jaw. "With you and I seeing each other more often, the timing isn't the best, I'll give you that."

She leans back in her chair and grunts. "And I thought my night was bad."

I glance over at her with a frown, searching her face for clues as to what she might be referring to. "How was your night bad? I know I was late, but—"

"It was nothing. Just . . ." She groans and bites her lip, and I can sense her hesitation when she says, "It's Chance."

I stiffen at the name.

"What about him?"

"He showed up at my parents' place looking for my father before he got home, and my mother made him go out with us since you weren't there yet. I think she felt bad for me or—what?" she asks, taking in my murderous expression.

A prickling heat I recognize as jealousy floods my veins and shimmies up my spine. Every muscle in my arms coils at the thought of Chance fucking Lockhart rushing to take my place.

The fact that he knew I was running late tonight and showed up on Lane's doorstep is more than a little telling, and it settles in the pit of my stomach like a rock. "Nothing. Go on."

"Well, I didn't want him to come with us but I was stuck. Then to make matters worse, my mother said she'd tell you where I was if you showed up, so he knew I'd been waiting on you, and he said something that pissed me off."

"What did he say?"

She fiddles with the hem of her shirt. "Just something about how you weren't good for me and a bad influence." She winces. "Now that I know what happened tonight, I assume that's where he was coming from, but I told him in no uncertain terms that he didn't know what he was talking about and to get lost."

My good hand fists, my mind churning.

Interesting that he thought Coach would be there, when he knows damn well he stays after practice for more than an hour each night. Also interesting is the fact that he waited to speak with Coach until we were in the locker room. Normally, he'd do it right on the field after practice.

Come to think of it, he's never stopped him in the locker room before. Yet he did tonight. The same night someone planted booze in my locker, poised to fall out when I opened the door conveniently in front of Coach.

The timing is suspect at best, made more suspicious by the fact he busted ass to get to Lane's house in search of Coach when he knew damn well he wouldn't be there, then bad-mouthed me to her.

My jaw hardens.

Suddenly, it's looking a lot less like the booze bottle was some kind of honest mistake or a prank gone wrong and a lot more like someone put it there.

And I'd bet anything that someone was Chance.

I'm not surprised when Coach asks to see me after practice.

I jog off the field, hit the locker room quickly, then make my way into his office. The stitches tug and pull at the palm of my hand as I give the door a quick knock before entering.

Coach's tanned face lifts and he waves me in, folding his arms over the desk in front of him while he studies me like one of the plays in his playbook.

"Nichols," he nods toward the chair across from him, "have a seat."

I do as he asks, watching as he leans back in his chair. "How's the hand?"

"Fine, sir," I say, silently cursing the way my stomach ties itself in knots. I might have known this was coming, but it doesn't make it any easier.

Hell, he had me do ten extra sets of bleacher runs and one hundred push-ups after practice, and I'd do it all thrice more if it meant I could skip this confrontation altogether.

Coach sighs and scrubs a hand down his face. "Listen, Nichols, this isn't personal. Most coaches in the league would give you a warning and move on. Maybe that's what I should do, too, but I like to think I'm different. I care about my team. I value respect and hard work and personal responsibility. I'm not just trying to grow great football players, but great young men, too, and I don't think I need to remind you that you shouldn't be drinking during the in-season. And you sure as hell shouldn't have alcohol in your locker, especially when you're underage."

I clear my throat, sensing this is my cue to say something. "With all due respect, sir, the booze wasn't mine. I know that's hard to believe. It makes little to no sense considering very few people have access to our combinations, so I know how bad this looks, but it's the truth."

He stares at me for a moment like he's trying to decide whether to believe me. "I've seen drugs and alcohol ruin lives. I've also seen a lot of people in my time claim they didn't have a problem when they did. Denial can be a very powerful mental game you play with yourself."

I scoff. "You think I'm lying?"

He shrugs. "I don't know. Only you know the truth, but what I do know is that this is your second warning this season" He leans forward in his chair and picks a pen up off his desk, tapping it on the smooth hard surface. "And if you get another, well, it won't bode well for you. I've seen this happen before. A kid with talent starts getting in trouble here or there, just minor things, but each one worse than the last. Next thing you know, they're getting busted for something they can't crawl out of, and their ass is off the team. I'd hate to see that happen here. You have a lot of talent, Nichols. I don't want to see you waste it, and I'd like to be the one to help you reach your full potential. With a QB like Lockhart at your disposal"—he shakes his head—"well, the sky's the limit."

I grind my teeth. *Fucking Lockhart.* If Coach only knew what a dirty rat I suspect him to be. I'd love nothing more than to burst his bubble, but I suspect it would take a lot to make him doubt his protégé.

I've stewed over everything that happened since last night, and now more than ever, I'm certain it must've been him who planted the booze in my locker. The only thing I can't seem to piece together is *why* he did it. I'm not a threat to his spot on the team and I haven't given him any trouble on the field. The only thing I'm guilty of is spending time with Lane, so I have to assume there's a connection. He must know we're seeing each other and he's jealous.

But why not simply rat me out to Coach?

It's the only part of the argument I don't have an answer for.

I clear my throat, sensing Coach wants acknowledgment. "Yes, sir. I can assure you nothing else will happen."

He taps the pen on the desk again, eyeing me over a stack of papers. "On a personal note, I know you've been spending time with Lane and Sophie."

Oh shit.

I stiffen, every muscle in my body rigid as I wait to see where this is going.

"She seems to value your friendship," he says, and the tight line of his mouth tells me he's none too pleased about it. "Lane doesn't trust easily, so I can only assume by inviting you into Sophie's life she trusts you. Don't break that trust. And keep it . . . *friendly.* As long as you can do that and remain respectful, no drinking or funny business, we shouldn't have a problem."

My jaw clenches so hard my teeth ache.

I'm fucking falling for this girl, and her father—my coach—loathes me so much he feels the need to issue me a warning.

Fucking fantastic.

"I can assure you, I have nothing but the best of intentions where your daughter and granddaughter are concerned."

He leans back in his chair once more, eyeing me beneath a knitted brow. "I'm glad to hear that." Another couple taps on his desk and he says, "I think we're finished here."

"Yes, sir." I rise to my feet and exit Coach's office so fast, my head spins.

I'm not more than a few feet down when a hand clamps over my shoulder. I glance up to find Tommy hovering outside, his features twisted in concern. With a lift of his chin, he says, "Hey, a bunch of us are headed to Slice. You wanna join?"

I glance behind me, then back to him again and shrug. "I'll hang for a bit." The truth is the only place I want to be is wherever Lane is, but that isn't an option. Not with her at her parents' house tonight and me on Coach's shit list, so pizza with the boys is about as good as it's going to get. If I go back to the dorm, all I'll do is either miss her or stew over the whole booze-in-my-locker thing.

"Come on." We exit the tunnels and step out into the cool evening air when I feel Tommy glancing my way. "I haven't seen you since yesterday." He hooks a thumb back the way we just came. "How'd that go?"

"It wasn't fucking mine, man." I shove my hands in my pockets as I try to smother the urge to defend myself further.

Tommy raises his hands, eyes wide. "Hey, I didn't think it was. We've been rooming together since the beginning of summer. You think I don't at least know you well enough by now to know you wouldn't be caught dead with a bottle of liquor in your locker? Shit." He shakes his head and scratches the side of his stubble-covered cheek. I exhale, my muscles loosening.

"Can I ask you something?" I say, staring at the courtyard as we pass through it toward the edge of campus.

"Shoot."

"What are your thoughts on Lockhart?"

Until now, I've pretty been tight-lipped about the dude, mostly because everyone and their mother seems to fucking worship the ground he walks on. Unless they're from a rival team, and even then, they're begrudgingly in awe of his talent.

"As a quarterback or a person?"

"A person, I guess?" After all, his character off the field isn't necessarily tied to his character on the field. Unless you take into consideration our last away game against Alabama where he barely gave me the ball.

"I think he's an arrogant asshole." Tommy shrugs. "But I guess I figure that comes with the territory of being great."

I grimace. I don't trust Lockhart as far as I can throw him, and it bugs the shit out of me a dick like that is so good at what he does.

"I think maybe he stashed the booze."

Tommy chokes. "For real, dude?"

I nod, saying nothing as we pass the Bowman Center and take the walkway toward the sidewalk that leads into town. "If I tell you something, will you keep it between us?"

"Of course, man. Look, I know most of my free time is spent with Melissa, but I'm here for you if you need me. I just gotta prioritize in my downtime, you know?"

I wave him off. "Dude, I get it. Trust me. That's actually kind of what this is about."

Tommy frowns. "I'm not following."

"I'm . . ." Shit. How do I explain this to him. Technically, I'm not seeing Lane yet, at least not like that, but I *want* to be. I will be.

I run a hand over the scruff on my jaw. "Well, I've kind of been talking to Lane Turner and—"

"No fucking way." Tommy's eyes bulge and he halts in his tracks. "You have a thing for Lane? But on the bus, you insisted it was nothing, that you just had class together."

I shrug. "I lied."

Wasn't it obvious?

"Wait." Tommy frowns. "She's not the chick from the park, is she?"

"The one and only."

Tommy groans. "Damn, bro. You sure about this?"

"I mean, technically we're only friends. We haven't crossed any lines, if you catch my drift, but it's only a matter of time."

"You sure about this, dude?"

"Never been surer of anything in my life."

He stares at me for a moment, then starts to walk again, taking the sidewalk that leads into town. "Does Coach know?"

"He knows we're friends."

Tommy whistles. "He doesn't play around. I bet he wasn't happy about the booze on top of you and Lane hanging out."

"You could say that," I grind out.

"So, where's Lockhart come into all this?"

"You know how tight they are, right? Him and Coach?"

"Sure. It's pretty common knowledge among the team, and they don't exactly try to hide it. He coached him in high school, right?"

"Right. And maybe I'm paranoid, but I can't help but feel that ever since Lane and I have started hanging out, he's had a huge problem with it."

"Did he say anything to you?" Tommy arches a brow.

"Not specifically. But there are signs. Like the entire game at Alabama where he didn't give me the ball once. Some comments he made about the bracelet her daughter made me. Confronting Lane about hanging out with me. Extending game tape hours today so that I can't see her."

"You think he planted the whiskey in your locker, don't you?"

"I think it's a definite possibility," I say.

We cross the street and Tommy pauses on the sidewalk in front of Slice. "You really think he'd fuck with you like that over Turner's daughter?"

"I know it sounds crazy, but after I cleaned the glass up, changed, and had Mark bandage my hand, I busted ass to get to her place last night because I'd promised I'd go trick or treating with them, but guess who beat me there, 'looking for coach'?" I make air quotes with my hands.

Tommy's brows rise. "No shit."

The muscle in my jaw twitches. "And, according to Lane, when he found out she was waiting for me, he laid into her about how bad he thought I was for her."

Tommy whistles. "So, you think he has a thing for her? Or is it more like a brotherly, overprotective thing?"

Do I think he's interested in Lane? I don't know. The fucking pieces don't quite fit; it's like I'm missing something, but I'm not sure what. Then again, maybe he's an overbearing douchebag when it comes to Lane because of what she went through in high school. He would've been around when she was pregnant. It's possible he's worried I'm just another egotistical asshole that only cares about himself.

I want this theory to fit, and logically it makes sense, but for some reason, it doesn't feel right, like a pair of shrunken jeans. "I'm not sure," I say after a while.

My gaze finds the large window of Slice. I can already see several of the guys from the team inside, waiting to be seated.

Tommy follows my gaze, his brow knotted as he says, "It's gotta be the overprotective bit, right? Or maybe he's just pissed that you disregarded Coach's orders? I mean, it would be weird to go to such lengths just because he was into her when the dude could, literally, have any chick in the tri-state if he wanted."

Not Lane; never Lane.

"Right," I say.

Tommy claps me on the shoulder. "Maybe you should just talk to him, clear the air and let him know your intentions. It can't hurt, right?"

CHAPTER 31

LANE

I SIT DOWN AT the formal dining room table with Sophie. Years ago, when I was a kid, Mom decided we didn't use this room enough, and her Sunday brunches were born.

It's ten o'clock. I already spoke with Teagan, and though I wish he were here, I understand why he thinks it's a bad idea after what happened at practice this week. Better to play it safe and not poke the bear. Besides, I'd rather have him alone, which is precisely why I'd asked my mother to watch Sophie for me. The second I've choked down my food, I plan on heading to the lake house where Teagan is meeting me.

Only two more hours until I get to see him. Two hours for the day alone, a first for us.

My stomach twists with nerves at the thought, and I bite my lip.

All I have to do is get through brunch, which shouldn't be much of a hardship since Chance isn't here. Looks like he heeded my warning and smartly stayed away.

Mom places the last of the platters on the table heaped with trays of bacon, fruit, crepes with fresh strawberries and whipped cream, quiche, and even fried chicken.

My stomach rumbles. I haven't attended one of her brunches since summer break, thanks to Chance, and it's easy to forget how amazing they are.

Dad ambles into the dining room, takes one look at the place settings, and says, "I don't think Chance is going to make it today, hon."

"Oh?" Mom steps back, her gaze lifting to my father who's sinking into a chair at the head of the table. "Well, we'll have room for one more just in case."

The second the words leave her mouth, the doorbell rings.

Dad frowns and starts to rise, but Mom is already on her feet and heading into the hallway while I strain my neck to see.

Maybe Teagan decided to come, after all?

I have half a mind to follow my mother to the door to see for myself. It would be just like him to hang up with me after promising to see me at noon, then show up here to surprise me.

The thought makes me smile, but the second Mom bustles into the room with Chance beside her, it vanishes.

What the hell is he doing here?

The synapses in my brain fire, trying to make sense of it because the Chance I know is scared to death of my secret.

My jaw tightens as I watch my father rise and clap him on the back while pulling him into his chest in one of those bro hugs men do, then sits back down. "Have a seat, son," he says, waving to the empty chair beside him, the one across from *mine*.

Suddenly, I'm not so hungry, which really pisses me off because . . . crepes.

My gaze tracks Chance's every move as he slides into his chair. I don't even bother to hide my disgust for him as he sits and nods in Sophie's direction. "Hey, Sophie," he says, and I have the insatiable urge to both pluck his eyes out for looking at her. Instead, I pull her under my arm to protect her.

On the rare occasion he's at our house and not huddled in my father's office watching game tape or discussing new plays or anything football related, he barely acknowledges her existence. It's been like that since the day she was born, and I think I like it better that way.

"I'm so glad you could make it, honey. Ed just got done telling us he didn't think you would. And look, Lane is actually here for a change. It's the first time in forever we've all been together for brunch. Gosh"—she glances over at me—"when *was* the last time?"

"It's been about four years," I say, deadpan.

Chance stiffens before his eyes flicker between my mother and me. "Uh, yeah." He clears his throat. "I didn't think I was going to be able to come, but then at the last minute, everything worked out." His gaze settles on mine, his voice lowering. "Now that I know Lane's here, I'm really glad it did."

Rage boils my blood as I stare him down. Clearly, he's calling my bluff. He doesn't think I'll tell my parents the truth. And much to my dismay, he's right.

Guess he knows me better than I thought.

I don't know if anything would push me to tell my father the truth when I know how completely devastated he would be. Especially not when I'm so close to having Chance out of my life for good.

All I have to do is get through the rest of the year. With any luck, he'll be drafted early and gone. I won't have to see him all the time. I won't have to hear about him every day or see the pride in my father's eyes when he mentions him by name.

No more pretending like seeing him doesn't fill me with a toxic combination of resentment and guilt at hiding the truth.

I tear my eyes from his, no longer wanting to look at him. He doesn't deserve my attention, but luckily, I don't have to do much except eat because Dad turns the conversation to football as everyone begins to fill their plates.

I take care of Sophie first, cutting a crepe into bite-sized pieces to make it easier for her to eat before I start on my own plate, all while ignoring the disgusting amount of praise my father heaps on Chance for his performance at the last game. Part of it stems from his own pride; I know this. My father shaped Chance into the football player he is today, and now he's going places. I don't blame him for being proud of that, but it still sucks to sit here and listen to it.

My mother, God bless her, does what she always does best and listens raptly, smiling and commenting in all the right places.

I used to be able to do that.

I used to be able to go along with it.

But I can't anymore.

I'm done, not to mention irritated with sheer arrogance at the man across from me as he tries to catch my eye and smile.

"Teagan had a great game, too," I say, glancing up from my plate to offer my father a pointed stare. Across from me, Chance's glare bores into my skull. "He had some incredible blocks, not to mention the touchdown he got. Oh, and if he hadn't recovered that fumble by the Lions, we'd have been seriously screwed considering we only won by three points."

My father's forehead creases, and he hesitates before saying, "That, he did. I have to admit, I didn't give him much play time after, uh . . ." He clears his throat. "I've had some doubts about him, especially after an incident at practice the other night, but he proved to me yesterday afternoon how much he wants this. His performance wasn't lost on me."

I nod, shifting to lock eyes with Chance. "I'll be sure to tell him when I see him next," I drawl as a slow smile curves my lips.

Chance's cheeks flush, and if the firm set of his mouth is any indication, I succeeded in pissing him off.

Good. Now we're even.

"We've had better tight ends," he says, squaring his shoulders.

I roll my eyes. I so badly want to say we've had better quarterbacks, too, but it wouldn't be true, and I'd just sound like a jerk.

Besides, Chance is doing a good job at showing his hand all on his own.

"Is that so?" I prop my chin on my fist and stare. I have no idea what kind of game he's playing, but it's obvious he's trying something; I just haven't figured out what.

Chance nods. "Yeah. The kid's a loose cannon if you ask me."

Kid?

My brows rise. He acts so fucking superior, it makes me sick. Meanwhile, he's half the man Teagan will ever be. I only wish I could tell him so, right here, right now, in front of my parents without sounding like I'm the one in the wrong.

Out of the corner of my eye, I see my father take a bite of his food, his forehead creased in concentration. "Teagan has a lot of spirit and a damned lot of potential. He's stumbled a bit off the field, but it's no reason to discount him, at least not yet. If he keeps his head in the game, I think he'll go far."

The pleasure at the irritation sliding through Chance's features hits me like a branding iron, hot and sharp.

I grin, knowing this wasn't what Chance wanted to hear. But that's the thing about my dad. He may be tough, and he may love Chance like a son, but he's fair and more than diplomatic. In many ways, he views all of his players as his children, prides himself on shaping each and every one into not only damn good players, but also decent men.

I stab a strawberry and pop it in my mouth, feeling more than a little smug. "Did you know he has a twin sister?"

"Really?" Mom smiles over at me.

I nod. "Her name is Brynn and she goes to Ann Arbor University. She also happens to be dating one of their star receivers, Jace Taggart?"

"Taggart?" My father perks up, eyes on me.

"Yup."

My father grunts. "He's a hell of a player. Didn't he play for a school in Ohio before college?"

"Yeah. Riverside. He and Teagan played on the same team. They're best friends actually."

"How lovely," Mom says. "So, Teagan's best friend is dating his sister?"

"Yeah." A quick glance at Chance's pinched expression and red face encourages me to go on. "He's still good friends with a couple of guys from his old team, actually. I think it's kind of cool," I say, knowing Chance no longer talks to *anyone* from his high school team. The minute he got a scholarship to CU, he dropped them all like a hot potato. Kind of like when I got pregnant. "Another one plays college ball, but I forget his name. He plays for Ohio State."

"No shit." My father stares off into the distance. "I'll have to check out their roster, but if he's a freshman, I know Atlas Scott has been making a ton of headlines. They're predicting he'll be a first-round pick."

"The name sounds familiar," I say, at least I think it does. But regardless, I say it because the steam coming from Chance's ears has me giddy.

Aw, poor Chance Lockhart isn't the center of attention. Boo-hoo.

The fact that Chance seems to loathe Teagan so much is practically an endorsement of his character.

"What's Teagan's major?" Mom asks, and I give her a mental high five for prolonging the conversation.

"Education. He wants to be a high school teacher and hopes to coach football."

Chance snorts and my father spears him a look. After all, he was a teacher until he got the gig at CU.

I smile at Chance's blunder, wishing I had a hidden camera to capture this on film; I'd study it like one of my father's game tapes.

"That's wonderful." My mother's gaze flickers to Chance and her posture stiffens before she changes the subject.

An hour later, brunch is over and the dishes have been cleared from the table. I pass by the living room where my mother sits with Sophie in her lap, cuddling with a movie on. I round the sofa and press a kiss to the top of Sophie's head, then tell my mother I'll be back tonight but not to wait up since it'll likely be late.

"You're sure you're okay with her?" I ask one last time. When she shoots me a glare, I hold my hands up and laugh. "Got it."

I back away and head for the hallway when someone steps out of the shadows.

I practically jump out of my skin, and my hand flies to my chest where my heart bangs furiously against my ribs.

"What are you doing here?" I hiss as I open the closet door beside him and pull out a jacket. "Aren't you supposed to be going over game tape with my father in his office?"

Chance shoves his hands in his pockets, staring at me a beat before he says, "He's waiting on me."

I slide on my coat, not in the mood for whatever this is, and try to push past him, but he steps in front me, blocking my path.

My eyes turn to laser beams, directed right at his face. If only I could eviscerate him with a glare. "You don't listen well, do you? I told you not to come. I told you that if you showed today and didn't leave me alone—"

"You were bluffing." Chance shrugs, his cocky expression bordering on smug. "You and I both know that if you were going to tell your parents, you would've done so years ago."

I hate that he's right, absolutely loathe him for it.

"I have to go." I dart to my right, but Chance follows. I try the left, but his arm stretches out, catching me.

I loosen a breath from deep in my lungs, frustration building inside of me like a geyser ready to erupt.

"What do you want, Chance?" I snap. "Is it just your goal in life to piss me off? Make things harder for me? Do you hate me that fucking much?"

Chance flinches, which only pisses me off more. As if my words could possibly hurt him. "Does your father know you're fucking Nichols?"

I suck a breath between my teeth. "You're an asshole."

"Does he?"

My stomach sinks at the implication, though I guess I shouldn't be surprised. First, he caught us together at Slice, then I showed up to the team bus to hand deliver a good luck charm. And then, there was Halloween. Even I can admit we look like a couple from the outside looking in, and that's without our afternoons working together in the basement of Wyndham Hall on Teagan's lunch break.

I force down the seed of fear sprouting in my chest and stare him in the eyes. "Not that it's any of your damn business, but I'm *not* sleeping with Teagan."

His eyes brighten like the fact I've kept my legs closed is a revelation. His gaze slides over my body, a hunger in his eyes I recognize, and I want to punch him in the face, serve him a right hook to the jaw.

I hate that he knows what I look like under my clothes. And I absolutely hate that he's the only one who does.

"So, you're seeing him, but not sleeping with him?"

"I don't see why you care. My love life is none of your business," I snap.

His eyes narrow and my chest pinches. "You see, I think it is."

I scoff. He's even more of a dick than I thought he was.

"You and I have a history," he says, taking a step closer.

"With a piss-poor ending."

"See, that's where you're wrong. It's not the *end*, Turner."

I laugh, the sound incredulous even to my own ears.

My frustration mounts inside of me, a jockey ready to ride. "What the hell are you talking about?"

"I told you when we were kids, after I found out you were . . ." he waves his hand toward me, and I want to laugh because he still can't utter the word pregnant. "I told you then I wasn't ready."

I shrug. *What the hell is he getting at?*

"So? I remember. Trust me, I was there. I remember every single second of that conversation." It was etched in my mind like a weighty tome. I replayed that conversation over and over in my head for fucking days.

"Right. But you're missing the point." Chance reaches out, but I dodge him. "The point is, I will be ready one day. Once I get drafted and have a few years under my belt." He rakes a hand through his hair, his tone serious. "Maybe once I'm older and I—"

"Please tell me you're joking." I choke over the words. "Please tell me that you're not standing here telling me I'm your fucking backup plan."

My body vibrates with anger.

"*Lane . . .*"

"No!" I point at his face, finger trembling. "You can stop right there, because I am no one's backup plan. Do you honestly think we could just pick up where we left off? Be one big happy family after you abandoned us for years? And what about Sophie? Do you think she'll just accept you, then? Years later, after you've been right here all this time? Chance, she doesn't even *know* about you." I shake my head and take a step back, away from him. "*No.* I deserve better."

I've found it, too.

"And you think Teagan is the one to give you that?" Chance scoffs. "Who are you kidding? You're a single mom, and you don't even have a degree yet. Your whole life will be an uphill battle. But once I'm pro, I can make things easier."

Rage swims in my veins, a shark with teeth, threatening to rip through flesh and bone to get to the heart of its prey. My vision turns red as I stare him down, shocked we're even having this fucking conversation, and though I don't want them to, his words pick at old wounds that have only begun to heal.

All the fears that I'm not good enough, all my insecurities, everything I've told myself these last four years rise to the surface, bobbing in the tumultuous sea of my thoughts.

"Maybe it will be an uphill battle," I say, my voice eerily calm compared to how I feel inside. "But I'd rather climb a fucking mountain alone than free-fall with you." I start to turn, then stop myself, glaring at him one last time. "And you're wrong about one thing. Teagan cares about me. Not every guy sees baggage when they look at me and Sophie. Some see so much more."

Because I *am* worth it.

I'm still furiously replaying my conversation with Chance in my head when I step back from the wall, now painted partly with bright ivory paint. The living room with its large windows overlooking the lake will be so much brighter with the lighter color, but it's not until I hear the knock on the door that I smile.

Setting my roller back on the tray of paint, I hurry toward the living room and fling the front door open. Teagan's wide smile and dimples greet me, completely evaporating my sour mood as I lunge toward him and wrap my arms around his neck.

With a laugh, he draws me into his chest, squeezing me tight as he lifts me off my feet before setting me back down again. "Happy to see me?"

"You have no idea."

He places me back on my feet and glances around the room.

"I just got started," I say, when his eyes focus on the fresh paint. "I needed something to occupy myself while I waited."

Mostly to keep my mind from wandering to the confrontation with Chance.

Teagan stares at me as if trying to gauge my statement but simply nods, then stretches his arms out, and it's then I notice how good he looks in his worn jeans and an old faded Riverside Rebels T-shirt. "Well, I came to help, so put me to work."

"I guess you can jump right in. I've got an extra roller and paintbrush," I say, suddenly wishing we were doing more than painting.

Teagan nods. "Where's Soph?"

"Uh, I forgot to tell you. I asked my mother to watch her so we could get more painting done." I shrug. "I figured it would be easier."

I bite my lip, cursing the flush of heat in my cheeks.

Right. Because that's *why you asked. So you could get more painting done. Definitely* not *because you wanted to get him alone.*

"Damn. I wanted to show her this cool video I saw the other day. It was all about T. rex with these cool digital recreations. Did you know that baby T. rexes were actually super cute. They were about the size of a skinny turkey and covered in down feathers—what?" he asks, stopping his monologue to run a hand over his face. "What's that look for?"

Liquid heat blooms inside my chest, spreading like a massive hand, its fingers reaching toward my heart. "You were watching dinosaur videos?"

"I mean, they were more like documentaries."

"That's . . ." I shake my head, the words lodged in my throat.

Sweet. Thoughtful. Sexy. So fucking irresistible I don't even know what to do with it.

If I ever doubted whether Teagan Nichols had my heart in a choke hold, this would be all the confirmation I need. I'm tired of letting fear in the driver's seat, tired of running from something I know is real.

My chest tightens and I take a step closer, a cheeky grin spreading my lips. "Should I be jealous you're disappointed she's not here?"

His eyes heat as they flicker over me. Reaching out, he snags my hand in his and pulls me toward him.

I stumble, nearly crashing into his chest. "*Surprised.* Not disappointed. Because if she's not here, that means I have you all to myself."

My heart beats against my ribs. My breathing hitches.

I wonder if he'll try to kiss me before I shake the thought off.

Of course he won't. Other than a few moments of weakness, I've made it perfectly clear all I want is friendship.

Teagan's phone starts to ring, and I catch my breath. My lungs fill. "You gonna answer that?" I tease.

Teagan grimaces, then pulls his phone from his pocket and frowns down at the screen. "Just give me a minute," he says as he accepts the call.

I hook a thumb toward the kitchen, needing a moment to think.

Or panic, same thing, because I can feel the fissures in the walls around my heart coming down, and I'm not sure what to do about it.

"I'll just . . ." I trail off. "Make some coffee."

Sounds good, he mouths, then I turn and rush from the room.

I busy myself in the kitchen with the little coffee pot I got for a steal at a garage sale last year and start to fill it with water.

Teagan's voice trickles toward me, only separated by a half wall I fully plan on tearing out to expand the kitchen and create an open concept space.

"What do you mean we have a meeting today? What the hell for?" he grinds out.

My shoulders sag with disappointment as I add the coffee grounds. A flick of the switch and seconds later, it starts to splutter while I lean against the counter with nothing left to busy myself but my racing thoughts.

I hate that Chance has gotten to my head. Absolutely detest the fact that he opened wounds and insecurities Teagan had begun to heal.

But the conversation in the other room I'm trying hard to ignore isn't helping.

It's wrong to eavesdrop, but I justify it by telling myself it'll be better this way. If Teagan has to leave early and I'm prepared for it, I'll be less disappointed. More capable of handling the letdown, rather than catching me off guard.

"So, let me get this straight," Teagan's voice carries to me. "Lockhart calls a last-minute strategy session to watch game tape and go over new plays on our only day off and everyone is just going to fucking jump when he says jump?"

I stiffen while my stomach lurches somewhere in the vicinity of my throat.

Chance called a last-minute meeting?

He knew I came here to meet Teagan. I don't know how I know that, but I do; I'm sure of it. Maybe this is his way of getting even after I poked the bear at brunch? Worse yet, maybe this is his sick way of trying to prove to me Teagan's the same as him, that he's no better and in the end, he'll prioritize football.

I chew my thumbnail, thinking.

If Lockhart called a meeting, everyone would be expected to go. The game next weekend against Florida State is huge, and it wouldn't bode well for any players not willing to put in the extra work.

"Fuck that!" Teagan seethes. "Yeah, well, I don't care if he expects everyone to be there or not, I'm not going. Today's our only day off and I plan on spending it with Lane."

I step forward, risking a glance at him to see him standing, one hand on his hip as he listens to the person on the other line. "So fucking be it!" he says then hangs up.

I jump back, turning away from him and toward the coffee pot as I try and wrap my head around the conversation.

A moment later, I register the sound of his footsteps behind me, feel the heat of him at my back and close my eyes. "Everything okay?"

"Yeah. Sorry about that. I guess some of the team is getting together."

I slowly spin around to face him, not wanting to assume. "Do you need to go?"

An almost imperceptible shake of his head. "No."

I swallow over the heartbeat in my throat, almost afraid to believe my ears. Missing today's strategy session would put even more of a target on his back as Chance has made it very clear to me he has a problem with him already.

But Teagan doesn't seem to care; he seems completely at ease with his decision as he hovers above me, a smile curving the corners of his mouth.

He chose me.

Over football.

Over his obligation to the game.

My conversation with Chance threatens to surface once more, and I mentally give it the middle finger because Teagan chose me despite the fact that I have a child and no degree and am still figuring things out.

He chose me despite my father being his coach, messy life and all.

All of the things Chance said about no one wanting me completely evaporate. I told him I wanted someone who looked at me and Sophie like a gift and not baggage.

And I got him.

He's standing right in front of me, and he's . . . *immaculate,* so much more than I ever could have asked for.

Whatever remains of my walls crumbles around my feet, carried away by the tide that is Teagan.

I close the gap between us and my gaze falls to his mouth.

I should tell him Chance was at brunch today, mention my conversation with him. Even if I can't share the paternity of Sophie's father, I should at least give Teagan a heads up that Chance considers me his backup plan. In his warped mind, he thinks we have a future. After all, you can't build a house on a rocky foundation, so he should know the truth if I'm going to take this next step. If I'm going to push friendship in the rearview mirror for good.

But the last thing I want to do is talk about Chance, let alone think about him. Not right now when we're here alone, together. Not when he's looking down at me with so much adoration in his eyes, I could drown in it.

"Ready to paint?" Teagan gently takes my hand, threading his fingers through mine, and his lips quirk.

"Not yet." I shake my head, and mustering every ounce of courage I possess, I step closer and fist his shirt in my hands. "I have something else in mind," I whisper.

His sapphire eyes flare, flecks of green and midnight sparking to life inside the blue as he licks his lips, eyes on my mouth. "What did you have in mind?"

I stretch, my mouth inches from his as I breathe him in. "*This.*"

Our lips meet, and it's like sparks to kindling.

We ignite.

CHAPTER 32

TEAGAN

THE MOMENT SHE PRESSES her lips to mine, I claim her. She's mine. There's no going back to friends after this, and even if I had any hesitation or doubt about where her heart lies, I'd claim her, anyway.

"Fucking finally," I growl.

I show no hesitation as I kiss Lane back.

She and I were on this path from the moment I met her. From the moment I saved Sophie in the park, we were inevitable. It was just a matter of time until we got here.

And fuck, am I glad we finally got here.

I cradle the back of her skull, spearing my fingers into the long, lush auburn locks that drive me wild. A tilt of my head and I'm taking the kiss deeper, parting her lips with my own.

She sighs, and I swallow with an answering growl.

This. I've wanted this *for so long.*

I swipe my tongue over the seam of her lips, then sweep inside her mouth, tasting her like she's something to be savored. Like she's the best fucking meal I've had in weeks, because she is. She is *everything*.

I bite her lower lip with a little tug, drawing her closer until we're flush against each other, so I can kiss her harder. I say all the things she's afraid to hear, telling her how much I want her. Not her body; though, fuck, do I want that, but *her*. I want every fucking thing she has to offer—her mind, her heart, her thoughts, her words—anything she's willing to give.

And in return, she tells me everything she's afraid to say.

Her lips tell me she wants me, too.

Her soft sigh tells me she's falling like I am.

The goose bumps over her skin tell me she likes my touch.

The frantic gripping of my shirt means she can't get close enough; she wants more.

My mouth slides to the corner of her lips, pressing one soft kiss there before I move to her jaw, her neck, and to the shell of her ear, breathing in her sweet scent.

Her breath turns shallow, ragged, matching pace with the pounding of my heart. It hammers against her hands as she splays them over my chest, and when I can't take it anymore, I return to her mouth, and she meets me with equal enthusiasm.

Her hands drift to my back, sliding beneath my shirt, and my muscles clench in response. Her touch is like lightning, sinking beneath my skin, frying my senses and obliterating my thoughts.

We stumble back toward the living room, my hands on her waist anchoring her to me as we fall to the pile of cushions that serve as a makeshift couch.

My ass hits first and I drag her down with me where she shifts, straddling my lap.

I groan, fingers digging into her hips as I move her over the bulge in my pants while bucking against her.

She feels so fucking good.

My hands slide beneath her shirt and up her back, over miles of smooth, soft skin while my mouth explores the curve of her jaw, her neck, and the skin at her throat where her pulse pounds wildly.

With a growl, I thrust against her, and she answers with another roll of the hips.

My teeth graze her lower lip, nipping and licking, before swallowing her soft moan as I palm her breast.

Slow down, asshole.

Slow. The. Fuck. Down.

With a groan, I reluctantly remove my hands from under her shirt and slide them into her hair instead where I hold her, milking the kiss for everything its worth.

I want to explore everywhere, beneath all her clothes, every fucking inch of her. I crave the feel of her curves beneath my palms, her skin, hot against my own, but the last thing I want to do is move too fast too soon. I don't want to take more than she's ready to give. Not when her head is finally catching up to her heart and she's finally put herself out there.

I slow the kiss, brushing my lips over hers in a languid rhythm before I use every ounce of restraint to pull back.

I stare into her eyes, hooded and clouded with lust, and it's like a giant fucking gut punch; it makes me want her even more.

I run the pad of my thumb over the curve of her jaw, taking in the sight of her swollen lips and her sparkling eyes, every bit as blue and beautiful as sapphires, and all I can think about is how I want to see her every fucking second of every fucking day. Football is the furthest thing from my mind. Classes, Coach, and my fucked-up trust issues because of Knox are a distant memory.

I am absolutely fucked over for this girl.

CHAPTER 33

LANE

T HE DAYS THAT FOLLOW that Sunday afternoon I broke our friendship truce are a whirlwind. With only a month left in the semester, finals are approaching as well as projects and deadlines. Between our classes, my work, and his crazy football schedule, Teagan and I see each other every spare second we can manage, which isn't easy considering we're keeping our relationship a secret. It's all look, don't touch for the foreseeable future. It sucks, but the last thing I want to do is interfere with football or explain to Sophie what having a boyfriend means.

Now that I've lifted the lid on my tightly contained feelings, it hurts to feel like I'm stuffing them in a box again, but I know it's for the best.

Also like I know we're moving way too fast.

One second, I was standing on the edge of a cliff, armed with a parachute but afraid to jump, and the next, I'm in free fall.

Now all I can do is pray it doesn't hurt when I hit the ground. *If* I hit the ground.

There's always a chance this thing between us might actually work.

In the blink of an eye, we've gone from friends to meeting in my car before class and finding dark corners of the library whenever we have a spare moment. It's like I'm sixteen again, all raging hormones and roaming hands.

My teeth sink into my lower lip as I remember him pushing me into the large-print section of the library just this morning where we made out like it was our dying breath.

My phone rings, jolting me from the memory.

I reach inside my messenger bag and fish it out only to see the number for campus day care flashing on the screen.

Panic fists at the base of my spine as I answer, pressing it to my ear. "Hello?"

"Hey, Lane, it's Cindy."

The director. Oh, shit.

"Is everything okay?" I ask, even though I know it's not. She wouldn't be calling if it were.

"First, I want to stress that Sophie is doing okay. She's calm and watching a show on a tablet."

I blink my eyes closed, trying to take solace in her words as I nod. "What happened?"

"She fell on the playground at recess, and I'm afraid she split her knee pretty badly. It's a pretty deep wound. We're holding a compress to it, but I'm afraid she's going to need stitches.

Unfortunately, we can't leave with her because we'd be under-staffed, which means if you can't come and get her, we'll have to call an ambulance."

My stomach clenches, bile rising to the back of my throat as I tell myself Sophie's all right.

She'll be okay, and that's all that matters.

I exhale, pinching the bridge of my nose as I try to figure out how I can be in two places at once. The last thing I want is for an ambulance to transport her for what will likely be a frightening experience over a minor injury, but I can't afford to miss my presentation either.

Shit.

"Just give me one minute, will you? No matter what, someone will be on the way," I say.

"No problem," Cindy says, her voice soft. "We'll see you in a minute."

I hang up and waste no time dialing my father. But he doesn't answer.

I curse under my breath as I try him one more time, mind racing with my options. Missing my presentation on such short notice will be considered a no-show, and the professor made it perfectly clear anyone who ditched would be given an automatic failing grade.

Voicemail picks up for the second time, and I groan. "Where are you?" I shout, startling a passing student.

Worrying my lip with my teeth, I try my mom, but she's a physical therapist's assistant and when I get no answer from her either, I assume she's in with a patient.

Gabby's in class, so she'll be no help.

I squeeze my eyes closed and tip my head back, resigning myself to either flunking my presentation and ending up with a D in the class or allowing the day care to call an ambulance for something as minor as a split knee.

Unless . . .

My thoughts drift to Teagan at the same time a warm arm slides around my waist as if conjured by my subconscious.

"Hey there, beautiful," the familiar voice murmurs.

"Teagan!" I whirl around, panic filling my veins as his arm falls.

Instantly, his expression transforms. His smile dims, replaced with a frown. "What's wrong?" His forehead furrows. "Is it the presentation? Breathe, baby," he says, sliding his hands up and down my arms.

He called me baby.

I shake my head, refocusing my thoughts. "No. It's not that. I . . . God, I hate to do this, but I need a favor."

"Anything. Just name it."

My breath stalls, the words lodged in my throat.

In all the years since I had Sophie, I've never needed a favor from someone outside my parents, and even then, it's a rare exception.

But there's a first time for everything, and I can feel things changing with us like the shifting of sand through an hourglass. Maybe I don't rely on Teagan in the same way I would if he were Sophie's father. I don't need a paycheck, or for him to tuck her in at night. But there are other ways to rely on someone. Ways not tangible and hidden from the naked eye. I'm relying on Teagan to be there and show up, to *love* us.

A shockwave ripples through me at the revelation.

Because I love him; I know I do.

I don't know when or how it happened, but somewhere between the day he flashed me his dimpled smile and insisted he was going to be the best damn friend I could ever have and now, I've fallen for him.

I've just been too damn scared to admit it for fear the second I let my guard down, I'll get hurt.

My pulse races as the revelation settles in my bones because I have more pressing matters to handle right now.

Just say what you want, Lane. Ask for help.

"I need you to take Sophie to urgent care," I blurt.

His expression tightens with worry, his tone ominous as he asks, "Where is she? What happened?"

"She's at day care and she's okay, but she fell and needs stitches in her knee. If I don't get her, they'll take her by ambulance, and I hate the thought of her riding with strangers to the hospital. But if I do take her—"

"You miss your presentation. Don't worry, I got this."

He answers so quickly, it gives me pause, sure he doesn't understand. "But you'd have to go *now,* which means you'll miss your morning class."

"Lane," he gently presses his hands over my shoulders, "I said I've got it."

"Okay." I nod through the swell of guilt in my chest. "You're sure?"

"Positive. Even if I had practice, I'd leave to take her."

I blink, startled, and let the thought settle, somehow easing a little bit of the heaviness inside my chest. "You know I wouldn't be upset if you couldn't. I can just give my professor a doctor's note and hope he accepts it."

He shakes his head, his expression stony as he tightens his hands over my shoulders. "No way. You've been practicing your spiel all week and working on the presentation even longer. If you miss, you'll screw your grade. So, I'm going to grab Sophie and get her through the stitches like a pro while you ace your project."

My heart melts, and I start to move again. "I don't deserve you."

"You absolutely fucking do, but if you want to show me just how much you appreciate me, I can think of a few ways." He winks, and I bark out a laugh.

"I'll call Cindy from the center and let her know you'll be there. Here." I rummage in my bag for my keys, "Take my car, so you can use the car seat." I place them in his outstretched palm with a flutter of nerves. "You know where I park, but do you know where the day care is?"

"Outside Simon Hall," he says, already backing away. "It'll only take me two minutes to get there."

I bite my lip and he must see the worry churning in my gaze because he says, "I've got your girl, Lane. Don't even give it a second thought. Now get in there"—he nods at the hall—"and kick some presentation ass."

CHAPTER 34

TEAGAN

THE DOCTOR LEAVES THE exam room to grab a nurse and supplies before she stitches Sophie's knee, leaving me alone with her.

The scent of antiseptic and Clorox fills the air, stinging my nose. So far, Sophie has put on a brave face, but I can tell by the quivering of her chin and the fear in her eyes, she's two seconds away from a meltdown.

"Hey, you okay, kiddo?" I ask, taking her little hand in mine; it's so soft and small with little dimples at each knuckle.

Her little round face tips, and the trust I see in her eyes grips at my heart. "Is it gonna hurt?" she asks, lip curling like she might cry.

Fuck stitches. If I could take them for her, I would.

I squeeze her hand, trying my best to reassure her with a calm, steady tone. I don't want to scare her, but I also won't lie to her, either. "It's just going to be a tiny pinch, kind of like a bee sting, then the magic numbing medicine will work, and you won't feel anything."

"Is that what they did to your hand?" Her blue eyes drop, focusing on my bandaged hand.

"Sure is, except I'm a big boy, so I didn't take any magic numbing drops." Slowly, I remove the bandage and hold it out for her to see the dozen sutures in my palm. "A few of them are even starting to dissolve already."

She stares intently, then asks, "Does it hurt now?"

I shrug. "Not really. It's a little sore, but just because I think my hand is healing and it's ready for the stitches to start coming out."

Her brow furrows, and for a moment, I worry I said the wrong thing.

Should've just said no, asshole.

But then she bobs her little head, seemingly accepting this new information in stride. "Can I touch it?" she asks, blinking up at me.

"The stitches? Sure."

She reaches a tentative hand out and touches the sutures so lightly I barely feel it.

"See? Doesn't hurt at all." I nudge her with my knee. "And you wanna know the cool part about stitches?"

"What?" Her eyes brighten slightly, her expression earnest.

"You're going have the coolest scar after. Then everyone will know how tough you are, and you can tell them about the time you fell off the monkey bars onto a big, jagged rock."

Her brow furrows. "Do you have scars?"

"Sure do." I roll up the sleeve of my shirt, revealing a pink line just below my elbow.

"Wow. Did you fall off the monkey bars, too?" Sophie pokes it, and I can't help but laugh.

"Almost. It was a skateboard in my driveway." I grimace, leaving out the part where I was doing stupid tricks and goofing off. I'm lucky I didn't crack my head open.

A knock on the door interrupts us, and all the blood drains from Sophie's face, leaving her ashen. "Ready?" the doctor asks, pushing into the room with a nurse trailing behind her.

Sophie's small throat bobs, and her eyes glisten as they meet mine.

"You know what always helps me when I'm scared?" I ask, my stomach clenching into a fist.

"What?" her tiny voice wobbles as she watches the doctor prep her tools.

"Look at me, Soph." I snap a finger. "Look right here."

She turns her attention to me, brown curls bouncing.

"Just look at me the entire time, and if you're scared, squeeze my hand." She takes my hand and I motion with my other for the nurse and doctor to start. "That's what my mother used to tell me to do when I was little."

"Just a small pinch," the doctor warns.

"I'd just squeeze my mother's hand." The doctor moves in with the Lidocaine, and Sophie clenches my hand, her knuckles turning white while I continue, trying to distract her. "And it would help me to not be so scared anymore. I did that with the stitches near my elbow after I fell off my skateboard. Barely felt a thing. You know what else helps?"

Sophie shakes her head, her mouth tight.

"Ice cream," I say, deadpan. "Lots and lots of ice cream. Do you think after this we need to stop at The Frosty Cow?"

Sophie nods animatedly, and I pinch my lips together to fight a smile. "I bet I can eat more ice cream than you can," I taunt.

"No way!" Sophie shouts, accepting my words for the challenge they are. "I *love* ice cream."

I narrow my eyes like I don't believe her. "But do you love ice cream as much as I love pizza?"

"Yes. Definitely, yes!"

"Wow." My eyes round. "You must love it a lot."

"Chocolate peanut butter is my favorite."

I shake my head, eyes glistening. "You are a girl after my own heart because nothing, and I mean *nothing*, beats chocolate peanut butter. And The Frosty Cow has the best chocolate peanut butter ice cream I've ever tasted."

"Can I get it in a sugar cone?"

"Is the sky blue?" I scoff. "Of course you can!"

Sophie beams at the same time, I hear the snip of scissors and the doctor steps back. "All done."

I glance down to her knee at the same time the nurse places a giant bandage over the now-stitched wound.

"Done?" Sophie blinks, mouth agape.

"Yep. All done." The doctor smiles, glancing up at me. "Good job distracting her, Dad."

I carry Sophie in my arms out of the urgent care center and onto the sidewalk outside as we head to Lane's car. Maybe I'm being silly or overprotective, but I had to park a ways from the entrance and don't want her walking with her bum knee.

I shift her above my hip, taking care to not touch her knee while she prattles on about the prizes she got, and though I should be listening, I can't seem to focus on anything other than the doctor's words echoing inside my head.

Good job distracting her, Dad.

My heart clenches at the memory.

She called me Dad. *Dad.*

Until now, I hadn't thought about how Sophie and I might appear like a father-daughter duo to the outside world.

If Sophie noticed the doctor's blunder, she certainly didn't show it, which is just as well. I'm sure Lane would prefer to be the one to handle any conversations about Sophie's father, or lack thereof.

But that doesn't mean I can get the sound of it rolling off the doctor's tongue out of my mind.

Being mistaken for Sophie's father should make me uncomfortable. I'm only nineteen, a freshman in college. Six months ago, I was still living with my parents, partying with my friends back in Riverside, and generally acting like a jackass without a care in the world.

I'm not ready to be a father, or at least, I shouldn't be.

But instead of being freaked out at the prospect, the notion of being there for Sophie as her father turns my insides liquid. Everything inside of me melts at the thought. It's as if that single word has tipped my world on its axis because, the fact of the matter is, I love Lane. I'm head-over-heels, truly, deeply, and madly in love with her. And I love Sophie, too.

I'm fucking proud to be a part of their lives. I'm not afraid of what a serious relationship with Lane means or where it might lead. I'm not worried about going from zero to three-sixty because I'm already there.

From the moment I laid eyes on Lane Turner, before I realized she was the coach's daughter and a single mom, I knew.

She's it for me.

As crazy as it sounds, as quickly as our relationship has progressed, I know deep down that she's the one. And Sophie feels more like mine with every passing day.

I pause at the edge of the sidewalk, ready to cross the parking lot toward Lane's car when a voice calls out.

"Nichols?"

I grit my teeth and turn, all thoughts of Sophie and what the doctor said vanish as I curse my dumb luck. What the fuck are the odds of running into Chance Lockhart outside urgent care on a fucking Tuesday?

"Chance?" I angle myself toward him where he stands outside the pharmacy doors, assessing me through narrowed eyes.

His gaze flickers from me to Sophie, then back again as he draws closer. "What are you doing here?"

"Just handling a cut on Sophie's knee."

"I got stitches," Sophie announces proudly, then resumes playing with her prizes.

"We have game film in thirty," Chance says.

The muscle in my jaw twitches. "Good thing I'm only ten minutes from campus, then."

He stares at me for a moment, his gaze cold, expression stony. Stepping to my side, his shoulder pressed to mine, he whispers, "Just what the fuck are you doing here, Nichols?"

"I told you—"

"You know what I mean," he hisses so Sophie can't hear. "Fucking around with Lane, taking her daughter to the doctor. What are you getting at?"

I meet his eyes, my gaze calculated. "Are you threatened, Lockhart?"

The vein in his forehead bulges, and I see a flicker of something in his expression that tells me I hit my target. "Why don't you stop worrying about everybody else and focus on yourself, huh?" I clap a hand over his shoulder, mostly because I know it'll piss him off. "Lane's a big girl. She can handle herself."

Before he can say anything else, I step off the sidewalk into the parking lot with Chance's voice at my back. "You don't know what you're doing here, Nichols."

I wave at him and keep walking, thankful for the girl in my arms. If not for her, I'd be in his face, doing a lot more than giving him lip.

Hell, I'd probably do something I'd come to regret and earn myself a warm spot on the bench come Saturday.

There's something I fucking hate about that guy.

My phone rings, breaking through my thoughts, and I check the screen to see Lane's name. Grateful for the reprieve, I press the speaker button and hold it out as we approach her car.

"It's your mom," I whisper to Sophie, before I say into the phone, "Sophie's driving service, can I help you?"

Sophie giggles in my arms.

"Are you still there?" Lane asks, sounding slightly harried and out of breath.

"Lane?"

"Yeah?"

"Breathe," I remind her.

"Right. Sorry." Lane pauses, and this time when she speaks, her voice is steadier, stronger. "So, how did it go?"

"It went really well. She's all sewn up. Took her stitches like a champ."

"And I'm gonna have a scar!" Sophie yells so Lane can hear.

"See? You hear that? She's gonna have the coolest of scars."

Lane lets out a breathy laugh. "You're amazing."

My heart flips inside my chest. "Maybe just a little."

"I'm serious." Her voice is a throaty rasp, a bedroom voice—the kind that makes me wish she were here and I could have her alone. "Teagan, thank you."

"It's no problem. I was glad to help. How'd your presentation go?"

"The first couple of minutes were a little shaky because my mind was on Sophie, but after that . . . I think I nailed it."

"Thatta girl." I smile, and my thoughts drift back to Chance.

A glance at the sidewalk confirms he's gone, but I can't help but feel like I should mention it to her.

"Where are you headed now?" she asks, breaking through my thoughts.

"Uh . . ." I purse my lips, glancing down at Sophie as I debate telling her now or later that we're getting ice cream before lunch.

"The Frosty Cow!" Soph screams.

"You little turncoat." I laugh, mouth open.

"Did she say—"

"Okay, so I might've promised her ice cream on the way back to campus as a bribe to be brave, but it worked, so I think I should get a pass."

"Just don't eat too much." Lane laughs, and I'm relieved she's not pissed about me feeding Sophie dessert before an actual meal.

She's exactly the kind of loving, laid-back yet firm parent I'd want for children of my own.

Shit.

Did I really just think that?

I just got out of the friend zone, and here I am, already planning my fucking future with this girl.

I shake my head at myself and when I set Sophie on her feet, Chance Lockhart is the furthest thing from my mind.

CHAPTER 35

LANE

I LEAN AGAINST THE archway to the living room of the lake house where Teagan lounges on the brand-new couch that was delivered just this afternoon, courtesy of my parents as a housewarming gift. His broad shoulders and long arms spread over the back of the couch, the remnants of the take-out pizza I ordered on the second-hand coffee table I scored at a flea market last month.

With his gaze fixed on the television, he laughs at an old rerun of *The Office* while I ponder how normal this feels, having him here. After practice, he stopped by for dinner and a movie, then spent the majority of the last hour painting Sophie's nails a bright pink and playing dinosaurs.

Talking, dinner, and Sophie's bedtime, all of those ordinary things are made extraordinary just by his presence.

I clear my throat and he glances my way. "Hey," he says, a smile curving his lips.

I nod toward the hallway. "She was hoping you'd tuck her in, say good night."

"Absolutely." He rises, drawing closer and towering above me as he grabs my hand and walks with me down the hallway toward her bedroom.

Pausing just outside, I let him go in while I wait beside her doorway, head against the wall as I listen to him tell her good night. "Sweet dreams, Sweet Sophie," he murmurs, and my heart swells.

A rustling sound followed by footsteps signals his approach, and when he steps out into the hallway and shuts her door behind him, I soak him in.

He's all tousled blond curls, tan skin, seaside eyes, and dimpled smiles.

God, he's beautiful.

And my little girl is every bit as smitten as I am.

The thought should scare me, but somehow it doesn't. Not anymore. Not like it did.

"The kid had quite the day," he says, leaning back against the wall across from me, tucking his hands into the pockets of his gray sweats. "I think she'll be out in minutes."

I hum in response as I glance down at the monitor, then turn it toward him, so he can see. "I think maybe she already is."

He chuckles, a soft rumble I can feel vibrating in my chest even though we're feet apart.

"Thank you again for today," I whisper, not wanting to wake Soph. "You have no idea how much your help meant to me."

He offers me a lazy shrug. "No big deal."

"It's a big deal to me," I say.

Tell him you love him.

The voice inside my head startles me, and I swallow, my throat dry.

I'd known my feelings had been on a downward spiral for quite some time now, but to have them intrude so suddenly shakes me.

Heart pumping wildly in my chest, I debate my options, but my tongue is leaden, too heavy to speak as Teagan curls a finger, beckoning me forward. "Come here."

I suck in a breath, then close the gap between us without hesitation, coming to stand directly in front of him.

His hands lift, trailing his fingertips up my arm, over the delicate skin of my collarbone to either side of my neck before sinking into my hair at the base of my skull.

I whimper, a shiver racking through me at his touch.

Nerves coil in my stomach, a viper waiting to strike as his gaze flickers to my mouth.

I rise on my toes, knowing what comes next and not wanting to wait another minute to have his mouth on mine.

His hands tighten in my hair as he dips his head, and our lips meet. Fingers gently press into my scalp as his tongue brushes the seam of my lips, begging for entrance, and I open for him at the same time, he spins me around and pins me against the wall all while his mouth claims me.

He takes his time, angling my head and deepening the kiss while my heart beats wildly.

His tongue glides against mine, tasting and coaxing me into submission before he lowers his mouth, lips skimming over my jaw.

I bite down to stifle the moan threatening to erupt from my chest while my hands slide beneath his shirt. Hot skin meets my palms, and his abdominals clench under my touch before he grinds his hips to mine.

"Sometimes I think you're too good to be true," I confess.

He grunts, his lips and tongue hot on my skin as he continues his perusal, scraping his teeth over my collarbone, my neck, before he lifts his head to meet my hooded gaze. "I'm very much real, Lane, and I'm here, right where I want to be. With you." He leans his forehead against mine, his breathing ragged. "And if I'm too good to be true, then so are you. You have no idea how fucking special you are."

I exhale a breath as his lips lower, brushing over mine slowly before releasing me again. He makes it so hard not to believe him that he almost has me convinced. Somehow, I'm worthy of this man.

Everything about the time in-between the day when we met in the park and now has been perfect.

"Teagan . . ."

I love you. I almost say it, the words on the tip of my tongue, but I stop them. For reasons I can't explain, I hold them back.

I suck in a breath when he tugs my earlobe with his teeth before whispering, "You know I'd do anything for you, don't you?"

I nod, breathless as I shiver under his touch. "Yes."

"I want you to feel safe with me, Lane." He presses his body into mine, his hips grinding, the hard length of him against my hip sending a ball liquid fire from my stomach south.

"I do," I say, realizing I mean it.

I feel safe with Teagan in a way I never thought I would with a man.

Closing my eyes, I meet his lips once more, drowning in the sensation of his mouth, his touch.

His hands slide beneath my shirt and when he unclasps my bra, I moan.

He grunts in approval as one hand comes around me to palm my breast, and I exhale a shaky breath, so turned on I can't think through the pounding of blood in my ears.

"Tell me what you want from me, Lane, and it's yours," he whispers over my lips.

"I want you," I choke out. "*All* I want is you."

He shifts his hand to my other breast and rolls his hips into mine with a groan. "You already have me."

His mouth moves to my neck, and when his hands retreat from beneath my shirt, I mourn the loss until he's lifting me up, scooping my hips to straddle him as he walks us back into the living room toward the couch.

A hiss of pain wheezes through his lips at the same time he stumbles. "Shit. Fuck."

He loses his footing, somehow managing not to drop me while hopping on one leg. "Fucking Spinosaurus," he growls.

I glance down at the floor to see one of Sophie's dinosaurs, and laughter erupts from my chest as Teagan struggles to regain his footing.

"You think that's funny, do you?" he asks, a glint of humor in his eyes.

I clutch my stomach with my hands, trying to contain my laughter. "Kind of."

"I could drop you, you know." He arches a brow, and I run a hand through his hair, lacing my fingers through his curls.

"You wouldn't," I murmur.

He lowers his head and sucks my lips into his mouth, and I gasp. "No. You're right. I wouldn't. I'll never let you down."

My heart cartwheels when his lips meet mine.

He just barely sidesteps a spike-backed stegosaurus before lowering me to the couch. My legs wrap around his waist while the delicious weight of him presses into me, and my tongue finds the hollow of his throat.

A raspy moan splits the silence encouraging me to move my hands between us where I grab the hem of his shirt and tug.

Sitting back on his haunches, Teagan helps me, ripping his T-shirt off in a single motion and tossing it to the floor before

I fumble with the waistband of his pants, too shaky to make quick work of them.

His hand clamps over mine, a tremulous breath escaping him as he meets my eyes. "Are you sure?"

I nod fervently, then reach up to nip on his lower lip, tugging with my teeth, watching as he closes his eyes and groans. "Positive."

He blinks, searching my eyes for the truth. "But are you really, really—"

I press a finger to his lips, silencing him. "I'm sure."

He only hesitates a moment before he growls. "Thank fuck."

He lets go of my hand, and I shove his pants off his hips before he sinks on top of me, the delicious weight of him pressing me into the cushions.

His hands spear into my hair and he claims my mouth, kissing me until I'm dizzy. Kissing me until the world spins and everything leading up until this moment seems inconsequential, like a distant memory because this is where we were always meant to be, here, in each other's arms. I'm sure of it. Sure of *him*.

My heart pounds so hard against my ribs, I fear they might crack as I move beneath him, wanting him closer, wanting him inside of me.

I moan when I can't get close enough, and Teagan's mouth retreats.

"What's wrong? Do you want me to slow down?" he asks, lifting his head, breathless. "I don't want to rush with you, Lane, but my body and my brain are on two separate tracks."

"No." I shake my head, pulling him back to me.

"Because we can take our time. We can—"

"A lot less talking, and a lot more doing," I say, my patience waning.

I want Teagan more than anything I've wanted in my entire life.

One hand drops, cupping my breast, and I whimper, arching into him.

I feel his grin against my mouth. "Damn, baby, you're sexy."

He called me baby. And sexy.

I shiver, goose bumps covering my skin at the gravelly sound of his voice. Every inch of my body heats as he unbuttons my blouse and pushes my bra off my shoulders, then lowers his mouth.

I gasp, writhing beneath him.

My entire body pulses, a pressure building within me as his hands move south. He lifts his hips, sliding down my jeans, my panties, until I can feel every glorious inch of him pressed hard against me.

"Shit. I'm not prep—"

"My purse," I mumble. "Kitchen table."

He pushes up on his arms, holding his weight off me as he stares into my eyes, and I know what he's thinking. I can read it on his face. He's surprised I planned for this, considering I refused letting him into my heart for so long.

Inevitable, I want to tell him.

You and I, we were always inevitable.

He presses another soft kiss to my mouth and stands while my eyes rake him in, and I blush.

He is . . .

He disappears into the kitchen, then returns, purse in hand.

. . . fucking incredible.

I take my purse and pull out the little foil packet, then hand it to him.

But instead of rushing to take it, Teagan cages me between his arms. He stares down at me between his muscled biceps, dropping a slow, gentle kiss to my lips before retreating once more. "You're magnificent."

My throat bobs.

He brushes the hair from my face, cupping my jaw in one of his large, calloused hands. "So fucking magnificent," he whispers again. "Every single thing about you. Your heart." He drops a kiss to the center of my chest. "Your mind." He brushes his lips over my forehead, and I shiver. "Your body." His eyes darken, and he takes my breast into his mouth while I arch against him. "Your kindness," he murmurs, against my skin.

"The way you are with Sophie," he whispers into the shell of my ear. "Your loyalty. Your strength." He leans up again and shakes his head, his brow furrowed. "You're so fucking strong, Lane."

Reaching out, he traces my lower lip with his thumb. "I wish you could see what I see," he whispers. "Because if you even saw half the woman I do, you'd never doubt your worth a day in your life."

My eyes fill with tears, until he blurs above me, a living watercolor. A masterpiece.

I open my mouth to speak, but all that escapes is a whimper.

I swallow over the lump in my throat, trying again, saying the only three words I can say at this moment because if I don't, they might burst from my chest.

"I love you," I murmur, pulling him flush against me. "I love you, Teagan Nichols."

His eyes widen, his breath catching as he stares down at me as if afraid I might take it back. He blinks, and then his eyes soften. "I love you more."

He drops his mouth to mine, and I push his boxer briefs off while the crinkling of foil fills my ears.

Anticipation balloons in my chest as the weight of his body lessens for a moment, never breaking contact with his mouth as we kiss, before he lowers himself once more and I arch against him.

His hands find my body, exploring, touching me everywhere before he chases each caress of his calloused hand with his mouth.

My breath fills my ears.

My heart soars.

Hips buck. The pressure inside me yearns for release as he hovers above me, close but not close enough.

Sliding his hands up my arms, he pins them above my head while his hips roll, and I gasp. "You're mine, Lane Turner."

I nod, unable to speak through the sensations rippling through me and the glorious pressure of his hips.

"Say it," he growls. "Say you're mine."

His mouth finds my neck, his breath hot and his tongue even hotter as he tastes me inch by inch, scraping his teeth over my skin as he reaches my breasts.

"I'm . . ." I trail off, shaking my head. I can't think let alone speak.

I don't even know what the fuck I'm saying as his free hand slides between us and my eyes flutter closed. Sensation consumes me as his fingers find their target.

"Say it," he says again, tone husky.

My thighs clench. "I'm . . . I'm yours," I choke out.

Every single part of me belongs to this man and him to me.

He lifts his head, approval in his hooded eyes. "Good girl," he growls as he rocks against me, hand still firmly in place, still torturing and teasing.

I cry out and he presses his palm to my mouth, stifling the sound.

And just when I think I can't take anymore, he pushes into me and takes me over the edge.

CHAPTER 36

TEAGAN

THE SOUND OF THE shower switching on in the other room coaxes a smile out of me.

It's late, half past one in the morning, and I'm probably a glutton for punishment because I only have about four and half hours until I need to be up for conditioning.

Still, I can't bring myself to regret tonight if I tried.

Being with Lane was everything I thought it would be and then some. Like cracking a code or solving an impossible puzzle, Lane and I just . . . *fit*.

And she loves me.

I shake my head at the thought, my grin spreading.

We spent the better part of the past four hours memorizing each other's bodies, and when we weren't doing that, we talked.

We talked and we laughed and we kissed, until the kissing turned into more and we stopped talking entirely.

With a contented sigh, I grab my sweats from the living room by the couch, slip them on, then return to Lane's bedroom where I settle onto the makeshift bed on the floor, resigning myself to having a sore back in the morning since Lane has yet to buy bedroom furniture.

Fuck. Maybe I'll buy her a bedroom suite and surprise her with it.

If I have any say in it, I'll be spending a lot of time helping her break it in, so I might as well be the one to buy it.

Inspired, I reach for my phone on the stack of boxes beside me to search nearby furniture places when I knock one of them to the floor.

Shit.

I sit up, stretching to pick up the contents of the box, which I quickly realize contains photographs and mementos, snippets of Lane's life, such as a baby's knit cap and a tiny sock I assume belonged to Sophie. Movie stubs. A school photo of a younger Lane with a toothy grin.

Smiling, I scoop a pile of pictures into my hands and place them back in the box, pausing when I start to close it as one of them catches my eye.

I hold my breath as I pluck it out from where it's wedged partially beneath a few others, and a chill skitters down my spine.

My smile fades, hands instantly shaking as I stare at the photograph, half expecting it to change like it's merely a figment of my fucked-up imagination. But when I inhale through my nose, count to ten, and blink twice, it's the same two faces staring back at me—a younger version of Chance and Lane.

Both of them are smiling, with Chance's hand wrapped around her waist, and though there's nothing incriminating—it could be any two friends or a family member—it's not their proximity to each other or even the hand gripping her waist that makes my stomach churn. It's the look in her eyes that eats me alive. Because neither of them are looking at the camera. Instead, they're staring into each other's eyes. And the expression on Lane's face is so intimate and so filled with longing, it makes my heart ache.

I lie in the dark, head pressed into a pillow as I hear the sound of Lane's bedroom door creek.

I close my eyes, pretending to sleep as she settles onto the blankets beside me.

Pressing her body next to mine, she snakes her arms around my waist, propping her chin on my shoulder. "You awake?"

I focus on the steady rhythm of my breath in the silence, feeling like the world's biggest asshole for pretending to be asleep when I'm not, but I can't open my eyes. I can't turn to face her. Not when my head hurts and my chest feels like it might explode.

After a moment, she lays her head down on the pillows beside me, and relief washes over me before it's replaced with the icy fingers of fear.

Chance and Lane.

Lane and Chance.

I can't seem to erase the picture from my head. No matter how hard I try, it's right there, dancing behind my eyelids.

I clench my hands beneath the blankets until my fists ache as bad as my heart, as if I can erase the image of them with the pain.

Surely if there had ever been anything between them, she would have told me.

I love her, and she loves me. I'd know it even if she hadn't said it.

We've been intimate.

She trusts me now.

Or at least, I thought she did.

But the more I think about it, the more doubt creeps in.

The memory of how pissed Chance was when he saw us together for the first time. Purposely fucking with me during games by switching up plays. The booze bottle in my locker. Showing up on Halloween in my place. Calling last-minute meetings when he knows she and I are together.

The confrontation today on the sidewalk.

Suddenly, it all makes sense.

It's not like I've advertised to her the shit Chance has given me, but if he and Lane were ever together, it certainly explains his behavior.

My thoughts take an immediate detour to Knox and despite my best intentions, I can't help but compare him to Lane. All these years we were friends, and I had no idea he was really the enemy. All the years I thought I knew him but never really did.

This is different, I tell myself.

Not if she lied.

My stomach roils. I don't even know Lane is hiding anything. I'm probably just a jealous asshole, reacting to a stupid photograph for no reason. Maybe I'm reading into the picture, seeing things that aren't there. Maybe Lane had a crush on Chance when they were younger. As much as I fucking hate the idea, it's not out of the realm of possibility. And it's certainly not a crime, nor is it an indictment.

I need to get a grip and calm the fuck down. Get some sleep.

Maybe everything will look differently in the morning.

Maybe I'll realize I have nothing to worry about.

I'm letting my exhaustion get the better of me.

All I can do now is close my eyes tighter and pray for sleep.

CHAPTER 37

TEAGAN

I INHALE, PREPARING MYSELF to face Lane.

Sleep did little to ease the anxiety gnawing on my chest. If anything, it intensified as if the passing of time somehow confirmed what I saw.

I'm standing outside Lane's front door after waking in her bedroom, only to find a note asking me to sneak out and knock because Sophie thinks I'm coming for breakfast.

I know she just doesn't want to confuse Sophie. Explaining why I spent the night with a child's mother isn't on my top ten of things I ever want to fucking do.

But with the photo fresh in my mind, I can't help but feel like an afterthought, a mistake.

You're being ridiculous.

Lifting my fist, I knock on the door and wait as I hear footsteps from within. A minute later, a beaming Sophie swings open the door. "Mom's making bacon!"

I grin and my heart does a slow roll as she reaches out to grab my hand and drags me inside to where Lane stands in front of the stove, a gorgeous smile lighting up her whole face.

"Hey." I lift a chin and smother the anxiety ballooning in my chest when I realize I'm squeezing Sophie's hand a little too tight.

Exhaling, I force myself to relax, telling myself, once again, that it's just a picture. Probably nothing. I'd asked her from the start if she and Chance ever dated and she said no at a time when she had no reason to lie to me.

But a picture's worth a thousand words...

My free hand clenches.

Lane turns and reaches out, drawing me into a hug which feels a little like she's holding me together. "Hi, again," she whispers in my ear.

My face falls to the top of her head and I inhale, breathing in the floral scent of her shampoo. I could get high off this scent, but instead of soothing my nerves, it only amplifies them.

She draws back and cups my face in her hands, and I don't even have to force a smile; it comes all on its own. Lane draws the best out of me every fucking time.

"Glad you could join us for breakfast."

"Uh, yeah, sure. No problem."

"You're lucky little Sophie, here, never sleeps in," she says, pointing at her with a spatula. Then she leans into me again and whispers, "I wish I could kiss you right now."

"Me too," I choke out. So fucking much; she has no idea.

"Hungry?" She spins around and checks the bacon, then begins to pile it on a paper plate lined with napkins. "I know football works up an appetite," she says with a wink.

"Starving." I rub a hand over my stomach despite the heaviness in my chest. "I did a little extra conditioning last night."

"Is that so?" Lane arches a brow, then turns and sets the plate of bacon on the table and grins, a mischievous glint in her eyes. "Well, then you better eat up because I sense *a lot* of extra conditioning in your future."

Her cheeks flush, and the smile she gives me is so genuine, her gaze so soft, I can almost convince myself my fears are nothing more than a result of an overactive imagination.

Almost.

Me

I need one of you to tell me I'm fucking crazy.

Jace

You're fucking crazy. There. You're welcome.

Graham

I can get on board with this assessment.

Atlas

I sense this has to do with Lane.

Chris

Because in the end women make us all fucking crazy? I concur.

Me

No. I need you to tell me I'm fucking crazy after I explain why I'm fucking crazy. Otherwise, it's a moot point.

Jace

sigh

Me

I found a picture of Lane and Chance Lockhart, and it looked . . . I don't know, intimate?

Chris

Oh, shit. Was it a nude?

Me

NO, IT WASN'T A FUCKING NUDE!

Chris

Whoa. No need to yell. In my defense, you said it looked intimate.

Graham

You seem stressed.

Atlas

Highly.

Jace

So, we've established they were clothed and you're stressed. Were they kissing?

Me

No.

Jace

In bed but clothed?

Me

NO! Look, it wasn't anything so incriminating. They were just staring into each other's eyes and smiling. But she looked fucking in love with him, okay?

There. I said it.

And it doesn't feel any fucking better voicing my thoughts than it did by holding them in.

Jace

Oh, shit.

Atlas

Ouch.

Graham

> Staring longingly into each other's eyes is worse than a kiss. So, you think they used to be an item or what?

Me

> I don't know. I asked her about it shortly after we met, and she led me to believe they've never been romantic. In my head, I kept thinking she'd told me no, but I've given it a lot of fucking thought since yesterday afternoon and realized she sort of brushed off the question.

I inhale and pinch the bridge of my nose as I recall the photograph. I wasn't imagining the chemistry between them or the affection in Lane's eyes. No way. Just remembering her lovestruck expression makes my stomach pitch.

An unbidden thought rises to the surface of my mind.

I try to shove it down, but it's like a fucking buoy, rising to the surface no matter how much I hold it back.

I grip my phone tighter and stare at the screen.

Just type it.

Fucking ask.

Then they can tell you you're crazy, and you can move on.

My heart lurches in my throat as my fingers move over the keypad of my phone, and I punch out the question before I can stop myself and hit send.

Me

What if he's Sophie's father?

Atlas

Oh fuck.

Chris

Damn. If that's her baby daddy, you're toast. He's so much better than all of us.

Jace

Hey, speak for yourself, fucker.

Graham

Do you really think that's a possibility?

Me

I mean, he was around then.

Jace

What did she tell you about the father?

Me

Early on, she told me he was from out of state and attending one of her father's summer football camps before her senior year. They had a summer romance, and she never saw him again.

I give it some more consideration and her explanation doesn't sit well with me.

Now that I think about it, Lane isn't the type to have a fling. She's conservative. Thoughtful. A rule follower. It doesn't jive that she would fall for someone that quickly and jump into bed with them. It would make more sense if she knew the father for a lot longer.

Fuck.

Okay, but what reason would she have to lie?

I exhale, running a hand over the back of my neck while I think.

Why *would* she lie?

To protect Chance? That didn't seem right.

Every time I've seen them interact, she's made it clear there's no love lost there, at least on her end. So, it doesn't make sense she'd hide paternity for his sake.

There has to be another reason. One I'm not seeing.

Are you sure you're not just being para-noid?

Or, there's that.

Me

I don't know. Maybe?

Graham

Jealousy can be a bitch. I know from personal experience. LOL

Jace

Except you were right to be jealous.

Graham

Fucker.

Atlas

In all seriousness, that'd be a pretty big secret to keep if her father and Lockhart are as tight as you say.

Graham

And even if they did date, it doesn't make him the father.

Me

You're right.

A wave of relief crashes over me. I'm being paranoid, a jealous prick.

Me

Damn. I feel like I'm losing my fucking mind. What's wrong with me?

Jace

You're in love with her.

Chris

He would know. Ask him how nuts he was when he was fighting his feelings for Brynn. LOL! Fucking hilarious.

Jace

Dick.

Atlas

Am I the only one paying attention? Dude's been in love with her since the moment he met her.

Graham

True. He went from happy and single to stepfather in minutes.

Jace

Bahahaha!

I roll my eyes as I imagine them snickering behind their screens.

Me

Fuck off.

Jace

Dude, just talk to her, man. You probably just got jealous when you saw the pic, but chances are it's nothing. If

I lift my head from my phone and click it off because they're right. I need to talk to her. Come right out and ask her.

Even if Sophie's father is the one thing I promised never to talk about, the one thing she said is off-limits.

CHAPTER 38

LANE

Though Tuesday got off to a rough start, the next couple of days fly by despite barely having any time to see Teagan. So I'm particularly thrilled when he enters the basement of Wyndham Hall where I've begun working on the team's practice gear.

After the perfect night we spent together, I've been dying to see him again, and the few stolen moments we've had between classes aren't enough. With only a month left in the semester, schoolwork is ramping up and deadlines are approaching, which means he's taking advantage of any spare time he has to catch up with assignments while my nights have been busy picking out renovation materials for the lake house.

Everything in my life seems to be coming together, and I can't help but step back in the rare quiet moments and look at my life in awe. It's like all at once, my dreams have been answered. Dreams I didn't dare to wish for, like falling in love.

Scratch that.

Because I've already fallen.

I am completely and hopelessly in love with him, and he loves me.

I hadn't planned on telling him so soon but I couldn't help myself, and my heart squeezes every time I think about hearing him say those words.

"Hey, stranger." I turn to him with a smile and sigh as he pulls me close, then cups my face in his hands and leans into me, thighs touching, heart pounding in tune with mine. He brushes a soft kiss against my mouth. That's one of the things I love about Teagan; he kisses with his whole body, not just his lips.

Butterflies awaken, floating through my chest even as he takes a step back and says "hey" in a tone that sounds *off*.

"Big game this weekend," I say, wondering if that's what's weighing on his mind.

Teagan exhales, releasing a fraction of the tension I see in his face. "Yeah. Florida State. It's gonna be a tough one."

"You'll win. I know it."

He nods and the muscle in his jaw flickers before he asks, "You'll be there?"

"It's a home game, so I wouldn't miss it for the world." I smile back at him, but his throat bobs, and I wonder if he's nervous about something else or if it really is just the game.

"Can I ask you something?"

My brows rise but instead of meeting my eyes, he avoids my gaze and steps forward, taking one of the jerseys I finished scrubbing to wring it out. "Sure," I say, ignoring the uneasy feeling fisting at the base of my spine.

"You said Sophie's dad isn't in the picture, right?"

I stiffen and my defenses rise like a drawbridge over water. "I think you've been around enough to know that for a fact."

"Yeah," he says, but his tone and the way he chews his lower lip tells he's not convinced. "Do you ever see him anymore or talk to him?"

Ice chinks in my veins as I try to wrap my head around the sudden line of questioning and the timing of it all when it's the one topic I told him was off-limits.

"Why are you asking now? What is this really about, Teagan?"

He leans forward, gripping the edge of the plastic wash bin while the muscles in his arms and back flex. "I just . . ." He trails off, lifting his head and finally turning to me. "I told you early on that the one thing I couldn't take is you withholding the truth or lying to me about—"

"I'm not lying. He really *isn't* a part of our lives."

"Okay, but—"

"Do you *think* I'm lying?" My voice rises an octave, and the guilt swimming in my veins colors my cheeks. "Because if you do, I'd appreciate it if you just came right out and asked what you really want to know instead of beating around the bush, because I told you all of this already."

"Fine." His nostrils flare and he pushes his shoulders back as he asks, "Were you and Chance ever together?"

My heart flies into my throat and I swallow, trying to dislodge it.

I should tell him the truth. I know I should.

I love him.

I want him in my life, which means complete transparency. We can't build a future off lies, but I can't bring myself to form the words any more than I can change the truth, though God knows I wish I could.

"No," I choke out.

I justify the lie by rationalizing. In reality, Chance and I never really *were* together. I spent the better part of a year after I found out I was pregnant coming to terms with the fact that what I thought we had was all a lie, a figment of my imagination, and a product of the fanciful whims of a teenager with a crush.

He stares at me for a long moment while I prepare for him to call my bluff, but he doesn't. "Okay. And Sophie's father is . . ."

"I already told you." I throw the wet jersey in my hands onto the counter with a loud thwack, angry he won't just let it drop even though I have zero right to be. "Just like I told you this was the one topic off-limits, my hard no. I won't talk about him. He's not a part of our lives, and that's all anyone needs to know."

Including you.

My unspoken words are louder than the ones coming from my mouth, and I hate myself for them.

Teagan grips at his hair, and the pain on his face is so acute, it makes my chest ache. "I can't help but feel like there's this giant shoe waiting to drop. Like there's something I'm missing. Maybe I'm crazy to think Chance might have—"

"Yeah, you are." I scoff.

Liar.

Liar.

Liar.

"It's just that he's been fucking with me, and the other day in your room, I saw a picture of the two of you and—"

I suck in a breath. "You were looking through my things?"

"I wasn't snooping, if that's what you're asking. The box fell and everything spilled onto the floor. I was picking the photo albums up when I saw it."

I should've burned any pictures I had of the two of us long ago. God, why didn't I?

"You know he and my father are close. In high school, he was around a lot. We were friends once."

He stares at me for a long moment. "You're right," he eventually says, running a hand over the back of his neck. My chest tightens. "But I guess I just don't understand this need to keep the paternity a secret." His gaze hardens when it returns to mine. Did her father—did he force himself on you? Is that why—"

"No." My mouth drops open in shock. "God, no. Nothing like that." My hands ball into fists, fighting the tightening in my chest. "Looking back, I think he manipulated me, told me everything I wanted to hear, but he would never . . . He may be selfish, but he's not *that* kind of man."

"Then, what, Lane?" He steps forward, arms outstretched, tone pleading. "Help me understand why you can't open up to me." He reaches out and grabs my hand and places it on his chest, over his racing heart. "I'm the one person you should be able to trust the most, and I've never given you a reason to doubt me."

"Because I just can't," I cry.

But God knows I want to.

And that should be enough. It should be that simple.

But somehow, it's not.

I yank my hand away, unable to touch him any longer, afraid the guilt might kill me if I do.

My limbs shake with the flood of emotions running through my veins, and I begin to pace. I feel like a trapped animal, wounded and bleeding and *scared*. Unable to quell the strangling fingers gripping my lungs and strangling the air from them.

"I love you, Lane. And I love Sophie, too."

His words strike like lightning.

It's the second time he's said them, but my heart jolts all the same because I love him, too. So much.

Yet I feel him slipping from my fingers. And I know how to hold on, but it's like I can't physically do it. I can't give him the one thing he wants, the one thing he needs—the truth.

Instead, I convince myself that's okay. He doesn't need it. We can survive on lies if they're well-intentioned.

"I love you too," I say, my voice thick.

Tears prick at my eyes, and I shake my head as if that will shake them off. My gaze drifts to his mouth, those full lips I know so well.

He closes the gap between us, reaching me in two strides. One hand cups the back of my head while the other squeezes my waist as if he's afraid of losing me even though I'm standing right here.

He dips his head, pressing his forehead to mine.

I hear the shallow sound of his breath, his audible swallow. "Say it again, Lane? *Please.*"

"I love you." I breathe.

I'd say it a million times over if he asked.

This I can give him.

This one truth I can share.

"I love you, Teagan. I love you so much it hurts. Why can't that be enough?"

He sucks in a breath and releases me, scrubbing a hand over his face. When his eyes return to mine, the pain in them is so sharp I feel it lance through me like a knife. "Are you ever gonna tell me?"

My heart lurches.

Fear bubbles inside me, warring with my anger as we stand there, locked in each other's eyes. Both of us battering rams with our horns locked.

"I told you in the beginning. You *knew* this topic was off-limits." I cross my arms over my chest as if I can protect my heart from the blow I know is coming. "And you agreed. It's unfair of you to push me now when you understood from the start."

"I know. You're right. But feelings change." His shoulders slump, whether in defeat or resignation, I'm not sure. "And I guess I just don't understand why you're protecting him."

"I'm *not* protecting him," I snap.

I'm protecting someone else—my father.

And I owe my parents *everything*.

"Well, you're protecting someone, and if it's not him then it's yourself, which means you don't trust me. I've done nothing but lay my heart on the line since I met you, proven myself to you over and over, but you still don't trust me."

He takes another step back in retreat, his blue eyes wet with emotion.

As selfish as it is, all I want is for him to wrap his arms around me and tell me that it's okay. That he doesn't need to know. That I can keep this *one thing* and he'll still love me.

"It's not that simple," I say, desperate for him to stay.

He lets out a shaky breath and averts his gaze. "See that's the thing," he replies. "It really is." And then he walks away.

CHAPTER 39

LANE

I PRESS ONE LAST kiss to Sophie's head, then quietly make my way to the door where a sliver of light from the hallway spills inside the entryway to her room. Turning, I take a moment to watch her curled up in bed, eyes closed, lashes fanning against her chubby cheeks.

The slow rise and fall of her chest and the steady sound of her breath tells me she's already asleep, which is no surprise. With me working for the team, our nights are later than they used to be. By the time I get her home and fed and in bed, it's past her bedtime. Add in weekends at the lake prepping the house, and our weekly routine with Teagan at Slice, she's exhausted most nights.

I bite my lip at the thought of Teagan.

She asked for him today, wanted to know if she'd get to see him after practice, but I had to tell her no.

After our argument this afternoon, I knew he wouldn't want to see me.

Maybe he's done with us entirely.

I swallow over the pain this thought causes.

I thought about our argument for the rest of the day. When Teagan and I first met, I couldn't tell him the truth about Chance. It was too soon. I didn't trust him yet, and I needed to get my bearings.

At the time, the identity of Sophie's father felt like an insignificant detail. Chance wasn't a part of our lives or our future, so he didn't matter.

But now, it feels so much bigger than that.

My head has caught up with my heart.

Would I stick around if I knew Teagan was keeping something from me? If he told me there was a piece of him he could never share with me, but asked me to trust him, anyway?

I know I wouldn't.

Yet I somehow, I expect—*hope*—that he will.

But what if he decides I'm not worth the hassle or the energy it takes to love me? As crazy as it sounds, when I see my future, I see him in it. I *want* him in it. My stomach clenches at the thought of losing him to this.

How can we withstand all the coming storms with this divide between us?

I want Teagan in my present, but I want him in my future even more. Which means I need to tell him the truth.

I inhale a shaky breath and pause in front of the doors to The Buzzy Bean.

A patron leaves, sending the nutty scent of coffee wafting toward me while I fight for the courage to step inside those doors.

I'd planned on seeking Teagan out today and apologizing. But he beat me to the punchline with a text already waiting for me when I woke, asking if we could meet for a coffee before conditioning—*alone.*

My stomach sinks as I wonder for the hundredth time in the past hour if this is it, the moment he finally crushes my heart beneath his palm. It's the moment I've feared since the day I met him, because I knew, even then, he had the capability to make me fall. And with that comes the power to unravel me completely.

I shake out my hands, then take a deep breath; I can't stall any longer.

If he's going to dump me, I'm just delaying the inevitable, and it doesn't matter whether it happens now or an hour from now, it'll hurt all the same.

My feet carry me inside the coffee shop, but the usual buzz I get simply from the smell of the coffee and pastries is absent. Instead, I search for him with what feels like a water buffalo sitting on my chest. And when I spot him at a small table by the window, my heart kick starts, a revving engine rumbling to life, before I remember why I'm here and that I have no idea what he wants to say.

I take a step toward him, and the movement draws his attention. His head lifts, and our eyes lock.

I'll tell him the truth.

He'll understand.

I can trust him; I know I can.

And he'll forgive me for not telling him sooner.

But even as I come to stand at the foot of the table and he rises from his seat to greet me, I can't help the little niggling feeling of doubt in the back of my mind. The one that reminds me he and Chance are teammates and my father is their coach. Athletes are passionate, and football is a harsh game where emotions on the field can make or break you. What if he gets pissed off and says something to Chance in the heat of the moment, or God forbid, to my father? What if, in a moment of desperation, he tells a teammate who Sophie's father is, and it gets back to my father?

I've sacrificed for years to keep this a secret so as not to destroy my father's dreams. Am I really willing to risk it now?

Shut up and stop overthinking. For once in your life, Lane, do something for you. Preserve your relationship for you.

I swallow and my muscles lock into place as I wait to see what Teagan will say upon seeing me. But when he steps forward and pulls me into his arms, I sag into him, relief loosening my limbs.

He kisses the top of my head, his strong arms holding me to him while my heart goes wild.

We stand there like that, wrapped up in each other for I don't know how long before he pulls back, and I blurt, "I have some things I need to say."

His jaw tightens, and I wonder if he's every bit as anxious as I am as he motions to the table. "So do I. Why don't we sit? I bought you a coffee," he says sliding a paper cup toward me.

"Thank you." I try to smile but I'm too nervous and it comes off more like a grimace.

If he notices, he says nothing as he pushes a couple creamers my way. Even though I'm not sure I can stomach anything right now, I doctor my cup anyway, needing something to do with my hands.

Teagan's quiet as he watches me, his gaze steady on my face, and when I finish, I glance up at him, steeling myself for whatever's about to happen.

"I'm sorry," we say at the same time, and we laugh.

The band gripping my chest falls away completely when Teagan reaches out, taking my hand in his. "Can I go first?"

His eyes spark like blue flames and I nod as his hand encapsulates mine.

"I'm so sorry, Lane." His tone is firm, steady, like him and the grip on my hand. "I never should've pushed you. From that very first day, when I convinced you to give me a chance, you told me the stakes. You flat-out told me to never ask about Sophie's father, and I agreed. I accepted the terms because I wanted you so badly you could have asked me for anything, and I would've given it. But then I saw that picture and it just""—his jaw tightens—"it freaked me out. But I shouldn't have pushed and demanded anything from you that you're not willing to give. That's not how love works. Love doesn't demand *anything*. It gives."

"Teagan, I—" A hand fists in my throat, choking my words.

"You don't have to say anything. Not yet," he says, and I hate myself for staying silent. "I've never been the insecure type, and I hate that's how I came off. But you need to know that it's only because you're the most amazing woman I've ever met, and I want you for keeps." His throat works with emotion and I want to reach out, to pull him into my arms and erase all his fears and make them mine, because lord knows, I have plenty for the both of us. "Fuck it, I'll just say it. I was acting like a jealous idiot, but it won't happen again."

"Oh, Teagan." My throat constricts. "You don't owe me an apology because I get it. I understand. But I want you to know that you have *nothing* to worry, no reason to be jealous, because I feel exactly the same way you do. I want you for keeps, too."

His lips quirk. "Good to know." Then he grimaces. "But I was kind of a dick about it. You were right. You were upfront with me about it from the beginning."

Guilt gnaws on my chest.

If I'm going to tell him, now's the time.

I worry my lower lip with my teeth.

Just blurt it out and deal with the repercussions later.

"God, I love you," he whispers as he leans across the table, clasping the back of my neck as he brushes his thumb over the side of my jaw.

"I love you too," I croak.

He grunts in response and closes his eyes before he blinking them open again. "I fucking hate that we fought about this."

"Me too."

His gaze drops to my mouth, and I want to kiss him more than anything. I want to drown my fears in his taste, lose myself in his touch.

But the window of opportunity to tell him is slipping past me with each passing second. If I don't say something now, I will seal my fate. I may never get another chance where he's ready and willing to listen with an open heart and open ears. After today, the lies I told will only grow and fester like a tumor, larger than the both of us. I need to cut it out entirely. Now, before it's inoperable, too late to heal.

I open my mouth to say the words, to tell him he was right about everything: Chance, and the fact that he needs to know the truth if we're to have a future. "The thing is, Teagan." I glance down at my hands. "I know I told you not to—"

"You know what?" Teagan places his fingers under my chin, lifting my head so his gaze meets mine. "Let's just forget it. Strike it from the record."

"But . . ."

His thumb brushes over my lower lip. "We're all good, Lane. I promise. We're all good."

I let myself believe it.

CHAPTER 40

LANE

THE REST OF THE week passes in a blur as Teagan and the team get ready for the big game against Florida. While Teagan's spending extra time conditioning and going over game tape, I'm preparing for Christmas. Even though we haven't officially moved into the lake house yet, this will be our first Christmas here, and so I want it to be perfect.

My mind whirls with all the things I need to do. Buy Christmas lights, finish shopping for Sophie, decorate, plan the food . . .

The arm around my waist tightens, and the masculine rumble of Teagan's voice turns my skin to gooseflesh. "Morning," he says before pressing a kiss to the side of my neck.

I smile and sink further into his arms. Last night, I brought more of my belongings to the lake house and finished the last of the painting while Teagan helped me with Sophie. It didn't take much convincing to get him to spend the night, and I could certainly get used to waking up in his arms.

"The door is still locked," he whispers into the shell of my ear.

A shiver ripples up my spine as his hand slides up my waist, thumb brushing the underside of my breasts. "We could—"

"Mom!" Sophie's voice calls out, amplified in the staticky sound of the monitor.

I turn my head into the mattress and stifle a groan while Teagan laughs. "Well, shit," he says.

"Mom!" Sophie yells again.

"Duty calls." I whip the covers off, padding my way to my overnight bag and grab a pair of joggers to slide beneath the oversized T-shirt I'm wearing, before calling out, "I'm coming!"

"Funny. That's what you said last night, too." Teagan props his head on his hand, a salacious smile curving his lips while he watches me with glittering eyes.

I swat at him with a laugh before I head for the door. "Meet us out front." I motion toward the window.

He nods, watching me as I go.

Once I'm out in the hallway, I pad my way to Sophie's room in my bare feet and swing the door open. "Hey, baby. Ready for some breakfast?"

She nods and rubs her sleepy eyes. "Can I watch a show?"

"Sure. I'll put something on while I make pancakes. Teagan should be here soon, too. He promised to stop by before practice."

It's not entirely a lie. After all, he *did* promise to have breakfast with us before his game; he just never left.

"Do you think he'll still be wearing his lucky bracelet?"

"Of course he will." I pick her up and hold her in my arms. It won't be too long before I can't do this anymore because she's too big or too old for cuddles.

I carry her into the living room, squeezing her a little tighter. "He hasn't taken it off since the day you gave it to him. It's probably why he scored last game."

Sophie beams. "Maybe I should make him another."

I chuckle under my breath, knowing I've opened a can of worms. If Sophie had her way, she'd make him a thousand more.

I can picture it now, his arm covered in brightly beaded bracelets from wrist to shoulder. "Well, it would probably be a little hard to hide since he has to keep them covered. They don't like the players wearing jewelry."

"Why?"

I sigh. I've explained this to her already, and she'll ask why a thousand more times more before I'm through, so I pick up the remote and flick on the television, then sit Sophie on the couch.

The knock on the door sends a spike of joy surging through my chest, and I marvel at the fact I spent all night in his arms and I still can't get enough of him.

I hurry to answer it, swinging it open to find him standing there with sleep-rumpled hair, wearing gray sweats and a hoodie. The dimples in his cheeks deepen when he sees me, and my heart softens.

"Teagan, you're here!" Sophie yells from a few feet away. "Mom's making pancakes!"

"Really?" He steps inside and I close the door behind him. "I had no clue. Looks like I arrived just in time." He winks at me, and my insides turn to mush. "Pancakes are in my top ten foods."

Sophie gasps. "Mine too."

"Along with pizza and ice cream?" I laugh. "Obviously."

Teagan walks up to where Sophie's perched on the couch and offers her a fist bump. "That's why we're best buds. Because we like the same things."

"I thought Mom was your best bud."

"Uh, well . . ." Teagan's forehead knots. "She is, but I guess she's a special kind of buddy now."

I press my lips together, suppressing another laugh, but surprise myself when I say, "Actually," I glance at him, "Teagan is Mommy's boyfriend."

The words slip out without preamble and the second they do, my pulse kicks into high gear, wondering if I made a mistake telling her.

"Boyfriend?" Sophie gapes.

I nod.

Even though her concept of romantic relationships is limited, she has a vague idea of what a boyfriend is from being around Gabby who talks about all her failed relationships incessantly.

"Mmm-hmm," I murmur, barely looking at her because I'm too busy focusing on Teagan whose eyes glitter darkly, a gleam of joy in their cerulean hewn depths.

"Teagan, is it true?" Sophie asks, staring up at him like she always does when she asks him a question—as if he hung the moon and the stars, and holds all the answers to the universe.

"Yep, it's true." His grin splits into a smile, and his dimples deepen as he straightens and makes his way toward me, pulling me into his chest for a hug. "Your mom is my girlfriend."

He brushes a kiss against my cheek. "Thank you," he whispers, leaving a trail of fire in his wake. "Is that okay?" he asks Sophie, stiffening slightly like there's even a remote chance she'll reject him.

Little does he know, Sophie loves him just as much as I do.

She nods, her curled head bobbing. "This is way better. Mommy can be your girlfriend, so I can be your best friend."

A toothy grin splits her cherubic face, and if my heart wasn't completely gone before, it is now.

CHAPTER 41

TEAGAN

T HE TEAM IS HANGING in the locker room with our practice gear on, ready to take the field when our assistant coach, Mulvaney, asks us to stay. Apparently, Coach Turner wants a word with us prior to practice. Tomorrow is probably the biggest game we'll have in the regular season so we're all jittery with nerves, and the simple request only heightens the pressure we're all already feeling.

"What do you think he wants that he can't say on the field?" Tommy asks beside me, his voice low. "Since when does he hold pre-practice huddles in the locker room?"

I shrug, shaking off the ominous tone of Tommy's voice. "It's probably just about tomorrow," I say, even though I'm not so sure.

Tommy's right. Any pre-game strategizing, speeches, or peptalks happen once our feet hit the turf.

The door to the locker rooms opens with a bang. The heavy oak wood slams against the wall, reverberating throughout the tight confines of the locker room. Beside it, Coach Turner peers at us from the entryway, his gaze roaming the men standing before him, and if the pinched set of his mouth and tomato face are any indication, he's pissed. *Really pissed.*

Everyone straightens, eyes forward. Every sound inside the room ceases almost instantly, a palpable tension taking its place.

Coach ambles forward until he's front and center, all eyes on him.

The wrinkle in his brow deepens above hard, assessing eyes.

I suck in a breath and hold it, sensing that whatever he's about to say will severely fuck up our day. "It's come to my attention, by a source at Florida State, that someone gifted them a copy of our playbook."

It's like being in a vacuum; all the air is sucked from the room.

The silence that follows is deafening.

Whole minutes pass with Coach standing there, staring out at us as if waiting for Judas to show his face.

Eventually, a rumble of voices spreads, a low hum that builds around me. Words and phrases are tossed out. *Stolen. Impossible. No fucking way.*

When the tone starts to shift and rise, he raises a hand to silence us. "Like you, I didn't believe it at first so I came to my office early. I'd just had the playbook last night, but when I checked this morning, it was gone."

"Holy shit," I mutter under my breath, stunned.

"Fuuuuck," Tommy echoes.

"They're lying," someone shouts. "Ain't no way."

"How?" another demands.

"No way, Coach," Greene says. "They're fucking rats. They know we can beat them and they're trying to shake us, turn on each other."

"I wish that were the case." The muscle in Coach's jaw flickers. "But my source is a good friend, an old friend from college, actually. We've known each other for more than twenty years. Played football together. Helped each other at the start of our careers. He's a confidant of mine and he works at the university, so I have every reason to believe what he's telling me."

"Who was it?" Chance demands across the room, arms crossed over his chest.

His stony gaze slides to mine where he holds it for a few beats before glancing away again.

"I don't know," Coach bites out. "I can only imagine it has to be someone who has access to the facilities."

"Like a player?" Chance asks.

"Or a staff member, yes," Coach says.

"No way. We've worked too damn hard to get here," Tommy says beside me. "None of us would do that."

Coach holds a hand up. "I have every intention at finding out who it was. In the meantime, practice is canceled for today."

Protests rise around me, some calling for the turncoat's head on a pike. Others insisting we need the practice now more than ever.

"Quiet!" Coach snaps, and the ruckus fades. "Quite frankly I don't give a fuck what you think we should do. The damage is done. I've seen the copy of the playbook they have, and it is in fact, ours. So, I'm going to spend the next twenty-four fucking hours in my office trying to come up with a plan, new plays, whatever it takes to do some damage control while also trying to figure out how the fuck this happened and who the hell is responsible. I expect all of you"—he points at each of us, moving across the room—"to keep your ears to the fucking ground and if you hear so much as a peep about this or have an inkling of who it was, I expect you to come to me tomorrow before the game, and no sooner. I don't want to be bothered until then because I'll be working around the clock to do damage control. It might seem like this effects only one game, but the ramifications could be far reaching if someone from Florida got it in their head to pass the book along. You might as well kiss the championships goodbye. Is that understood?"

He pauses and a cacophonous "Yes, sir!" trickles through the room.

"Good." He nods and backs toward the door. "You're on your own for the day. Do whatever the fuck you want."

Once he's gone Greene slams his fist into a nearby locker and turns on us. "Whoever the fuck it was better turn themselves in right now, I swear."

A rumbled ascent fills the room while I stand there shell-shocked. Any hope we had of pulling out a win tomorrow have all but vanished. All our hard work is for nothing.

Tommy sighs and slides two hands into his hair. "Well, there goes tomorrow." He kicks the bench in front of us, then curses.

"It makes no sense," I say with a shake of my head. "Why would someone do that?" And more importantly, who the hell would have access to Coach's office to even snag his playbook in the first place?

"Maybe the mole got fucking paid?" Tommy throws out.

Maybe. I'm sure it wouldn't be the first time money exchanged hands to ensure a win. Or maybe the same person who managed to gain access to the locker combinations also has access to Coach's office.

The thought detonates inside my brain like a hand grenade, and when my gaze lifts in the direction of Chance Lockhart, our eyes lock.

My heart pounds a frantic beat as I run laps around the track. I've lost count of how many I've done, but it doesn't matter. Most of the guys hit the weight room and finished conditioning more than an hour ago but I, for one, couldn't leave. Not yet. Not with my mind racing in a million different directions.

So, I run until my muscles burn and my lungs ache.

I run until the thoughts in my brain muddle and fizzle to nothing more than a blissful hum.

Slowing my pace, I come to a stop, bending at the waist to catch my breath before I do a few quick stretches, then head for the locker room.

I can't imagine what Coach is thinking right now. Even if he can create a whole new fucking playbook, we don't have time to learn them for the game tomorrow. Instead, we'll be flying by the seat of our pants, with last-minute plays being hurled at us; it's about the only thing we can do to try an earn a win other than pray like hell.

I shake my head as I enter the tunnel and head for the locker room, still unable to believe one of my teammates or a staff member sold us out.

Did someone offer them money?

For the life of me, I can't come up with a reason good enough to hand our rival the blueprint for beating us, and monetary gain is the only thing that makes even remote sense.

Regardless of the reason, the betrayal cuts deep. Teammates are a band of brothers, and even though I'm nowhere near as close to these guys as I was with my teammates back in Riverside, if I'm feeling the sting of this, I can't imagine what the veteran players on the team are feeling. The seniors must be shitting bricks right now.

And Coach . . . If I were him, I'd be beside myself.

It's the best season he's had in years and now, because of one selfish asshole, the team will take a massive hit.

It's quiet as I duck under the archway into the hall that leads to the locker room. Hours have passed since Coach made the announcement about the playbook, and most of the guys have probably gone home by now.

I tug open the heavy metal door, my thoughts drifting to Lane. I hadn't planned on hanging out with her tonight on account of how important tomorrow's game is—or was—but I can't help but wonder what she'll think when she finds out what happened.

I lift my head as I round the corner and freeze.

My eyes widen, trying to make sense of what I'm seeing. Seconds pass, but my brain still won't compute.

Chance stands at my locker, a gym bag at his feet as he pops the combination lock off my locker, then bends and removes an item I'd recognize anywhere. The one I've seen Coach clutch during practice every fucking day for the last four months.

His playbook.

The realization is a bucket of cold water to the face.

Ice chinks in my veins, a glacier in my chest.

"What the actual fuck?" My mouth hangs open as Chance's head whips in my direction. Surprise flickers in his eyes as he straightens. The hand holding the playbook lowers.

I can see the panic in his stony gaze moments before he holds the playbook out, waving it in front of me like evidence. "It was you!" he exclaims.

"Are you fucking kidding me?" I scoff, motioning to my locker. "I just fucking watched you open my locker and remove it from your bag, ready to stash it there."

"No." He shakes his head and turns fully toward me, squaring his shoulders. "I had a feeling you were the rat, so I figured I'd check it out. Sure enough, I was right."

"Like hell you did." My hands fist as I step forward, muscles coiled, ready for a fight.

The fucking audacity of this guy is mind boggling.

"If you saw anything different," he says with a smirk, "you need to get your fucking eyes checked."

I take another step closer, my mouth a tight line as I try and determine his angle. To get me off the team? To fuck with me because of Lane?

It's hard to be one step ahead of your enemies when you don't know they're fucking motives.

Fury blazes through my veins. "What's your endgame, Lockhart? What are you trying to pull?"

"I don't know what you're talking about." He scoffs.

"Ever since you saw me with Lane that first night, I've had a target on my back. The liquor bottle in my locker. Then showing up at her place and bad-mouthing me. The impromptu mandatory Sunday meetings when you knew damn well we were together. Your threats when I saw you the other day with Sophie, and now this?"

He huffs out a laugh. "You're fucking paranoid, Nichols."

My gaze sharpens on his face. "Am I?"

I'd love nothing more than to punch his fucking lights out, imprint my knuckles on his face, but something tells me that's what he wants. One more reason for Coach to kick me off his team.

Another step closer, and Chance slaps the playbook into my chest, leaning in so I can smell the cloying scent of his cologne. "Good luck explaining to Coach why you have the playbook," he says. Then he removes his hand as he backs up, and the playbook nearly falls to the ground before I fumble for it, catching it before it has the chance. And by the time I lift my gaze, he's gone.

CHAPTER 42

TEAGAN

I SPEND THE REST of the day with an anvil in my chest.

After spending a disgusting amount of time debating on what to do with the playbook, I took it with me.

When it comes down to it, my integrity is what matters to me the most. Even if I left in the locker room for someone to find, Chance will pin it on me. Clearly, it's what he wants, and nothing is going to stop him. Instead, I'm better off taking it to Coach myself, explaining to him what happened, and hoping like hell he'll believe me.

By morning, nerves coil in my stomach like a bed of snakes.

After tossing and turning all night, I'm exhausted and feeling pretty shitty about how my showdown against Chance will go. Having the truth on my side is all I've got while he and Turner have history.

I sling my gym bag over my shoulder and tell Tommy I'm heading to the field early to take care of something, then set off across campus. It's a cool morning, cloudy with a chance of rain, which suits me just fine considering the ominous gray clouds match my mood.

When I finally reach Coach's office, I want to puke. Any confidence I had before is long gone, replaced with the certainty that he'll take one look at the book in my hands, condemn first and ask questions later.

If I'm lucky, he'll give me a chance to explain, but in the end, he still might not believe me.

I take a deep breath and draw closer, hovering just outside his office door. It's cracked open, but I assume he's alone since it's so early. That is, until I raise my hand to knock and hear a familiar voice from inside and my stomach drops.

Chance.

I knew he'd come after me, but I'd hoped to beat him to the punch.

I peek inside the door, careful not to show my face as I make out a sliver of the room, enough to see Coach clap Chance on the back. "It's been my pleasure to watch you grow over the years, son, and no matter what happens out there on the field today or the rest of the season, you've earned your success. You're gonna go far."

Lowering my hand, I swallow over the bile rising in the back of my throat.

I knew Turner and Chance were close but hearing him call him "son" makes my skin crawl.

Turner thinks of Chance as family.

He'll take his side every time.

Which means I'm fucked and not just with football, but Lane, too.

"I appreciate it," Chance says. "I never would've gotten to where I am without you."

The sound of footsteps startles me and I scramble back, hovering in the shadows of the hallway as I try to catch my bearings.

The door swings open, and Chance steps out.

My pulse skitters. His grin widens. "Nichols." He saunters closer, a picture of casual ease. "Come to talk to Coach? I assume you have information about the playbook."

My nostrils flare. "You smug son of a bitch."

"Guess it's your word against mine." He taps his chin. "Wonder who he'll believe." He starts to brush past me, but I block his path.

"At least I have my integrity. At least I didn't throw my whole fucking team under the bus just to prove some kind of point."

All the amusement in Chance's expression vanishes and he shrugs. "I'll still get drafted."

"You're a dick."

Chance smirks, something dark and dangerous gleaming in his eyes as he leans into me and whispers, "Tell me, does it bother you that her father thinks of me as a son? That he'll *always* be Team Lockhart?"

The muscles in my jaw flex. My fists vibrate with the need for release, knuckles turning white as my nails bite into the palms of my hands.

This is what he wants, to goad me into a response.

He's probably hoping I'll snap and get my ass benched.

Instead, I lift my chin and smile. "Does it bother you? That Lane chose me?"

There's a flicker of anger in his eyes, and I know I have him.

This *is* about Lane.

Disgust curls my lip as I look him up and down. "I wonder what it would be like to pine after a girl for years, only for her to choose the rookie?" I say, throwing Chance's words from months ago back in his face.

"You think she *chose* you?" Chance bites out. "Newsflash, Nichols, you were her second choice, only because I walked away."

My eyes widen, a low hum in my ears as I try and make sense of what he just said. If I'm to believe Lane, she never had feelings for Chance. Nothing happened between them.

"Tell me," he murmurs, "does it haunt you knowing I got there first? That *I* was the one to pop her cherry."

My heart seizes in my chest.

Time stops.

The world tilts.

Impossible. It's fucking impossible.

I try to breathe, but fire fills my lungs as pain lances through my chest.

Everything hurts.

Chance hums in approval, then delivers the death blow as he chuckles and bites his lip like he's recalling a memory. "Damn, she was responsive. Or, at least she was with me. She was so fucking—"

I lunge for him, blind with rage as the roaring in my head spills from my mouth. My fists meet his face. Not once but twice, catching him off-guard before he gets in a punch in of his own.

His knuckles catch my mouth. My lips splits and blood coats my tongue as I deliver a right hook of my own.

Behind us, a door creaks, but I'm too busy blocking a punch to make sense of it, too angry and preoccupied with tearing Chance fucking Lockhart limb from limb to give a fuck.

My pulse pounds along with the throbbing of my fat lip.

I vaguely register the presence of several people now in the hallway watching, their faces a blur as Chance and I dance around each other, fists raised at the ready.

I barely make out Tommy as one of the onlookers before Chance barrels toward me, body cocked like a weapon as his shoulder catches me under the ribs and slams me back into the wall.

The air whooshes from my lungs, and I struggle for breath.

"I don't believe it," I manage. "There's no fucking way you and Lane—" The words form a lump inside my throat, but I push past it. "She told me you were never together."

Chance laughs, raising his fists in a protective stance as my left darts out again, barely missing him. "What? You think she somehow had a baby on her own? Damn, Nichols, that's basic sex ed. What do they teach you in those Podunk-ass schools of yours? Let me fill you in. Girl meets boy. Girl likes boy. Girl and boy fuck. Was fun. It's just dumb luck the condom broke."

"Chance, stop!" Lane's voice breaks through my rage like the crack of a whip.

I turn, startled, to find her standing in the din of the hall, a Wildcats jersey with my number hanging off her petite frame, her long auburn hair striking against the blue. And when her eyes meet mine, the sorrow I see in their jeweled depths tell me everything I need to know.

She lied.

My ribs crack, cleaving my heart in two.

Suddenly, I'm standing back in my living room months ago, finding out Knox was the one who hurt my sister. One of my best friends. Someone I *trusted.*

"Why?" I ask as I stare at her.

She says nothing as her gaze shifts, fear replacing the sorrow I see as she glances behind us, her voice soft as she says, "Dad?"

I spin around, dizzy with the whiplash of emotions as my eyes find Coach Turner, and I remember the sound of the door.

He saw the whole thing go down.

His mouth is drawn, his face pale like he's seen a ghost. Apparently, I wasn't the only one she lied to, but this knowledge does little to stanch the bleeding.

"Dad, I can explain," Lane pleads behind me.

I glance at Chance and watch with little satisfaction as the blood drains from his face.

"Tell me it's not true," Coach croaks out, straightening his spine as if preparing for the blow.

"Dad, I . . ." Lane swallows. "It's true."

My lungs don't want to work.

I tell myself to breathe, but I still can't seem to draw a breath; it's as if someone punched me in the gut, knocking the wind out of me. Whoever came up with the expression "it's as easy as breathing" clearly never experienced this kind of soul-crushing heartbreak because there is nothing easy about it.

I manage a small sip of air at the sound of footsteps approaching. Somewhere behind us, the assistant coach's voice cuts the tension. "Hey, Turner, you're needed down here on the field."

Coach nods, his gaze empty, emotionless. "Go on. I'll be right there," he tells Mulvaney.

He sighs, shoving a hand through his thinning salt and pepper hair, and I recognize the same pain in his eyes as the one currently ripping through my chest.

"What a clusterfuck," he mutters.

It's the most honest thing I've heard all day.

He bows his head then lifts it again, as if he can't decide what to do with himself, which emotions to allow. "Get to the locker room," he barks. "Both of you. I'll be there in a minute. We have a game to play. There's no delaying it, not even for . . ." He waves his hand in front of him, then drops them and turns toward his office. "We'll sort this shit out later."

"Dad—" Lane tries again, her voice thick, but Coach ignores her, slamming his office door in reply.

When I turn, Tommy and the other spectators are gone. Only Chance, Lane, and I remain.

I can't look at him; it makes me physically ill to even be in his presence right now, and I have a moment of panic wondering how the hell I'm supposed to play football. How am I supposed to pretend the last hour of my life never happened?

"How could you?" Lane asks, her voice trembling.

Of course, she's addressing him. Why wouldn't she?

My stomach sours and I take a step back, afraid I might lose the protein shake I downed on the way here.

"Doesn't affect me any. I'll have a spot on the draft either way. In fact, I'm supposed to get called up early."

Lane scoffs. "Of course. It's always about Chance. You got what you wanted, so now you don't care who you hurt in the process, all because of some misplaced jealousy for something you never wanted in the first place. Because you don't want me and Sophie. You never did. You just can't stand the thought of someone else having us."

I take another step back.

I can't be here.

Can't bear to hear this.

"I might. One day," Chance says, and my stomach heaves.

I throw my hands up in front of me as if shielding myself from whatever else they're going to say. "I can't do this," I choke out. "I can't fucking do this," I say and then I turn.

I push past Chance, knocking into his shoulders in my haste, and take the hall in long strides, but before I can reach the locker room door, Lane's voice calls behind me.

Her footsteps pound on the cement beneath her feet as she runs after me, and I have half a mind to dodge her and keep going. I could walk away. Get in my car and drive until I'm far away from here. Hell, maybe I'll never come back.

Maybe the physical distance will somehow give me the strength to face everything I just discovered. Maybe then it won't hurt so fucking bad.

I reach for the locker room door at the same time a small hand clamps down on my shoulder, and Lane blocks my path.

"Move," I grind out, but she doesn't. Instead, she just stands there with watery, red-rimmed eyes while I try my best to avoid her gaze.

"Teagan, you have to understand. I—"

"You *lied!*" For the first time since she appeared in the hallway behind me, I meet her eyes. "You lied straight to my face when I asked if you and Chance were ever together. And for a minute, I thought, what if he's the father? But when I brought it up, you were so insistent it was some nameless, faceless guy from summer camp, and I felt like a fool for even thinking it. But this whole time I was right. Or maybe I knew all along, but I just wanted to be wrong so badly that when you lied, I believed it."

"I know. God, Teagan, I'm so sorry. If you'll just hear me out, let me—"

"Explain?" I take a step back, away from her reach, as I run a hand over my mouth. "I told you lying is a deal-breaker for me. You knew my past. You know I can't handle secrets and that I need transparency."

"I know." Tears streak down her cheeks, and damn if my first instinct isn't to make them stop.

And that's the fucking problem. I'd do damn near anything for this girl. I'd take a bullet. Walk through fucking fire. Stand on a bed of nails. *Anything.*

But I've made a big enough ass of myself these last few months and all it got me was a broken heart.

"Do you, though? Because the one thing I needed, Lane, the *only* thing I asked for, was the one thing you couldn't give me."

I skirt around her to get to the locker room door while she follows my movements, slamming a hand over it as I grip the handle. "Don't leave things like this. Please, Teagan. I love you."

My knuckles whiten with my grip, her words sending shockwaves through my heart until the ripple effect is felt every-fuck-ing-where.

My throat works, and I wonder if it's my heart lodged in the back of it. I wonder if it'll ever settle back inside my chest.

"I have a game to play," I say.

Then I open the door and disappear.

CHAPTER 43

TEAGAN

W E'RE ONLY TEN MINUTES into the game when Coach puts me in.

I have no idea what the hell he's thinking, or maybe he's not thinking and that's the point. His eyes are glazed over, like he drank a fifth of whiskey. And he'd have to be drunk to put me on the field with Chance because being on a football field with him is the last place I want to be.

I want to rip his heart out with my bare hands. Break his ribs. Punch him in the nose. Gut him with a blade like he gutted me outside Coach's office.

But I can do none of those things.

Instead, I'm supposed to run and block and evade and catch the football as if my world hadn't been turned upside down just minutes ago.

Fuck. That.

I barely glance his way as he calls out the play. It's a passing play in which I get the ball. Any other game, I'd be thrilled. I love an opportunity to score. Love the thrill of outsmarting my opponents and taking the ball home, but I feel nothing. No joy. No anticipation. Only a heaviness in my chest I can't shake.

I crouch low at the line of scrimmage, my eyes fixed on Chance as I await the snap. He hikes the ball, and muscle memory takes over while my mind reels.

I explode off the line, my legs pumping as I run for the goal line, surging past defenders. My focus narrows and I turn in time to see Chance ready for the throw. But instead of putting my hands out and readying for the ball, all I can think about are his hands—the same ones clutching the football—touching Lane, pleasing Lane, holding Lane.

Time slows and I close my eyes as a fresh wave of pain rips through me.

How long were they together?

Would they still be a couple if she hadn't gotten pregnant?

Did she love him?

Does she still?

And why? Why, why, why, a million times why?

Why did she lie to me?

Chance's arm snaps back and the ball flies, but I'm too distracted.

My feet and arms are full of lead.

I'm late as I shift my stance and reach.

My vision files away the blur of maroon and white—a defender—coming straight for me.

I tell myself to pivot but I'm too late.

Something crashes into my side. My hip explodes and my legs fly out from under me. I'm airborne—weightless—floating like a feather through the air until the moment I hit the turf with bone-jarring force.

My head slams on the ground. Teeth rattle.

Pain explodes in my back like a cannon, strong enough to outpace the throbbing ache inside my chest.

I cry out and try to roll on my side for relief, but I can't.

I can't fucking move.

It's my last thought before the world goes dark.

CHAPTER 44

LANE

I HATE MYSELF A little more with each passing second as I try and focus on the game. All I have to do is get through the next few hours, and then I'll make Teagan listen. I'll find a way to explain myself that he can understand.

He has to understand; he just has to.

Teagan takes the field, and my pulse skips a beat.

I watch as they hike the ball and Chance takes his time setting up for what I think is going to be a pass to him.

But something goes terribly wrong.

Teagan stops.

He pauses when he should be moving his feet.

It's as if his mind is elsewhere.

Panic seizes my chest as the ball leaves Chance's hands and soars through the air. It flies toward Teagan just as he finally shifts, positioning himself to catch it, only it's a fraction too late because the defender is already there. And just as the ball is within reach, he plows into Teagan with the force of a freight train.

My heart stops as the defender's helmet hits him hip high.

Teagan's feet fly out from under him, his body launching to the ground at an unnatural angle.

He falls backfirst with an impact that reverberates through the stadium.

I yelp and hold my breath, waiting for him to get up, but he doesn't.

I count the seconds that pass. Far too long for him not to be immobile.

"He's not moving," I say out loud. "Why isn't he moving?" I scream.

Medics take the field while all players—both ours and the opposing team—take a knee. Everyone else in the stadium goes quiet as the medics get to work, and still, Teagan does *not* move.

No, no, no, no!

I stand, craning my neck to see, as if it might somehow change what's in front of me. Blood pounds in my ears like a herd of buffalo, drowning out whatever the announcers are saying over the loudspeaker.

I cover my mouth with shaking hands, muffling a moan.

Get up.

Get up.

I repeat this mantra in my head as if I can make him move out of sheer will.

The EMTs shout, cutting through the sound of my pulse, and suddenly, I hear everything in wild technicolor.

The sound of a siren.

My father screaming as he runs onto the field with his assistant beside him. The low murmur of fans around me as an ambulance appears, taking the field and parking just feet from Teagan's prone form.

Wait.

I need to see him. I need to.

My eyes fill with tears as I race down the stands, pushing my way through fans and spectators, all of them watching with bated breath.

I take the stairs quickly, as fast as my feet will carry me, which still isn't fast enough when I push through a throng of onlookers surrounding the fence in front of the field. "Excuse me. Out of the way!" I dodge another person. "Move. Fucking *move*!" I cry.

I'm not gonna make it.

I break through the crowd, and icy fingers grip my chest at the sight of Teagan strapped to a board as they load him onto a stretcher and into the ambulance.

Shoving at the gate, I try to get through, but security stops me with a beefy arm to my chest. "You can't get onto the field ma'am."

I ignore him, pushing and clawing at his arm. "That's my boyfriend!"

Another guard comes to help restrain me, but I fight him, too. "My father is the coach. *Please*," I wail as tears clog my throat. "I need to go with him. He's hurt. He needs me," I cry.

The guard wraps his arms around me from behind, pinning my arms to my side while I try to shake him off like a madwoman. "Ma'am. You need to stop!"

"Let go of me! Let go. I work here, and he's my—" The words die in my throat as the ambulance pulls off the field, and I fall to my knees, a keening sound erupting from my chest while the sirens blare in my ears.

And all I can think is, *this is all my fault.*

CHAPTER 45

TEAGAN

I'M FLOATING.

Weightless.

Everything is dark. Until it's not.

I wince, squinting through bleary eyes, but the light hurts, so I shut them quickly.

In the background, someone is talking, but I can't make out the words.

My eyelids flutter again, and I open them, sending a wave of nausea ripping through my gut. The room spins, turning with the pounding agony in my head as I try and remember what the hell happened, sensing it's right there on the edge of my brain, but the memory slips through my fingers like sand.

Wincing, I focus instead on the hushed voices around me and make out one word: football.

That's right . . .

I got hit.

The memory sweeps through me at once. It happened so fast it's a blur—the defender coming at me, then the ground rushing up to meet me, and the sickening thud.

I try to move, but everything fucking hurts. Every twitch of my muscles sends sharp jolts of pain through my back like I'm driving railroad spikes through my bones.

And then I remember what my heart wants to forget, and it's like waking from a bad dream.

My chest pounds at the memory of my confrontation with Chance. *And Lane . . .*

Aw, fuck.

I don't want to remember.

I want to go back to sleep. To forget.

The ache in my chest intensifies, wrapping around me like a vise, five times worse than the hammering in my head or the daggers in my spine.

I squeeze my eyelids tighter and my thoughts scatter.

I can't think about this right now, so I allow the grogginess to take over and dream.

The next time I wake, the pain in my head is merely a dull throb, background noise to the real pain in my back.

I inhale and open my eyes, glancing around at the hospital room, far more conscious of my surroundings and everything that happened to me at the game than I was the first time I woke.

Sadness sweeps over me, but I have no time to dwell on it because a nurse chooses this exact moment to appear at my bedside, eyes bright, tone soft as she says, "I called for the doctor since you're awake. He'll be here in a minute to explain everything. Also, you've been cleared for visitors and you have quite the crowd waiting for you. I hope you don't mind, but your coach is here." She steps aside to reveal Coach, his face slack and pale as he sits in a chair by the window.

He rises and my thoughts immediately go to Lane, but I block them out. I can't think about her right now. It's too much.

"My parents?" I ask, turning back to the nurse.

"Mr. Turner called them as soon as it happened and we've also been in touch with them. They know that you're okay, but they're on their way here."

I nod, and try to tell her thanks, but all I can muster is unintelligible mumbling.

"Water?" the nurse asks, and I nod again suddenly realizing the fire in my throat is thirst.

She turns to the little bedside tray where a pitcher of water sits, waiting for me to wake I guess, and pours me a cup, then hands it to me.

I take huge gulps, drinking until I drain the cup, then set it back down on the tray at the same time the door to my room opens and the doctor—or at least, I assume it's the doctor—walks inside, dressed in green scrubs and a white coat, a stethoscope around his neck.

"Mr. Nichols," he says, his tone far more chipper than I feel, "glad to see you awake."

"How long have I been out?" I ask, my voice slightly garbled, but stronger than a moment ago.

"Just a few hours in and out."

Fuck. It felt like a century.

"Do you want privacy for this, or—" the doctor's gaze flickers meaningfully to my coach and back.

I shake my head. What the fuck do I care? He was there. He saw what happened.

"It's fine." It'll save me from an update.

"You suffered a Grade II concussion. That and the pain is what had you going in and out of consciousness, but there's no swelling or anything to be concerned with as far as your head goes. Still, we'd like to keep you for observation overnight, seeing that you did lose consciousness."

A concussion. That's nothing.

"Is that all?"

He spears me a look, and I stiffen, waiting for whatever else he's about to say. "You had a pretty good fall, and the impact to your spine was severe enough that you have a compression fracture in your back, your T2 to be exact."

I straighten at the news, shocked as I push myself up with my hands.

Wrong move.

A knife twists in my back, and I hiss. *Fuck.*

The doctor holds his hands out, and his calm expression alone alleviates some of my fears. "I know it sounds scary," he tells me. "When people hear they broke their back, they immediately think of paralysis, but that's not the case with this kind of injury. You'll be fine with some care and rest. No heavy lifting for at least eight weeks. No sports. Mobility will be limited, and you'll have to wear a back brace for two months. Even small tasks will be painful. Putting on a shirt, brushing your teeth, but overall, the pain shouldn't be severe. It will be annoying and frustrating for an active man like you, but it should heal up on its own. No surgery. No PT. If you're going to break your back, this is the way to do it."

My brain quickly computes, the doctor's words echoing in my mind and clanging through my head, while I try to wrestle them into submission.

I broke my fucking back?

Shit, that sucks.

But I'm fine. Or at least, I will be. No surgery. Just a back brace and limited activity.

Nothing life altering.

Except . . .

My brow creases. "So, football. You said I'm out the rest of the season, but what about . . .?"

The doctor's expression answers my question before I even finish. "I'm sorry, but I highly recommend you get another hobby. Any time you break a bone or have a fracture, that spot will be vulnerable, more susceptible to future breaks."

Get another hobby. Like it's that easy.

I exhale a rough breath, feeling a little like the walls are crumbling around me.

Across from me, Coach is eerily silent.

The doctor places a gentle hand on my shoulder, meeting my eyes as he says, "You're lucky to be walking away from this hospital. Next time, you might not be so lucky."

I'm still reeling from the news when the door to my room closes.

The doctor is gone with the promise to discharge me in the morning just as a precaution, leaving me alone with Coach.

Football has been such a big part of my life for so long, I'm not sure how my life looks without it. I'd always known college was endgame for me, but now the thought of it ending so soon fucking hurts.

I swallow, staring straight ahead at the ugly painting on the wall across from me as my thoughts drift to Lane.

My chest instantly throbs, and I have half a mind to call the doctor back, to ask him to check my heart, too.

A throat clears, and my head jerks toward the sound.

Coach draws closer, hands shoved in the pockets of his joggers. It almost hurts to look at him, and when his gaze meets mine, the raw emotion in his eyes is enough to have me glancing away again.

"Hey, Coach," I mumble.

"Teagan." He clears his throat, his Adam's apple bobbing and the realization that he's no longer my coach, not after today, hits me square in the chest.

I won't ever step foot on a football field again, at least not in a uniform.

A burst of pain explodes inside of me, a round of fireworks hitting in succession, each one bleeding into the next.

I lost a lot today.

Lane.

Sophie.

Football.

It feels like every-fucking-thing.

Knowing it could've been worse, that I might not have walked out of here, does little to ease the sting.

Coach removes his ballcap and glances down at his hands where he wrings it like an old rag. "I'm sorry, son." He clears his throat. "I can't help but feel like part of this is my fault."

I frown.

I might feel like shit, but none of this is on him. That's just plain stupid. "No." I shake my head, my tone firm. "This was all on me, sir. I was distracted, not thinking right. Hell, I stopped mid-play. My mind was elsewhere and I just fucking froze. I wasn't even thinking about football or catching the ball.

Otherwise, I never would've gotten struck in the first place. I should've told you where my head was at, that I couldn't play."

"As nice as that sounds, I'm your coach." He places the wrinkled cap back on his head and our eyes lock. "I knew you were emotionally wrecked, or at least, I *should've* known. I never should have put you out on that field. Not after . . . after everything that happened."

He inhales a sharp breath and glances away for a moment, composing himself, his voice stronger when he says, "I know how to read a player, but I was so damn stuck in my own head, I ignored everything and everyone just so I could shut everything else out, pretend like it never happened."

I understand that more than he knows.

"Maybe," I tell him, "but I still should've told you I was in no condition to play. This one's on me."

He bows his head, shoulder slumping with the weight of the world as he says, "You were a damn good player, Nichols."

I swallow, unable to choke anything out through the tightening in my throat as I nod.

"Well . . ." He taps a hand on my bed rail. "I'll let you rest, but I'll be back to check on you in the morning before they discharge you." He turns for the door, and I'm more than grateful when he leaves without mentioning Lane.

My gaze slides to the window overlooking the city below and I stare out of it in an effort to numb myself. Traffic lurches along, stopping at lights and zipping between lanes. Pedestrians walk over the sidewalk, to and from work, to shops and restaurants.

I hear a knock on the door, and I turn my head to see the nurse from earlier peeking inside. "Mr. Nichols, there's a young lady here to see you, a Lane Turner? I didn't know if you wanted any other visitors yet?"

I shake my head as my chest cleaves in two, then I turn back toward the window while I focus on the simple task of breathing.

"Not now," I say. "Tell her I don't want to see her."

CHAPTER 46

LANE

THE SECOND MY FATHER appears in the waiting room, I'm on him. "How is he?" I blurt, knowing he saw him.

He barely looks me in the eye as he mumbles, "Not great." He swallows while my stomach drops to my knees. "He had quite the hit to the head when he hit the ground, but his concussion is mild. It's his back that's the problem," he chokes out.

"His back?" I straighten, chest tight.

He nods, staring in the direction of the elevators, like he can't get away from me fast enough. "He fractured his T2. He's able to walk, but it will limit him and likely hurt like a bitch until it heals."

His back.

Tears prick my eyes as I think about how much pain he must be in on top of the betrayal I handed him, and when my father starts to move past me, I grip his arm, stopping him. "What about football?"

My father bows his head and shakes his head. "He's finished."

I drop my hand from his arm, too numb to stop his retreat as he strides away from me.

Everything that happened today is my fault.

It's my fault Teagan was distracted. I could tell the moment he stepped onto the football field, he wasn't himself.

It's my fault he's lying in a hospital bed.

It's my fault his heart is hurting.

And it's my fault he'll never play football again.

My fault. It's all I can focus on as when I note a nurse headed toward the hallway and rush to stop her.

"Can I see Teagan Nichols?" I ask. "I don't know what room he's in, but—"

"The football injury?" the nurse asks, her tone soft.

"Yeah." I swallow.

"I was just headed there. Visiting hours are over for tonight, but I can ask if he's up to one more. And you are?"

Oh God, what if he doesn't want to see me?

"Lane Turner," I say, my voice feeble.

"I'll see what I can do." My hopes plummet the further she gets down the hall. The thought of going home without laying eyes on him and telling him how fucking sorry I am is unthinkable. If I could go back and redo things, I would. I'd tell him everything from the beginning. But I can't, and so I'll do anything to make things right, no matter how long it takes.

When I spot the nurse returning, I hurry toward her, meeting her halfway as she glances at me with sympathy in her eyes, and I know.

He doesn't want to see me.

The knowledge shouldn't surprise me, but it hits me in the chest all the same.

"I'm sorry," the nurse starts, her gaze soft.

I nod, unable to speak through the lump in my throat.

"He went through quite the ordeal. He's probably just tired," she says.

"Yeah," I murmur, even though I know better. Teagan isn't just tired; it's personal, and I can't say I blame him.

I stay in the waiting room until dusk falls and night settles over the city like a heavy cloak. I can't go home until I see him, and yet I know at some point I might have to. There's a real possibility Teagan and I are finished. Done.

He might never want to speak to me again.

You lied straight to my face when I asked if you and Chance were ever together.

I hang my head in my hands, willing the sharpness of the memories to fade and hating myself a little more when they don't.

I'd been so scared of what the truth might do to my family, I never stopped for one second to think of what it would do to me.

And now it's too late.

A sob rips through the back of my throat. Tears drip down my cheeks.

Because of me, Teagan is lying in a hospital bed alone, hurt and heartbroken.

I destroyed everything.

I wallow in my grief a little more, replaying the entire scene over and over again in my head.

I'd come to talk to my father to voice my suspicions about Chance. Little did I know they'd already beaten me there.

I remember the smug look on Chance's face, the agony in Teagan's eyes.

There's a special kind of pain in knowing you were the one to break the heart of the person you love. It's a special kind of torture with no escape route.

The knowledge of it wraps around you, squeezing like a boa constrictor, and stealing the air from your lungs. But instead of dying, I'm here, living with the pain of it instead.

The hours pass slowly. It's around three a.m. when a middle-aged couple hustles into the waiting room, heading directly for the nurses' station, and I wonder if it could be Teagan's parents. If I look close enough, there's a resemblance there. But then, maybe I'm seeing things.

Regardless, I feel a pang of longing for the woman as I hear her prattle on in a hushed tone, clearly worried as her husband takes her hand and sits beside her.

Sometime after six a.m., I nod off, but I'm awakened with a jolt at the scent of coffee and commotion a few rows down.

I rub the sleep from my eyes and blink to find it coming from the vicinity of the couple, and when I finally focus on them, I see the source. A young woman close to my age is pulling each of them into a long hug, a tray of coffees clutched in her hand.

A minute later, she releases them. When she sits our eyes meet, and I gasp.

Even through the haze of sleep, I can see the striking resemblance. She doesn't just look like Teagan. She *is* Teagan, only a feminine version of him, same blue eyes and all. She has the same honey blonde waves as Teagan, and they share the same straight smile. Same cheekbones. Same nose shape even though hers is smaller with a slightly more feminine slope. Even their mannerisms are similar, letting me know exactly who I'm looking at: Brynn, Teagan's twin.

She holds my gaze for what feels like an eternity before I finally glance away, self-conscious under the scrutiny. I have no idea if he's told his parents about me, but I'm absolutely certain, based on the way she stared at me just now, she somehow knows who I am.

I slump down in my chair at the same time she starts toward me.

Oh, God. I cover my face with my hand as if I can shield myself from her line of vision.

My heart races as I stare straight ahead, praying she doesn't come up to me and introduce herself.

She probably has no idea it's my fault Teagan's here, but she will soon enough, and I can't bear the thought of what his family will think of me then.

My hands turn clammy. Sweat pricks my brow as I take shallow breaths.

She's only a few feet from me when the nurse intercepts her. I can't hear what she's saying but whatever it is must be good news because Brynn's face splits into a wide smile and she's waving her parents over. Together, the three of them, with the nurse at the helm, head for the hallway and I know they'll get a visit.

Jealousy stabs my chest before it occurs to me Brynn might mention to him that she saw me and what his reaction might be.

Bile rises to the back of my throat.

If I'm not gone when they come out, I'm not sure I have the strength to face them.

An hour later, I get a text from my mother asking when I'm coming back home. It's the second one in three hours, and I know I can't stay any longer.

If I were any other college student, staying would mean some missed classes and nothing more. But I'm not. I have Sophie to consider, and she's been with my mother since early yesterday afternoon when I left for the game. Even if my mother didn't have a job, it would be wholly unfair to ask her to keep Sophie any longer.

Motherhood doesn't wait because life throws you a right hook.

Instead, you're forced to roll with the punches and go through the motions, even when everything around you is falling to pieces.

Even with a broken heart.

CHAPTER 47

LANE

I OPEN THE FRONT door and stumble inside. Now that I'm home, I know I'll have some answering to do. My parents are going to expect it when what I really need is space to lick my wounds. If I can't have that, then a shower, hot meal, and some sleep before unraveling the events of the past twenty-four hours would be nice. But I know I'll get none of those things seeing as how Sophie's already up for the morning and I'm just getting home.

Removing my jacket, I quickly hang it in the coat closet as my stomach rumbles. Despite my bleeding heart, my empty stomach is catching up with me. If I'm to parent at all today, at the very least, I'm going to need some toast and the largest mug of coffee I can find.

I head toward the kitchen, wondering when I ate last, only to decide it must've been yesterday morning. I'd been in too much of a hurry to find my father before the game started to stop for lunch and too sick to my stomach to eat after what happened with Teagan.

I exhale as the hallway ends and opens into the kitchen, and my steps falter.

Dread settles in the pit of my stomach as I my gaze falls to my parents, sitting around the island with a pot of coffee in front of them, along with the remnants of breakfast. Either they waited up for me all night or woke with the intention of addressing everything my father overheard yesterday. A quick sweep of the living room across from me confirms my suspicions when I find Sophie oddly absent.

Shit.

I swallow the nausea rising in the back of my throat when I realize I won't even have a reprieve over breakfast. Though I'm not sure why I expected anything different. They deserve answers, and I can't blame them for wanting them now.

"Where's Soph?" I ask, feeling slightly sheepish. I'm five years old again, in trouble and afraid to look them in the eye.

My arms hang limply at my sides. I'm a shell of the person I was on Friday night when I was in Teagan's arms—beaming, happy, full of life. I hate everything that's happened in-between then and now, but there's no going back, so I put one foot in front of the other.

"She's over at Gail's house next door," my mother says. "She's helping her rake leaves."

I nod. I know how much Mrs. Miller misses Sophie since putting her in daycare. I've been promising I'd drop by for days but haven't had the chance. I guess this time, it worked out.

Lucky me.

"Have a seat." My mother motions to the chair beside her, her smile forced.

Beside her, Dad won't even look at me.

I slide into the seat next to Mom and risk another glance at my father, noting the pinched forehead and angry slash of his mouth, and I wonder if he plans on ignoring me forever. Maybe he's going to let Mom do all the talking and sit there like a mute. Or maybe he's simply biding his time to tell me how much I've disappointed him. I'm not sure which is worse.

I reach out, ignoring the nerves tangling in my chest like a thicket of brambles, and grab the coffee carafe, along with the empty mug sitting beside it, and pour myself a cup. Steam curls from the lip, and the nutty aroma instantly soothes the tiniest of nerves.

I doctor it with cream while my mother rises from her chair, piling an empty plate with fresh fruit and a muffin, which she then slides toward me as she reclaims her spot.

My stomach churns. I might have been starving a moment ago, but I'm not so sure I can choke anything down now. Not with the air of disapproval hovering over me.

Still, anything is better than meeting their eyes or starting a conversation I don't know how to have, so I force myself to take a bite of fruit while I wonder what advice I'd give Sophie in this situation.

I suppose I'd tell her not to lie to the ones she loves, but it's too late for that. Been there, done that, and now it's ruined several lives. Not just mine but also the lives of my loved ones.

Maybe it's time I start following my own parental advice.

Silence surrounds us. I can only guess what they're thinking, how shocked and crestfallen they must be to discover I've hidden the truth right under their noses.

I can feel Mom's probing gaze on the side of my face, sense Dad's pain and anger radiating from him like the steam rising from my cup, and I decide all at once that the silence is so much worse than whatever they could possibly say.

"I'm sorry," I blurt after a moment, unable to take it anymore. "I'm so sorry I lied, that I didn't tell you the truth. I never meant to hurt anybody. I was just doing what I thought was best for everyone involved."

Mom inhales sharply. "So, it's true? Chance *is* Sophie's father?"

I find the courage to tear my gaze from my plate and glance over at her and nod. "Yes."

Emotion flickers through her eyes and it's a moment before she speaks again. "How did it happen . . .?" She grunts and waves her hands out in front of herself. "I mean, I know *how*." Dad winces. "But what I mean is, when did you two start seeing each other? How long were you involved, and how did we not know about it?"

I swallow, wondering where to start. I've held this secret for so long, it's like I don't know where it begins and where it ends.

"It was toward the end of junior year that it started to feel like maybe there was something there. Then early that summer, I felt a spark, but I never thought he'd be interested in me. He was so popular and at the top of his game. A million girls wanted him. And maybe that was part of the appeal. Feeling wanted by someone everyone else wished they could have puts kind of a spell on you. I don't know."

I shake my head and breathe before continuing, trying not to think about it too hard. "But we'd known each other for years, so we were already comfortable with each other. That summer, at football camp, I went to help Dad and we saw each other almost every day. Conversations deepened. Feelings grew. He said he loved me." My throat catches on the words. "And I believed him. I thought maybe I loved him, too."

Of course, now I know better. What Chance and I shared was never love. Infatuation, maybe. Lust, certainly. But not love. Not like with Teagan. Not the kind of all-consuming, soul-crushing, tear-your-heart-out, can't-imagine-my-life-without-you kind of love.

Pushing the thought of Teagan away, I lift my chin and wait for my parents to say something because I'll never get through this if I dwell on him.

"Why didn't you tell us?" Mom asks after a moment.

For the first time since I sat down, I feel my father's eyes on me, but I don't dare to look. If anyone has the power to draw my tears, it's him, and I've shed enough of those for one night.

I exhale slowly, trying to find a way to tell them in which they might understand, but all I have now is the truth. I won't make the same mistake twice; I won't lie to them again.

"When I found out I was pregnant, I was so scared to tell you. The last thing I wanted to do was disappoint either of you, but I thought maybe with Chance by my side, it would be easier. We'd do this together. But when I told him, it didn't go over well and certainly not how I'd expected. He told me we were too young. That he wasn't ready to be a father. To his credit, both of those were true. But he also told me that if I chose to keep the baby, it was on me. She was mine to raise because he wanted nothing to do with her."

I shrug, noting for the first time the shadows beneath my father's eyes.

"So that's what I did," I continue. "After I processed everything he said, I accepted full responsibility for Sophie from that day forward. I chose to have her, to keep her, and raise her. He made his choice very clear, and I know how close you are to Chance, especially Dad, so I knew he wouldn't accept Chance walking away scot-free." I glance at him and quickly glance away again, the turmoil flickering in his gaze more than I can handle. "Then, a day later, I overheard a conversation between Dad and Kyle Bradley, the director at CU. I heard him promise Dad that if he brought Chance with him, he'd hire him as head coach."

Dad curses under his breath and places his head in his hands, but I can't stop, no matter how much the truth hurts.

Telling them is like popping the cork on a bottle of champagne. With each word, the pressure in my chest eases a little more.

"So I lied," I continue, chin quivering. "When you asked who the father was, I simply told you it was one of the out-of-state kids from camp. It was so much easier than the truth. My life was already being flipped on its head and I wasn't taking yours with it. As it was, you went from nearly being empty nesters to having a grandbaby at home overnight, and if you had known it was Chance, it would've made it so much worse. I know how Dad is. First, he would've demanded Chance take responsibility, and when that didn't work, he would've washed his hands of him in spite of his dreams. Chance would've gone elsewhere to college, and Dad's dream job would've passed him by, and I couldn't have that. You were already sacrificing so much—your home, your time, your reputation—for your pregnant teen daughter, and I couldn't let you sacrifice this one thing, too."

Mom grips her coffee cup, her knuckles turning white, "You should've told us upfront. Even if you wanted to wait a year until your father started at CU, why not tell us then? It's not a small lie, Lane. Were you going to hide it forever?"

"I know!" I yell, startled by my own outburst. "I know," I repeat, softer.

I exhale as guilt roils in my stomach. "The damage was done at that point. The lie was already out there, and nothing was going to change with Chance, so it made the most sense not to disrupt your lives over something that wouldn't change. How would Dad feel knowing he got his dream job on account of the guy who knocked me up and left me? How would he look him in the eye and coach him every single day knowing he wants nothing to do with our Sophie?"

Silence settles in the space between us while I toy with the muffin in front of me, tearing it into pieces.

"But all this time, you could've made it easier on yourself. Even if he didn't want Soph, like it or not, she's still his. At the very least, Chance had a financial obligation to—"

"Mom," I huff out a breath. "He was a high school student with no job, same as me. What could he possibly have done for us?"

"You held a job, and he should've, too. He would've been forced to work, at least a little bit."

"What would be the point?" I ask, my voice rising slightly, tired of this conversation.

All I want is to crawl into bed and sleep for a year, until all of this is over and I can open my eyes without the claws of guilt wreaking havoc in my chest. Without the pain of knowing I've probably pushed Teagan away for good incinerating my insides to dust.

"You shouldn't have had to do this alone!" Mom says, digging in her heels.

My gaze softens and I reach out, taking one of her hands currently squeezing the life out of her coffee cup in mine. "I didn't. Mom, I had you and Dad." I give her hand a little squeeze and her eyes glisten. "You could've thrown me out on my butt. At the very least, you could've easily shamed me or told me I was a disappointment. Do you have any idea what you've done for me? How much you've helped by just *being* here? You guys are my rock."

"It was a simple mistake; one a lot of people have made before you." Fire blazes in Mom's eyes, and her voice shakes.

"While that may be true, not all parents would have been as understanding. You allowed me to stay here so I could scrimp and save my money. You threw me the biggest graduation party on the face of the planet, so I could get the most graduation money possible. All of those things allowed me to put a down payment on my dream home, a home for Sophie. If not for you guys, my situation would have been so much worse. Sophie and I would've turned out a lot different. The least I could do was return the favor and give Dad his dream—"

"Fuck my dream!" A bang collides with the harsh rasp of my father's voice, and I jump.

The breath freezes in my lungs as I turn to him. His balled fist rests on the table, eyes swimming with pent-up rage. "Do you *really* think I'd choose football over you? That a game is more important?"

"No," I choke out. "Which is exactly why—"

"You are *always* number one, Lane. Always." His voice trembles as he jabs a finger at me. "You should've told us and let the chips fall where they may. You're our *daughter,*" he says, like it pains him. "You're more important to me than some stupid job could ever be."

My eyes fill, and I curse myself when the first tear falls. "But the truth would've changed *nothing*," I manage through the tightening of my throat.

"Maybe not." Dad leans forward and grips my face in his large hands, wiping away a tear only for it to be replaced by one of his own. "But at least we could've been there for you. At least, I wouldn't have invited Chance in here every fucking Sunday during the season for brunch or to my office to go over plays. A mistake I can forgive but abandoning my grandchild"—he shakes his head—"not taking responsibility for his actions, that I cannot. At the very least, *he* should've told me. He should've been a man and come clean."

He releases me and it's like a weight I didn't know I was carrying has been lifted from my shoulders. "You're not the only one who lied, Lane. Remember that," Dad says.

I blink over at him, coming to terms with the fact this changes a lot for him.

"I treated him like one of my own." Dad scrubs a hand over his face. "We invited him into our home, our lives. I *trusted* him. But the whole time, every time I saw him and he didn't own up to being Sophie's father, he lied to me. It's making me question *everything* I thought I knew about him as a man."

Mom shakes her head, face pale. "To think of all the times he was around Sophie, and this whole time he knew . . ."

"It's unforgiveable." Dad clenches his jaw, gaze lifted as he stares out the windows behind me. "Chance Lockhart is dead to me."

CHAPTER 48

LANE

I TUCK SOPHIE INTO bed after a bath and books. It's been two days since I left the hospital. Two more days I haven't heard from him.

Thanks to my father, I've gotten updates, but I still yearn to see him myself. I think about him every moment I'm awake and when I lay my head down to sleep. It's probably half the reason I'm so exhausted. My brain is running a twenty-four-seven Teagan marathon.

The dozens of texts I sent since he got injured have remained unanswered, so I'm not holding out hope for a reconciliation anytime soon. In fact, I probably need to come to terms with the fact I won't get one at all.

I'm pulling the blankets up to Sophie's chest and giving her a kiss goodnight when she yawns and asks, "Can we see Teagan tomorrow?"

I freeze, my heart lurching at the sound of his name. I've yet to address Teagan with Sophie, mostly because I'd been hoping he'd at least say *something*, but he hasn't and now that she's asked, I have no idea how to respond.

Unprepared, I swallow over the lump in my throat as my mind races.

This is the exact scenario I'd hoped to prevent by avoiding a relationship. Over the course of the last two months, Sophie's grown every bit as attached to Teagan as I have, and it absolutely kills me that she's going to feel the same heartbreak I feel now when she finds out we're no longer seeing each other. Knowing I'm mostly to blame only makes it worse, second to the fact I can't shield her from this even if I wanted to.

I inhale through my nose, staring down at her cherubic face. "Um, I don't know, baby."

"What about Friday? Can he come to the lake house with us?"

I brush some errant curls off her forehead, and my throat bobs. "Well, remember when I told you he got hurt in the game Saturday?"

She nods.

"He's probably going to need a lot of rest, so I'm not sure he'll be going anywhere for a while."

Her eyes brighten. "He doesn't have to do anything. He could sit with me and we could read."

"Oh, yeah. Maybe." I try for a smile, but it falls flat.

"Maybe means probably not." She pouts.

Smart girl.

"Well, it's just that . . . there's another reason," I say, and my stomach clenches. "See, Teagan's kind of upset with Mommy about something right now, and I'm not sure he wants to see me just yet."

"Why?" Her eyes widen. "Did you do something to him?"

Tears clog the back of my throat, stinging my eyes. "Kinda, yeah."

"What? Mom, what did you do?"

I didn't want to get into all of this with her, at least not now. When no one knew the truth, I figured I'd keep the secret forever, but now that it's out, I'm not sure what's right anymore. I know there will come a time when Sophie asks about her father, probably sooner rather than later, and I'll have to address it somehow. But it's one thing for my parents to know who Sophie's father is, and it's quite another to tell a four-year-old, who's incapable of managing her emotions. Telling her isn't a decision I can make on the fly. I need to think about it, mull it over with my parents, since I no longer have to struggle through this alone.

"It's complicated," I say. "Grown-up stuff."

She seems to digest this, a furrow between her brow as she says, "Just say you're sorry. Then he can come over and play with me."

I exhale. "Oh, baby, I wish it were that simple, I really do."

"Does this mean he's not your boyfriend anymore?"

I swallow over the ache in my chest. "I'm not sure."

She starts to ask another question, but my heart can't take it, so I reach out and place a finger on her lips. "Just get some sleep, okay? We need to give Teagan time to heal right now." Both physically and emotionally. "And I promise I'm going to do everything in my power to make things right."

Even if it's too late and he won't give me another chance, I need him to know how much he means to me. I need him to know I'm sorry and why I lied.

"Promise?" she asks, lifting her pinky finger for a pinky promise.

"Promise." We link fingers before I kiss her goodnight, then hurry out the door, closing it behind me before I lean onto the cold, hard frame.

I press my eyes closed, and the pain sweeping through me threatens to take me out at the knees. A sob catches in the back of my throat, but I hold it in.

Squeezing my lips together, I cover my mouth with my hand, pressing it against my lips as I wrestle for control. Each breath feels like razor blades in my throat. Every beat of my heart a metronome counting the seconds that slip by and Teagan and I are apart.

I gasp, chest tightening with the effort of holding myself together.

I can't breathe. Can't move.

My hands turn clammy, my forehead beaded with sweat as my legs buckle out from under me, feet numb as I slide to the floor.

I'm having a panic attack; I know this, but it feels like I'm dying all the same.

I bend my knees and drop my head against them as I try and focus on something positive, but it's hard when my life has been turned on its ear and the one person I want the most in this moment, the only one who could draw me out of this, is the one person I can't have.

I breathe in through my nose, out through my mouth until the pain in my chest lessens, until my head stops spinning and the feeling returns to my feet.

With shaking hands, I pull out my phone and find Gabby in my contacts, then type out a text: *Gabs, I need you. I'm at home.*

Then I hit send and wait for her to come.

Twenty minutes later, I'm standing in my bedroom when Gabby pulls me into a hug. "I hope I didn't interrupt anything important," I say with a sniff.

"Are you kidding?" Gabby pulls back, taking a good look at me as she says, "Lane Tuner needs no one, so when you get a text from her saying otherwise, you don't walk, you run."

Right. My shoulders curl and I let out a shaky breath as I drop down onto my bed.

"Now, tell me what's wrong." Gabby walks over to my desk and pulls out the chair so she's sitting directly in front of me. "Spill."

"My parents know," I blurt.

Frowning, she starts, "Your parents—*oh*!" Understanding ripples through her features and her gaze softens. "They know about Chance."

I glance down at my hands and nod.

"Does this have anything to do with the rumors I heard about your father taking a leave of absence for the remainder of the season?"

"Yeah," I croak. "Oh God, Gabs, everything is a mess. Teagan knows, too, and now he's hurt because of me. It all came out right before their game, so he was distracted on the field. He won't speak to me, and I don't blame him. Just weeks ago, he asked me if Chance and I had ever dated and I said no. Then he asked me about Sophie's father, and I refused to tell him anything, angry he was even asking."

I take a deep breath, ignoring the churning in my stomach as I remember Sophie's sweet face as I tucked her into bed. "Sophie misses him already and is starting to ask about him. My father met with Chance in what I assume was an extremely tense and unpleasant confrontation. He's no longer allowed in our house, not that I care about that. It's a relief, actually, not to have to see him anymore. My father doesn't even want anyone speaking his name, and effective as of yesterday, he's taken a leave of absence from coaching until next season."

My secret did everything I feared it would; it blew up and took everyone with it.

"This is the part where you say *I told you so*," I quip.

"Like I would ever do that." Gabby sighs, staring at the wall in a way that only inflates the hopelessness living inside my chest.

"I fucked up. Everything is broken and it's all my fault, and I don't know how to fix it all."

"Maybe you can't."

My eyes lock with hers. "But I *have* to."

"Lane," Gabby says as she reaches out and squeezes my shoulder, "there are some things that can't be fixed once broken, but they heal over time. Your parents love you. They're just shocked and hurt. But they'll get over it. In a few years, it'll seem like just a blip in the radar."

"And Teagan?" I ask, fear coating my words.

The sadness in her eyes speaks volumes as she shakes her head. "I don't know. But what I do know is you can't beat yourself up over this. What's done is done. It's out there now, and there's a certain kind of freedom in telling the truth. Embrace it. Learn from this and move on. It's all you can do. And if Teagan doesn't want you afterward, well . . ." Gabby trails off, her words leaving scales on my heart.

"But it can't be over," I whisper.

Exhaling, Gabby reaches out and grabs my hand. "Listen to me, Lane. I watched you beat yourself up over getting pregnant. Part of me thinks you've punished yourself ever since. You made one mistake, Lane. *One.* You think you're the only person who had sex a little too young? You think you're the only person who regretted it after? Who should have waited and wished she had?" Gabby shakes her head. "Hell, Lane, if I counted every person

I know that matched that description, I wouldn't have enough hands or fingers. The only difference is you got pregnant, and those other people didn't. But they could have. Every single one of those people who match that description could've easily been in your shoes, myself included. It doesn't make any of them better than you. You're not less than them because the fucking condom broke."

My cheeks heat, and I glance away from her. The urge to rebut everything she just said runs so deep I have to press my mouth closed to keep from arguing.

"But guess what? You took responsibility. You did right by yourself, by Sophie. Hell, ever since then, you've spent the last four years trying to prove yourself like you're on some kind of redemption mission. I've watched you run yourself fucking ragged to ensure you're not a burden on those you love because of the weight of your choices. I've watched you refuse to let your mom watch Sophie or even let me to take her for a day, just because we *shouldn't have to,* or you don't want to be an *inconvenience.* The only problem with this line of thinking, the one thing you seem to ignore, is that we fucking *want* Sophie."

She pulls away from me now, on a rampage as she shoots to her feet, pacing in front of me.

I open my mouth to speak, but I don't dare stop her when she points and glares. "It's like you've been punishing yourself for four fucking years. And to what end? You're hellbent on doing everything on your own like you're not worthy of help because of one bad choice made years ago."

My insides twist at the truth in her words. I throw my hands up, frustrated and defensive and . . . *lost.* "So, what's your point? What are you even trying to say?"

She pauses, eyes like darts finding their target when they lock with mine. "I'm trying to say that you need to stop punishing yourself and start fucking living, Lane. Meeting Teagan was the best damn thing that ever happened to you because for the first time in your life, I watched you give up a little of that control. I've watched you release your foothold on this idea of perfection, or that you're not worthy."

"That's ridiculous." I scoff, crossing my arms over the frantic beating of my heart. "What is it I think I'm not worthy of?"

"Hell if I know." Gabby throws her hands up. "Time, help, love, or whatever the fuck else you have in that head of yours. These past two months, I've watched you not only openly accept help but ask for it instead of being so damn stubborn and doing everything yourself. You've taken the proverbial bull by the horns and I fucking love it."

My guts twist painfully. "Yeah, well, that's over now. Thanks for the reminder."

"Maybe it is. Maybe it isn't. But what I do know is we accept the love we think we deserve. And ever since you found out you were pregnant, you think you don't deserve anything good, Lane, unless it's fucking hard-earned by you."

Her words hit me like a sledgehammer, knocking the air from my lungs. I open my mouth to speak, to deny it, but she beats me to the punch.

"And maybe that's the problem. From the moment Teagan met you, he gave himself freely. He was smitten with you from day one. Hell, I could see the love in that boy's eyes from the start, but you didn't think you deserved him. You didn't think you deserved love or a relationship or happiness, telling yourself no one wants a young, single mom. And so, you pushed him away. And once you could no longer do that, you did the one thing that ensured you'd self-destruct. You withheld the truth from him, the one person you should've confided in."

She flops back down in the desk chair, and her whole body sags. "Self-sabotage is a bitch."

CHAPTER 49

LANE

M Y THOUGHTS CHURN IN my head like freshly tilled soil. It's as if, with one swift movement, Gabby up-rooted all my weeds and exposed them to the light.

Is she right?

Have I been so focused on being perfect, all while punishing myself because of one mistake? Was I so blinded by my own shame that I pushed Teagan away?

Self-sabotage, that's what Gabby called it.

I hate to say it fits. This whole time, I've blamed keeping Chance's secret on preserving my father's future, but when you love someone, you tell them everything.

And I trusted Teagan. Enough to tell Sophie we were dating. Enough to allow him a place in my life with her. I should've told him, yet didn't. Why?

We accept the love we feel we deserve.

It's the one phrase that keeps running through my head and every time I think about it, I feel a little piece of me crack.

How many times did I tell myself no one would want me because I'm a young, single mom?

A thousand. A million. Every time a man dared to look in my direction with even the slightest hint of interest.

Yet it was a lie.

I *lied* to myself time and time again, because Teagan *did* want me. I was just too damned stubborn to give him all of me when he asked.

I drop my head back against the headboard of my bed, staring at nothing when my gaze falls to my nightstand and the leather-bound journal I've kept since junior high. The binding is cracked. Pages have been added and old ones glued back into place. Inside, are hundreds of entries, and though I don't use it all that much anymore, there was a time when I did. When I used it nearly every day, spilling everything I couldn't bear to say out loud onto its pages.

Reaching out, I pick it up and run my fingers over the worn leather cover, then crack it open. Each entry is labeled with a date at the top, making it easy to find *that* day—the one that changed everything.

I'm pregnant.

I can barely believe it.

The word rolls around in my head like a bowling ball every time I think about it, thoughts scattering like pins at its impact.

I'm still shocked, but I have the pregnancy test to prove it. Two pink lines and my whole world is about to change.

How could I let this happen? How could I be so dumb?

I'm so disappointed in myself, I can barely look in the mirror.

Stupid, stupid, stupid.

I know better.

My heart clenches as I turn the page on my journal and find another entry, skimming it and reading only the parts that jump out at me with a kind of sick fascination as I relive all the big moments in my life□days, weeks, months.

I'm going to tell Chance today. I don't want to wait. Waiting won't make this any less real, so there's no point in it. Besides, he loves me. What could go wrong?

He's coming over in about an hour to go over the playbook with Dad and then we were going to steal a few moments together like we always do.

I'll tell him then.

It will be okay.

We'll face this together.

I close my eyes for a brief moment, thinking about how I'd felt. I really thought it would work out, that Chance and I would ride the wave of parenthood together and everything would be okay.

The next page tells another story.

Chance doesn't want the baby.

When he told me, I didn't even know what to say. I was speechless, stunned into silence. After I recovered, I told him it was okay, that I understood. And I do, kind of. He starts at Cumberland University next year, and there's a lot riding on him to excel as a rookie quarterback. Most think he'll go pro.

Still, I'm not sure where that leaves us. Me and the baby in my belly.

But it's my decision to keep her. Not that I know it's a her. I suppose it could very well be a boy. Either way, I'll do this alone. I have to.

I just hope God blesses me with a really easy baby because this is surely going to be the hardest thing I've ever done. And though I'm trying to be brave, I'm scared. So, so scared.

I told Mom and Dad today.

I don't know what I expected. Disappointment? Screaming? Yelling? Judgment? For them to kick me out of the house?

I received none of those things.

Shock, yes. Sympathy, absolutely. And, yeah, maybe they're a little disappointed even if they won't say so, but it was nothing like I'd feared.

Overall, they were just really supportive, which makes me feel even worse because I didn't tell them the truth about the father.

But how could I?

A few weeks ago, I overheard Dad on the phone with the athletic director at CU, and I know he's been promised the coaching position there next year if he signs Chance and brings him with him.

My dad's dream has been to coach college football for as long as I can remember. He's worked so hard, but I know what he'll do if I tell him. He'll confront Chance and refuse the spot. But Chance will only be around for a handful of years while my father's career will last five times that. I can't let my mistake destroy his dream. I just can't.

My life isn't the only one that's about to change, and the gift of ignorance is the least I can do for them because my parent's lives will change with this baby, too. People will stare. They'll talk about how their teen daughter got knocked up. They'll have a newborn in the house, crying and crawling and making a mess. Since I'm under their health insurance, my medical bills from the pregnancy and birth will be theirs. Instead of preparing to be empty nesters, they're starting all over again. Well, not quite because she's mine, but close.

All those reasons and more are what make me even more determined to make this as easy as possible for them. They shouldn't have to suffer because of my mistakes.

So, I'll handle everything, do everything myself. I won't ask them for a thing, and they won't have to lift a finger. After my hospital bills are paid, I won't ask them for a dime.

It'll be as if I truly am a single mom, living on my own. The things I can control, I'll control. And all the other things . . . I'll just have to make up for them.

My chest tightens as I lower the journal. There it was. The moment I decided I'd keep the burden from them and shoulder everything myself. Only, I did so to the point of destruction, like I'm some kind of fucking martyr.

I flip the pages quickly, only picking up words and phrases as they blur together before my eyes.

Today, Danny Connors called me a slut . . .

I thought Kiera, Jenny, and Amanda were my friends, but today, I overheard them at the lunch table laughing at me and talking about me when they thought I couldn't hear.

Gabby told them to fuck off.

Guess they're not my friends, after all . . .

Prom is only a couple months away and I really want to go, but I'm not holding my breath. Most of the kids treat me like a pariah. My old friends see me coming and they do everything they can to avoid me, even crossing the hall to walk on the other side.

I'm five months along now and showing, which is probably part of the problem. Like a fool, I thought maybe Chance would take pity on me and ask me to the dance. After all, I am *carrying his baby. But then I heard Mira talking with a friend in study hall. Turns out, they're going together.*

It stings just a little.

He and I made a mistake and yet I'm the only one paying for it.

Sometimes it seems unfair, but then I remind myself not to dwell on it since I can't change it.

Gabby asked me to go with her, but I don't think I will. I know she likes Kevin Rooney, and rumor has it he's going to ask her. The last thing I want to do is be the pathetic pregnant friend and play third wheel.

At least I got to go to junior prom . . .

I'm counting down the days until graduation, which is only a couple weeks before my due date. Maybe I'll even go into labor first, and then I won't even make my ceremony.

Either way, it'll be a relief. I'm huge. I can now say with confidence I know how Hester Prynne from The Scarlet Letter *must have felt. I might as well have a giant A on my back for how much everyone stares at me . . .*

When I returned to my seat after receiving my diploma, the group of kids in front of me snickered. I was so embarrassed . . .

My hands clutch the journal, my eyes watery as I remember how hard those days were. Reading the entries over for the first time feels like reliving them all over again, but I know there are happier days in store, so I flip forward a few pages where the entries morph and change.

After the birth of Sophie, the entries brighten. My words are full of joy and love, instead of despair, and my eyes well with tears just reading them.

She's so beautiful, the most beautiful thing in the world . . .

I'm three months postpartum, and it's amazing what breast-feeding can do. I'm back to my pre-pregnancy size, which my doctor also says has a lot to do with how young I am and my body's ability to bounce back so quick.

I guess there's at least one perk to having a baby at seventeen.

I was feeling pretty good about myself until I was walking to class and a guy from Sociology came up to me. He has sandy hair that brushes his collar and bright green eyes. The old me would totally think he's cute, but new me knows better than to even entertain the idea of finding a man attractive when I know it could lead nowhere. Even if I wanted to date, I don't have time. I barely have time as it is between my gig working from home, classes, and Sophie. But I also know better than to think a college freshman would want to date a single mom to a newborn.

As if to prove myself right, when he asked me out, I told him I wasn't sure I could get a sitter for my three-month-old and he blanched. Every ounce of blood drained from his face as he took three giant steps back, voice shaking as he said that could be a problem, and, actually, he was busy, anyway.

Never mind the fact he asked me out.

Then he turned and ran like his pants were on fire.

I document several other similar experiences, not that I was even looking to date, but the more I read, the more I see how right Gabby was. It's not hard to read between the lines. From the moment I got pregnant, I decided I wasn't worthy of love, and with the exception of Gabby and my parents, the world around me seemed to agree. All I saw were the weight of my mistakes, and ever since, I've been hellbent on correcting them. I used to think I was proving to everyone else—the cruel kids at school, the girls who used to be my friends, all the boys who ran when they found out I had a child—that I was worth something, that I had succeeded and made something of myself.

But now I wonder if maybe this whole time, I was trying to prove it to myself. *I* needed to know I was worth it. I needed proof.

The epiphany hits me like a ton of bricks.

Maybe this whole time, I've felt unworthy of love, which is why when it smacked me in the face, I did everything in my power to run away.

The thought sits heavily on my shoulders as I turn back to the journal.

I read about Sophie's first smile and her first taste of baby food. I read the joy of milestone moments like crawling and her first steps. I read about late nights studying, then waking to a crying baby. I relive scrimping and saving to throw her a first birthday party. I relive the day I found the lake house and solidified my dream. Doctor's visits and work and laundry and meal prep.

I fucking did it all.

Me.

Not only did I bring the most beautiful, sweetest, intelligent little girl into the world, but I did it with a fucking smile. I worked and saved money and went to school. And, yeah, it was hard, but I proved I can do hard things.

By the time I close the journal, I'm so fucking proud of myself, my heart is bursting.

This whole time, I've never given myself any credit for what I'd done up to this point, and maybe I was lucky. I have wonderful parents who supported me every step of the way, but that doesn't negate my hard work. It doesn't take away from the sacrifices I had to make to get to where I am now.

I inhale, breathing through the swelling in my chest as I remember the first time I met Teagan. The spark of interest in his eyes and the way he flirted made it clear he was interested. And then he asked for my number and I immediately wrote him off. In my mind, he didn't stand a chance because there was no way he'd want me—a single mom with a messy life.

But he did want me.

And now I can see why.

I've always known Sophie was a blessing and anyone I welcomed into her life was lucky to have her, but what about me? It's been *four* years, and I still haven't forgiven myself for not being perfect. The problem with self-criticism is it blocks out the ability to see all the good because you're so focused on the flaws.

And I have so much to offer someone.

But now I might've lost the man I love, all because I couldn't believe in myself enough to tell him the truth.

Because we accept the love we believe we deserve.

I stand, clutching the journal to my chest, my heart pounding. "Our story can't end like this," I murmur to myself. "It just can't."

CHAPTER 50

TEAGAN

T HE FUTURE LOOKS PRETTY dismal from this angle.

Brynn is gone, having left after hovering over me for four excruciatingly long days, my parents left last night, too.

Tommy is at class, which will bleed into practice. If I'm lucky, I'll see him tonight, which means I'm alone for the next eight hours.

I'm not sure if that's a blessing or a curse.

I lie in my bed, far later in the morning than I'm used to—but then, I have nowhere to fucking be—and stare at the wall while my thoughts churn.

Come summer, this room will no longer be mine. It's a hard pill to swallow, one I've tried to choke down during the handful of days since I left the hospital on Sunday.

As of this moment, my name on the roster for the Cumberland Wildcats is merely a technicality. I'm no longer a college football player. My days as a Wildcat are over.

Finished.

I've worked so damn hard for so long to get to where I am. Most guys dream of playing at the college level, and though I'm grateful for the time I had, it wasn't nearly long enough. I might not have had dreams of playing beyond college, but it still stings to have it end so soon.

In the blink of an eye, I lost something I loved, and there's no getting it back.

What will I do without football?

Living the normal life of a college student without athletics was never something I pondered, but one I'm now being faced with.

No more scholarship. No more football.

Next year, I'll have to figure out financial aid, not to mention changing my living arrangements. I'll be forced out of the athlete dormitories into regular student housing, unless I got an apartment off campus. My mornings will no longer be filled with conditioning and training. No more afternoons watching game tape. No more two-a-days in the summer or practices into the early evening. What the fuck am I supposed to do with my time?

To say adjusting to a life without sports will be a challenge is an understatement.

My thoughts drift to Lane, and my heart squeezes.

I'm not sure what hurts worse—my fucking back or my heart, but my pride takes a close third.

The one thing I told Lane I needed from her—the only thing—was her honesty. No secrets. No holding back.

And in the end, it was the one thing she couldn't give me.

I've replayed the events of the past two months, along with game day in my head more times than I'd like to admit. All the clues Chance was Sophie's father were there. I'd suspected as much, and I think the only reason I believed Lane when she said she and Chance had never been together was because I so desperately wanted it to be true.

I wanted to trust her, even if my gut told me I was right.

How could she lie straight to my face?

And, fuck, why did it have to be *him?* Of all the men in the world to be Sophie's father, it had to be him.

I already hated the dude, and now I fucking despised him on a level that borders on unhinged. How he could stick around for almost four years and ignore Sophie's existence, lying to Coach day-in and day-out, is beyond me. It's in-fucking-comprehensible.

Set aside the fact all the trouble Chance has caused for me was on account of my interest in Lane, I'm not sure where to go from here. How can Lane and I possibly work when I can't trust her to tell me the truth?

Knox's betrayal has made me hate liars. I told myself I'd never be fooled again, that I'd never befriend one, let alone be with one. But I can't seem to put Lane in that category beside him, even though I know she technically belongs there.

My heart can't seem to let go because I love her.

I fucking love her. And I love Sophie, too. If I didn't, this wouldn't hurt so damn much.

I scrub my hands over my face and hiss at the stab of pain the movement causes.

Everything fucking hurts all the damn time. Brushing my teeth, reaching in the fridge for a drink, making a sandwich, taking a shit, showering, putting on my shoes. And the pain is a constant reminder of the heartbreak. They go hand-in-hand like peanut butter and fucking jelly, one reminding me of the other because heaven forbid I forget for even a moment.

Dropping my hands, I grit my teeth and reach for my phone on the nightstand, expecting the electric prod in my back this time.

Once I have it in hand, I open my unread texts. I have about a dozen from the guys in the group chat which I've left unread, most of them checking in and asking for updates, worried I might lose my mind between coping with the injury, Lane, and my inability to play football.

The Sunday I was released from the hospital, after my parents went out to grab us all some lunch, I got Brynn alone and told her everything.

I needed to spill my guts about as much as I needed my spine intact.

So, I filled her in on Chance and all the shit he had been giving me. I explained about Lane and how she lied. I told her about the confrontation before the game, how distracted I was, and how I have no idea what the fuck to do about it all now.

The whole time Brynn listened with zero judgment. She didn't offer me advice I wasn't ready to hear. Instead, she only asked if I wanted her to tell the guys about everything that transpired between the day I got laid-out on the field and now, and I'd said yes. They knew I'd been hurt, but that was the extent of it, and I just couldn't bring myself to tell them the rest. I was too tired. Too in my head.

And now, as I scroll through their messages, I'm more grateful for Brynn than ever that I can open my phone and talk to them without having to relive the horror of my injury and everything that happened before it.

Instead, I can focus on now.

Because that's where my head needs to be. In the present, the future.

I can't go back and change what happened. All I can do is look forward.

My fingers hover over the keys on my phone, debating what to say to the guys. I only know I need to hear from them, and if I want to reach them before tonight, now is the time. Most of them should be done with football for at least the next couple of hours before practices start back up.

I chew on my bottom lip, trying to decide how the hell to open this conversation when I decide for a little levity because it's better than the fucking morose thoughts swirling in my head.

Leave it to Graham to cut to the chase.

I sigh and tip my head back against the headboard while I think of my answer.

How the fuck am I?

I'm not really sure.

Jace

> Some more than others. Perks of being her personal love slave.

Me

> Seriously, dude?

Jace

> What?

Chris

> Yeah, and I heard the evidence of those perks last night. Kept me up for fucking hours.

Me

> I did not need to hear that.

Chris

> You're telling me. The worst part is I didn't know whose yelling I was hearing, Jace or Brynn.

Jace

> I don't sound like a fucking chick in the sack, dude.

Chris

> Whatever helps you sleep at night.

Me

> Can we refocus, please? This conversation is making me sick and I already

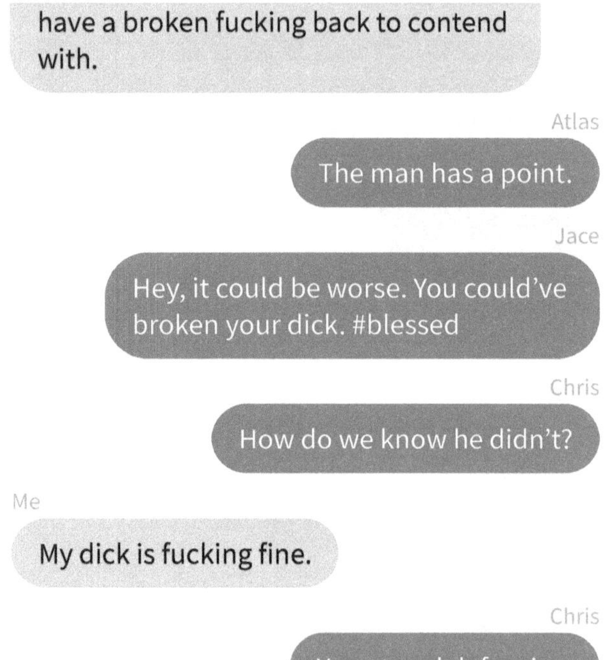

I close my eyes and let my head fall back against the head-board.

Why did I text them? Why?

When my phone pings again, I'm almost afraid to look at it.

Damn. Graham hit the nail on the head.

I suppose I shouldn't be surprised. He went through a hell of a time last fall with his best friend, Mackenzie.

I'm sure he does. Graham had his whole future mapped out for him since he was a kid. His father played in the NFL and expected Graham to follow in his footsteps. It wasn't until Graham had his heart broken, then found Skylar and fell in love with her that he had the courage to admit what he really wanted. He turned down an opportunity to play in the Big Ten, walked away from football, and never looked back.

Jace

And we're here for you, man.

Me

The worse part of it all is I just want her. With her by my side, I could handle any-fucking-thing. Losing football means nothing compared to the thought of losing her.

Atlas

Have you talked to her?

Me

No. She's tried calling and texted me dozens of times, but I just can't bring myself to respond when I don't know what to fucking say.

Jace

Maybe it's time, man.

Me

Probably. But every time I think about how I asked her point-blank if she and Chance were ever together and she lied straight to my face, I shut down. I can't even think about it without getting sick to the stomach. All I can think about is how Knox lied right to my fucking face for years. I had no clue he hurt Brynn. No clue he was fucking guilty. Since then, lying is a hard fucking no, and it's so hard to get past that.

Shit, I get it. You're in a tough spot, bro. Not sure what I'd do if I was in your shoes.

I grimace.

Helpful.

Sorry, man.

Okay, so if the roles were reversed, and it was your girls. What would y'all do?

I'm basically Brynn's bitch, so unless she cheats on my ass, she's not getting rid of me that easy. ☒

Do you know who you're talking to?

I frown just as another text comes through.

Oh, shit. That's right. He's a liar and Mackenzie forgave him. I almost forgot. Bahahahaha!

Atlas

Asshole.

I scrub a hand over my jaw, thinking about it. I know what happened between him and Mackenzie, but the details are foggy.

Atlas

I found out my father was responsible for the car crash that killed Kenzie's mother and didn't tell her about it even though I *knew* she wanted to know.

Damn, I almost forgot.

They broke up over it, and it took months and a lot of other shit happening to mend those bridges.

Me

But I point-blank asked Lane and she lied. You omitted the truth. It's a little different.

Graham

Shades of gray, man.

Jace

True. And though I get it, Lane isn't Knox. I don't think she would purposely hurt someone. What Knox did was unforgiveable no matter how you cut it.

He's right. I know he's right, but . . .

Atlas

Do you know why she lied?

Me

Does it matter?

Graham

Maybe.

Atlas:

Intention matters, at least with me. I was selfish for not telling Kenzie, but I never meant to hurt her. I was just so damn afraid of losing her, and I thought she wouldn't be able to look at me without seeing my father.

Jace

Maybe Lane has a damn good reason.

Me

Like protecting that asshole, Lockhart?

Atlas

Maybe. Maybe not. But you won't find out until you talk to her.

Graham

You're hurting anyway, and you have to face this at some point. So sit down and ask her why. Maybe her answer will surprise you and you'll find a way around it?

Me

And if I can't?

Graham

Are you really ready to lose her?

Chris

I just want you all to know that I resent all these references to things I know nothing about. It's rude.

CHAPTER 51

LANE

THE AIR SEEMINGLY TURNED cool overnight as if autumn waited until this exact moment to make its presence known, so when I step out of my car beside the athlete dormitories, I'm unsure whether it's my nerves holding my lungs in a vise or the cold.

I exhale, clutching the messenger bag to my side as I remind myself that no matter the outcome, I can do hard things. I'll be okay.

A girl with long blonde braids steps out of the building in leggings and a Wildcats jacket. She glances around her as if looking for something and I know that's my cue. She's just as Gabby described, so I swallow the tangle of nerves in the back of my throat, close the car door, and cross the remainder of the parking lot toward the front of the building.

"Are you Stacy?" I ask as I grow closer.

She smiles. "Lane?"

I nod. "That's me."

Gesturing to the building, she says, "Come on," then turns and swipes her student ID in the card reader, holding the heavy oak door out for me as I step in behind her.

Once we're inside, there's another set of doors that leads to either wing of the dormitories. If I'd sat in the parking lot long enough, I could've followed someone in, but my nerves are frazzled as it is. I didn't want to be left waiting. Or worse, denied access. So instead, I'd asked Gabby for a favor.

She phoned up one of her friends and in seconds, I had a way into the athlete dorms and a babysitter for Sophie.

I have no idea how this will go. Teagan's silence speaks volumes. I can only assume he's not ready to talk to me, and maybe he'll never be ready, but the way I see it, my best chance of getting him to listen is by coming to him. Besides, I'm not letting another day go by without seeing for myself that he's okay.

Stacy pauses at the front desk, talking to the resident adviser as she signs me in on a clipboard, then turns to me and says, "They need an ID."

I startle. "Oh, right." Digging in my bag, I pull out my student ID and slide it across the desk.

The RA glances at it, confirms my name, and then sets it on the desk. "When you leave, just sign out and you can pick it back up then."

"Okay, thanks."

"Ready?" Stacy says from behind.

I turn and nod, too nervous to speak. In seconds, I'll be standing in front of Teagan's dorm room, praying he won't slam the door on my face.

We push through the glass doors and bypass a small lobby. "The boys' wing is the left," Stacy says, walking toward it. Turning, she waits for me to catch up. "Do you know what floor your boyfriend lives on?"

Boyfriend.

I wonder if I still have rights to that word.

"Um, the second?"

"Okay, just take the elevator here, then." She motions to the right. "It'll take you to the lobby and the hallway to the rooms is right off it."

"Thanks," I say, ignoring the jumping jacks in my stomach.

"Sure thing." She waves goodbye and turns, heading toward the girls' wing and leaving me on my own.

I stab the button to the elevator and the doors slide open. Stepping inside, I block everything out except the sound of my heavy breathing and count in my head as the car rises to the second floor.

The doors open and I step off, more than grateful to find the lobby blissfully empty. The last thing I need is to see one of my father's players and get drawn into conversation when all I want to do is get this over with, say my piece, and let the balls fall where they may.

Hurrying down the hallway, I pass the door numbers until I find room 204 and pause. I stare at the grains in the wood for what feels like hours, afraid of what will happen the moment I knock. Every possible scenario runs through my head in quick succession, until my heart is pounding so hard, I don't even hear the door when it opens.

Tommy steps out and startles. It takes him a moment to compose himself, but even so, his dark eyes widen like the moon when he sees me. "Uh, hey, Lane."

I swallow, my throat turning dry. "Is, um, Teagan here?"

"Yeah." Tommy nods, his gaze darting behind him. "He's in his room. I just came back for lunch, but I have to leave for practice," he says, looking sheepish, like he's guilty for still being able to play. "We go over game tape and plays in the afternoons."

I muster a smile. "I know."

"Oh. Right. Yeah, I guess you would." He rocks back on his heels. "Anyway, you can go ahead in if you want." He hooks his thumb toward the room. "I should probably get going."

I watch him leave before taking a step forward and opening the door. I knock on it for good measure, then enter.

The space is small with two doors on either side of the bath-room, leaving me to guess which one is his. I turn toward the one on the right, but I only get two steps before it swings open. "Hey, Tommy did you see my—" Teagan stops mid-sentence, frozen in place.

His eyes make quick work of me. Shock and disbelief melds into joy and then a wary apprehension as shoves his hands in the pockets of his joggers and says, "Lane."

"Um, hey," I manage with a weak smile.

The sight of him punches me in the gut. His torso is thicker than normal, all weird angles jutting from the cotton of his t-shirt, which I realize must be some sort of brace.

I swallow and motion toward him. "Does it help?" I shake my head, flustered when he frowns. "The brace, I mean."

"It helps," he says, softly. "I was actually just looking for my keys. I wanted to come see you."

"You did?" My heart beats faster, and I try not to read into it as my gaze sweeps over him.

He looks good. Maybe a little tired if the dark half-moons beneath his eyes are any indication. But despite the brace, he's in one piece, on his feet, and walking. His blond waves curl around his ears and a week's worth of stubble covers his jaw, giving him an irresistibly sexy scruff. Leave it to Teagan to take a broken back and heartache in his stride and come out looking even sexier than ever.

I swallow, feeling suddenly self-conscious in the silence. I have no doubt I don't look half as good as him and I don't have a serious injury to blame it on, just myself. "Um, Tommy told me to just come in. I hope you don't mind."

My gaze flicks to the yellowish bruise on the edge of his jaw. More evidence last Saturday went sideways.

"Uh, no. It's fine." Teagan stares at me for a moment, his brilliant blue gaze drinking me in as if he's forgotten what I look like. "What are you doing here?"

My stomach twists and all at once, I doubt my plan. Maybe this wasn't such a good idea after all. Maybe I shouldn't have come, but I'm here and there's no going back, so I straighten my spine and strengthen my resolve. "I came to see you," I tell him.

Obviously, Lane.

I fight the urge to roll my eyes.

Of course I'm here for him. Now strap on your big girl panties and tell him why.

Fucking talk, Lane.

I puff my chest and unearth the last of my courage. "Listen, Teagan. Maybe you're glad I'm here, or maybe I'm the last person you want to see. I don't know. But what I do know is I couldn't go another day without talking to you, and even if you had answered one of my calls or returned one of my texts, this was something I had to do in person. So, I hope you don't throw me out."

I hold my breath, waiting for his reaction.

His eyes search mine for a heartbeat before he drawls, "I'm not going to throw you out, Lane."

I nod, awash with relief. It might not be much of an endorsement. I would've preferred a smile or some words of encouragement, but he's not throwing me out on my ass, so I guess I should be grateful and take it.

"Right. Good." I shift on my feet. I've never been more nervous in my entire life as I open my mouth and begin. "I know I lied to you, and that is absolutely inexcusable. You confided in me about what happened with your friend and your sister, and so I knew dishonesty was where you drew the line, but then I never expected your hard no and mine to collide. That's not an excuse. It's just . . ." I wring my hands in front of myself.

Shit. I'm doing a piss poor job of this.

"What I'm trying to say is, I should've told you the truth earlier, before you even had to ask, and I certainly should have told you the truth when you did. I am *so* sorry I didn't," I say, chin wobbling. "I'll probably live the rest of my life and regret that one decision because somewhere along the way, I completely fell for you, and there's no turning back. That's not a secret you keep when you love someone. Not when I saw a future with you."

Teagan bows his head and shrugs, then winces with the movement.

My hands flutter toward him, then stop. "Are you okay?"

"Fine," he grinds out. Exhaling, he raises his head again. "Maybe deep down you just weren't sure about me."

"No." I clench my jaw, hating that he's in pain because of a situation I caused. Hating this whole damn thing. "No, that's not it. I didn't tell you, Teagan, because I was protecting my father."

His gaze snaps to mine, and the curiosity in his eyes is enough to keep me going.

"When I was pregnant, I overheard a conversation between my father and Kyle Bradley, the athletic director at CU. The job at Cumberland was his, *only* if he brought Chance with him. It was promised to him on that one condition and after all my parents sacrificed for me, after everything they did and how they supported me, I couldn't allow him to pass up his dream or worse, piss it away because he was furious with Chance for being an asshole."

My whole body shakes with the memory, remembering the sinking feeling in my chest. The knowledge that I'd need to lie to my parents because it was the only way I could give them something in return.

"This one thing was the only thing I could give them, and so I deluded myself into thinking it was okay to lie to them, to everyone. So I made up the story about the guy at summer camp, which wasn't entirely off-base, and when they believed it, I never looked back. I told myself I'd take this one to the grave because I allowed myself to believe my father would prefer his dreams over his daughter." A sob threatens to escape my lips, but I hold it back. "I was wrong."

I glance down at my hands and then to the messenger bag at my side and open it, pulling out the old leather-bound journal. "What I realize now is it wasn't just about protecting my father. Somewhere along the way, I became obsessed with this road to redemption, like I needed to prove myself and make up for the mistake I made. I was so blinded by this idea that I fucked up, that I wasn't good enough, and I convinced myself no one would ever want me. *Me,* Lane Turner, a single mother with a toddler and a full-time job, still working on my degree. I was so focused on all my faults and all the ways I fell short that I didn't see how much I actually have to offer someone. And I let the one person I fell in love with slip through my fingers because of it. And because I was fucking scared. I was so scared, Teagan."

I hold the leather journal out, hand shaking while I fight the tears pricking at the back of my eyes. I can't look at him or I might lose it right here. "This is my journal. I don't write in it much anymore, but I used to."

When he doesn't make a move to take it, I meet his gaze and motion with the book. "Take it. Read it. It's all in here, everything I just told you and so much more. It's the only way to make you see. Maybe then you'll understand."

He reaches out and takes the journal in his hands, staring down at it with intensity.

"You once said you were going to make me see what you see. That you'd make me see just how special I am and how fucking lucky you are to have whatever piece of me I'm willing to give." I swallow. "Well, I see it, Teagan. I see it, and I'm ready to give it all to you, every piece of myself if you still want it."

I take a step back, memorizing how he looks in this moment before turning for the door and praying like hell it's not for the last time.

CHAPTER 52

TEAGAN

I STARE DOWN AT the journal in my hands, stunned.

I'd just been trying to find my keys so I could hunt Lane down at work and talk to her, when she appeared in my dorm room.

Shocked doesn't begin to describe how I felt when I saw her standing here, looking every bit as incredible as I remembered, and it took everything inside me not to take her in my arms, to erase everything that happened.

But I needed to hear her out. I had no idea how things were going to work out between us, but I owed it to myself to see if what we had could be mended.

I blink down at the book, heavy in my hands.

She didn't lie to protect Chance.

Hell, she didn't even lie for herself.

She lied to give her father his dream.

Coach Turner doesn't strike me as the type to turn a blind eye. Coaching the father of your grandchild, knowing he wanted nothing to do with her or your daughter would be a hard pill to swallow, and I have no doubt he wouldn't have done it.

I crack the journal open and start reading the first entry Lane marked with a ribbon. It's from the day she discovered she was pregnant.

I quickly skim the entry, then pause and lift my head.

By giving me this journal, Lane basically handed me a window to her soul.

If she'd been guarded like Fort Knox before, this is the equivalent to throwing a hand grenade at all her walls and watching them fall at once.

This journal reveals her inner belly, leaving her exposed and vulnerable. And she'd given it to me freely, consequences be damned because she loves me, because the thought of losing me and what we have is worse than the thought of rejection.

Are you really ready to lose her?

I swallow, snapping the journal shut as Graham's words dance in my head.

What the hell am I waiting for?

I hurry down the hallway, cursing my back the entire way. I can't even run without the constant stab of a knife in my fucking spine.

The elevator opens immediately and I thank God for small favors as I get on and furiously press the button to close the doors.

Once they slide open again, revealing the first-floor lobby, I amble out, pushing my way through the heavy-ass glass and oak doors that shoot lightning into my spine and step outside into the cool autumn air.

My gaze makes quick work of the parking lot, zeroing in on the flash of auburn, and the hand gripping my chest releases its hold.

"Lane!" I yell, but she doesn't turn. I start for the parking lot, closing in on her when she pauses by her car and gritting my teeth the entire way.

Even from here, I can see her profile, make out the silvery track marks from her tears that tug on my heart.

"Lane," I try again and this time, she turns, her blue eyes wide as she looks at me.

"Teagan?" She swipes at her cheeks as if she can hide the evidence.

"Damn," I say slightly out of breath. "Don't you know I have a broken back? Where's the fire?"

She blinks at me, mouth parting as if she doesn't know how to take me. "Oh. I, uh—"

"Relax, Lane. I'm joking," I say with a smile.

The stiff set of her shoulders loosens. "Oh."

She fiddles with her hands out in front of her, clearly nervous, as the scent of her floral perfume hits my nose, beckoning me closer.

I stop just feet away. She's all pouty lips, soft curves, and smooth skin, and I want nothing more than to crush my mouth to hers. Claim her in all the ways I couldn't before, because even when we were together, there was always a little piece of her holding back. This secret between us.

But now . . .

She's offering all of herself to me. Her past mistakes, hopes, dreams, and all her inner thoughts and vulnerabilities. And I don't want to waste another fucking moment.

I reach out, a hiss of pain escaping my parted lips as I cup my hand beneath her head.

"Teagan, your back . . ." Lane's eyes widen with concern.

I bite back a groan. "Fuck. Sorry. This was a lot sexier in my head. You'll have to work with me here." I inhale, relieved when it's pain free. "I'm going to lean in slow as fuck to kiss you, but imagine me completely destroying you with my mouth in an alpha move that makes your head spin instead, okay?"

Lane nods, throat bobbing, lashes fluttering. "Oh, yeah, okay."

I grin and lean in, the anticipation killing me in the moments before my lips brush over hers.

The kiss is feather soft, sweet. It's full of promise and love and everything fucking in-between, and when I finally pull away, our eyes lock, and it's like a riptide pulling me away from shore, lost in all that blue.

"So, what does this mean?" Her gaze shifts nervously.

"It means that I still love you, Lane. I never stopped, and I'm sure as fuck not going to stop now."

She sighs, closing her eyes and pressing her forehead to mine. "I thought I lost you. And I screwed everything up. Your back, football—"

"My back will mend." I press a kiss to the top of her head. "And it's not your fault I got hurt. It's football. It happens. I might have been distracted, but it was my job to tell Coach I wasn't fit to play, and I didn't. And as for football . . ." I brush her cheek with my thumb. "Yeah, it's gonna be fucking weird not playing, but football was never my endgame. *You* are."

She reaches up, placing a hand over mine as a soft whimper escapes her lips. "But you haven't even read the journal yet. Are you sure?"

"Oh, I'm gonna read the journal," I say as I pull back. "I have every intention of doing so the second I head back into my room." I brush the hair from her face and her cheeks flush. "But I don't need to read it to know what I have, because I'm holding something fucking precious in my arms, and I'm not about to let it go."

"But I lied."

I nod. "You had your reasons, and though I wish you hadn't, you laid them all out for me on a silver platter, and they're reasons I can live with, ones I can understand. My family means a lot to me, too, and I don't know . . ." I shrug. "If I had been in your shoes, I might have done the same."

She slides her hands down to the collar of my shirt and grips it like a lifeline. "I can't believe I get to keep you," she says, her voice thick.

"Believe it, Lane Turner." I brush a soft peck on her forehead. "You were right. I did tell you someday I would make you see your worth. But I've always seen it. And I've been yours since the moment I met you. You just didn't know it yet."

Epilogue

TEAGAN

WE PULL INTO THE driveway of my childhood home and turn off the ignition. The ground is covered in a bed of white, the snow glistening like diamonds under the golden rays of the early morning sun. Several cars line our driveway, ones I recognize belong to my friends, and though I'm always glad to be home, today is different. Today is special because of the two girls seated beside me.

It's only a few days before Christmas, and we plan on spending the next two days here with my family and friends before returning to Cumberland where I'll spend Christmas morning at the lake house, watching Sophie and Lane open their gifts.

"We're here," I announce, turning to Lane.

She sits in the driver's seat, her posture rigid and her face a mask of nerves as she stares out the windshield.

I reach out and softly touch her hand. "Lane?"

She turns, blinking. "What if they don't like me?"

"Impossible." I shake my head.

"But—"

"I love you," I say, lifting her hand to my lips where I press a kiss. "So they'll love you, too. It's that simple."

"Mom," Sophie whines from the back seat. "Stop worrying so much. Just be yourself and it will be fine."

I chuckle under my breath while Lane shoots Sophie an incredulous look. "I'm the parent. Aren't I supposed to give *you* advice?"

"Sometimes Mommies get scared, too." She shrugs.

My lips quirk. Sweet Sophie is so full of wisdom, I sometimes wonder where she gets it until I remember who her mother is—fucking amazing woman that she is—and it all makes sense. "You ready to meet everyone?"

Lane pales, so I squeeze her hand. "It's going to be fine, I promise." Sensing she's still not convinced, I lean across the seat and place a soft kiss over her lips, then look her in the eyes. "You trust me?"

She nods, her teeth sinking into her lower lip, and if it weren't for the child in the back seat, I'd be freeing it with my own. "Then, come on."

I slide out of the car and help Sophie from her booster seat as Lane joins us and we walk to the front door, but I don't even have to knock. Before we've even made it to the porch, the door flings wide open.

"Brother!" Jace yells, arms spread out in front of him. "You've made it."

"Shut up, you big buffoon!" Brynn hisses behind him, her blonde head bobbing. "You'll scare Sophie." Turning her attention to us, she offers a little wave and says, "We'll just wait inside." Then she ushers him down the hall while he grumbles about beating everyone else to the punch.

I snicker as we mount the porch, holding Sophie's hand in my left and Lane's in my right as we step inside and make our way into the kitchen where a burst of commotion ensues. My mother rushes to me and gently pulls me into a hug, being careful not to hurt my still healing back. Dad ruffles my hair like I'm still two years old, Jace offers me a fist bump, and Brynn a side hug. Atlas and Graham amble forward, each of them placing a hand on my shoulder while Mackenzie and Skylar follow closely behind.

"Good to see you in one piece, man," Graham says.

"Good to be here."

My heart swells as I glance at the people around me. I've always been lucky to have so many people in my life, but I feel even luckier with the women by my side. "Everyone, I'd like you to meet two very special people."

"Wait for us!" a small voice yells and seconds later, both Trista and Sable, my little sisters, are bustling into the room, looking five times older since summer break when I last saw them.

Once everyone's settled, I clear my throat. "As I was saying, everyone, this is Sophie." I run a hand over her little curly head while she hugs my leg, suddenly shy in the presence of so many strangers. "And this is my Lane." I reach out and clasp her hand in mine, glancing at her with so much love and adoration I think I might explode from it.

When I turn back to my friends and family, I point, going through each name and introduction, and by the time I'm finished, I can practically see how overwhelmed Lane is before my mother and the ladies whisk her away to the kitchen for girl talk while Sabel and Trista take Sophie up to their room.

Later, after dinner is finished, and we've caught up, I hover by the stairs as my parents wish everyone goodnight.

My mother pulls me into another hug, whispering in my ear, "You did good."

"Thanks, ma," I murmur before they retreat upstairs, leaving me to lean against the wall and wait for Lane.

A creak on one of the wooden risers alerts me to her presence, and I turn to her with a smile. "Everything good?"

Her blue eyes sparkle as she takes the last step to meet me on solid ground. "Sophie is officially passed out in your sister's bottom bunk next to Sable. Trista was worried she'd fall off the top, so they insisted on bunking together."

I chuckle. "They got along well, huh?"

"I think she has two new idols." Lane grins.

I bite my lip and pull her into my arms with slow, careful movements so as not to jar my back. After more than six weeks of healing, it's not as painful as it was, but I still need to be careful. "I told you everyone would love you. *Both* of you."

"Do you always have to be right?"

"About you? Yes." I smooth a hand over her hair. "Thank you for being here."

"Thank you for wanting me here."

I smile and brush a thumb over her lower lip. "I'll always want you, Lane, whatever piece of you you're willing to give."

"How about all of me?" Lane rises on her toes to meet me, and our lips collide. She tastes sweet, like the wine she and my mother shared after dinner, and I want to drown in her.

I was already in love with Lane Turner, but having her meet my family and friends brought my feelings to a whole other level.

Turning, I press her against the wall, cupping her face with my hands as I lose myself in her, groaning when her hands slip beneath the front of my shirt, tracing the ridges and grooves of my stomach with her fingertips.

Pulling back, she says, "Should we get back to your friends?"

I press a kiss to her jaw, then her neck. "Fuck my friends," I say, claiming her mouth with another heated kiss. "I have other things in mind."

"Like?" she asks, breathless.

Like taking her up to my room and getting her naked.

My fingers grip her hips as I sink into her touch, and I'm about to hoist her up and wrap her legs around my waist, when I remember my back and curse my injury.

I suck her lower lip instead, and she lets out a soft moan when someone behind us clears their throat.

I lift a hand, giving them the middle finger, and it's worth the momentary twinge of discomfort because I know for a fact my parents are upstairs, which means it must be one of the guys.

Another throat clears, then Jace's voice calls out. "It's fine. We only get so much time together before we all go our separate ways again, but I'm kind of enjoying the show, anyway, so we can wait."

I mutter a string of obscenities as I pull away from Lane, whose cheeks are flushed a bright shade of red, and adjust myself in my jeans before turning. "This better be good."

Jace stands next to Atlas, and his eyes flicker south. "Well, it's confirmed. His cock isn't broken. Congrats, man."

I scrub a hand over my face and groan. "Seriously?"

Beside him Atlas chuckles, and Lane snorts.

"What? As your best friend, I was concerned for you. Can you blame me?"

"Yeah, I can, actually. Because it was my fucking back, not my dick that got hit."

Jace shrugs. "You just never know with these things, but I'm glad to see he's back in business." He slaps a hand on my chest. "How does that work with a broken back, anyway? Her on top, right?"

"Let it go, man," Atlas says beside him, stifling a grin.

"What?" Jace shrugs. "I mean, because he can't—"

"Say another word, and you'll be the one with the incapacitated dick," I deadpan.

Jace raises his hands, palms out. "Sheesh. You don't have to get so violent. I was just wondering," he grumbles.

Beside me, Lane bites her lip to hide a smile, her cheeks pinken as we rejoin the others in the living room. Between the armchairs and the massive sectional, everyone is spread out and coupled up.

I gingerly sink down onto the sectional and pull Lane beside me as Jace announces, "His cock works."

"Give me that." I motion to the throw pillow at Lane's side and when she hands it to me, I chuck it at his head, wincing as I hit my target.

His mouth gapes, hand flying to the back of his skull. "I hope that hurt."

"It did. But it was worth it." I smile.

Graham snickers, and they launch into a story about the time Jace ran out of the showers in the locker room, slipped, and almost face-planted into Graham's genitals.

I sit back in my seat, laughing along with them as they give Lane the highlights reel of our friendship over the years like they're sharing a greatest hits album.

The last time we were all together in the same room was my mother's barbecue, the day I found out the truth about Knox. It feels like it just happened yesterday, yet so far away at the same time. The night we all said our goodbyes around a fire at Crow's Creek before we parted ways last summer, feels like a lifetime ago.

I can't help but think of how much everything has changed since then. The crazy boys of Riverside have grown up. Our bond may be stronger than ever, but we're no longer the boys we started as. We're men, forged through the fire of tragedy, heartbreak, loss, and everything else life has thrown in our paths.

I glance over at Atlas, his dark gaze glittering as he smirks at some dumbass thing Jace is saying, one arm slung around Mackenzie's shoulders.

When he bulldozed into our lives more than a year ago and stole Mackenzie from Graham before he could confess his undying love for her, I thought he'd break us. He was arrogant and jaded and tough as fucking nails. As it turns out, it takes a whole lot more than a girl, football, and Graham's asshole father to tear us down.

And Graham . . . My gaze shifts. His sandy hair falls in his eyes as he presses a kiss to the top of Skylar's head.

I remember sitting with Sky at our senior football banquet and being so fucking grateful she found a way to bring him back to life when I thought we'd lost him.

Shit, he went to hell and back, and still came out on top. A broken heart, gambling debts, his parent's infidelity, a surprise half-sibling, thugs, and fires weren't enough to keep him down, and we were right there with him, every fucking step of the way.

"Babe, you know you love it," Jace croons, drawing my attention.

Beside him, Brynn slaps him on the chest and rolls her eyes. "Okay, maybe I do."

"See?" Jace grins like an idiot, and I shake my head.

"Do I wanna know?" I ask, having missed the punchline.

"Trust me when I say, you don't," Graham supplies.

"That's what I thought."

I tighten my arm around Lane as I watch my best friend eye my sister like she hung the moon.

When I discovered he'd been secretly seeing her behind my back, I lost my shit. He'd always been a player, and after everything Brynn had gone through in high school, I was so damn afraid of her getting hurt. She deserved whole-hearted devotion and loyalty, and I'll admit, it took me a hot minute to realize just how much Jace loved her. Turns out, he's exactly the man to give her everything she needs.

We've been through break-ups, funerals, injuries, betrayals, victories, infidelities, loss, and so much more.

And now, here we are.

I lift Lane's hand to my lips and press a kiss to her palm.

Ever since the day she showed up at my dorm, we've seen each other every single day, and though I fucking miss football like I'd miss an arm or a leg, I have to admit, having my schedule open up has its advantages. No more squeezing in time on my lunch break or sneaking around. No more travelling for weekend games or early morning conditioning. Now, I'm building a life for myself outside of football, instead of around it, with Lane and Sophie at the helm.

"Teagan?"

At the sound of my name, my head snaps to Graham, pulling me from my thoughts. "What's up?"

"I have something for you." Digging into his pocket for his phone, he pulls it out. "Cal sent me an email I thought you might want to see. Consider it a Christmas gift." He rises from his spot on the armchair and hands me his phone while I instantly sober.

If Graham's father sent an email regarding Knox, it must be good.

My gaze homes in on the text, and I quickly skim the short message.

Hope this email can give the Nichols some peace and healing this holiday season.

My hand shakes as I click on the attachment and an article loads.

I read, almost afraid to believe my eyes.

"They brought Knox in on charges for sexual assault and sexual battery," Graham explains, confirming what I'm seeing. "He's going to be indicted."

I scrub a hand over my mouth and drop the phone, searching for my sister. "Brynn—"

"I already know," she says, from her perch on Jace's lap. "Jace told me as soon as we got here. You know he can't keep a secret." She rolls her eyes.

My chest tightens. "And you're good?"

She nods with a smile that reaches her eyes. "I'm good." She glances down at Jace and threads the fingers of their clasped hand together. "Better than good."

"I figured you guys could tell your parents tomorrow. Together," Graham adds. "Merry Christmas, bro."

I nod, overwhelmed with emotion as I turn and place a kiss on Lane's cheek, heart full. "Yeah. Merry Christmas."

Silence settles over the room, and I imagine everyone is lost in their own thoughts, likely thinking about the stab of betrayal like I am, and how it's finally over. We'll have justice, and the four of us are stronger for it.

"I think this calls for a group hug, am I right?" Jace asks, breaking the silence, a wide grin stretching his face as he rises. "Bring it in, boys." He reaches out and yanks Graham to his feet, then heads straight for me. "Come on, right to Daddy." He motions toward himself while I stand before he can do anything stupid and hurt my back.

One of his heavy arms falls over my shoulders. "Call yourself Daddy again while you're touching me, and I'll fucking throat punch you," I deadpan.

"I think I just gagged." Graham shifts closer.

Unfazed, Jace tips his chin at Atlas. "Come on, Mr. Macho, let's go. You too."

Atlas groans and curses under his breath, but he rises to his feet and joins us, completing the circle as Jace tries to squeeze the life out of us like a human boa constrictor. "Damn, I missed this," he murmurs.

"Watch my fucking back, man!" I snap.

"I feel the love, don't you?" he murmurs.

"Okay, now this is getting weird," Graham says.

"*Getting* weird?" Atlas blinks across from me, his arms around Graham and Jace. "It's *been* fucking weird."

"When do we break?" Jace whispers, ignoring them. "Is it time to break? The chicks are all watching us, and I feel like we've held too long now for a casual release."

Graham flinches. "Casual release? The fuck you talking about?"

"Okay, we'll break on three," Jace whispers. "One, two . . ."

"Oh, dear lord . . ." I close my eyes.

"Three!"

LANE

SIX MONTHS LATER . . .

It's funny how all of life's miracles happen when you least expect it.

Getting pregnant with Sophie.

Finding Teagan.

I've been blessed enough with those two things alone to last me a lifetime.

I glance over at Teagan's profile in the sunshine while he watches Sophie try and bait a fishing hook, chuckling when she sticks her tongue out in concentration, and I smile.

On days like today, while we're sitting on the dock of the lake house with the water stretched out before us, I glance over at the two of them and I feel so full I might burst. Life without Teagan Nichols was fine, manageable, but life *with* Teagan Nichols is nothing short of incredible.

Everything is falling into place.

Teagan found an amazing apartment just off campus—though it's more a formality than anything considering, since we moved in a few months ago, he spends most of his time with us here. And I don't see that changing anytime soon, especially with spring semester having come to an end and summer starting. All Teagan has been able to talk about is everything he hopes to do with us between his summer classes and my work schedule, including teaching Sophie how to fish, which is why he's currently helping her cast a fishing line into the lake.

They've been at it for hours, and though she's getting better, she still needs help.

"Last one," I call out, "and then we really need to get going."

Today is Sunday, which means brunch with my parents, and instead of avoiding Sunday afternoons at my childhood home, I actually get to enjoy them now. No more Chance. No more tiptoeing around the house, uncomfortable encounters, or the guilt of keeping secrets from my folks.

Ever since his injury, Teagan has earned himself a permanent place at their table, and I'm not sure who's happier about it, him or my mother. She loves his voracious appetite, and he loves her cooking, and though he and my father talk football, it's no longer the only point of conversation at the table.

Once Sophie reels her line back in, we pack up the tackle box Teagan bought for her birthday last week and head for the car.

The drive to my parents' house is filled with laughter and chatter from the back seat as Sophie talks about the zoo trip Teagan promised her next weekend during Brynn's much anticipated visit. By the time we pull into the driveway of my parent's house, she's practically bouncing with excitement.

We head inside, and the comforting scent of crepes and strawberries wraps around me like a warm blanket. We're not more than three steps into the kitchen when my mother pounces.

"Teagan, love!" Mom crosses the room and pulls him into her arms for a hug before she holds him at arm's length, looking him over like she hadn't just seen him last week. "All that sun you've been getting at the lake this week agrees with you. You look dashing with a tan."

"*Mom.*" I blush, completely mortified at the way she fawns over him all the time, but also in complete agreement because Teagan is heart-stoppingly handsome with all that smooth, golden skin.

"What, darling, I have eyes." She winks and my mouth gapes while Teagan chuckles beside me.

"Thanks, Dolly. You don't look so bad yourself. Getting ready for your trip to the Virgin Islands?"

"Yes! We're all set. I still can't believe Ed surprised me with *three* weeks away. What will I ever do without my Sweet Sophie?" she asks, using Teagan's nickname for her as she wraps her up in a hug.

"Sitting on an island, sipping Painkillers? I'm sure you'll manage." I laugh.

True to his word, Dad took the rest of the season off football, and despite his plans to return in the fall, he surprised Mom with a trip for their anniversary. A thank you, he said, for putting up with him through years of football.

"I'll miss your Sunday brunches, though," Teagan says, eyeing the platter of crepes behind her on the island while he pats his flat stomach which I know firsthand is rippled with muscle.

Mom laughs. "That's why I made extra today, so Lane can freeze the leftovers and feed you while I'm gone."

"If I didn't already love your daughter, I would now," he says in reverence.

I snort at the same time Dad enters the room in a hurry. "Sorry. Got caught up on a call. Where's the food? I'm hungry," he says, glancing into the dining room, looking all forlorn.

"We're coming. We just got to chatting." Mom hands us each a platter of food to take to the table while Dad places a kiss on my head, gives Sophie a squeeze, and Teagan a pat on the back.

Once we're seated, we begin to eat when Dad clears his throat. "So, I have something I want to discuss."

I tense, my body instantly rigid. Though it's been months since Chance's name has been mentioned, it's still conditioned in me to expect these Sunday brunches to be hyper-focused on football and all things Chance Lockhart.

Shortly after Teagan's injury and my father's leave of absence, the athletic board decided not to press charges against Chance for the stolen playbook, but they *did* suspend him from the team indefinitely.

He had to sit out the last month of the season, including quarterfinals, and just this past week, instead of getting drafted to a team in the Big Ten on the East Coast like he'd hoped, he was drafted to the Los Angeles Chargers as second string.

Looks like *he's* backup plan now.

I smirk to myself before I sober, hoping this isn't what my father wants to discuss.

"I just got off the phone with Harvey O'Neil," Dad says, and I instantly relax.

"The athletic director at John Marshall high school?" Mom asks. "Gosh, we haven't heard from him since you left your spot there. What did he want?"

"I guess they lost their assistant coach this summer. Moved to Colorado with his family."

I stare at my father for a moment while I chew my food. I know him well enough to know he's getting somewhere with this, I'm just not sure where.

"So Harvey wanted to know if I had anyone in mind." He shrugs, then lifts his head, his gaze finding the man beside me. My heart beats faster as I realize what my father's getting at. "I was wondering if maybe you'd want it," he says.

Teagan's eyes widen. "Me?" he chokes out.

Dad nods, his gaze steady as he waits for Teagan to process what he just proposed. "I think you'd be a great fit. You have a season of college football under your belt, and you're good. More than good. It would be a shame to waste all that talent when it could be put to good use coaching young men. Plus, it would be a foot in the door at John Marshall High for a teaching gig once you graduate and great experience for a head coaching spot someday, should you want it."

Stunned into silence, my heart swells as I glance between them.

If Dad's willing to put his neck on the line for Teagan professionally, it speaks volumes of how highly he thinks of him.

"Uh, I mean," Teagan's throat bobs. "I'd love to talk with them about it, yeah." He turns his baby blues to mine. "What do you think, Lane?"

As if he has to ask.

I offer him the biggest smile I can manage. "I think they'd be really lucky to have you."

"Okay, great. I'll set up a meeting, then." Dad grins, then turns back to his food while I hold Teagan's gaze,

Reaching under the table, he clasps my hand in his and I mouth, *I love you*, to which he mouths back, *I love you more.*

The rest of brunch flies by with the five of us sitting around the table long after the food is gone and the leftovers tucked away. Eventually, we wander to the back porch where we play cards for a couple hours while Sophie plays on the swing set.

After a while, we head home where we grill on the back patio, then catch fireflies with Sophie before tucking her into bed.

I step out onto the dock where Teagan waits for me, a bottle of wine and two paper cups behind him on the tattered wooden boards, and I grin to myself. Seems we haven't upgraded our choice of tableware since those many months ago.

He glances up at the sound of my footsteps and smiles, a radiant, beautiful smile that brings out his dimples and sinks straight to my bones.

I settle down beside him, taking the paper cup he offers me, smiling into the brim as I take a sip and stare out at the setting sun.

"I see those wheels spinning. What are you thinking about, Lane Turner?" he asks.

I turn to find him staring, thinking how we've come full circle.

Humming, I rise to my feet and grip the hem of my shirt.

His gaze darkens, zeroing in on the movement, before drifting back to my face where I arch a brow. "Want to go skinny dipping?"

Teagan hops to his feet and grabs me so fast, I squeal. His mouth finds mine while he helps me out of my shirt, whispering against my lips, "And they say there's no such thing as a stupid question."

Want more college football romance from Gracie?

THE LOVE PLAYBOOK brings you back to Ann Arbor University with a reverse grumpy sunshine romance featuring Chris and Charlotte from *Tell Me You Love Me* and cameos with the whole Boys of Riverside crew!

BLURB

Charlotte Baker is the grump to my sunshine and the star of all my unrequited fantasies.

She checks all my boxes while all I seem to do is piss her off.

But I'm a wide receiver in the Big Ten. I'm used to winning, and my golden retriever personality is sure to wear her down.

Those cutting looks she gives? Just a cover. Secretly she wants me; she's just loathed to admit it.

Those snarky comments? They're simply a way to hide her attraction; she just can't see it yet.

Oh, and did I mention I just discovered her father is engaged to my mother?

Now she's saltier than normal.

But I won't let this forbidden romance get me down. I have a plan, a way to win her over and secure my mother's engagement to her father at the same time.

On paper, my plan is foolproof: I'm going to show her what it's like to be romanced. I'm going to woo her. I'm going to throw the Love Playbook right at her.

Lettie might have made it clear that she's not interested in me, but I'm nothing if not persistent.

All she needs is a little persuasion.

Right?

ORDER NOW

About Gracie

Gracie is a contemporary young adult author who loves romance and writing fictional characters. When she's not busy telling lies for a living, she's likely wrangling her three kids, cooking subpar meals, and procrastinating. Feel free to reach out to her on social media! She loves talking to readers and chatting books!

Gracie's Gang (FB Group)

Facebook Page

TikTok

Instagram

Pinterest

Afterword

So, here we are. The Boys of Riverside series has come to an end, and I can't help but feel a little sentimental about it, if I'm being honest. I'm sad to see them go, but I'm so grateful for the joy I experienced while writing their stories. I'm not sure I've ever connected with characters I've written so deeply to the point of missing them when they're gone, but that's certainly the case for this crazy group.

I'm so grateful for everyone who has joined me on this ride—editors, designers, and especially readers—and I hope you'll follow me on my next venture. Even though the series is over, I don't think it's the last we've heard from them. Their voices are too strong and far too loud in my head to be silenced for long.

So, even though this is goodbye, it's goodbye for now, not forever.

www.ingramcontent.com/pod-product-compliance
Lightning Source LLC
Chambersburg PA
CBHW061102310726
48974CB00002B/363